the BOY & his RIBBON

NEW YORK TIMES BESTSELLING AUTHOR

PEPPER WINTERS

The Boy
&
His Ribbon

by

Pepper Winters

The Boy & His Ribbon
Copyright © 2018 PEPPER WINTERS
Published by Pepper Winters

Published: Pepper Winters 2018: **pepperwinters@gmail.com**
Cover Design: Ari @ Cover it! Designs
Editing by: Editing 4 Indies (Jenny Sims)

www.pepperwinters.com

OTHER BOOKS AVAILABLE FROM PEPPER WINTERS

Dollar Series
Pennies
Dollars
Hundreds
Thousands
Millions

Truth & Lies Duet
Crown of Lies
Throne of Truth

Pure Corruption Duet
Ruin & Rule
Sin & Suffer

Indebted Series
Debt Inheritance
First Debt
Second Debt
Third Debt
Fourth Debt
Final Debt
Indebted Epilogue

Monsters in the Dark Trilogy
Tears of Tess
Quintessentially Q
Twisted Together
Je Suis a Toi

Standalones
Destroyed
Unseen Messages
Can't Touch This

Chapter One

REN

2000

"STOP! WILLEM, SHOOT him. Don't let him get away!"

Bolting from the farmhouse with its broken paint-chipped shutters and rotten veranda, I swung the large backpack straps higher on my shoulders and leapt the small distance from hell to earth.

The weight on my back wasn't balanced, sending me tripping forward.

I stumbled; my ankle threatened to roll. My useless ten-year-old legs already screamed it wasn't possible to outrun a bullet from the wife of a killer and slaver, especially with such a cumbersome burden.

Even if it wasn't possible, I had to try.

"Come back here, boy, and I won't cut off another finger!" Mr. Mclary's boom cut through the humidity of the night, chasing me with snapping teeth as I darted into the thicket of leaves and stalks, weaving like a worm around maize twice as tall as me.

My tiny fists clenched at the thought of living through that pain again.

His threat only gave me more incentive to escape—regardless if a bullet lodged in my spine and I died in the middle of their cornfield. At least this excruciating nightmare would be over.

"Kill him, Willem!" Mrs Mclary's voice screeched like the crows she liked to shoot with her dirty rifle from the kitchen window. "Who knows what he's got pilfered in that bag of his!"

A noise sounded behind me; a sudden cry jerked into silence.

An animal perhaps?

A cat?

I didn't care.

I ran faster, putting my head down and using every remaining drop of energy, pain, and hope in my wasted, skinny body. The bulky backpack dragged me down. The weight far heavier than I remembered when I'd slung it over my shoulders during a test attempt two nights ago.

I'd planned this for weeks. I'd scratched my escape route into the dusty floorboards beneath my cot and memorised the location of canned beans and farmhouse churned cheese so I could grab it in the dark.

I'd been so careful. I'd believed I could vanish from this rank place I'd been sold to.

But I wasn't careful enough, and I hadn't vanished.

Bang.

Corn stalks shivered in front of me, cracking in place where a bullet wedged at head height. The cry came again, short and sharp and close.

Gulping air, I leaned into the soupy skies and kicked my burning legs into a sprint. The backpack bounced and dug into my shoulders, whispering that I should just drop my supplies and *run.*

But unless I didn't want to survive past a day or two of freedom, I needed it.

I had nowhere to go. No one to help me. No money. No direction. I needed the food and scant water I'd stolen so I didn't perish a few measly miles away from the very farmhouse I'd flown from.

Bang.

An ear of corn exploded in front of my face. Mr. Mclary's voice warbled words with out-of-breath growls, giving chase in his precious field. My ears rang, blocking out another cry, amplifying my rapid heartbeat.

Just a little farther and I'd pop out on the road.

I'd find quicker escape on the sealed surface and hopefully flag down aid from some oblivious passer-by.

Perhaps one of the same people who drove past daily and smiled at the quaint rustic farmhouse and cooed at the diligent hardworking children would finally open their eyes to the rotten slave trade occurring in their very midst.

Bang!

I ducked and fell to my knees.

The backpack crushed me to the earth with sharp edges and sloshing belongings, yet another noise chasing me. I was strong for my age, so why did I find such a thing exhausting to carry?

Shoving away such delays, I sprang up again, wheezing as my stupid little lungs failed to grant enough oxygen. My limbs burned and seized. My hope quickly dwindled. But I'd become well acquainted with pain and threw myself head first into it.

This was my one chance.

It was life or death.

And I chose life.

* * * * *

Dawn crested on the horizon, its pink and gold daring to creep under the bush where I'd slid a few hours ago.

The gunshots had stopped. The shouts had ceased. The sounds of vehicles or people long since vanished.

I shouldn't have turned off the road and entered the forest. I knew that. I'd known it the minute I'd leapt off manmade pathways and traded it for dirt, but Mr. Mclary had chased longer than I'd expected, and I was starved, beaten, and not prepared to give up my life by running in full sight of his rifle scope.

Instead, I'd scrambled into the bushes of private, untended land and fought exhaustion until the hairs on the back of my neck no longer stood up in terror, and the thought of earning a bullet in the back of my head was no longer enough to keep me awake.

The bush had offered sanctuary, and I'd fallen asleep the moment I'd burrowed beneath it, but it wasn't the dawn that had awoken me.

It was my backpack.

A mewling, muffled cry came again, sounding alive and not at all like water and cheese.

The noise was familiar. I'd heard it as I'd run, but I'd been too focused on living to notice it came from the very thing I'd stolen.

The heavy rucksack was ex-army canvas with faded green stitching and buckets of room for bed rolls, ammunition, and anything else a soldier might need.

I'd barely used any of the available space with my meagre supplies, yet it sat squat and full in the dirt.

Another wail sent me scrambling into a squatting position, ready to bolt.

Leaning forward with shaking hands, I tore the zipper open and fell backward.

Two huge blue eyes stared up at me.

Familiar blue eyes.

Eyes I never wanted to see again.

The infant bit her lip, studying my face with a furious flicker of attention. She didn't cry louder. She didn't squawk or squirm; she merely sat in my backpack amongst canned beans and squished cheese and waited for…something.

How the hell did she get into my bag?

I hadn't put her there. I definitely wouldn't steal the natural born daughter of Mr. and Mrs Mclary. They had sixteen children working their farm and only the girl in front of me was theirs by blood. The rest of us had been bought like cattle, branded like a herd, and forced to work until we were begging for the abattoir.

The baby wriggled uncomfortably, sticking her thumb in her mouth and never taking her eyes off me.

"Why are you in my bag?" My voice was far too loud for my ears. Something small scurried off on tiny feet. Bending closer to her, she leaned back, wariness and fear clouding her inquisitive gaze. "What the hell am I supposed to do with you?"

A stream gurgled not far in the undergrowth. My thirst made my mouth water while merciless practicality made me think up other uses for the river.

I couldn't take her back, and I couldn't take her with me.

That gave me no option.

I could leave her unattended for a wild animal to make a meal of, or I could dispatch her humanely by drowning her just like her parents had drowned a boy three weeks ago for not latching the gate and letting three sheep escape.

She twirled a faded blue ribbon around her teeny fist as if going over the conclusions herself. Did she know I contemplated killing her to make my escape easier? Did she understand that I would treat her no better than her parents treated me?

Slouching in the bracken beneath my chosen bush, I sighed heavily.

Who was I kidding?

I couldn't kill her.

I couldn't even kill the rats who shared the barn with us.

Somehow, she'd crawled into my backpack, I'd stupidly ran with her even though I'd known something was wrong, and now my impossible task at staying alive just got even harder.

Chapter Two

REN

2000

I'D KNOWN I might face death if I ran.

If not from a bullet, then starvation or exposure.

That was why I'd waited far longer than I should have. Why I'd lost weight that I needed and strength I couldn't afford to lose. I'd been sold to the Mclarys two winters ago, and I should've been smarter.

I should've run the night they filled my mother's fist with cash, stuffed me in a urine-soaked car, then shoved me in the barn with the rest of their kiddie prisoners and introduced me to my education the very next day.

The night I was sold was hazy, thanks to a strong cuff to the head when I'd dared to cry, and these days, I couldn't remember my mother, which was fine because I never knew my father, either.

I only knew that we'd been made to call Mr. and Mrs Mclary Ma and Pop.

I'd obeyed out loud, but in my head, they were always the hated Mclarys. Just as hated as their blood relative currently foiling my escape plan.

I glowered at the baby girl, adding another level of intensity, doing my best to work up enough rage to kill her and be done with it.

Just like I didn't know my father, I didn't know how she'd ended up in my backpack. Had she crawled in by herself? Had another kid put her there? Had her mother even placed her inside for some reason?

The bag wasn't mine. The scuffed-up thing belonged to Mr. Mclary who filled it with booze and thick sandwiches when it was harvesting time. It sat bold and dusty by the door, hanging out with its friends the musty jackets, broken umbrellas, and well-worn boots.

I scratched my head for the hundredth time, trying to figure out the riddle of why my carefully plotted escape had somehow ended up with an unwanted passenger.

A passenger that couldn't walk or talk or even eat on her own.

Tears pricked at my scratchy eyes.

I should be miles away by now, but I still hadn't solved this problem. I still didn't know how I could run quietly and hide secretly with a baby who would, at any moment, start screaming.

Just because she'd been deathly quiet and serious since I'd found her didn't mean she wouldn't expose me and get me killed.

I cocked my head, studying her closer, hating her pink clean skin and glossy golden curls. Her cheeks were round and eyes bright. She was a mockery to every kid in the barn with sunken faces and withered bodies that looked like trees poisoned by petrol.

She was lucky. She'd been cared for. She'd slept in a bed with blankets and teddy bears and hugs.

My fists curled, reminding me all over again of my one missing finger on my left hand.

Would they miss her?

Would they search for her?

Would they even care?

I'd lived my life with one existence: where parents were cruel and beat their children, branded them with hot cattle irons, and fed them by trough and pail.

Up until a year ago, I'd believed that was how *all* kids were treated. That we were all *vermin only fit to toil*—Mrs Mclary's words every night as we crawled exhausted into our mismatch of cots and pallets.

It wasn't until the night Mr. Mclary cut off my pinkie for stealing some freshly baked apple pie that I saw a different story.

I'd tempted fate by sneaking back into the farmhouse—which was the very reason I had nine digits and not ten anymore. After passing out and coming to from the pain, I'd exhausted my search for a cleanish rag to replace the blood-soaked undershirt around my severed finger, and decided the farmhouse would have a tea towel I could borrow.

It was that or drip blood everywhere.

Mrs Mclary was screaming like a shot rabbit somewhere upstairs. She'd been as fat as a sow for months and I guessed her time to give birth had finally come. I'd seen enough animals and the grossness of new life to tune her out as I tiptoed toward the kitchen.

Only, in the raucous of babies arriving, someone had left the TV on and I became spellbound by its magic.

Moving pictures and colours and sounds. I'd seen the thing on before but had been chased out with a broom and starved with no dinner for sneaking a peek.

That night, though, I morphed into the shadows, holding my throbbing stump of a finger, and watched a show where the kids laughed and hugged their parents. Where healthy dinners were cooked with smiles and lovingly given to plump children at a table and not thrown in the dirt to be fought over before the pigs could eat our scraps.

Mr. Mclary constantly told us that we were the lucky ones. That the girls he dragged by their ponytails into the farmhouse after Mrs Mclary had gone to bed were the chosen angels bestowed an important job.

I never found out what that job was, but the girls all returned white as milk and shaking like baby lambs on a frosty morning.

In fact, having my finger cut off was my worst and best memory.

Having him grab my hand and snip off my pinkie with his fence cutters as if it was nothing more than a stray piece of wire had made me buckle and vomit in agony. The fever, thirst, and throb while watching that TV show had stolen my wits.

I was beyond stupid to stay inside the home where the devil lived.

But when he'd found me passed out from infection and blood loss in his sitting room the next morning, he'd taken me to the doctor.

On the ride over—in a truck filled with sloshing diesel for his tractor—he'd yelled at me not to die. That I still had a few years of use left and he'd paid too much to let me quit yet.

When we'd arrived at the hospital, he'd stuck his reeking face in mine and hissed at me not to say anything. My role was to be stupid—a mute. If I didn't, he'd kill me, the doctor, and anyone else who helped me.

I'd obeyed and learned what kindness was that day.

The tale spun to the medical team was my clumsy ass had

severed it with a columbine blade while cutting hay. My dirty face and knobby knees were used as Mclary's evidence that I was a reckless, unruly child, and thanks to his reputation around town for being a good farmer, civil neighbour, and regular churchgoer, no one questioned him.

No one asked me how badly his lies stunk.

The infection was bad, according to the nurse, and after shivering on her table with teeth chattering and stomach heaving, she'd sewn me up, pricked me with an injection, and given me a look that made me want to spill everything.

I'd bit my lip, fear stronger than I'd ever felt welling in my chest.

I *wanted* to tell her.

I wanted so, *so* much to tell her.

But I kept my mouth shut and continued living Mclary's lie.

In return, she'd told me I was so brave, kissed my forehead, and gave me a bag of jelly beans, a sticker with a gold star, and a little teddy bear that said *Get Well Soon*.

I'd hugged that bear harder than I'd hugged anything as I reluctantly climbed into the fumy truck and buckled in to return to hell.

The moment we were away from view, Mclary snatched the bear and jelly beans from my hands and tossed them from the moving vehicle.

I knew better than to cry.

He could take my teddy and candy, but he couldn't take the kind smiles from the nurse or the gentle tutting of the doctor as they'd made my finger all better.

Not that I had a finger anymore, just a useless stump that itched sometimes and drove me mad.

I should've run that night.

I should've run a week later once I'd finished my antibiotics and no longer flashed with heat or sickness.

I should've run so many times.

The funny thing was that out of sixteen children at Mclary's farm, the sea of faces constantly changed. When a girl or boy grew old enough to harbour a certain look in their eye or gave up the fight after years of struggle, a man in a suit would come, speak pretty words, touch trembling children, then both would vanish, never to be seen again.

A few days later, a fresh recruit would arrive, just as terrified as we'd all been, just as hopeful that a mistake had been made, only to learn the brutal truth that this wasn't temporary.

This was our life, death, and never ending all in one.

My thoughts skittered over the past in spurts, never staying on one subject for long as the dawn crept to morning and morning slid to afternoon.

I didn't touch the baby.

She didn't cry or fuss as if she knew her fate was still fragile.

Halfway through our staring contest, she'd fallen asleep, curling up in my backpack with her tatty ribbon in a tiny fist and her head on my crumbling block of cheese.

My stomach rumbled. My mouth watered.

I hadn't eaten since yesterday morning, but I was well-versed in withholding food from angry bellies. I had to ration myself if I stood any chance of surviving.

I knew that at least.

Mrs Mclary called me stupid. And I supposed she was right. I couldn't read or write. I'd been hidden away in some dark and musty place with my mother until I was sold and brought here.

However, I knew how to talk and use big words, thanks to Mrs Mclary calling herself *a well-read and intelligent woman who liked to decorate her vocabulary because this town was full of simpletons.*

I got the gist of what she said some of the time, but most of the time, my brain soaked up the word, sank its baby teeth into it, and tore it apart until it made sense, then stored it away to be used later.

I forgot nothing.

Nothing.

I knew how many hammers Mr. Mclary hung in the tool shed and knew one had gone missing two weeks ago. I knew three of the four cows he had planned to slaughter were pregnant to his neighbour's bull, and I knew Mrs Mclary skimmed money from the pig profits before telling her husband their tally.

All stuff that was useless.

The only thing I knew of value was my age because according to Mr. Mclary, I was the same age as his prized mare that was born ten years ago during a mighty lightning storm that cleaved their oldest apple tree in two.

Ten years old was practically a man.

Double digits and ready to conquer a new existence.

I might not have traditional schooling and only been taught how to work the land, how to skin game, or drive a tractor using a stick to compensate for my short legs, but I had a memory that rivalled everyone's in the barn.

I might not know how to spell the months or seasons, but I knew the flavour of the sky when a storm was about to hit. I recognised the fragrance of summer compared to winter, and I remembered the passing of days so well that I could keep a mental tally even if I couldn't count.

I also remembered the night my stowaway arrived into the world.

Mrs Mclary's labour had been long and I'd been woken by a screech the evening after returning from the hospital, standing on my cot to peer out the barn's only window as the farmhouse lit up and a car spun into the driveway.

I didn't know why Mr. Mclary didn't take his wife to the doctors, but eventually, the screams stopped and a thin wail pierced the night, sounding so young, so small.

My finger throbbed with its stitches and phantom itch as I listened to the baby's arrival, my feverish mind tangling with pictures of sheep giving birth to lambs and sows giving birth to piglets until I collapsed back on my cot, convinced that the baby Mrs Mclary had delivered was part animal, part human.

I narrowed my eyes, inspecting the napping girl in front of me.

Her ears were cute like a human, not floppy like a cow. Her nose was tiny like a fairy, not shiny like a dog. Her skin was encased in a pink onesie, not downed with fur. She was as girly and as rosy as the well-cared for kids on that TV program, and it only fuelled my hate more.

* * * * *

Dusk stole the sharpness of the undergrowth, making shadows form and worries fester.

I'd been here too long.

And I still had no answer.

I'd left the baby an hour or so ago, slipping silently through the undergrowth to check out the river gurgling happily in the distance. I'd sat on its mossy banks for ages, staring at the ripples, imagining myself plucking her plump infant body from my backpack and shoving her beneath the surface.

Of the pressure I'd need to hold her under.

Of the ice I'd need to kill her and not falter.

And as try as I might, I reverted to the same conclusion I'd had this morning.

I couldn't kill her.

Even though I wanted to.

And I couldn't leave her to be eaten.

Even though I wanted to do that, too.

And I couldn't take her back because even though she was loved by the devils who hurt me, she could never be permitted to grow up to be like them. She couldn't be allowed to trade in lives or make money from unlucky kids like me.

I also couldn't take her back because by now the Mclarys would've given up looking on their own estate and headed three farms down for the deer hunter dogs that could sniff out prey for miles.

The river wouldn't be taking a life tonight, but it would be saving one.

A quiet scream cut through the trees and bracken, followed by a hushed cry. Unless I'd heard such a thing, I wouldn't believe a scream could be quiet or a cry hushed.

But Baby Mclary managed it.

She also managed to haul my ass up and send me rocketing back to her to slap my hand over her gaping little mouth to shut her up.

The hounds would be on our tail.

I hated that I'd left it this long to remember that would be the next step of Mclary's plan. We didn't need any more bad luck on our side by her calling out to them.

"Shut up," I hissed, my fingers gripping her pudgy cheeks.

Her blue eyes widened, glistening with tears and uncertain as a fawn's.

"We need to leave." I shook my head, cursing her for the thousandth time for making *me* a *we*.

I should be leaving. *I* should be running, swimming, hiding.

But because I couldn't solve this problem, she'd have to come with me until I could.

She hiccupped behind my palm, a tentative tongue licking the salt from my skin. She squirmed a little, her two miniature hands reaching up to latch around my wrist, holding me tighter, slurping wildly as if starved for any nutrition.

Which she was.

So was I.

I was past the point of hunger, but I was used to such a condition.

She was a spoilt breast fed baby who didn't understand the slicing pain in her chubby belly.

Tearing my hand away, I bared my teeth as her bottom lip wobbled and tears welled again.

Pointing sternly between her eyes, I snarled, "If you cry, I'm leaving you behind. You're hungry? Well, so are many other creatures who will gladly eat you for supper."

She blinked, wriggling deeper into the backpack and crushing my cheese.

"Oi!" My fingers dove into the bag, pushed her aside, and rescued the badly sat on cheese. "This is all we have; don't you understand?"

She licked her lips, eyes wide on the unappetizing curdled mess.

I hugged it to my chest, possession and unwillingness to share rising in me. Feeding time in the barn meant the tentative bonds we might have with the other slave children were non-existent. We might trade holey blankets or borrow fourth-hand shoes, but food? No way. You fight for a scrap or you die.

There were no hand-outs.

Her fingers clutched at her blue ribbon, over and over again as her belly gurgled almost as loudly as mine. Her ugly face scrunched up with the beginnings of another scream.

My shoulders tensed. Violence bubbled. I honestly didn't know what I'd do if she cried and didn't shut up.

But as her lips spread and lungs inflated for noise, she tilted her head and looked right into my soul. She paused as if giving me a choice, a threat—a conniving weasel just like her mother and father.

And once again, I had no choice.

Tension slipped from my spine as I sank into realization that from here on out, I would have to share everything. My shelter. My food. My energy. My *life*. She wouldn't thank me. She wouldn't appreciate it. She would expect it just like every filly, calf, kitten, or puppy expected their parent to ensure its survival.

"I hate you," I whispered as I looked through the trees for any sign of company. My ears twitched for any sound of baying hounds as my fingers tore open the plastic and pinched the warm, smelly cheese between them.

My mouth watered so much I almost drooled as I raised the morsel out of its bag. My legs shook to eat, knowing they had a long trek ahead of them.

But blue eyes never left my face, condemning me for even thinking about eating.

"I hate you," I reminded her. "I'll always hate you. So don't you ever forget it."

Ducking on my haunches, I shoved my hand in her face.

Instantly, a grimace twisted her lips in a strange sort of smile as her hands came up, latched once again around my wrist, and a tiny, wet mouth covered my fingertips.

She pulled back a second later, spitting and complaining, red fury painting her blotchy cheeks. She scowled at the cheese in my fingers then me, looking far older than her young age.

I scowled right back, fighting every instinct to eat what she'd refused. "This is all we have until we get somewhere safer." I pushed it toward her mouth again before I could steal it. "Eat it. I won't give you the chance again."

She took a moment. An endless moment while she cocked her head this way and that like a sparrow, then finally swayed forward and licked the cheese from my hold.

Her fingers never stopped twirling her ribbon, hypnotizing me as she quickly lapped at the miniscule offering and sat back in silence.

I didn't speak as I broke off another cube and placed it on my tongue. A moan of sheer delight escaped me as my body rushed to transform taste into energy and get me the hell away from here.

I wanted more.

I wanted the whole thing.

I wanted every can of beans and every bottle of water I'd been able to steal.

But even though it cost me, even though my hands shook with a brutal battle to seal the plastic and place it in the backpack with her, I managed.

Grabbing the sides of the canvas's zipper, I looked her dead in the eye. "We're going for a swim, so the dogs can't smell us. You're probably going to get wet and cold, and there's nothing I can do about it, so don't cry. You cry, and I'll leave you for the bears."

She blinked and stuck her thumb in her mouth with her ribbon dangling from her fist.

"Good." I nodded. "Don't...don't be afraid."

With a final look at her silky hair and innocent trust, I yanked up the zippers, drenched her in darkness, and swung her substantial weight onto my back.

She cried out as she thumped against my spine.

I stabbed her side with my elbow, striding fast toward the

river. "Della Mclary, you make one more sound, and it will be your last."

She fell quiet.

And I ran...for both our lives.

Chapter Three

REN

2000

THE FIRST FEW nights of something strange and new were always the toughest.

I'd learned that the hard way, and the lesson came again as I crashed to my knees next to a falling down shed in the middle of an untended field.

Adaption.

That was what I'd done when I'd been sold to the Mclarys, and if I didn't remember the struggle it took to fall into routine, accept the inevitable, and find a new normal, then I probably would've curled into a ball, yelled at the vanishing moon, and suffocated the damn baby in my backpack.

Those first days at the farmhouse had been the worst because I kept expecting something *more*. Something kinder, better, warmer, safer. It wasn't the conditions I'd been thrust into or the back-breaking work I was assigned, but the hope that all of it would vanish as quickly as it had arrived.

But once that hope had been eaten away by my starvation, life had gotten easier. Acceptance had been smoother, and I'd saved up my tears for when they truly mattered.

Breathing fast, I peered into the dawn-smudged gloom for signs of a hunt.

My clothes were still wet from walking thigh-high in the stream for as long as I could physically stand it. My muscles had bellowed from the chilly water, my ankles threatening to snap every time I slipped off an unseen rock on the bottom.

It would've been far easier to sink below the surface and let the ripples take me. To lie on my back and rest.

But I couldn't do that because the baby zipped up tight would drown in the wet canvas, thrashing like the fish Mclary caught in his pond.

She'd cried a few times in our night-time journey. Once, she'd whined due to me slipping up to my waist and getting her wet. Twice, she'd mewled like a kitten, hungry and tired. And at some point, as the straps of the backpack cut into my shoulders and I leaned more and more into her weight, forcing myself to put one more step in front of the other, she'd squalled loud and angry as if in protest for her conditions.

I'd elbowed her again.

She'd fallen quiet.

And we'd continued on until I couldn't walk another step.

Rolling from my knees to my ass, I reached up with stiff arms and seized fingers to slip the backpack off my shoulders and scooted away to lean gratefully against the weathered boards of the shed.

The long grass kept us hidden. The light breeze kept us quiet. And the morning light revealed it was just us in the sea of rye that hadn't been cut or baled in years.

That meant the farmer didn't tend to his crops, and we were far enough away from the Mclary's holdings to be safe for a few hours of rest.

I barely managed to unzip the bag and let little blue eyes and blonde hair free before slipping to my side and dreaming.

* * * * *

Three days.

Three days of broken sleep, sore limbs, and the never-ending need to run as far as possible.

Three terrible days of learning what a baby ate reappeared ten times worse a few hours later. I'd had the gag-worthy task of figuring out how to remove a wriggling annoyance from clothing and clean up a mess that needed a hose rather than dry grass.

I didn't have a replacement diaper and didn't want her getting my backpack and food disgusting, so I ripped up my only spare t-shirt and Frankensteined a covering for her squashed little butt.

On the fourth day of hard-won freedom, Della Mclary crawled from the backpack and waited by my nose until I woke from exhaustion. I hadn't even thought of her wandering off while I slept, and her shadow hovered over me, creating horrors of farmers and enemies and guns.

My survival instincts, already on high-alert, lashed out, and I shoved her away from me.

She rolled away, silent with shock until she came to a roly poly mess covered with leaves.

And then she cried.

And cried.

And *cried.*

The code in the barn was to stick to yourself. No one got too close because no one wanted to risk getting hurt, either by Mclary punishing the friendship or because of the inevitable ticking clock that meant everyone left eventually.

Della had no such qualms.

She'd sat in her pink onesie, stinking like shit and chubby legs kicking in dirt, while her midget finger poked at my cheek; over and over until blurry sleep became blurry awake.

And now, I'd struck her.

I tore at my hair, not knowing what to do, itching to shut her up by any means necessary.

Crawling over to her, I cringed against the ripe smell and plucked her from the ground. Her weight felt heavier in my arms than on my back.

I twisted her closer, ready to slap my hand over her mouth, frantically looking at the horizon to see who or what had heard us, but the minute my fingers went near her tear-stained face, she clutched my index and sucked on it.

Her crying stopped.

Her sniffles and flowing tears didn't.

But at least she was silent, and there was no way I wanted to shatter that miracle, so I sat with her uncomfortably, letting her do what all baby creatures did when seeking comfort—nuzzling and suckling, creating another layer of frost on my hatred rather than thawing.

"Why did you mess this up for me?" I growled. "Why couldn't you have stayed with your awful parents?"

I would be so much better off without her.

I should've left her behind days ago.

We'd already gone through the food far faster than I'd planned. The cheese was gone and two cans of baked beans. I had one left.

I didn't even know if babies could eat beans, but I'd smashed it up and fed it as a paste, and she'd wisely never refused anything I offered. Not after my threat the first time.

Feeling trapped and useless and totally unprepared, I rocked my nemesis to sleep, both our empty tummies cawing as loud as the crows in the trees.

Chapter Four

REN

2000

EVERYTHING I HAD in the world now fit into two cargo pants pockets and an empty backpack.

I had no food or water.

I had no tent or blanket, no spare clothes, no medicine, no toothbrush or soap.

I'd done a terrible job at stashing away important things I'd need for this journey and regretted my stupidity on not planning better.

I'd done my best to keep us semi-clean by washing in the river we followed by day, and tried my hardest to keep us fed by hunting rats and rabbits and cooking them over the smallest fire I could by night.

Della screamed the first time I bashed in the head of a rabbit caught in my snare and skinned it in front of her. Unlike the previous times she'd cried, sucking on my finger didn't shut her up.

She'd cried and cried herself into a stupor until her gasps and hiccups trailed into sleep, and I'd woken her a few hours later with stringy overcooked meat.

Her golden curls had turned brassy with grease. Her pudgy pink cheeks white and sallow.

I wasn't used to seeing health slip so quickly from someone I saw every day. The kids in the barn all looked like filthy skeletons with wiry muscles and bleakness in their gaze.

No one changed inside that place once they'd given up hope and accepted their new fate. Della, on the other hand, switched from inquisitive infant to cranky monster, and my hate billowed bigger every day, swarming in size until I rubbed at my ribs, trying to dislodge the suffocating pressure whenever I looked at her.

If she cried, my hands curled to shut her up permanently. If she shat my t-shirt, my gag reflex begged to vomit all over her. If she crawled from the backpack while I was sleeping and burrowed into my side, my desire to shove her away was so strong I had to leap to my feet and back away to avoid hurting her the way I wanted.

I didn't want this.

I didn't want *her*.

I wanted my freedom, and she was just another form of imprisonment.

Sighing heavily, I once again rubbed at the ball of loathing wrapped around my throat and forced myself to relax. I was hungry enough without burning through more precious energy.

Ten days.

I'd made it ten days.

I could make it ten more—even with a no longer fat baby and an ever-increasing need to rest, eat something decent, and change into cleaner clothes.

Sitting in the shade of a massive oak tree, I scanned the horizon as I always did and split my attention three ways.

One, on Della as she lay on her back, twirling her dirty blue ribbon while wriggling in fallen acorns; two, on our surroundings and any sudden motions or noises, and three, on the measly tools in front of me.

I'd hoped by spreading out my worldly possessions, I would see an alternative for their use or have an epiphany on how to make life better. How to actually survive rather than continue what we were doing and slowly dying day by day.

My fingers stroked the nicked and tarnished blade that I'd stolen from the sheering shed last season. Mclary had whipped all of us for its disappearance, but no one knew I'd taken it, and I'd buried my guilt deep enough to justify everyone being punished on my behalf.

Along with a knife, I had a ball of baling twine, an oversize sewing needle meant for repairing sacking and tarp, a hay net that had come in handy making small animal snares, and a tin cup that had been assigned to me to drink from the well on the farm.

My one set of cargo pants, faded green t-shirt, and holey sneakers were days away from falling apart and covered in filth from living in the wilderness. And Della's pink onesie was now a disgusting shade of putrid brown from diaper mishaps, mud, and pathetic attempts to rinse in the river.

Like I said, utterly measly and totally lacking.

I should've grabbed a tarp at least for shelter, a blanket from my bed, cutlery, painkillers—not that I had access to those—and so many other handy things I missed.

The only thing we had on our side was the weather.

The temperature had stayed muggy and warm since leaving Mclary's and a small layering of leaves at night was enough to stay comfortable. With the river as our guide, we might be hungry, but we were never dehydrated, which I suppose was something to be thankful for.

* * * * *

I'd lost count of the days and nights.

I'd forgotten how long I'd lugged a baby through forest and farmland, putting as much distance between me and the Mclary's farm as I could.

All I knew was I needed something other than fish and rabbit to curb my ravenous appetite. I needed a brush to clean the fur from my teeth. I needed clothes that didn't reek. I needed a break from the girl making my life a living hell.

When I'd first run from Mclary, I shouldn't have entered the forest for fear of getting lost or dying, but thanks to my will to survive and basic education, I'd excelled better than I hoped. I didn't know what direction I travelled in most of the time, and I didn't know where I was going, but each day was a success if we ate, drank, and slept in safety.

Now, I was about to leave the sanctuary of the wilderness and do something else I probably shouldn't do. In fact, something I most *definitely* shouldn't do in my current stinky state with a listless baby who slept more often than cried these days.

If I'd survived better, I wouldn't need to do this.

If I didn't have an unwanted passenger, I wouldn't *have* to do this.

Cursing Della all over again, I gritted my teeth and took the first step from twigs and branches, trading it for paint and concrete.

Nothing happened. No one noticed. No bullet lodged in my skull.

I waited, twitching like a deer, sniffing the air, testing the waters.

When the night sky stayed silent and nothing suspicious

moved, I gathered my bravery and slunk farther from the treeline.

Using the cover of darkness, I sneaked closer toward the small township in the distance.

Just like I didn't know where I was, I didn't know the exact time, but most houses were dark, no cars on the road, no people or noise or life.

The perfect time to steal the supplies I needed and then split.

Hoisting the backpack further up my shoulders, I stiffened, waiting for Della to make a sound. She'd been quiet all afternoon in her dirty carrier, and it was past time to eat.

Normally, by now, she'd grizzle and squirm enough to make me give up travel for the day and find somewhere to sleep.

Tonight, she didn't make a peep.

That ought to have relaxed tight muscles instead of digging my worry deeper.

I still hadn't forgiven her for making my escape so hard, but I'd lasted this long, and I'd fought too hard to ensure she lasted, too.

She owed me.

I didn't talk to her often, but when I did, I always earned a sunshine smile or serious stare. I supposed this would be a good moment to speak kindly, to reassure both her and myself that we wouldn't get caught and would be better equipped once this visit was over.

"Don't worry, Della Mclary. I'll get you something yummy to eat tonight." I patted where her butt would be and strode onward.

I didn't focus on how much lighter she was these days or how hard running had been on both our bodies.

Sticking to the shadows, I stalked through suburbia. Pretty, well-kept houses with tidy lawns and painted garden furniture—so unlike the paint-peeling unkemptness of the farmhouse—welcomed me in silver moonlight.

I kept going, heading deeper into family territory and totally unfamiliar concepts of slides and swings and paddling pools left unguarded on front lawns.

I didn't stop. I didn't dally.

I was hunting for a supermarket. Something I could smash my way into, stuff my backpack full of things, then vanish back into the forest unseen.

But the deeper I travelled through manicured verges and swept streets, the more my hope deflated. I wasn't in the heart of the town where such things as stores and restaurants existed.

I was in sleepyville where children from the TV show slept soundly in safe beds with kind-hearted parents to watch over them.

I continued down the road, no longer finding the houses pretty but mocking. Mocking me with everything I'd been denied and everything I ever wanted.

One particular house hurt my stupid ten-year-old heart as I stopped on its pavement and stared. Its blue and white paint, warm wood veranda, and large bay windows whispered of peace and somewhere to rest.

The large doorknob begged me to turn it and stroll right in, to claim a bed as my own, and forget all my worries forever.

Della's knee dug into my spine as she wriggled.

"Quit it." I growled over my shoulder.

A tabby cat shot from a pruned rose bush, darting past my feet and sending my pulse jumping. With the adrenaline shot came hunger so vicious and slicing, I stumbled and clutched my empty middle.

A small cry came from within the backpack. A cry that mimicked my craving. A cry she knew she shouldn't utter but couldn't help escaping.

I didn't even have the energy to elbow her into quietness again.

Who was I kidding?

There wasn't a supermarket or dumpster or any hope of a large area of food ready to be stolen. The only choice I had before I buckled on the sidewalk was to pick one of the dozing households surrounding me, and I'd already made my selection.

The house in front of me.

The one that welcomed me to take what was inside as if it'd been waiting for this very moment.

Once the idea popped into my head, I didn't think twice.

"Be quiet." I jiggled the straps on my shoulders. "You hear me?"

Silence was my answer.

"Good."

Looking left and right, I bypassed the blue fence and pebble pathway guiding to the entrance and slithered through the shadows toward the back door. Even the service side of the house was well tended with clean rubbish bins.

Slipping into the backyard, I saw a basket of toys neatly placed, and a large umbrella wrapped tight, guarding its family, the table and chairs.

Della hung heavily on my back as I stooped as low as I could to avoid the sensor light and made my way as carefully as I could to the back door.

I had my knife.

I could smash a window or jimmy a lock.

But as I climbed the deck to investigate, my eyes fell on an oversize cat flap. Ducking, I tested it with my hand, punching it quickly.

The plastic flopped open, letting me stick my head into the warm scents of cooking, clean linen, and happiness.

I practically drooled on their welcome mat.

For once, I was thankful for my small size and skinny frame. It would be a tight fit, but I could contort myself to gain entrance. Hell, I could do anything if it meant earning a full belly tonight.

Shrugging the backpack off my shoulders, I shoved it against the side of the house out of the way. Unzipping it a little, I placed my hand on Della's dirty blonde curls as she popped up like a jack-in-the-box. "No. You're staying here."

Her blue eyes searched mine, achingly hungry and begging for any scrap of attention, food, or whatever else kids like her were used to getting.

Her helplessness did not work on me, and my heart grew ever harder. "I'm going inside to fetch supplies. Do. Not. Move." Her head ducked beneath my hand as she slouched sadly back into the bag.

I didn't know if she understood what I was saying, but I didn't take my hand away. I squeezed her tiny skull with my fingers. "I'm warning you. If you run off, I won't search for you. You'll die and get eaten by a dog. Do you want to be eaten by a dog, Della Mclary?"

Her nose wrinkled and tears welled, making her eyes glow blue.

"No crying. I don't like cry-babies." Grabbing the zippers, I pushed my face almost to hers. "If you're good and sit here quietly, I'll bring you fruit and chocolate and even new clothes, okay?"

The tears teetered on her bottom lashes but didn't fall. Twirling that confounded ribbon around her tiny fist, she plonked down and ducked her head.

I took that as a yes.

"Remember, be quiet as a mouse, and no one will hurt you."

I zipped up the bag and crawled through the cat flap before I could change my mind.

Chapter Five

REN

2000

ONLY A FEW minutes I spent in that house, and I made the first mistake of my short life within thirty seconds of them.

The kitchen was freshly scrubbed from cooking, the dishwasher sloshing quietly in the corner, a gold fish bowl humming with a night light revealing lazy, glittery fish.

A cat sprang onto the granite countertop, its yellow eyes glowing in the darkness.

I waved a hand at it, not daring to speak just in case the heavy silence carried my voice to wherever the people slept in this place.

It ignored my command to leave, never blinking, its whiskers prickling at my invasion.

Giving it the finger, I slunk deeper into its home. The cat followed me, flicking its tail, silent paws hunting my every step.

Goosebumps trailed down my spine as I entered the dining room which spread out into a family room with comfy golden couches, large TV, and a shaggy rug full of toys. The mess on the rug was the only thing out of place with large artwork staring down from neatly painted walls and dust-free figurines judging me as I spun around and headed back toward the kitchen.

I didn't need to steal anything of value, just things of practicality.

Like food.

Delicious food.

And that was when I saw it.

The booster chair wedged up against the breakfast bar ready for someone of Della's size to hang out with their much larger family members.

This family had kids.

This family had a baby like Della.

Unlike my backpack baby who sucked my finger for lack of food and slept with a stained ribbon for comfort, their baby had a cat to squeeze and fish to coo at. Unlike Della who slept beneath trees while blanketed in moonlight, their baby had a comfy crib, soft sheets, and all the food it could ever want.

My fists curled to think of his luck and Della's misfortune. Whoever this baby was I hated him because he had something Della never would.

Consistency...familiarity...*home*.

My feet froze to the crumb-free floor.

The idea unravelled too fast to stop it.

Leave her here.

I'd been begging for a way to be rid of her ever since I'd found her squishing my cheese. It wasn't that I hated her because she was the blood of my enemies but because, day by day, she was robbing me of my only chance at making something of myself.

I couldn't run far. I couldn't travel fast. All my ideas of finding a new place to call my own had been scrapped because of her endless needs.

She would end up killing us both, and a solution had just landed squarely in my lap.

The cat meowed, weaving around my legs as I strode quickly toward the back door. Shoving the creature away, I ducked on all fours and wriggled my shoulders back through the tight rectangle.

I'd have bruises tomorrow, but I wasn't counting. I already had more than normal along with scars and bumps and missing fingers.

With my body half in the kitchen and half on the deck outside, I strained to reach the backpack and dragged it unceremoniously toward me.

Della grumbled as it tipped sideways.

"Hush up." I yanked her closer, so I could unzip the top. Ripping it down too fast, a blonde curl got caught in the zipper's teeth. Her face scrunched up with indignation, her mouth wide and ready to scream.

My heart jack-knifed as I clamped a hand over her tiny mouth. "Don't you dare," I hissed in her ear. "It's just a little pain. It's nothing."

She wriggled beneath my hold, little whimpers and struggles

unmatched for my wiry strength from working the land and wrangling unhelpful livestock.

The cat swiped at my ass still lodged in its exit. I tried to kick it and lost my grip on Della's mouth.

I stiffened, already preparing to run the moment she cried.

Lights would flick on, feet would pummel stairs, and I'd be caught stuck in a cat flap like a failed, stupid thief.

Why didn't I use the door?

I could've unlocked it from the inside.

Hating and cursing my idiocy, I didn't breathe as the moment stretched so long my teeth ached. My body already vibrated with her scream. But slowly, her lips closed, anger faded from accusing eyes, and her teeny hand rubbed her scalp with her ribbon clutched tight.

I let out the breath I'd been holding.

"Good girl," I whispered. "You're very brave."

The transformation in her entire body blinded me. A smile spread. Cheeks pinked. Spine straightened. Any sign of sickness and starvation from living in the wild deleted, all because of one morsel of praise.

There was a key in that.

A message that all humans—tiny or ancient—needed nutrition in the form of love as well as everything else.

It made my recent decision even easier because I was not capable of feeding her everything she needed. I'd gotten her this far. My job was done.

"Get out of the backpack." I pushed the canvas sides to collapse on the deck.

Giving me a sideways look, she bit her lip uncertainly.

"Get. Now." Pulling her once chubby arm, I knocked her off balance and dragged her out. She didn't make a sound, not caring her filthy onesie got caught on a deck splinter or that the only place she'd found safety in was now tossed out of reach.

Keeping my fingers locked around her midget wrist, I backed through the cat flap, pulling her with me. "Come on."

It took a few attempts with the cat trying to squish past me and Della wriggling the wrong way, but somehow, I managed to get her inside without too many grizzles.

I really should've just unlocked the door, but we were inside. The cat shot outside. And the house slept on none the wiser.

The minute all limbs were inside the kitchen, I stood and stretched out sore muscles, ignored my growling stomach, then scooped her from the clean floor.

The novelty of not having to knock off leaves from her ass or check her for beetles and ants was nice as I carried her into the lounge and placed her on the rug with all the bright plastic toys.

Instantly, she latched sticky fingers around some sort of ring with rainbow disks slipping and sliding. Once again, she gave me a smile so blinding, so pure, so *grateful*, I buckled under a different type of hunger.

A hunger for the same thing I couldn't give her.

A hunger for something that offered safety even if everything around us was dangerous.

"Don't make a sound." I pointed at her, backing away to the kitchen. "I mean it."

She watched me go, blue eyes never leaving mine as I ducked around the breakfast bar and wrenched open the pantry.

She stayed quiet as a chipmunk as I grabbed packets of crisps and chocolate biscuits and brightly wrapped lollies. The foils and wrappers made a horrendous noise in the quiet, making my ears twitch for company and eyes flicker to the dark corridor beyond.

Abandoning them on the counter, I turned to quieter things.

Knowing I was on borrowed time, I yanked open the fridge and fought every instinct to dive straight into the cool crisp shelves full of deliciousness.

Grapes dangled with a cheese platter wrapped in cellophane. A chunky pink leg of ham smelled of smoke and honey. Beer clattered in the door along with apple juice packs and little glass jars with a picture of a baby on the front.

I couldn't read what flavours they were, but one was orange, another green, and one a greyish pink. Grabbing all three, I shoved them into my cargo pockets, grabbed the platter with cheese and grapes along with the ham, and somehow balanced my haul back to the living room.

Plonking them beside Della, I dashed back to the kitchen drawers to pilfer a spoon for her. I didn't need cutlery. I was too hungry to eat with manners.

"Sit still," I ordered as I landed next to her on the plush comfy rug. I wanted to take this rug. To sleep on it. Wrap myself up in it in the forest. I never wanted to leave its comfy-ness.

But it was too big, too heavy, and after tonight, I would be travelling light.

I'd no longer have a baby to haul across the country.

I could fly.

My stomach growled at the enticing smells, and I ripped off the cellophane, dug dirty nails into the ham, and ripped off a handful.

Della licked her lips as I tore it apart with my teeth, swallowing before properly chewing, forgetting I was human and becoming an animal instead.

Her smacking grew louder as she squashed herself against my leg, reaching for the ham. I didn't stop her as she copied me, powerless fingers clawing at the meat, little tongue licking air for a taste.

Even though part of me wanted to strike her for touching my food, I fought those instincts and tore her off a piece. She snatched it as if possessed by the same feral obsession, sucking and mouthing the smoky meat, frustrated tears filling her eyes as she failed to chew.

"Ugh, you're so useless." I grabbed another handful of ham, feeding the monster in my belly so I could at least find some compassion to be kind.

Content, if not annoyed with her lack of progress, Della sat quietly and let me eat. She never tore her eyes off my mouth and swallowed when I swallowed and smacked when I smacked, and when that crawling, tearing emptiness inside was sated, I shoved as many grapes into my mouth as I could then twisted off the lids from the baby food jars.

With ham-greasy fingers, I scooped up a bit of orange slop with the spoon and held it in front of her nose.

She gagged and fell backward.

I snickered. "That good, huh?"

I didn't help her up. She'd been the one to tumble; it was up to her to figure it out, but I did shove the spoon in my mouth to taste what she'd refused.

"Yuck." My lips puckered at the overly mushed paste that tasted vaguely like pumpkin. Nothing like the sun-ripened, freshly picked pumpkin that we'd grow at the farm, but a vegetable pretending to be a close cousin.

Tossing it to the side, I pulled a strip of ham off the bone and waited as Della figured out with her hopeless legs and arms how to sit up and wave her hands for something to eat.

I placed the ham on my tongue and chewed it. I chewed until the meat was juicy and tender, and then I passed it to her.

Instantly, the ham vanished from my hand to hers, then disappeared into her tiny mouth.

She bounced on the spot as she swallowed, eyes bright for more.

I didn't know if it was the familiarity of the routine from living in the forest together—eating rabbit and rat—or if I'd turned her into a carnivore with our previous measly choices; either way, I tried offering the pumpkin on the spoon again, only to have it splattered over my cargos with demands for more ham.

Seeing as this would be the last time I ever saw her, I obeyed. Stripping ham, chewing, and giving it to her until she'd had her fill.

When her eyes finally grew heavy and the sparkle of dinner and toys dimmed, I stood and returned to the kitchen.

Della did her best to watch me as I reached outside the cat flap for my backpack and stuffed it with as much food as I could. But by the time I'd finished squashing in apple juice cartons and filling up a few empty bottles I found in the recycling bin with water, she was curled up on the rug, snoring gently.

The cat slithered past me, giving me a cold glare before trotting over to the baby on his rug. He sniffed her, investigated every inch, then curled up beside her as if accepting this new human in his home.

She didn't need me.

Soon, when the sun rose, she'd have brothers and sisters and parents who would raise her as one of their own. For now, she had a cat to watch over her, fish to blow bubbles at her, and a kid who'd never meant to be in her life disappear.

She'd forget all about me.

She'd stay alive and bug free.

This was where she belonged.

"Goodbye, Della Mclary."

With a final look, I unlocked the back door and strode out of her life forever.

DELLA

Present Day

INTRODUCTORY ASSIGNMENT FOR: Creative Writing Class
Professor: Diane Baxter
Brief: To write a non-fiction piece about our lives that reads like fiction

Dear Professor Baxter,

I know you asked us to write something true that reads as fake, but I have a problem.

I'm not trying to be difficult and refuse to do the assignment but…well, this problem of mine…it's a fairly big problem.

You see, I'm not allowed to tell the truth.

Ever.

Like literally, forbidden on pain of death.

Ever, ever, ever.

You want us to write a story based on reality, but my entire life I've lived a reality based on a story.

Every town I ever lived, every school I ever went to, every friend I made, and enemy I crossed, they all got told a tale.

That's probably why I'm so good at your class. Because creative writing wasn't just something I was interested in but a skill that ensured I stayed alive.

I know I'm not making any sense, but you'll understand by the end.

If I do this assignment, of course, which I'm still debating whether or not I can.

It's not that I'm afraid anymore. I know nothing can hurt me (now).

And I know if I don't do it, it will affect my grade and possibly even my graduation.

What I'm worried about is what will happen if I tell the truth, and what will happen if I continue to live the lie I've been living since the day I was born.

Then again, if I don't write it, no one will ever know how unbelievable real life can be. But if I do write it, I'll probably never show you.

Round and round I go, Professor Baxter. Hopefully, I'll make my decision very soon, but whatever choice I make, whatever story I tell...my life?

You'll never believe me.

Even if I tell you the truth...

Even if I reveal every secret...

You'll never believe me.

No one ever does.

Chapter Seven

REN

2000

FOR FOUR DAYS, I hung around that town.

I didn't know its name.

I didn't know how many people made it their home or the names of those I stole from.

All I knew was I missed the trees and open spaces and the smells of dirt and rain and sun. Concrete, paint, and petrol covered the softness of nature, hinting that I might have been sold to a farm, but my soul had found sanctuary there. I missed fields and animals and even the toil of turning seed into crop.

I was too wild for a city and struggled with what that meant. I had no recollection of my life before I was sold, and now that I was free, all I wanted to do was return to what I'd run from, but on *my* terms, not Mclary's.

I wanted the caw of cockerels at dawn.

I wanted the bay of cattle at lunchtime milking.

I wanted to be free to make my own way, and unfortunately, the city was the opposite of freedom.

It had rules that came with punishment—just like the farmhouse.

It had expectations that came with penalties—just like the farmhouse.

Civilization was a foreign, scary place for someone like me who had no urge to become a clone, co-existing in the town's matchy-matchy houses.

All I wanted was to be left alone, and that was the heart of my problem.

I didn't want to be touched or talked to or cared for or told off. I didn't need company because company came with future complications.

All I wanted was *life*.

And it left me with only one solution.

Along with hurting my body, Mclary had hurt any chance I had at finding safety in normal society because how could a nine-fingered ten-year-old kid who'd seen things that he could never unsee, who couldn't read or write, who'd never been to school or learned how to make friends...how did that kid become one of these adults? These shallow adults who scowled at messy children and laughed in condescending tones?

The answer that I grudgingly came to was...I couldn't.

I was in a town surrounded by homes, yet I was homeless.

I was a kid, but I didn't want parents to feed me or give up the tiny shred of independence I'd claimed for myself.

I was free, but I breathed and twitched with claustrophobia to *run*.

And so, that was what I planned to do.

Even though my heart pounded to leave immediately, I forced myself to sit down and plan. I wouldn't make the same mistake twice, and I wouldn't leave this place until I had better supplies.

The one silver lining was life was infinitely easier not having a baby screaming at random times or having to carry her heavy ass through car parks and hedgerows.

For four nights, I'd slept beneath slumbering houses or even sprawled on a lounger if the yard didn't have a security light. I chowed through my stash of food and returned twice to different homes, slinking through cat flaps to restock my smelly backpack.

I'd washed in paddling pools left on front lawns. I'd stripped and scrubbed my filthy, scrawny body, diligently cleaning between every toe, every finger, and even my belly button. Crystal clear water was left a murky, muddy brown ready to be explained by confused parents and wailed over by angry kids.

I hoped they knew that even though I was a pest to them, their belongings were a godsend to me. Their food was appreciated. Their deck chairs highly rated. And the paddling pools wrenched utmost gratefulness from every bone.

I'd never had a bath at Mclary's—unless I sneaked a dip in the pond—but then I'd end up smelling of algae and duck shit and be beaten for it anyway.

Paddling pools were much better, and I despised the feeling of slipping back into rank, grubby clothes after scrubbing so clean. I hadn't gotten around to stealing a new wardrobe just yet, but soon. Very soon.

Clothes were yet more items on the long mental checklist I kept adding to. I was thankful for my good memory because without skills to write what I needed, I couldn't afford to forget anything vital.

During daylight hours, I rested out of sight or wandered streets unvisited by locals, going over my upcoming vanishing act back into the forest.

Occasionally, my thoughts tripped back to Della, and I'd stop short, wondering if she was safe. Was she fed, clean, warm? Had she forgotten all about me?

The hatred in my heart slowly faded, leaving behind an uncertainty that I'd done the right thing.

On the third night, I was tempted to return to the house with the bay windows and welcoming blue paint to see if she was happy. I let my thoughts convince me that I was responsible for her future even though that was an utter lie.

She was the daughter of my enemies, and I shouldn't care about someone who had such tainted blood running in their veins.

Besides, she *wasn't* my responsibility.

She was never supposed to get mixed up in my life.

She was better away from a kid who didn't have a plan apart from staying hidden, staying alive, and figuring out what he wanted to become.

Did I want to be Ren? The kid with no last name, no parents, no home? Or did I want to be someone else? Someone who had every right to walk down neat streets and sit at fancy restaurants?

Someone who was *someone* not *something*.

I did want that, but I also wanted *more*.

I couldn't explain it, but whenever I looked at the treeline on the outskirts of town, the itch inside built until I physically scratched with the desire to disappear inside it.

I wanted twigs cracking beneath my shoes and grass swaying around my legs. I wanted the reward of hard living because every day was sweeter for having survived with no one and nothing.

Perhaps I was punishing myself, or maybe I'd lost all trust in people.

Either way, on my fourth night, I found myself in front of a camping store in the middle of the shopping district of the sleepy little town.

My fingers smudged the glass as I pressed my nose up and stared past the streetlight reflections to the tempting merchandise beyond.

Tents and sleeping bags and everything I'd ever need to turn the wilderness into my home.

It didn't take me long to figure out how to break in, spying the back delivery door with a flimsy lock and no reinforcement. All it took was a twist of my dull blade and the mechanism gave up, swinging the door open with a whisper of invitation.

No alarm shattered the night.

No security guard grabbed me by the scruff of the neck.

I spent the rest of midnight wandering aisles, staring at pictures on packets and squinting at words I didn't understand.

I tested the weight of tents and camping stoves. I snatched sharp knives and Swiss army blades and stashed them deep in my pockets. I stole a foldable saw, small hammer, and a handy toolkit with screw drivers, pliers, and other miniature hardware I'd no doubt need.

Scooping up two first-aid kits complete with everything from needles to painkillers, I gathered a pile of water purifiers, strange dried food, bendable plates, cups, and cutlery, and finally, after much deliberation, I chose the smallest one person tent I could find that weighed less than Della.

Trading my dirty backpack, I upgraded to a cleaner one with waterproof flaps and hardwearing zippers. Khaki green with navy blue stitching, it fit my tent, sleeping bag, and everything else I needed with plenty of space left over for food.

Once I'd exhausted my checklist, I headed toward the clothing racks and helped myself to two of everything.

Two long sleeves. Two t-shirts. Two undershirts. Two trousers. Two belts. Two jumpers. Most were too big, but they were well-made and warm and would last me a lifetime if I took care of them.

For the heavier things, I deliberated far too long, doing my best to make the right choice. Eventually, I settled on a windbreak, waterproof duck-down jacket along with tramping boots a size too big, a four-pack of woollen socks, and some underwear.

At the last minute, I also shoved in a pair of flip-flops for reasons I wasn't entirely sure of, along with a beanie, scarf, gloves, and sunglasses.

Dawn slowly blinked fresh eyes and yawned away the night,

giving me a heads-up that it was time to leave.

Hoisting up my new bag of possessions, smoothing my stolen wardrobe, I crept from the camping store, pulled the door closed behind me, then headed to the supermarket across the street.

* * * * *

I had everything I needed.

I was ready to trade closed-in civilization for wide open spaces.

For the first time in my life, I felt an unfurling of excitement.

No one had caught me raiding the supermarket. No one saw the small smashed window in the staff bathroom even though they'd opened an hour ago and customers came and went.

I strolled boldly down Main Street in my clean earth-coloured clothes and dared them to say I didn't belong.

My eyes latched onto the horizon where beckoning trees and twinkling sunlight promised a new beginning.

And then, I made the second biggest mistake of my life.

I glanced to my left, toward an appliance store selling computers, stereos, and TVs, and there, on the four giant screens in the window was Della.

Her scrunched up face, purple from crying, her fists flailing, her mouth wide in an ugly scream.

My legs shot across the street before I could stop myself, slamming to a stop with my heavy backpack bashing against my spine as I pressed a shaking hand against the window.

Della.

Why was she crying?

Why was she on TV?

And where the hell was her ribbon? Her little fists were empty of her favourite belonging.

Her blue eyes shot red with tears, her little legs kicking as some strange man held her with a heavy scowl.

I wanted to kill him for holding her with such disgust and inconvenience.

My fingernails clawed at the glass, trying to comfort her even though I'd been the one to throw her away.

Then screaming Della was replaced with a severe woman in a pink suit.

Her mouth moved but no sound came.

There was nothing more important to me. I *had* to hear what she said.

Shoving my way past a customer exiting the store, I stomped

my way inside and latched onto the closest TV. The sound was turned down but loud enough to make out words I never wanted to hear.

A few nights ago, a baby girl was found in Mr. and Mrs Collins home. No sign of forced entry, no note explaining who she is, no hint where she came from or if whoever left her plans on coming back.

Mr. and Mrs Collins kept the child for a few days, hoping whoever had left her would see the error of their ways and return, but when no such visit occurred, they contacted local authorities and requested she be collected by Social Services until a foster family can be found.

If you or anyone you know is missing a baby girl, approximately one and a bit years old, blonde hair, blue eyes with a birth-mark similar to a sunburst on her left thigh, then please, ring the number below or call the police.

For now, the baby girl is having one last night in Prebbletown before facing an unknown future tomorrow.

Social Services.

Unwanted.

Unknown future.

My knees turned to water as images of Della being sold, same as me, to a fate worse than me crashed through my mind.

She'd end up being the girls with ponytails forcibly taken into the house by Mr. Mclary to do special tasks. She'd become broken and rageful and full of vicious hate at a world that'd failed her.

At a boy who had failed her.

My heart traded hate for something else.

Something that tasted like obligation, commitment, and a tiny thread of affection but most of all, like sour seething possession.

Della Mclary had become mine the moment she ended up in my backpack.

I was the only one who could hurt her.

Not that man holding her. Not Social Services. Not Mclary or false parents or men who might buy her for special tasks.

Only me.

I spun in place, the cutlery clanking loudly in my backpack.

"Hey, what are you doing in my shop? Where are your parents, buddy?" an elderly shopkeeper waddled from behind his desk, but he was too late.

I bolted from his store as the little bell jangled my departure.

I ran down the street.

I sprinted all the way to the pretty blue and white house

where something of mine waited for me.

Chapter Eight

REN

2000

SCENARIOS RAN IN my head as I careened to a stop outside the house where Della Mclary waited for me to fix what I'd broken.

Midmorning meant people inside would be awake. Bright sunlight meant I wouldn't go unnoticed.

I could wait until darkness and steal her back, but then I ran the risk of stumbling into the wrong bedroom and being caught. I could wait until Social Services arrived tomorrow and grab her, but then I ran the risk of being grabbed myself.

Or—and this was really my only option—I could march up to the front door, knock, and demand Della be given back to me.

I looked over my shoulder at the forest in the distance, seeing my dream of living alone vanishing bit by bit.

I wasn't afraid of darkness or predators or being completely vulnerable with no one to rely on but myself. But I was afraid of taking Della to such a place.

She was useless.

She was a *baby*.

I already knew she didn't fare well in the wild thanks to the previous few weeks we'd survived. She'd inched closer toward death every day.

Only because you weren't prepared for her.

Only because you didn't take what you needed.

It wasn't because I didn't know how to live off the land, and it wasn't because I couldn't provide for us.

She'd been a surprise.

And this time…I had shelter, tools, and equipment that meant we'd flourish not perish.

She wouldn't be a death sentence anymore, merely a complication I willingly chose.

I stepped back from the house.

Wait, did I willingly choose this, or was I doing it out of fear? Was living with me better or worse than living with another? Just because I'd been sold and the girls sharing the barn with me cried themselves to sleep every night, didn't mean that would happen to Della.

Perhaps the best thing for her *would* be to wait for a foster family to take her, love her, house her in a pretty little home and feed her with supermarket purchased food instead of being carried for miles by a boy then bedding down in a tent with a belly full of hunted rabbit.

After all, wasn't that what I tried to do by leaving her with a family who already had a baby? Why didn't they want her? They already had one. What was the difference in raising two?

Mclary had sixteen and managed.

The sun beat down on my head, making my back sweat against my pilfered gear. I had to make a decision. I had to leave town before I was noticed—before the owner of the camping store saw his merchandise walking down the streets unpaid for; before the supermarket manager noticed his broken window.

But…Della.

My eyes shot back to the house.

The front door swung open, revealing a woman with a lemon dress and a blue dish cloth in her hands. Her brown hair hung down her back while pink spots decorated her cheeks from chores.

I froze.

We stared at each other.

We stared some more.

Slowly, she lowered the dish towel and stepped off her porch then down the pebbled path to the front gate.

My knees jiggled to sprint. My thighs bunched to flee.

She smiled, cocked her head, and said, "Hello."

I swallowed.

I hadn't spoken in days. I'd almost forgotten how. Before I could be polite, she added, "I saw you in the window. Are you okay? Are you lost?" Her gaze landed on my backpack, questions scrolling over her face. "What's your name?"

Her questions were landmines, and I didn't want to get blown up.

Looping my fingers under the straps of my bag, I raised my chin, narrowed my gaze, and said coldly, "You have something of mine."

"Excuse me?"

"I made a mistake."

"What mistake?"

"I left something behind."

She frowned. "Left what—" Realization widened her eyes. "Wait, are you talking about—"

"Della Mclary." I nodded sternly. "She's mine. I want her back."

I noticed my stupid error too late.

I'd given her true name.

I'd revealed her family—the name connecting her to everything I was running from. Once again, I looked over my shoulder at the forest with its waving leafy arms and the message on the wind to hurry, hurry, hurry.

"Give her to me." I wiped my mouth with the back of my hand. "Now."

Her gaze slid over me from head to toe. "But...but you're a kid. What do you mean, she's yours?"

My heart sped up. I hadn't thought this through. How could I tell a stranger the truth of how Della and I ended up as a we?

The reality...I couldn't.

So, I told the first lie of many.

I boldly looked into a stranger's face and spun the beginnings of a tale that would last the rest of our lives.

"She's my sister. And I want her back."

* * * * *

It took what I assumed was fifteen minutes or thereabouts.

I couldn't tell the time, but the sun's shadow didn't move from the beginning where I stood on the street and demanded a baby, to the ending when I bolted from the house with her in my arms.

The woman was home alone with two of her own children, harried and split in all directions, so I was yet another mess to her already messy morning.

A boy about half my age drew on the walls with her pink lipstick—only for her to scream at him to stop. Another boy, a little older than Della, tossed his mug of milk from his booster seat, spraying the kitchen and his mother with white.

Two little devils, undeserving of love and protection and a life littered with possibilities.

They didn't know how lucky they were.

They didn't know how evil the outside world could be.

And then, there was Della.

Forgotten and alone on the very same rug where I'd placed her, her little shoulders sank almost to her tiny hips. She was a puddle of despair, and it tore me up inside.

Her hair was cleaner than I'd last seen but not sparkling like the two boys causing mayhem. Her cheeks were a little fuller, but her colour wasn't perky, just blue.

Blue eyes, blue heart, blue aching sadness.

Left behind and unwanted, she sat sadly, silently, staring at the rug with no toys in front of her, no cat to cuddle, no fish to coo at, no love or friendship or company.

And I'd done that to her.

My feet glued to the kitchen floor as an axe cracked through my ribcage. I wasn't much older than the boy running circles around his mother, yet in that moment, I felt like a man.

A man who'd made a terrible, heart-clenching mistake. A man who'd left behind a baby but had returned for a friend.

The woman said something, but I didn't hear her. All I could hear was the eternal emptiness, the sucking vacuum, the crippling need to fix all the pain I'd caused little Della.

My backpack crashed to the floor, clanking and clunking, uncared for as I took my first step toward a future that would mean a life of struggle, hardship, unpredictability, uncertainty, and an unbelievable consequences.

She looked up as my newly booted feet stomped onto the rug.

For a moment, she stared at me blankly. Her mouth pressed together, her blue eyes distrusting, wary, and hurt.

But then a change happened in her.

A change that stole the sun and radiated from her every golden strand and poured from every infant pore.

Something physical slammed into my chest.

Something unmentionable and powerful and so damn pure, I'd never felt anything like it before.

I thought I'd wanted to be on my own.

And I did.

But I wanted to be on my own.

With her.

And then, she cried.

Her arms swept up, her lips spread wide, her joy manifested into tears and gurgles and a crawl so fast and lurching, she looked like a drunken crab desperate to reach the ocean.

I ducked on my haunches and waited for her to scramble into my arms.

And when she did, I knew I would never let her down again. I would die for her. I would live for her. I would kill for her.

In my ten measly years on this unforgiving, cruel, terrible earth, right there I found home, and no matter where we ended up, I'd always be home because I would never let her go again.

"I'm sorry, Della Mclary." I hugged her tight, squishing her face into my chest, pressing a kiss to her strawberry smelling hair.

That would be the last time she'd ever smelled fake. The next time she'd have a bath, she'd smell like streams and grass and silver-scaled fish.

As much as I didn't want to upset her by moving too swiftly, I also knew we couldn't stay here. Behind me, the woman was on the phone, muttering to someone, whispering about me and Della, telling them to come quick and stop whatever I was about to do.

Because she knew what I was about to do.

Della knew too, and the biggest grin split her tiny lips, revealing equally tiny teeth that I'd only just noticed. At the supermarket, I'd grabbed a toothbrush and two tubes of paste. She'd have to share mine. She'd have to share everything of mine.

Yet there were some things she couldn't share.

I stood upright, and she squalled in fear, wrapping fierce arms around my legs.

Ducking down, I patted her head. "It's okay. I'm not leaving you. I won't do that again. You have my word."

As if she understood, her fear vanished, smothered by indignation and the glow of a pissed-off female. It was a look I'd seen multiple times on her mother as she'd swatted me with anything close by. It was surreal to have the same stare given in two completely different circumstances.

I chuckled.

I'd never chuckled before.

The mother hated me.

The daughter liked me.

I was stealing her for everything the Mclarys had stolen from me.

I would keep her, mould her, train her, turn her into the exact opposite of what they would have made her become, and I would change her name because she no longer belonged to them.

She belonged to me.

Yet something was missing…

I studied her, inspecting the brown trousers and grey long sleeve she'd been dressed in. I frowned at the micro-sized sneakers on her feet. She looked like a tomboy and was happy about it.

But still, something was missing.

Her hands.

They were empty.

No blue satin.

No ribbon.

Ripping her from the carpet with my fingers under her arms, I plonked her on my hip and turned to face the woman. "Her ribbon. Where is it?"

Her two boys continued to reap anarchy as she slowly put down the phone.

"What ribbon?"

Della squirmed in my arms. I squeezed her tight in warning. "The blue ugly thing she loves."

The woman glanced over my shoulder toward the trash can in the corner.

My teeth clenched. "You threw it away?" Marching toward the can, I manhandled Della so I could hold her with one arm, ripped up the lid with the other, then dropped it before ploughing my hand straight through eggshells and bacon rind until I found the slipperiness of her disgusting ribbon. The moment I pulled it free with new stains and old, Della snatched it.

I wanted to snatch it right back. It needed a wash, but for now, I had other problems to take care of.

Turning back to the woman, we stared some more until she finally admitted, "I called the police. You can't take her."

I stepped toward her. "I'm leaving."

"Just because I let you into my home doesn't mean I'll let you take anything out of it." She slithered from my path, putting the bench in our way. "You can't take her. You can't just steal a person like you stole our food."

Ignoring her tirade on my theft, I said calmly, "I *can* take her, and I am." Placing Della by the sink, I tapped her nose. "Don't fall off. It will hurt."

She planted her hands—complete with threaded ribbon through her fingers—on the granite and pressed her little sneakered feet against the cabinets below. Trusting her not to be stupid, I wrenched my heavy backpack from the floor.

She would no longer be able to travel on my back.

The extra complication should've layered me with doubt, misgivings, and hate.

Not anymore.

Now, I only looked for solutions.

Glancing around the welcoming space, I fell upon a laundry rack drying a mismatch of baby clothes and sheets.

Giving the woman a sharp look, I strode toward the rack and ripped off a few t-shirts, shorts, and jumpers all in blues, blacks, and browns for little boys.

They would fit Della. They'd be too big right now, but she'd grow. We both would.

At the last second, I stole a sheet then stuffed the baby clothes into my backpack, wrapped the sheet around my neck and back and copied what I'd seen Mrs Mclary do when she'd carried Della out to the fields to see her husband.

A sort of pouch on my chest to support Della's butt with her legs on either side of my waist and arms poking out the sides. She would be a nuisance. I wouldn't be able to travel far with her weight and our supplies.

But for now, my time had run out, and we were leaving.

Della gurgled something happy as I marched toward her and ducked a little to put her legs in the wrapped sheet first. Once in position, I slipped her into the hammock on my belly and tested the knots around my waist and neck.

Claustrophobia drenched my blood being so burdened, but my mouth watered for the forest.

Sirens sounded on the breeze, far enough away not to be urgent but close enough to warn they were coming. And quickly.

Storming past the woman, I stopped and stared. "You didn't want her. I changed my mind, and I do."

Her mouth opened and closed as I unlocked the back door.

"You're a kid. Where are you going to go?"

"Home." I shrugged. "We're going home."

"And parents? Do you have someone to take care of you?"

Heat filled my limbs, a fiery sort of scorn that put her beneath me. "*I'll* take care of her."

The woman shook her head. "But you? Who will take care of *you?*"

The door swung wide as a gust of sweet-smelling air swirled

in, leaves dancing over the welcome mat, tree branches bristling with speed.

I was being called just as surely as the sirens were running me out of town.

As the police wail grew louder, I stepped from her house and smiled. "I don't need anyone to take care of me. I have her. She has me. Family takes care of each other."

Not waiting for a reply, I half-ran, half-stumbled over her lawn, unbalanced with Della's weight.

I didn't look back as I raced through suburbia, chased the wind, and then vanished into the forest.

We were just figments of her imagination.

Ghosts she thought she saw.

Children she thought she'd met but would never remember.

Chapter Nine

REN

2000

THAT FIRST NIGHT, I travelled as far and as long as I could.

Della didn't grumble or squirm, no matter how many times I stumbled over tree roots that I couldn't see with her on my chest or ducked under low-lying branches.

Running on sealed roads was a lot easier than running through untamed wilderness, but no matter the strain on my back from carrying two different weights, and no matter the gradual aches and pains in my body the more miles I put behind us, I was happier than I'd been since...well, since I could remember.

And it didn't make sense.

Because I had nowhere to go, no guarantee of survival, and a baby reliant on me for every tiny thing.

I ought to feel terrified and trapped, not the exact opposite.

The same river we'd followed before welcomed us back, and I fell into step with the gurgle and ripple, occasionally tripping over slippery bracken but not wanting to travel too far from its banks.

I followed it for hours, silent and serious, delving deeper and deeper into the forest.

Digging my hand into my new cargo trouser pockets, I pulled out the last thing I'd grabbed on the way out from the camping store.

A compass.

I knew enough from farming that the sun was my biggest ally and greatest foe. The only letters Mr. Mclary thought to teach me were N, S, E, W for the four corners of the world where rain lived one day and drought lived the next.

Back at the farmhouse tacked to his wall in the kitchen, hung a large map with weird squiggly lines over hills and valleys. He'd caught me looking at it one day, and instead of cuffing me around the head and kicking me from the kitchen, he'd clasped my shoulder with dirty fingers and gloated. "That's mine, boy. Every boundary and treeline from here until as far north as Dead Goat Creek is all mine."

I'd done my best to study how to read such a magical piece of paper that showed every piece of property he owned, but the scale didn't make sense and the scratchings of words and numbers hadn't been taught to someone like me.

When I'd failed to respond in whatever way he expected me to, he'd twisted my ear, dragged me past his wife feeding Della in her booster chair, then threw me out, not caring I tumbled down the stairs to the dusty ground below. "The house isn't for the likes of you, boy. Boys stay in the barn." He slammed the door, making it rattle on its well-abused hinges.

I blinked aside old memories and focused on the compass. The needle pointed Northwest.

I didn't know what existed in that direction but it was the opposite of Southeast where Mclary's farm was.

Stopping in the middle of the forest with darkness descending rapidly and roosting birds all around us, I shoved the compass back into my pocket. "I'm tired. We'll sleep here."

Della's head raised from resting against my chest, her blue eyes bright and intelligent. Her little legs kicked and her hands raised, complete with filthy ribbon wafting in the air, as if to help me lift her out of the sheet sling.

"Wait." Stiffness already cramped my muscles now that I'd given my body permission to quit moving. It was always that way after a long day of labour. Keep pushing, keep moving, and the pain couldn't find you.

Stop…and it leapt on you like a herd of cattle.

I winced as I arched my back and let the backpack slip to the ground.

Hissing under my breath, I massaged the back of my neck where the sheet knot had dug into me for long hours. Fumbling with the tight bow, I gave up and bent myself enough to unhook it over my head.

Della slipped backward without the support.

I scowled. "Hold onto me. If you don't, you'll fall."

Her lips pursed as if trying to understand but didn't do what I asked.

"Ugh." Wrapping my tired arm around her, I held her tight as I undid the knot at my waist and the sheet tumbled down my front. Bending, I placed her on top of it, finally ridding my body of the weight it'd been carrying for so long.

It was sheer heaven.

All I wanted to do was leap into the river and fall asleep under the stars, but I had responsibilities now. And I had to do them before all my energy deserted me.

I was used to working on dregs. I was strong and stubborn and been taught by the land that to achieve anything you had to work and work hard.

This was no different.

For the next hour, I set aside the things we'd need from my backpack, fumbled around as I figured out how to erect the tent for the first time, and spread out the one sleeping bag inside it.

Once shelter was finished, I grabbed Della, stripped her of the boy clothes she'd been dressed in, stripped myself until we were both naked as furless animals, and carried her into the river. I couldn't let her go as the current was too swift, but I managed to at least rinse off the sweat from a long day.

Once we were semi-clean, I pinched her ribbon and used sand from the bottom to scrub it the best I could. She pouted the entire time I handled it as if not trusting me with her prized possession.

By the time we'd dried off, dressed in clean clothes, and eaten dinner of tuna fish on squashed, stolen bread rolls, my eyelids drooped and Della curled into a ball on the sheet by the small fire I'd made.

I curled up beside her.

The tent went unused that night.

* * * * *

We stayed there for three nights, getting used to the equipment I'd stolen, sunbaking in the dappling light through the leaves, eating squished bananas and apples, and growing fat on melted chocolate bars and deliciously salted pretzels.

I'd never eaten so well or had time off just to do nothing.

I didn't care we went through our rations crazy fast.

I didn't care we should probably keep moving.

This was every birthday that I'd never had, and I wanted it to last forever.

Della seemed to go through a growth spurt just like the lambs at Mclary's. One night, the baby sheep were all legs and skinny, the next they were fat and bouncy.

Della did the same thing.

The colour returned to her cheeks with regular food, and the sun browned the rest of her thanks to us barely wearing any clothes.

We learned to share the sleeping bag, clean our teeth with one brush, and scrub our clothes with the single bar of soap.

So many chores just to stay healthy and alive, but everything was so much more rewarding than fighting for scraps after a never-ending day raking, baling, feeding, milking, tending, mending…an eternal list of tasks.

In the evenings, we listened side by side to night crawlers and creatures and stayed dry and warm as a rain shower found us on the second night. The splatter of droplets on the tent lulled us to sleep instead of keeping us awake and shivering under a tree.

Life had never been so good.

And on the third night, when my mind was busy with plans of finding a new paradise, Della wriggled upright in the sleeping bag, pointed at my nose, and said, "Boy."

Chapter Ten

DELLA

Present Day

OKAY, I MADE my decision, Professor Baxter.

I'm going to do the assignment. I'm going write a non-fiction tale and make it read as fiction. However, I can't take all the credit as it already reads fake without any embellishment from me.

I suppose I should start this tale with the requisite address that's always used at the beginning of a story.

I don't know what sort of grades my biography will earn from you, and I'm still marginally terrified of the consequences of what he'll do for breaking my promises, but I'm actually excited to relive the past. To smile at the happy times. To flinch at the hard. To cry at the sad.

There are so many moments to sift through that it's like cracking open a jewellery box after decades of dust, pulling out gemstones and diamonds, and struggling to choose what to wear.

That was what he did to me, you see? He made my entire life a jewellery box of special, sad, hard, happy, incredible moments that I want to wear each and every day.

He always said the truth was ours, no one else's.

Well, now it's yours, so here it goes...

* * * * *

Once upon a time, there was a boy and a baby.

This boy didn't say much, he scowled often, worked too hard, cared too deeply, and nursed a deep distrust of people and society that nothing and no one could soothe. He had scars on his skinny body that clenched my heart the more stories he told. He had wisdom in his eyes that came from suffering, not age. And he had mannerisms born from a man who already knew his fate rather than a boy just beginning.

This boy and the baby were never meant to be together.

They were from different blood, different people, yet because of what the baby's father and mother had done, they were technically family in a strange, unexplainable way.

They say a child's earliest memories occur when they're as young as three years old, but those memories aren't there forever. There's a phenomenon called child amnesia that starts to delete those memories when they reach seven or so and continues to erase as you grow into adulthood. Only recollections of great importance are retained while the rest becomes a life-blur with no clarity.

I don't know about you, but I know that to be true.

When I was younger, I remembered more. I know I did. But now I'm eighteen, I struggle to recall exact days unless something happened so crisp and clear it's burned into my psyche.

I suppose you're thinking how then can I tell my life story starting as early as a baby? I don't know what happened, and my memory isn't a reliable witness.

Well...I can tell you because of him.

I can tell you every day from the day I came into this world because that very same night—or it might've been the night before—my father cut off his finger. I can retell every night we ran and every night we swam. I can tell you every moment until right now while I sit in my room typing this paper.

I know I'm not following the fiction-writing rules by breaking the fourth wall and talking to you as if you here beside me, but it helps this way. It helps trick me into thinking once I tell you the truth, it will be forgotten the same way I've forgotten so many precious things. It helps pretending I'm not writing this down, so there is no permanent scar on the secrets I promised to keep.

So with child amnesia and adulthood slowly stealing my past, how can I sit here confidently and tell you my tale?

I'll tell you again.

It's because of my favourite thing of all.

The thing I'd beg for, the thing I'd do anything he asked for, the cherished time of day that no one could steal.

A story.

A bedtime story meant to lull a frightened babe to sleep but turned into something so precious and coveted, I'd get goosebumps whenever he agreed.

You see, he was my only form of TV, book, radio, internet, or cartoon.

Without him, I would know nothing; I wouldn't have grown through the adventures he gave me. I'd still be a child born to monsters.

But I'm getting ahead of myself. Before I share his bedtime stories, I first need to introduce him.

The Boy.

That was my first word, you know.

He said it was because as a baby I would've heard my parents calling him Boy. They never used his name—probably never knew it. And because I was their little monster, unchanged yet by what he would make me become, I called him what they called him.

Boy.

A thing not a someone.

A possession.

I don't remember, but apparently the first night I called him that, he'd left me in a hurry. He'd stalked the forest on his own until his famous temper cooled, and he returned to me in the tent he'd stolen and the sleeping bag we shared.

I hadn't been sleeping, waiting for him to return with tears in my eyes and my ribbon wrapped around my fingers so tight they'd turned blue to match the satin.

He'd sat cross-legged in front of me, glowered with his endless dark eyes, and thudded his chest with his fist. "Ren," he'd told me. "Ren, not Boy."

It didn't occur to me until much later why he didn't have a last name. That night, he wouldn't let me sleep until I'd wrapped my infant tongue around those three little letters.

Apparently, once I'd mastered it, I never shut up.

I said it all the time, to the point he'd slap his hand over my mouth to stop me.

Even without his bedtime stories filling in the blanks and painting pictures I've forgotten, I can honestly say Ren is my favourite word.

I love every history attached to it.

I love every pain lashed to it.

I love the boy it belongs to.

I don't know if Ren looked the same when he was ten as he did when I started to remember him, but I can say his hair never changed from its tangled mess of sable and sun. Dark brown in winter and copper bronze in summer, his hair touched his shoulders one year then cut short the year after. But the tangled mess was always the same, shoved out of his coal-coloured eyes with nine fingers not ten, his nose slightly crooked from being broken, his cheekbones so sharp they were cruel.

Even as a boy, he was beautiful.

Too beautiful to carry the depth of suspicion and guardedness he never fully shed.

Too beautiful to be responsible for the wake of misdeeds left in his path.

Too beautiful to be normal.

Chapter Eleven

REN

2001

FOR FIVE MONTHS, we lived in that tent.

We walked to new campsites when we wanted a change or if I felt we'd overstayed. We never settled too close to civilization, and I always ensured we had enough supplies to last two weeks completely self-sufficient.

Della grew every day, to the point where she was too heavy to carry along with my backpack for long distances, and had to trot awkwardly beside me for short lengths.

The longer we chose trees to house us and stayed alive by hunting and foraging, the less fit for society I became.

I adored the open air, freedom, and ability to do whatever I wanted whenever I pleased.

I loved jumping in the river naked. I loved napping under a bush with the sun kissing my skin. I loved being quiet and not having to fight to survive.

Life away from people was the easiest path I'd ever chosen, and I wouldn't give that up.

For anyone.

But that was before winter hit.

For five months, the weather stayed consistently warm before gradually growing colder and colder. Our tent no longer kept the icy chill from our bones, and the sleeping bag wasn't warm enough to exist without other forms of weather protection.

My shorts and sunglasses were traded for jacket and beanie, and I ensured Della wore all her clothes, including a layer of mine, tied in places and pinned in others, to ensure she stayed as snug as possible.

One night, as ice started forming on the grass before we'd even crawled into the tent to sleep, I faced a decision I'd been putting off since my last hunt in a local town and a raid of their lacklustre supermarket.

I regularly visited towns to supplement our diet of meat and fish with things my body craved—sugar, salt, and carbohydrates. I had no qualms about stealing and did my best to break in as subtly as I could and only take things that would go unnoticed, so police would remain none the wiser.

We were a couple of days' walk from the last town and too far north according to the chilly air and the way Della shivered even hunched close to the fire.

Winter was fast approaching, and if I didn't change our circumstances, we wouldn't make it.

So I put aside my reservations of people and houses and began the long journey to the next congregation of matching homes and cloned society, doing my best to go south as much as possible to outrun the frosts determined to freeze us.

* * * * *

We found a township on the second day, and for a week, we hid in someone's garden shed where the rickety wooden walls and faded newspaper taped to the only window held the wintery blast at bay.

Our diet consisted of pre-packaged sandwiches and over-processed meats—thanks to a forage to a local store—and we chased the awful taste away with orange juice and soda.

Every hour spent in town, sneaking in shadows and staying hidden, drained me. I hated being surrounded by people. I hated watching my back and suspecting everyone.

I missed the simplicity of nature and the basic rules of win or lose.

Trees couldn't lie to you.

Bushes couldn't hurt you.

Humans were complicated creatures, and smiles were full of poison.

I didn't let Della come with me on any of my explorations, not because I worried she would prefer to trade our wilderness life for a family who didn't want her but because I feared she'd be stolen from me.

She was cute and smart and far too brave for her own good.

She'd make anyone an excellent daughter or special task giver like the girls Mr. Mclary invited into the house.

She had to be protected at all costs and kept hidden from everyone.

On my third scout for food, I ran past a bookstore with local newspapers displayed in the window. The black and white pictures stood out from squashed lines of unreadable text. Ever since seeing Della on TV, I'd studied the images of children on magazines and stories in newspapers, searching to see if the Mclarys were still searching for us.

I didn't know what I'd do if they were hunting for my one and only friend.

Over the past few months, Della and I had fallen into a habit we were both content with. She learned so fast—intently watching me do chores around the camp, until one day, she'd try to copy me as if she'd been doing it her entire life.

Collecting firewood—or more like fire sticks—she'd scatter them around instead of pile for an easy blaze. She'd fist the slippery soap and smear it on clothing without rinsing—mainly because she didn't fully grasp what she was doing and also because she was banned from going near the river unless I was with her.

She even tried to steal my knife one night after watching me sharpen the end of a stick to grill a fish over an open flame.

I'd drawn the line at that.

I liked her with ten fingers. She didn't need to copy me in everything and end up with nine.

Out of the two of us, Della talked constantly while I said hardly anything at all. She'd point at things all around us: sparrow, rock, plate, mug, water…waiting for me to name it before storing away the sound to be used later.

It hinted at yet another future complication in our life.
Education.

She was a sponge, and I only had a limited amount of knowledge for her to soak up. I could teach her how to live on nothing and not only stay alive in the forest but flourish, but I couldn't teach her the things that people learned in schools.

I couldn't show her what a real family was or how parents made you feel. I didn't know those things myself, so how could I pass on such details?

Throughout the months when she grew from baby to toddler, I grew harder and older but also softened thanks to her sweet innocence toward everything. She wasn't dragged down by hate or grudges. She didn't judge anything before she'd tasted or tested it for herself.

She taught me not to be so narrow-minded, granting a fleeting chance to be a child again when such a novelty had been stolen from me.

I often found my heart swelling with warmth for my young, tiny friend and cracking in pain knowing this life we shared couldn't go on forever.

She would eventually need more.

She would eventually outgrow me.

But for now, at least, I'd upheld my side of the bargain and kept her safe.

As we hung out, hidden and miserable from the weather in some stranger's shed, I played the naming game with Della and answered her eager finger as it flew from mower to sickle to drill to axe to rake. Rusted tools rested unused and forgotten, draped with cobwebs and dusted in beetle carcasses.

She repeated the words quietly like an eager parrot, her eyes aglow with learning.

We couldn't light a fire, so we spent our evenings huddled together in the sleeping bag, looking for ways to entertain ourselves.

This place reminded me of the farmhouse, and for the first time in a while, the fear I'd constantly lived with returned, and I locked my attention on the only entrance as Della grew drowsy and crawled into the tent I'd haphazardly put up amongst discarded household junk.

She grumbled some made-up language of baby tongue and badly phrased things I'd taught her until I obeyed her commands to come to bed and grudgingly agreed to tell another bedtime story.

Somehow, she'd latched onto the stupid retellings and stared at me with dreamy eyes and utmost contentedness on her pretty face whenever I succumbed to her demands.

The first one I'd told out of desperation when she didn't settle after something large and most likely hungry sniffed around our tent a few months ago.

I'd squatted on my haunches with two knives in two fists, ready to slice any creature that found its way into our sanctuary.

But whatever it was gave up after a while.

It didn't mean Della calmed down, though.

She'd whimpered and sniffled, clutching that damn blue ribbon as if it was her only friend in the world.

That had hurt.

I'd grown used to her seeking comfort from me—of her crawling unwanted into my lap at the worst times or snuggling too close in the night.

I wasn't used to contact from another and definitely not used to contact given so readily and often, but to have her deny what I'd grown accustomed to that night, especially after I'd been prepared to slaughter whatever it was to keep her safe reached into my chest and twisted.

Perhaps it was the feral mind-set I'd been in, already bathing in blood of whatever beast I would kill, or maybe it was the way my fists turned white from clutching the knives—whatever it was, her tears cascaded faster once the threat of danger had passed than they had when it'd been snuffling and pawing at our door.

So I'd done the only thing that popped into my head.

I'd placed aside my blades, pulled her into my lap, and told her a horror story to take her mind off the one we'd just avoided.

I told her about the farmhouse and what it was like at dinner-time. I let the fact that some animals wanted to eat us colour my retelling of starvation and helplessness in the barn. I'd killed rats and eaten them raw before. I'd torn pumpkin from another starving kid's hands. I sympathized with the hungry—human and beast—and did my best to make Della see that it wasn't personal. It was just nature's balance, and it was our responsibility to stay at the top of the food chain because we'd encounter so many that wanted to steal that position for itself.

She'd fallen asleep clutching me as tight as she clutched her ribbon, and although it shouldn't, although I was stupid to be jealous of a tatty piece of blue, I slept with a smile on my face and my friend in my arms all night.

Tonight, though, she wasn't satisfied with just a normal story.

She wanted the truth, and I was too young to think of sheltering her from it.

A few weeks ago, she'd noticed what I tried to forget every time I washed. She'd gawked at the marked piece of flesh on the side of my hipbone.

We always bathed together out of necessity and safety. I didn't care about being naked around her because all the other kids in the barn dressed and undressed to the point it was normal seeing each other bare. But there were some things I wished she didn't see.

Scars I'd endured.

Punishments I'd deserved.

Mistakes I'd made.

And that.

The one thing I could never run from.

The brand Mclary used to mark all his property from his horses to his cows to his bought and paid for children.

Della poked my hip with a tenacious finger, her face scrunched up as a stuttering please fell from her lips.

Before, I had more willpower about denying her things; I could easily say no and mean it. These days, I struggled *especially* when she threw back the same temper I used on her to get my way. She'd learned too well, and I sighed heavily, knowing tonight I would tell her just to stop her bugging me about it.

Keeping one eye on the shed door barricaded with an old generator and fallen apart rocking chair, I snuggled deeper into the shared warmth of the sleeping bag and began:

"A farmer with lots of cattle has only one way of making sure he can keep track of his inventory. With other farmer's stock sometimes wandering into his fields and rustlers stealing his herd at night, it makes sense to have a way to identify what belongs to him and what doesn't."

Della blinked, wriggling closer to pull up my jumper and push down the top of my trousers.

Instead of shoving her away like I usually did, I let her run her fingertip over the raised scar tissue on my hip.

While she studied the embossed *Mc97* in a neat oval stamped into my flesh, I said, "Your parents have a brand. I don't know entirely what the numbers are for, but I guess the *Mc* is for their name. Every single animal on Mclary's farm has the same brand. Their sheep, their cows…me."

Della let my clothing go to stick her thumb in her mouth and stroke her ribbon.

"Don't do that." I yanked her thumb from her tiny lips. "You'll have crooked teeth."

She was a pretty kid, but that didn't mean she'd stay that way if she had teeth as bad as her father's thanks to chewing tobacco and bad hygiene.

Slipping straight back into the story, I pushed her tiny hand into her lap. "The brand is found on all animals on their rump to the left, unless it's a sheep and then it's on their ear because of the wool."

Della nodded as if she understood every word.

I shrugged. "There isn't much more to say. It was the first morning I arrived at the farm. I remember being pulled from bed after crying myself to sleep and being stripped with four other boys in the crushing stall where the stock are wormed and drenched. There, he had two other farmhands hold us down, and branded us with his stamp of ownership."

I did my best not to let my mind skip down that painful memory lane, keeping my voice level and emotions out of it. "The smell was almost identical to that when he did the calves a few hours later. The burn hurt more than my finger."

Della's face fell as her little hand found mine. She squeezed with all the wisdom of a girl twice her age, full of sympathy I didn't want.

Snatching my hand from hers, I shrugged again. "It was fine. I was just like his herd to him. I got why he had to mark us. He said it was so no one could steal us because we belonged to him and he'd come claim us, but I knew it was so he could find us if we ever tried to run."

I rubbed the scar, wishing I could erase it permanently. "It doesn't matter, though. He'll never find me, brand or no brand."

Della smiled a vicious little smile.

I returned it, laughing under my breath. "He'll never find you, either. Will he, Della Mclary?"

I was a possession, and she was his daughter.

Both valuable in our own ways.

Both vanished, never to be his again.

Chapter Twelve

REN

2001

THAT FIRST WINTER was spent scurrying from one garden shed to another.

Sometimes, we'd find an abandoned house for a night or so, until the neighbours reported two stray children lurking around. Sometimes, we'd crawl through broken basement windows and boldly sleep beneath families who had no clue we lived beneath their feet.

For the coldest months of the year, I relied more on the humans I despised to feed and shelter us than the wilderness that lived in my blood.

As more time went on and the days grew shorter and the nights longer, I craved the scent of new leaves and sun-warmed bark.

I struggled to keep my discomfort and itch to be out of the city from Della, even though she suffered her own annoyance at being trapped in a place where the wrong people cared and the right people didn't open their eyes to two kids living rough right amongst them.

I liked that I could walk down Main Street with Della's hand in mine and only get a courtesy glance by those who believed all children had a family to return to and a warm meal to fill them.

I held my head high with arrogance when people stared at me and saw a kid not yet a man—a boy who would surely die if left alone and never know how wrong they were.

I liked being underestimated and enjoyed having a secret they didn't know.

What I didn't like were the men whose eyes lit up when their gaze slid from me to Della waddling beside me on her tiny toddler legs. What I didn't like were the cold glowers from women who judged me and pitied Della and believed I was the very same vermin that Mrs Mclary thought me to be.

The hairs on the back of my neck never relaxed from living close to people I didn't trust. My hackles stayed up, so when I crawled into bed at night, I was more exhausted than I'd ever been in the forest.

It all came to a head one night when lights flipped on and the door leading to family rooms above cracked open, and for the first time, we were at risk of being caught.

We had to make a choice.

Squatting in people's basements was just asking to be separated and sent to Social Services. So what if snow banks had gathered outside or snowflakes stuck together so heavy even the leafless trees bowed under their weight?

We couldn't keep doing this.

I couldn't keep doing this.

Luckily, I'd been smart and kept our gear tightly packed. Instead of setting up the tent and sleeping bag, I'd hidden us behind some cardboard boxes and used the musty smelling blankets found in the corner.

All we had to do was yank on our boots and bolt.

Whoever's house this belonged to clomped down the steps as I ripped the backpack off the floor and shoved it through the broken window. Scooping Della from the nest of blankets, I pushed her after it into the snow, then hauled myself up and out.

Instantly, the wind chewed through our jackets and gnawed on our naked hands and face. Della cried out as snow flurries danced in front of our eyes, obscuring our path, turning everything foggy and white.

A voice shouted behind us but we ignored it.

Working fast, I shrugged into the backpack and tore Della from the snow.

I wouldn't be able to run far but at least we hadn't been caught.

At least, we were still together.

* * * * *

That night was one of the worst and best of our lives.

Worst because we trekked through one of the coldest storms that winter. Worst because by the time I stumbled onto our new temporary home, Della shivered and shook with a cold, and not just the temperature.

And the best because, although we'd had to flee our last hidey-hole, the one we found to replace it was so much better.

I hadn't realised how close to the outskirts of town we'd been and only a few miles down the road, an old farmhouse rose from snow and ice, beckoning us closer.

I avoided the house even though no lights burned and no chimney puffed smoke, and carried Della into the barn farther down the gravel driveway.

The smells of hay and manure had faded, hinting that this farm hadn't been worked in a while. It made me sad to think of untended fields and forgotten livestock but grateful that the chances of being caught were slim.

Sneaking deeper into the barn, I deposited a sneezing Della onto the straw-covered floor and set about making an igloo out of brittle hay bales. It didn't take long, and the moment I spread out the sleeping bag and placed a piece of tarp over the entrance to our hay cave, the temperature warmed and the howling wind muffled thanks to the thermal properties of the dried grass.

The next morning, Della was achy and shivery, and I knew we weren't going to be leaving anytime soon. The supplies and first-aid kits I'd stolen didn't have soft Kleenexes for her runny nose or stuff to stop her coughing.

The storm had passed, so I left her tucked up tight and explored the farm in search of food and better medicine.

I didn't want to approach the house, but I had no choice if I wanted to ensure Della fought the virus as fast as possible. With a knife in my hand, just in case another man like Mclary lived here, I crept up the veranda and peered into dirty windows.

Nothing.

No furniture, no people, no knickknacks or signs of inhabitants.

It was abandoned.

And ours for the taking.

The front door was unlocked as I strolled in with shoulders braced and knife at the ready. I explored the three bed, one bath wooden farmhouse, doing my best not to see similarities with the Mclary's home but struggling.

The lounge was big with a large stain on the hardwood floor, hinting a coffee table had once lived there and someone had spilled something. The bathroom was peeling yellow with soap scum embedded in the claw foot bath. And the bedrooms were sad with their drooping curtains and mouse skeletons.

But it was dry, mostly weather tight, and had one queen mattress leaning against a wall in the third bedroom.

My thoughts turned to Della and getting her comfortable enough to fight the fever and stuffiness in a cosy bed in a proper house.

There was nothing to steal, and my raid on the pantry yielded an ancient can of peaches, an out-of-date box of Cocoa Puffs, and a sachet of noodles with a chicken on the front.

Mostly worthless but I could source other food.

I couldn't find other shelter.

Not in the middle of winter.

Leaving the meagre food on the wooden countertop, I didn't take them back to Della.

Instead, I brought Della to them.

I took the risk of claiming the unwanted house, bunkering down for the season, and doing what I needed to make her better.

I became a homeowner…however temporarily…for her.

Chapter Thirteen

DELLA

Present Day

WOULD YOU BELIEVE the boy and the baby lived three winters in that house?

No one noticed that the farm went from untended to small patches of veggies growing here and there. No one knocked when the chimney was swept and a fire roared, keeping its two illegal inhabitants warm inside. And no one cared when the empty house slowly filled with furniture, salvaged from rubbish piles and back alleys.

You see, humans are funny creatures.

The farmhouse was far enough away from society not to be an immediate concern but close enough that it was a stain on their otherwise perfect existence.

It was forgotten, ignored...just like us.

When Ren would return from scoping out tourists or seeking weaknesses on shop security, he'd smile a secret smile and feed me town rumours about the Old Polcart Farm.

You have to understand, Ren was a ghost when he wanted to be. The older he got, the more invisible he became. To a child, I found it utterly fascinating how adults just flat out ignored him.

He'd see things, hear things, steal things without ever being noticed.

And a lot of what he'd steal was information.

He'd spill unsugarcoated tales about how the son had shot the father before running off with two hundred chickens, geese, and turkeys. The father had rotted on the living room floor of Polcart Farm for weeks until the sweet smell of decay reached the town's noses.

The local police department removed every shred of furniture, paid a professional cleaner to delete the evidence of death, then put it on the market in foreclosure.

Only problem was, no one wanted to live in a house where a corpse had lain for weeks.

But us?

Ren and me?

Well, we were funny creatures, too, and we didn't mind the lingering smell or the dark ominous stain in the living room. We covered it with an old grain sack from the barn and placed a crate on top for our coffee table. A few bales of hay covered in blankets was our couch for that first year, while a few pallets beneath the mattress raised us from the floor, and Ren even made a lampshade for the single bulb from bent fence wire and old sheep wool.

He even found out how to turn on the electricity thanks to weathered solar panels and a broken wind turbine meant to operate water lines for stock. Thanks to his problem solving and determination, he learned how to redirect the naturally generated power to service the house.

In the summer, we never ran out of electricity. In the winter, we struggled but we didn't need much. Ren taught me to be grateful and to enjoy each little thing no matter how awkward or fleeting.

To me, Ren was magical.

He might not have been able to read and write, but he was the smartest person I knew.

Now, I know you're probably thinking, "Well that isn't high praise, seeing as you were a baby whose only friend and family was a farmyard boy" but I'm here to clarify that, even now as I'm about to cross the threshold into adulthood, I still maintain Ren is the smartest person I've ever had the privilege of knowing.

Everything he touched became useful or full of purpose. My days were spent waddling after him (his words, not mine) watching him endlessly, soaking up everything he did, squeezing my ribbon in awe as he wielded axes, planted seedlings, fixed hinges, and constructed fences.

He never stopped working.

He scolded me, berated me, and rolled his eyes at my need to follow, watch, and mimic, but I could tell he liked having me around. He called me a chatterbox, but that was only because he didn't say much, so I talked for both of us. But when he did speak, wow…my ears would throb for more.

His voice, even as a boy, was husky and low and almost dangerous with things he didn't say.

He had a fury inside him that scared me sometimes.

A single-mindedness that glittered in his eyes with dark ferocity.

I often wondered if he'd ever outgrow his savage tenacity, but he never did.

His relentless need to work and tend and toil was a product of his past that was so ingrained even I couldn't fix him.

I wish I could paint a better picture of how much I looked up to him.

How much I worshipped him.

How much I loved him even then.

He was everything *to me, and his intelligence didn't come from book smarts but life itself. He listened to its lessons, he excelled at its exams, and he gave me every piece of himself by sharing all that he knew.*

He didn't shelter me from things like other parents might have done.

He made me kill my first rabbit when I was two. He made me sew up his arm when he cut himself when I was three.

He treated me as capable and brave and bright, and that's what I became because I never wanted to let him down because he would never let me down.

Simple as that.

Chapter Fourteen

REN

2004

WINTER CAME AND went.

The sun warmed frozen land and sprouted new growth.

The trees rustled in the warm breeze and beckoned me back into their depths, yet whenever I looked at Della, I didn't have the heart to grab our already packed backpack and leave.

She'd sprouted over the past few winters from curious baby to independent person, and I didn't want to deprive her of the chance to grow up in a place where a roof meant stability and walls offered solid sanctuary.

She had free roam of the house—safe from drowning in rivers or being mauled by wildlife. I didn't need to watch her endlessly and enjoyed the freedom that gave me in return.

The veggies I planted in spring gave us enough variety to our diet that with regular hunting and a little patience, we didn't need to risk ourselves by heading into towns and stealing.

Realistically, it would be stupid to leave.

For over three years, no one had bothered us. No one noticed or cared.

We were as invisible as we'd ever been, and I was determined to give Della a home...if only for a little while.

Our first summer at Polcart Farm, I'd focused on better equipping the house for the next winter. I'd repaired the leaks in the roof; I'd salvaged old drapes from a local dumpster and hauled things back that made a house a home.

A table and chairs.

China plates instead of plastic.

A few discarded toys with tangled-haired dolls and missing-piece puzzles.

And, one night, when I cut through the back streets of the town after sizing up how easy a local corner store would be to break into if we ever needed emergency supplies, I stumbled upon a TV.

The screen was cracked in one corner and the picture jiggled in the other, but when I first plugged it in, using sun and wind as our power source, and Della snuggled up next to me with joy spread all over her face, it was worth the back-breaking trek back home.

When winter hit the second time, we were more prepared with rations and warmth, but boredom was a problem neither of us knew how to face. I'd already spent the time creating flowing water thanks to redirecting well water with the aid of a stock pump. I'd plugged holes in walls and cleaned dirty appliances.

The house was well cared for and didn't require much more.

I wished it did—if only to keep my brain from going stir crazy.

I wanted the chores of staying alive, of travelling, of learning a new place and circumstance. And if I couldn't have that, I wanted farm animals to tend, upkeep to dally with, and general busyness that kept my mind from the past and firmly focused in the now.

As fields were slowly deleted with more and more snow, Della became naughty, exploring areas she shouldn't, disobeying me, arguing with me, generally being a brat I wished I could toss out onto the frozen deck and teach her a lesson.

When she screamed in frustration because my lack of teaching failed her communication skills, I screamed right back. When she threw a corn on the cob at my face when I ordered her to finish every bite, I made her eat every kernel off the floor.

There were many things I permitted and indulged because she was my everything. My best friend, my little sister, my penance in real life. But if she ever wasted food…that was when my temper wouldn't be mollified.

We might have it easy now. She might have had it easy in the farmhouse while I wasted away in the barn. But there was no separation between her and me now. We were stuck with each other, and soon, when the seasons thawed and Della was bigger, stronger, faster, we would leave this place.

This wasn't a permanent solution.

And she had to know the value of things.

A TV wasn't something to be protected because it was worthless away from electrical sockets and satellites. A mattress wasn't special because it could never come with us when we ran.

But food? That was infinitely precious.

Our tent? That was priceless.

She might be young, but she was never too young to learn those lessons, and I gave her no leeway when it came to learning them.

She could cry all she wanted. She could hate me for days. We could fight until I stalked from the house and slept in the barn, but she would never win with me.

I was older.

I was in charge.

But I was also aware I was everything she had and wouldn't jeopardize that for *anything*.

Once the fire in her baby blue eyes simmered and the rage in my blood cooled, we'd awkwardly sit on our hay bale couches and slowly trade stiffness for solidarity.

She'd inch closer toward me with her ribbon trailing after her, and I'd open my arm for her to wedge tightly against me.

And there we'd sit, our apologies silent but completely heart-felt and true. I knew it was wrong to find such comfort in the sharp relief and drowning affection that came after an ugly fight, but I'd never had the aftermath before.

I'd had the shouting, the screaming, the striking, the kicking, but I'd never been held afterward or kissed on the cheek by an adoring little girl.

Just like we could cause each other's grief, we had the power to raise the stars. When Della was happy, I was happy. Her smile was infectious. Her eagerness to learn an absolute gift when I was desperate to teach.

To teach the opposite of what I'd been taught.

But I was also keenly aware that what I had to teach was extremely limited.

One dark winter's night, Della flicked through the TV stations at warp speed. We didn't get many channels due to bad reception, but sometimes, the weather allowed a snippet of movies and cooking shows, and now, a kid's channel.

She squealed and bowled toward me where I sat on the couch carving a stick into a lynchpin to be used as a new hinge in the gate I'd repurposed to keep critters out of our veggie patch. My knife scraped and shavings littered the floor.

Quickly, I palmed the sharp blade so she wouldn't impale herself as she bounced into my lap. I laughed and looked up at the bright TV where fake puppets and badly drawn cartoons wriggled around like idiots.

"Ren, look!" She waggled her ribbon-clutching fist at the TV. "Toons!"

"Cartoons." I pushed her gently off my lap so she sat beside me on the couch. It wasn't that I didn't like being touched; I just became overwhelmed whenever she did. It'd gotten to the point where I was afraid that one day, I wouldn't be able to breathe unless she touched me all the time.

She was my one weakness, and I was determined to stay immune to her for her own protection.

The TV squawked some stupid song, parading out knives and forks and bowls and fruit, flashing letters on the screen and screaming the name along with it.

Della jiggled to the song, repeating household items.

I returned to my carving, keeping one eye on her and one eye on whittling.

Time ticked on, and we fell into a comfortable rhythm; that was until Della exploded from the couch and ran to skid to her butt in front of the TV. Her little eyes danced over the brightness, her fingers drawing in the air the letter on the screen.

"A is for apple. A is for ape. A is for a great big *albatross*. Can you say albatross?" The cartoon puppet blinked as if we were a bunch of morons who couldn't say A.

I rolled my eyes, then froze solid as Della yelled, "Albwatloss." Turning to face me, she pointed excitedly at the screen. "Ren! A. It's A for appwle." She stood and traced the letter on the screen, then twirled around with her blonde ringlets bouncing and her blue ribbon twirling.

My heart stopped with how perfect she was. How smart. How kind. How brave. I'd never look at the colour blue again without thinking of her. I'd never hold another ribbon again without wanting to hold her.

Up until that moment, I'd kept a hardness inside me.

I'd treated her dearly, but I'd kept a piece of myself tucked away. But there, as she repeated the alphabet and started to excel me in every way, she nicked the fortress around my stupid heart, and I had no choice but to give it to her.

She was my Della, my ribbon, and I couldn't stop myself as I placed the knife back into its holder in my boot, crawled across the floor, and sat beside her.

She beamed and pointed at the letter S on the screen.

The one of four I knew thanks to Mclary and his compass lesson.

I repeated along with her and the stupid cartoons. "S is for snake. S is for snow. S is for a bright yellow *sun!*"

We lost track of time as we soaked up the knowledge gifted by ugly puppets. I didn't cringe at the childish songs. I didn't roll my eyes at the baby talk. I put aside my ego and imprinted every letter into my brain.

I did it for me but mainly I did it for her.

Because eventually, I would need to be more than the illiterate boy who'd carried her away in a backpack. I'd have to be a role model, counsellor, and friend. And I was determined to be a friend who could read and write.

As the night wore on and my eyes scratched and head throbbed, I glanced at Della, who'd turned drowsy and soft.

Normally, she was the one who instigated affection.

But that night, I was the one who dragged her droopy, sleepy body close and kissed her cheek. I nuzzled her sweet-smelling hair and murmured, "You're the one teaching me now, Della Ribbon. Please don't ever stop."

Chapter Fifteen

DELLA

Present Day

OOPS, I TOTALLY forgot to finish that last chapter.

It was a little off tangent I'm afraid, but at least, hopefully, it will help show you how special Ren was and how unique a man he became.

Now, before I lose my train of thought to such bittersweet memories again, I want to tell you three events that are so real to me.

I don't know if I recall them from my own experiences or if Ren was such a master storyteller, he manufactured the history to suit his own ends. Either way, they're some of my favourite, and this tale wouldn't be complete without them.

I suppose I'll begin with the very first one made at Polcart Farm where we lived for over three years. There were so many memories created there: antidotes Ren would tell me, jokes he'd spin from things I'd done, and lessons he'd remind me of from prior mistakes.

I knew Ren was happier in the forest away from society, but he put that need aside for me. He watched cartoons with me as we learned to read side by side. We cowered together when a hurricane threatened to tear the roof off, and celebrated when we cooked our first meal entirely self-sufficient.

So many things.

Too many things to mention in this assignment, so I'll only mention the three that totally stand out.

The first was when he finally called me something other than Della Mclary. I didn't have the words at the time to tell him how much I hated that name. That whenever he called me that, it was if he reminded himself that we weren't meant to be together and did his best to create distance.

But that night, when he finally called me Della Ribbon as we watched educational cartoons, he never once called me Mclary again. From then on, every time he called me Ribbon, my insides turned gooey, and I'd do anything he said—even if I didn't want to.

Amazing what love can make someone do, right?

In my toddler brain, I associated him calling me Ribbon with his admittance of loving me. He'd accepted me as his own. He no longer needed to remind himself that I wasn't born to be his.

The power of that nickname could stop my tears, cease my anger, soothe my fears, and to this day, he doesn't know how much it still affects me. How the gooeyness inside has morphed from child infatuation to adult intoxication. How gradually, over the years, my love has turned less pure, and I've kept that secret for years.

Anyway, moving on...

The second thing that meant the world to me was once we'd mastered the alphabet together, Ren left me at home one mid-spring afternoon and returned with his arms full of books.

Picture books.

Baby books.

Bibles.

Encyclopaedias.

And literary classics.

I'd spent the night curled around the musty delicious pages, stroking their pretty covers, gawking at the words I desperately wanted to know.

When he'd finally dragged me to bed, I'd clutched at a picture book about a lost little puppy trying to find his parents. Instead of a bedtime story made from truth and fact, I wanted Ren to read fiction to me.

I wanted the luxury of listening to his husky, throaty tone. Even before his voice dropped, I'd been addicted to it, and now that he sounded like a man and not a boy, I was obsessed.

Sometimes, and don't judge me for this, but sometimes, I would do something naughty just to have him yell at me. I know it was wrong, but when Ren yelled, he drenched it with passion.

He vibrated with the need to scold, and it thrilled and terrified me.

He'd bring that same passion to the tales he told while snuggled in bed. He'd regale how he'd helped birth baby lambs and how he'd once seen a foal being born. He was fluid and crisp and told a mean story that kept my attention for hours.

That wasn't the case when he cracked open the picture book and bit his bottom lip in panic. There was no husky voice. No story about a puppy finding his parents. Instead, there was a stutter and a pause and an attempt at sewing together the letters we'd learned into words we hadn't.

It'd been the first time I felt sorry for him. The first time my juvenile heart had the ability to think of him as hurting or helpless and not the *invincible, magical Ren I adored.*

It made me love him even more.

That night was the first night of many when we stayed up late and slowly learned how to read and not just parrot what the kid programs tried to teach.

And as we learned to read, we took turns stumbling over simple sentences until one of us would smooth it out and repeat it again and again until it was as effortless as speaking.

And finally, the third memory is a strange one. You'll think me mad for even mentioning it, but something about that night firmly fixed Ren as not just my father-figure and brother, but also my idol.

An invincible, immortal idol who I never ever wanted to be away from.

That first winter at Polcart Farm was bad. The icy freeze taught us that we might be able to live in the wild in summer but when the snow hit...unless we were able to grow fur and hibernate, we would die. That became even more apparent when I'd fallen sick with a simple cold the night we'd found the farm.

Due to the icy temperatures and my young age, it took weeks for me to come right, even with medicine Ren stole from the local pharmacy. He couldn't read the label so who knew if what he poured down my throat was the right dosage or the even correct drug, but he did his best, and I survived.

For days, he fed me stolen soup and cuddled me close so I could benefit from his body heat. Whenever I woke, he was ready with warm milk, medicine, and a story or two about life on a farm with sixteen children.

He didn't leave my side for longer than a few minutes, and when my fever finally broke and my chest no longer rattled with cough, he bundled me up in every clothing I had then carried me outside wrapped in the sleeping bag.

Snow covered everything, muffling sound and sight and senses. We could've been in a world completely uninhabited. We could've been the only two creatures alive, and I wouldn't have been happier because the boy who was my everything held me close and showed me the farm we'd borrowed.

He murmured how in spring he'd plant vegetables so we'd never have to risk getting caught stealing. He'd pointed out snow-softened bric-a-brac and said he'd transform rubbish into furniture and make us a home for as long as it took for me to grow strong enough so I was never sick again.

Like I said, that first winter was hard.

But the third winter at Polcart Farm was worse.

The fire never seemed to warm us, the mattress stayed damp from chill, the thrill of TV and learning—when we had electricity from meagre sunlight—was muted under the very real need to stay alive and not freeze to death.

One night, a blizzard blew so hard a window in one of the bedrooms shattered, spilling snow flurries all over the floor. I followed Ren upstairs, needing to be near him but trying to stay out of his way so he could fix it.

"I have to go to the barn to get wood and nails." He brushed past me, stomping in the boots that'd become too small for him and shrugging into his jacket.

"I'm coming too." I clattered down the stairs behind him, yanking on his beanie and wrapping his scarf around my tiny neck.

He grabbed me by the scruff as I went to dart past him into the swirling snow. "You're staying here, Della Ribbon."

"Nuh-uh. I'll help."

"You'll help by staying out of the cold."

"It's cold in here." I pouted. "No different."

"Della." He growled. "Don't argue. You know you won't win." The familiar angry light in his eyes pleased me. I enjoyed annoying him because it made him focus more on me than the many tasks and chores around the house.

Nodding once, I backed over the threshold and watched him vanish outside amongst eerie silver shadows and crunchy snow. My plan was to wait until he was too far away to throw me back into the house, then chase after him.

That was before a loud bellow echoed across the pristine white. My heart kicked and my little legs charged down the porch steps after him, tripping in the snow. "Ren!"

I fell splat on my face, scrambling out of freezing flakes to come face to face with a black and white monster. "Ren! Ren! Ren!"

The beast bellowed and nudged me with a shiny black nose.

"Ren!"

My scream tore through the night, bringing my saviour leaping over snow drifts and skidding to a stop in front of me. He shoved me behind his back, facing the monster on his own.

He'd be hurt.

Eaten.

Killed.

"No!" I scrabbled at his back, desperate to help but his dark laughter filled my ears.

His hand came up to land on the shiny nose as his voice lowered to a soothing murmur. "Hey, girl. Where did you come from?"

I couldn't stop shivering as Ren twisted to look at me over his shoulder. "It's a cow, silly Ribbon. It won't eat you."

A pink tongue lashed from its mouth, licking around Ren's palm.

"You hungry, girl?" Ren stood, reaching down to help me up while keeping his other hand extended to the cow. She didn't run off as I climbed to my feet and brushed away cold slush.

The black and white animal shivered same as me, her ears quaking in the blizzard.

"She doesn't have a brand," Ren said, searching her flanks with experienced fingertips.

My eyes fell to his hip where, beneath his many clothes, his own brand was a permanent link to my father.

Pointing at the house, he commanded, "Go inside before you freeze, Della. I'll be back soon." Not waiting to see if I'd obey, he nudged the cow with a soft hand and guided her through the storm to the barn.

Now, I know what you're thinking...I really should have obeyed and gone inside, but this was Ren—my idol. I couldn't let him out of my sight, not for a moment.

So I followed with soaking socked feet that quickly became numb as I trailed in the snow, falling over again and again until I entered the dark hay-smelling barn and watched Ren guide the skinny cow into a stall.

There she bellowed and shoved her face into past seasons bales, shaking off snowflakes and accepting Polcart Farm as her new home.

Ren closed the gate over her stall and jolted when he spotted me.

"Goddamn you, Della Ribbon, what did I say?"

I didn't care what he'd said because I was completely obsessed by the glossy-eyed black and white beast.

He scooped me from the shadows, tore off my ice-sodden socks, and kicked off his own boots to replace them. Once he'd jabbed my feet into his warm boots, he stood barefoot and glowered with the same black look he always gave me, and the look I always loved because it meant he cared for me fiercely even when I drove him mad.

"Do you want to die?" He waited for me to reply, and when I didn't, he huffed. "If you get sick again, I'm leaving you behind when it's time to leave. Don't say I didn't warn you."

I threw my arms around his neck and nuzzled him close.

He froze, permitting my hug but not returning it, his worry and anger keeping him stiff and unyielding.

But I didn't mind.

I never minded when he didn't return my affection because he loved me in other ways.

I was his, and he was mine, and through that bond, I felt things he never said aloud.

I mean, just the way he looked at me?

Wow, I wish I could draw instead of just write so you could see what I saw and feel what I felt.

The way Ren looked at you made you suffer beneath his expectation and glow beneath his praise. He touched you deeper than any hand could reach. He affected you harder than any spoken word ever could.

He cared with his entire soul and committed with entire being.

I might have been raised differently from so many kids. I might have missed out on things and probably lived through events that others would baulk at, but I was luckier than anyone because I had Ren.

I was never lacking for love.

I never felt unwanted or hurt or scared.

He was my entire universe, and he treated me like I was his in return.

Walking with bare ice-block feet toward a hay bale, he placed me down and commanded me not to move. I kicked my little legs and plucked prickly grass from beneath me and nodded with solemn promise to obey.

Muttering something under his breath, he left for a second but returned from another stall with a dinged up metal bucket. With a stern look, he entered the stall with the hay-chowing dairy cow and squatted down beside her.

"She's bruised from too much milk." His voice carried through the hushed barn. "She's wandered from her herd and hasn't been milked in days." His strong hands latched around her teats, and I hopped from my ordered spot to tiptoe closer.

Like I said, everything Ren did was magic.

Watching him milk a cow with strong sure pulls made my mouth fall open in awe. Hearing the slosh of fresh milk land in the pail made my tummy gurgle and thirst spring from nowhere. And bearing witness to that cow as Ren took away her uncomfortably full udder and left her empty and eating made me realise that Ren didn't just care for me with the fierce passion I recognised in his eyes.

Nope, he cared that way for every creature.

Every mammal, reptile, and beast.

He would bend over backward to protect, tend, and soothe.

But never humans.

Never people.

I was the one exception.

And that made me special...just like him.

Chapter Sixteen

REN

2005

I WANTED TO do something special for her.

I had no clue when her birthday was, or mine for that matter, but they fell sometime around summer. So far, we'd had a couple of weeks of perfect sunny weather, and I figured it was close enough to celebrate.

This time of year was the hardest for me.

Winter kept me grateful for the farmhouse we'd borrowed for the past few years, but summer made me *hate* it.

All I wanted to do was burn it to the ground and run away from its ashes.

The packed and ready-to-leave backpack mocked me for not having the guts to grab it and return to the life that lived and breathed in my soul.

If it was just me, I would have vanished the moment the nights turned shorter and the days became warmer, but it wasn't just me.

It hadn't just been me for four long years.

And although I felt trapped some days, although life would've been easier and simpler alone, I would never trade the little girl who trailed beside me as I guided her into town.

She blinked up at me, her blue ribbon tied in her hair today, keeping blonde curls from her eyes. Summer always made the blonde turn almost white, and her blue sparkling eyes seemed to grow in wisdom every day.

"Why we here, Ren?" she asked in her soft, childish voice. She glanced fugitively at the shoppers around us, some with supermarket bags and others with gift shop junk in their arms.

I hadn't taken her into town in almost a year.

We had no need to, and I preferred to stay as far away from these people as possible to avoid any disruption to our invisible world on their fringes.

But today was special.

And I wanted to *do* something special. If that meant something out of the ordinary and something we'd never done before, then I was prepared to do whatever it took to make this day stand out.

"It's our birthday." I squeezed her small hand in mine. "I think we deserve to eat something that we don't have to skin and scrub first, don't you?"

She slammed to a stop. "It's my birthday?"

Pulling her into the shadows of a bookstore—the same store where I'd stolen the books we'd studied and learned from—I nodded. "Yours and mine. Or at least...we'll pretend it is." I shrugged. "I don't know the exact dates but figured we should at least celebrate something."

A giant smile cracked her face. "We'll have cake like that TV show did when it was their birthday?"

"If you want."

"With candles and balloons?"

"Probably not."

Her face fell, then instantly brightened. "I don't care. This is the best day *ever*." She danced on the spot, her hair and ribbon bouncing. "Oh, wait..." She studied me, deadly serious. "How old are we?"

I fought the urge to tug her golden curls and pulled her back into walking. "Not sure but I was ten when I ran, and you were about one or something, according to the news reporter in the town I left you."

She scowled a perfect imitation of my scowl. "Yeah, don't do that again."

I chuckled. "I promised I never would, didn't I?"

"Huh. You might if I annoy you too much."

I chuckled harder. "You annoy me all the time, and I'm still here."

Her eyes widened with worry. "I do? I annoy you?"

"Yep." I spread my arms to incorporate a huge amount. "This much. Constantly."

Her lower lip wobbled. "But...you won't leave me...right?"

The barb of her sadness caught me right in the heart, and my joke no longer seemed funny.

Crouching to her level, I pressed my palm against her rosy cheek. "Della Ribbon, don't you get upset over something silly like that. You know I'm joking. I'd never—"

She shot off, squealing in laughter. "I win. You lied. I don't annoy you. You loooove me!" She spun in the street before I grabbed her bicep and dragged her sharply back onto the pavement.

Wild little heathen.

I ought to have been stricter on the rules, but somehow, I'd failed at creating uncrossable boundaries. I did my best to yell and bluster, but for some reason, my temper seemed to amuse and soothe her rather than scare the living daylights out of her.

Keeping her glued to my side with tight fingers, I muttered, "When you act like this, I second-guess that promise."

She blew raspberries at me, and for a second, two images slid over one another.

An image of a little girl with blonde hair and distraught eyes limping painfully from Mclary's farmhouse and crying herself to sleep, and then Della with her vibrant soul and fearless confidence.

Mclary lived to tear children apart.

I lived purely to ensure Della became everything she ever wanted.

It wasn't until a couple of years ago that I'd figured out what Mclary was actually doing with his 'special tasks.' That form of education came from a tatty, well-read magazine I'd salvaged from a dumpster.

I'd never seen so much nakedness in one place before and never naked adults.

And the things they were doing?

It made me sick. At least...the first couple of times I sneaked a peek. The first time I'd cracked open the glossy sun-bleached pages, I'd slammed them shut again, disgusted.

The second time, I'd been curious and looked at every graphic image cover to cover.

The third...well, by the third time, my body felt different— tighter, harder, strange.

After that, the sickness turned into more of a sick fascination, and my body burned with heat and need, swelling uncomfortably between my legs.

Over the past few years, my voice had dropped, I had hair

growing in places that embarrassed me, and now an undercurrent of hunger and searching for something I didn't understand lived deep in my belly.

It didn't happen overnight.

The familiarity of a boy's body slowly faded into foreign lands of a man.

Even though it took a few years to fully understand what the heavy ache in my groin was or why my heart beat faster when a pretty girl came on TV, it didn't mean I accepted it.

I *hated* not having control of my own body.

I hated having dreams of skin and touching and things that the magazine portrayed in explicit detail.

When I was younger, I'd woken to wet dreams with pleasure coursing through my body and not understood what happened. These days, I understood enough thanks to memories of helping Mclary breed his stock and watching bulls with cows and stallions with mares.

I'd come of age to reproduce, and I got the principal of why I hardened.

But I despised it.

I despised the complications it brought with it. I hated the random rage filling my blood and loathed the nasty demands, desperate for ways of releasing the pleasure lurking inside.

I didn't like lying frozen beside Della as she slept unaware. I didn't like having to hide my rapidly growing needs or lie to the one girl I promised never to lie to about why she wasn't allowed on my lap at certain times.

The body I once knew was now hijacked with desires I didn't.

For a couple of weeks, I'd watched Della to see if she felt different like me, but when I asked if parts of her were acting strange, she'd laughed and patted me on the head, saying if I was sick, she'd look after me.

But that was the thing...I wasn't sick. Unless, I was mentally sick because looking at that dirty magazine did things to my body that I kept hidden from Della at all costs.

I started bathing on my own because I couldn't control the hardness that sprang from nowhere. I started wearing underwear around her when before, we both didn't care—especially in summer if we went for a swim in the farm's pond or sun-baked on the porch.

That was another reason I wanted to do something different today.

I *felt* different, and it scared me. I didn't want to change because I knew my body. I knew its strengths and weaknesses. Now, I didn't trust it, and I was frustrated with the coursing newness and wants.

"Ren. Reeeeen. Ren!" Della planted hands on her narrow hips. She wore one of my sandstone coloured t-shirts as a dress with a piece of baling twine as a belt. She'd outgrown her clothes last year, and I'd yet to either make or steal new ones. "You're not listening."

"Sorry." Shaking my head free of the horrors of living in a sex-evolving body with no manual or anyone to ask if these urges were normal, I smiled at her tiny temper. "What? What am I not listening to?"

"Me. You're not listening to *me*." She stomped her foot.

I let her display of disrespect fly, finding it amusing rather than brattish. "And what were you saying?"

"Ugh." She blew a strand of hair from her eyes like an exasperated teenager—like me—and not like a five-year-old. "You didn't tell me. How old are we?"

Skipping back to our original topic as if my mind hadn't turned to less innocent subjects—like it did a lot these days—I said, "I'm going to say you're five, and I'm fifteen."

Thank God for the kid TV program; otherwise, I would still be a stupid farm boy unable to count his own age. Then again, who knew if my math was right. It probably wasn't and I'd just added or subtracted a year I shouldn't.

She wrinkled her nose. "Why can't I be fifteen, too?"

"Because you can't."

"That's not a reason."

"You haven't been alive for fifteen years."

"Neither have you."

"I'm closer than you are."

She studied me like someone studied livestock to purchase. "I don't think you look fifteen."

I returned her look of underwhelmed judgment. "And I don't think you look five."

"That's because I'm *not* five." She trotted off, heading toward one of the two diners in this sleepy town. "I'm fifteen, same as you."

If that was the case, she'd be going through the same crazy changes I was, and I'd have someone to share this minefield with.

But she wasn't.

She was still just a kid, and I was responsible for her happiness and well-being.

With her chin arched like a princess, she pranced right past the diner with its garish stickers of delicious looking food and loud jingling bell on the door.

I called, "Della Ribbon."

She spun instantly—like she always did when I called her that—her face happy, eyes glowing, body crackling with obedience and energy. "Yes, Ren Wild?"

I shook my head, chuckling—like I always did when she called me that. I didn't know where she'd come up with it.

For so long, I was used to her mimicking me and instantly recognising where she got certain mannerisms from and similarities in speech and tasks as it all stemmed from me.

But lately, she'd taken what she'd learned and adapted them to suit herself. She chose different words, spoke in different rhythms, and even attempted to do simple chores in her own way not mine.

Adding the word Wild to my first name had taken me by surprise.

I'd asked her why she called me that.

Her reply?

"Because you're wild like the bobcats we see lurking around our dairy cow sometimes. You're wild like the wind that blows in the trees. You're wild and don't have a last name so that will be your last name because it suits you and because you're wild."

Her child logic was simple and spot on and despite myself, my heart swelled every time she used it.

I was proud to be called Wild.

Proud that she recognised and understood me without having to spell out just how hard it was to live a domesticated life when I wanted to return to the untamed one we'd tasted for just a few short months.

"You went too far." I strode to the diner door and pushed it open, smiling as she gawked at the bell ringing our arrival. "This is the place."

She sidled close, tugging on my waistband for me to duck to her level. Whispering in my ear, she said, "But there are people in there. They'll see."

I stood and pushed her gently so she'd go ahead of me through the door and into the grease and sugar smelling diner. "I know. Don't worry. I have it under control."

I'd planned this for weeks. I'd ensured we both dressed smartly and didn't look like homeless ragamuffins who didn't eat or bathe. I'd dressed in a pair of shorts that were too short thanks to a growth spurt but still fit around my waist. My t-shirt was a little grubby with holes under the arms from scrubbing, but overall, it was presentable.

I'd even snuck out late one night while Della was asleep and broke into a house on the opposite side of town. I didn't stay long and didn't take anything apart from the cash in the wallet on the counter and coins from the handbag on the kitchen bench.

Thanks to a money section on the cartoon channel, I laboriously worked out I had forty-three dollars and twenty-seven cents to buy Della the best damn birthday lunch she'd ever had.

"Whoa." She slammed to a stop in the middle of the entrance, her blue eyes dancing over everything as fast as she could.

I knew how overwhelming this would be because it was just as overwhelming for me. We'd never been around this many people. Never been to a restaurant. Never had someone cook for us.

But thanks to television, we knew the principals of it, and as much as I wanted to stay off the grid and renounce my place in the human race and truly live up to the last name Della gave me, I couldn't.

For her.

One day, she would want to be normal.

She would want to have friends other than me.

A husband.

Children of her own.

She had to become used to people looking and talking and being cramped in a tiny space all eating together.

A woman in a purple and grey uniform with a stained apron spotted us lurking by the door. She waved with a pad and pencil, brown hair escaping her hairnet. "Grab a place anywhere you want, kids. I'll be right there." She returned to the people at the table before her, scribbling something down on her pad.

"Ren." Della tugged my hand, pressing her body against my leg. "I don't like it."

All around us bright lights flickered, plates clattered, people laughed and talked. The walls were painted the same purple as the waitresses' uniform, the booths wood and grey vinyl.

Not letting her fear override a new experience, I grabbed her hand and tugged her toward the closest booth by the door. I kept my own discomfort hidden, but I couldn't conceal the fact my hand trembled slightly in hers, matching her jumpy need to run.

"Get in." I pushed her onto the booth then sat beside her, gripping the table with my fingers. This was supposed to be fun.

It was terrifying.

Della scowled as if she was mad and hated me but cuddled close due to fear. "I don't like birthdays."

Sucking up my own issues with this outing, I kept my voice cool and commanding. "You're not a baby anymore. You have to deal with new things so you grow up."

My voice sounded hypocritical even to my ears.

My legs bunched and bounced beneath the table ready to bolt. My fists clenched to strike anyone who looked at Della wrong.

"I want to go home," she whined.

"And I want to go back to the forest," I snapped. "But we can't have everything we want."

Her eyes filled with liquid. "I want to go back to the forest, too."

"You don't remember it."

"Do too."

I rolled my eyes. "You were in diapers. Trust me. You don't remember it."

"Liar. I do. I do. I want to go now. I don't like it here." She scrambled at my arm, trying to raise it so she could climb into my lap.

I kept my elbow locked and remained unmoved by her terror of new things. "Della Ribbon, don't make me get angry."

She lowered her chin, her shoulders sagging even as her small body continued to quake with nerves.

"Now, kids. What can I getcha?" The waitress from before appeared, flipping her pad to a new page and looking at us expectantly.

I stiffened as her gaze slipped from my face to my chest then over to Della who'd turned into a tiny pouting mouse beside me.

I waited for her to recognise us.

For her to announce to the entire diner that we were the kids from Mclary's farm all those years ago.

But her eyes remained void of recognition, and no child snatchers appeared from the walls.

Della looked up with big blue distrusting eyes. Distrust that

I'd put there from my own distrust. I'd failed her in that respect.

She shouldn't fear her own species, and I needed to fix that error on my part.

The waitress suddenly leaned on the table, planting her elbows in the middle and reaching for Della.

Della shrieked and practically crawled into the vinyl booth while I couldn't stop my natural instinct to protect.

My hand lashed out, locking around the woman's wrist, stopping her mid-touch of the only thing I loved, the only girl I ever needed, the only friend I ever wanted. *"Don't."* My voice smoked with ice. Possession snaked in my gut.

Della was mine, and I would kill anyone trying to hurt her.

The waitress froze, leaving her wrist in my iron-shackle grasp. "I wasn't gonna do anything. She looks sad poor poppet. Only gonna cheer her up."

I let her go, narrowing my eyes as she straightened and rubbed her wrist. She glanced over her shoulder to see if anyone else had witnessed the vicious teen grabbing her.

I glanced at the exit already planning how to run.

This was a bad, *bad* idea.

"Look, sweetie." The waitress waved kindly at Della. "I only wanted to touch your beautiful hair and tell you what a pretty little thing you are." She smiled.

Della bared her teeth like a feral kitten.

The woman carried on unfazed. "You know...I work at the school down the road on weekdays and never seen you guys there. Are you new in town?"

I crossed my arms. "Something like that."

"What school do you go to?"

"Mr. Sloshpants and friends," Della whispered. "It's the program—"

I wrapped my arm around her tight shoulders, squeezing her in warning. "No school you will have heard of."

The woman pursed her lips. "Well, if you're new in town and don't have a school to go to, you should come to ours. We always have room for newbies."

Della perked up as the woman smiled bright as the sun. "We have finger-painting, playgroup, story time, maths and sciences and English—"

"Story time?" Della asked. "As good as the stories Ren tells?"

The waitress flicked me a look. "I dunno if they'll be as good as that, but they're pretty darn amazing." She winked. "You should come sometime. We'd love to have you. Show you around. You get a backpack full of crayons and colouring books and exercises. We even provide a uniform free of charge thanks to a grant from the government for small rural towns and our slipping education." She snapped her fingers. "Oh, and I almost forgot the best part!"

I didn't buy the sugary sweet delivery, but Della slurped it up like it was her new favourite food. "What?"

"You get homework and gold stars if you do well, and each class has their own pet. I believe there's a rabbit in one and a guinea pig or two and even a parrot. Pretty cool, huh?"

Della stopped shrinking into the booth, scooting to the end and beaming. "Whoa."

"I know." The waitress nodded solemnly. "It's awesome. Like I said, you should come along." Her eyes met mine. "You too, Ren. Brothers and sisters are all welcome."

Ignoring that she'd used my name thanks to Della giving it away, I opened the menu in front of me, unable to read most of the words but glancing at the pictures in record time. I wanted this woman gone. Now. "We'll have two burgers and anything else suitable for a birthday party."

"Oh, it's your birthday, sweetie?" She clapped her hands at Della. "How old are you turning?"

Della bounced on the vinyl. "It's me and Ren. We're fifteen."

The waitress laughed. "Wow, you look really good for fifteen. Bet when you're fifty you'll still look like an eighteen-year-old."

Della scowled. "I'm not fifty. I'm fifteen."

The woman laughed harder. "Okay, okay. Fifteen. Well, I better make sure the chef puts fifteen candles on your cake, huh?"

"Cake? There's cake?" Della's smile split her face. Her fear was gone. Her trepidation over new things vanished.

"Sweetie, there is *always* cake. Give me ten minutes and I'll have your bellies round as barrels."

I should thank this woman for making Della's first diner experience so easy on her.

I should smile at least for making *my* first diner experience more tolerable.

But all I could manage was a cool nod as she gave us one last grin and turned toward the kitchens with our order.

Chapter Seventeen

REN

2005

THE BIRTHDAY LUNCH cost me thirty-four dollars and ninety-one cents.

But it was worth a million, thanks to Della's happy squeals when the waitress brought out three iced-pink cupcakes all squished together with fifteen candles stabbed into them.

The cheery flames flickered all over Della's cute face as she stared, hypnotized.

Her sheer amazement made me forget we sat in public, and I grinned, loving her happiness.

It was the only time I dropped my guard. The entire meal, I'd watched, just like I did in the forest and at the farm, suspecting everything and everyone, making sure nothing could take me by surprise and hurt Della.

A little while ago, a family walked in with a girl about my age. She caught my eye and flipped her long black hair over her shoulder in a way that made my stomach clench. Not being around people meant I didn't have the worries of another version of my mother trying to sell me or another Mclary trying to buy me, but it also meant I didn't meet girls like her.

Like the dark-haired one who never took her gaze off me the entire time I sat steadfast beside Della.

She unnerved me—not because she stared and licked her lips full of invitation just like the dirty magazine showed, but because I didn't like my body's reaction to her.

I had no control over the hardening and tight discomfort in my shorts.

I hated that I had to push Della away with no explanation apart from a strict grunt not to come anywhere near my lap.

I missed simplicity when touching Della didn't make me feel dirty or wrong. When a hug was just a hug and not a moral struggle full of fear in case things happened outside of my control.

Glowering at the dark-haired girl, I did my best to ignore her. She made me feel as if I betrayed Della in some way, and nobody, under any circumstances, would make me break any promises I'd made to my blonde-haired best friend beside me.

I didn't know how long it took us to eat, but it had been longer than I wanted. Not through fault of the staff or food but because Della and I weren't used to being served. We flinched when our main course arrived. We jolted when Cokes and milkshakes appeared. And we froze in a mixture of disbelief and awe as the first mouthful delivered an explosion of different flavours instead of just one.

The waitress had been true to her word and went out of her way to make Della happy.

She brought placemats for her to colour in with bright rainbow crayons.

She laughed as Della tasted her first salty fry and promptly stuffed a fistful in her face.

And she kept her distance so I didn't feel trapped but remained attentive, never letting us run out of sauces or drinks.

This outing was for Della, but as I took my first bite of beef and cheese wrapped up in a buttery bun, I'd groaned with sheer pleasure.

Innocent pleasure.

Pleasure I was allowed to show and share with my tiny ribbon beside me.

And now, with bellies so full they hurt, Della crawled transfixed over the table to reach the glowing candles.

I grabbed her around the middle, holding her back from setting herself on fire.

The waitress beamed, waiting...for something.

When Della continued to gawk at the candles and I grew impatient with her squirming to get closer, the waitress said, "So have you made a wish? You need to make a wish, sweetie, and then blow out the candles."

Della scrunched up her face. "A wish? What's that?"

Even with the catalogue of words she asked me to give her on a daily basis and the TV, she still lacked so many. I hadn't thought to teach her what a wish was because to me, it was the constant urge to leave humans behind and hide in untouched wilderness.

And when I still belonged to Mclary, a wish was a desire for the long days, starving nights, and harsh punishments to stop.

A wish was hope, and hope killed you faster than anything. A wish was running away, and I didn't want Della to go anywhere.

The waitress gave me a strange look before answering. "A wish is asking for something you want so badly but don't know how you'll get it. It's a request for something you don't think will come true but believe in with all your heart anyway."

I gritted my teeth as Della nodded solemnly. "Oh." Her intelligent blue eyes met mine, studying me as if forming a wish full of complications and tough requests. "I wish for Ren to always be mine. To take me everywhere. And to give me more birthdays." Her white teeth flashed as she beamed at the waitress. "Do you make my wish come true now?"

"No, sweetie." The waitress giggled. "Now you blow out the candles, and it will come true by the power of pink icing and vanilla sponge!"

Della leaned closer and spat all over the cupcakes, blowing raspberries instead of air.

Not one stopped flickering with its mocking fire. I swallowed down my laughter as her joy deflated, and she looked at me forlorn. "Does that mean my wish won't come true, Ren?"

Ugh, this was what I didn't want.

Della lived in reality.

She knew the cost of hunting because she helped me kill what we ate. She knew the cost of shelter because she helped maintain the house we'd borrowed. But now she knew the cost of wishing for fantasies and the heartache when they didn't come true.

She didn't need a stupid wish to make her requests become real. I had no intention of ever leaving her again—I'd learned that lesson years ago. The next time we were apart, it would be because of her. She would leave me when she was ready. I would be the one heartbroken when she woke up one day and decided she needed more than what I could offer.

For now, though, she was still mine, and I wouldn't let her think for a moment she couldn't have everything she ever wanted.

Yanking her onto my lap—now that I was back in control of my thoughts and reactions—I dragged the cupcakes closer. "It only means the wish comes true faster and stronger." Giving her a smile, I said, "If we blow them out together, it will mean we're never apart. Want to do that?"

"Yes!" She bounced on my thighs. "Yes, please."

My chest ached that even in the middle of something as new as blowing out candles for the first time, she remembered her manners—the same manners I hadn't been raised with but learned were just as important as respect and discipline.

"Ready?" I puffed out my cheeks. "One, two, three…"

We blew out every candle.

We helped ourselves to our very first taste of sugar that didn't come from fruit and left the diner thirty-four dollars and ninety-one cents poorer.

Our crazy sugar high kept us chuckling and racing around the farm's fields, cannonballing in the pond, and playing with our dairy cow named Snowflake until the moon and stars appeared and we retreated into the house, exhausted.

* * * * *

Della watched me clean my teeth with a look in her eyes I hadn't seen before.

Scrubbing away the remnants of our overindulgence today, I spat mint into the sink and rinsed my mouth. She'd already cleaned hers thanks to the second brush I'd stolen her a few months ago.

Drying my hands on my shorts, I brushed past her to enter the corridor and head to our bedroom. She padded after me in my t-shirt without the baling twine belt—her version of pyjamas—still silent and staring at me with an intensity that made my skin crawl.

We shouldn't have had that nap on the couch before. She seemed just as wired now as she did when she'd stuffed a full-size cupcake in her tiny mouth.

"What?" I barked, climbing into bed and pulling the unzipped sleeping bag over me. She didn't crawl in beside me like usual. Instead, she stood by the foot of the mattress, crossed her twig-like arms, and announced, "I want to go to school."

I sat bolt upright, my heart racing. "School?"

She nodded, her button nose sniffing importantly. "Yes. I'm old now. I'm fifteen. I need to know what fifteen-year-olds know."

"I'm fifteen, and you know as much as I do."

"I want to know more than you do."

I fought the urge to crumple. I'd known this moment would come—I was thinking on it just a few hours ago at the diner—but to happen so fast?

Rubbing the sudden ache in my chest, I growled. "It's not

safe. You know that."

"*You* keep me safe."

"I can't keep you safe in school."

"Why not?"

"Because I don't want to go, and even if I did, we'd be in different classes."

"Why?"

"Because we're different ages."

She stomped her foot. "We're the *same*."

I rolled my eyes, dropping my hand as the fear of losing her was drowned out by the frustration of arguing with her.

Della had a mean temper—just like I did. We didn't often get into screaming matches, but when we did...I was grateful we didn't have neighbours because the police would've appeared on our doorstep.

"You're not going to school, Della. That's the end of it."

"No!" She raced from the bedroom, clattering down the wooden steps like a herd of sheep and not a barefoot five-year-old.

"Goddammit," I groaned under my breath. I didn't curse often because I hated the way Mclary had mastered the art of throwing words with such anger they had the power to make you flinch almost as much as a fist could.

I never wanted Della to be afraid of language or of me talking to her.

But when she acted like this...

Well...*fuck*.

Throwing off the sleeping bag, I charged after her in my boxers, racing down the stairs to find her cross-legged in front of the TV, flicking through the channels, desperately trying to find the educational kid's one.

She wouldn't find it.

The past few days' reception had been terrible, leaving us with hissing snow on most channels.

"Della," I warned. "Don't start a fight over something as stupid as going to school."

"It's not stupid! I want to go." She turned her back on me, crossing her arms. "I should've wished to go to school with the candles instead. Then I could go to school, and you couldn't stop me!"

Raking my fingers through my hair, I moved in front of her and ducked to her level. "You know why you can't go."

"No, I don't. We live in a house. We're normal! No one

cares." Tears welled and spilled down her cheeks. "No one cared we were in town today. No one said anything."

I shook my head, hating that my stupid idea of doing something special had already backfired. "It was a mistake to go. I'm sorry if I made it seem like we can have that sort of life, but we can't." I reached out, my hand trembling a little like it always did when we fought.

Fighting with her stripped me of every reserve I had, draining me to the point of emotional and physical exhaustion because I hated denying her things, but at the same time, she needed boundaries.

She would have everything she needed, but she would never be spoiled.

She wrenched away, crawling out of reach. "No! I want school. I don't want you. I want colouring and stories and painting."

"Now you're just being hurtful." I sat on my ass with my knees bent and feet planted on the floor in front of me.

"You're being mean. You won't let me go to school!"

"It's for your own safety."

"No. It's because you're mean!"

"I can't deal with you when you're like this. You're acting like a child."

"I'm not a child. I'm fifteen!"

"How many times do I have to tell you? You are *not* fifteen. Goddammit, you are five years old, and it's my responsibility to keep you safe and I can only do that if you stop arguing and being a brat and *listen* to what I'm saying."

She glared at me across the lounge, her legs and arms tightly crossed, her body language shut off and hating me.

I didn't care.

She wanted to know the real reason she couldn't go to school?

Fine, I'd tell her.

Keeping my voice chilly and cruel, I said, "You can't go to school because of me, okay?"

Her forehead furrowed, eyes narrowed.

I continued, "You don't have any parents to take you or meet with the teachers or sign any forms. You don't have any money. You don't have anything that the other kids will have, and people will notice. They'll ask why your mum or dad don't drop you off. They'll pry into your home life. They'll grow suspicious of who I am. They'll—they'll take you away from me."

My anger faded as, once again, the heaviness of missing her even while she sat in front of me squashed my heart.

Della sniffed back tears and scooted closer toward me—still wary, still angry, but her face lost its pinched annoyance. "Why would they take me away? You're Ren."

I smiled sadly. "Because I'm not your father or brother. I'm not your family, and they'll figure that out. They'll know I stole you and put you with another family who won't love you like I do. You'll be trapped in a house in the middle of streets and people, and I'll never find you again because they'll chase after me for stealing you. They'll try to lock me up, and we'll never be together again."

I tried to stop there. I didn't want to layer her with guilt for asking for something she should have by right, but I couldn't stop myself from whispering, "Is that what you want, Della Ribbon? To never see me again?"

She burst into noisy tears, speed-crawling across the floor to barrel into my arms. She curled into a ball in my embrace as I rocked her and kissed the top of her head. Her little arms wrapped around me tight and strong, and we both shook at the thought of losing everything we knew and cared for.

"No! No. No. *No.*" Her tears wet the side of my neck as she burrowed her face into me, and even though I'd earned what I wanted and had Della obeying me and wanting what I wanted, I couldn't help the awful taste in my mouth for being so nasty.

For shattering her dreams.

For denying her a future.

I froze.

What have I done?

Just because I was terrified of what would happen didn't mean it wasn't what was best for Della. There was no denying she would be better off with a family with healthier food and warmer beds. I'd always known that, yet my selfishness had stopped me from giving her up.

Della's tears slowly dried as I stroked her blonde hair and battled a war deep inside me. This was the first thing she'd ever asked for. The first thing she was passionate about. And I'd twisted the truth to kill her dream before it'd even been fully realised.

My shoulders rolled in horror. "I'm sorry, Little Ribbon."

Her face appeared in front of mine, and I studied the

beautiful blue eyes, button nose, rosy lips, pretty cheeks, and lovely little curls.

She was far too innocent, and because of that, I was far too protective.

If I didn't keep myself in check, I'd suffocate her.

"I'm sorry too, Ren." She wiped her tears with the back of her hand. "I don't want to go to school. I don't want to leave you."

Half-smiling, I held her close and stood. She weighed so much more than she had when I'd carried her in my backpack, but I still thought of her as a baby sometimes—completely helpless and tasty for anything to come along and eat.

But she wasn't.

She had claws even if they were short.

She had teeth even if they weren't sharp.

Carrying her up the stairs, I whispered, "I changed my mind. You can go."

Her entire body stiffened in my hold. "You mean it?"

No.

"Yes. I'll say I'm your brother and our parents are out of town. I'll lie and keep you safe."

She threw her arms around my neck. "Thank you, thank you, thank *you!*"

"You won't be able to go for long. Eventually, someone will ask questions, and then we'll have to leave."

"I'll go wherever you say."

I placed her on her feet in the corridor, needing her to hear how serious this was. "I don't mean leave school, Della. I mean we'll have to leave this place. This house. Once they know who we are, they won't stop. Do you understand?"

She backed away nervously. "But...I don't want to leave."

I shrugged. "We'd have to leave eventually. Someone will want to buy this place. We always knew this was temporary."

Fear filled her face then drained away as she straightened her spine. "Okay. I go to school, and we leave when you say."

I held out my hand. "Shake on it?"

She placed her small fingers in mine and squeezed with her tongue sticking between her lips in concentration. "Promise."

Letting her go, I padded toward the bedroom. "Let's go to bed. You and your temper have drained me."

She followed with yet another strange look in her eyes.

I groaned. "What now?"

"We don't have the same name."

I stopped, turning to face her. "Huh?"

She came as close as she could, grabbing my waistband above the brand embossed into my hip with urgency. "If you say you're my brother, we need the same name."

Goosebumps scattered over my arms at how smart she was; how effortlessly she saw the future and plotted potential problems at such a young age. "What do you suggest we do then?" I already knew what we would have to do, but I wanted to hear her theory first.

"Well…" She curled her nose, thinking hard. "You're Wild, and I'm Ribbon. One of us needs to change."

"Change?"

"Duh." She rolled her eyes, then her little lips widened in a brilliant smile, and she hugged my leg, her face going terribly close to the part of me I could no longer control. "I know!"

Tugging her away to put distance between us, I asked, "Know what?"

"You're my brother, so I need to be a Wild too. Can I? Can you share your last name with me?"

The amount of emotions this kid had put me through tonight was nothing compared to the crest of pride and love now.

"You want to share my name? The name you gave me?" I didn't know why that meant so much. Why I placed so much weight when really there was no weight at all. Why it felt so much more permanent and full of promises than a simple fix to an unfixable situation.

"Yes! I want to be Della Wild, and you're Ren Wild, and together, we're a Wild family."

I dropped to my knee and hugged her right there in the dingy corridor. "It would be a pleasure to share Wild with you and an honour to be yours."

It wasn't until Della snored softly beside me and dawn knocked on the horizon that I realised I'd deliberately not finished that sentence.

I'd meant to say it would be an honour to be your brother.

But I hadn't.

Because that wouldn't be enough.

Nothing would be enough because Della was more than just my sister and friend.

She was my world.

And I could already feel her slipping away.

Chapter Eighteen

REN

2005

FOR NINE WEEKS, Della went to school.

I accompanied her every day and waited for her every hour until she was back in my possession. The park across the road offered a convenient place to protect her without lurking outside and earning the wrong sort of attention.

That first day, I investigated every inch of the park and chose a tree high enough to look over the wall separating the school from the street and kept an eye on her. Trees and shade and shadows were my allies as I watched from afar, ready to run to her if she ever needed me.

It meant the chores at the farm went untended, that weeds grew in the veggie patch, and dinner was delayed due to later hunting, but the change in Della was one hundred percent worth it.

All weekend—as I freaked out how to handle her away from me for hours at a time—she'd talked about nothing but school, school, school. My ears rang with what she expected, and her dreams were full of happy thoughts as she tumbled into sleep with a smile on her face.

She'd laid out her clothes for her first day, and I'd swallowed my anxiety, knowing she couldn't go into public with what she'd chosen: a holey t-shirt and underwear far too small for her with the pair of flip-flops I'd stolen that I'd cut down to fit her.

No way.

That would be a sure way to announce we weren't a typical family and to invite deeper investigation.

So, as Della slept, I'd sneaked out and patrolled the town, looking for any laundry left on washing lines—hopefully a family with a little girl.

I hadn't found anything that easy, but I had found a house with a back door unlocked and a little boy's wardrobe folded neatly on the dining room table along with fresh sheets and towels.

I took two towels, some underwear, a pair of jeans, two t-shirts, and a jumper with a dinosaur on the front. They'd fit Della now that she'd outgrown her other stuff, and it wasn't like she'd grown up wearing pink princess stuff. She was used to navy, black, and brown.

At least she had clothes that weren't hand-me-downs and held together with plaited twine.

The morning of her first day, she'd been a vibrating bag of nerves, soaring with excitement to shivering with terror as we'd dressed, had breakfast of freshly gathered milk and eggs from the two hens I'd managed to steal from three farms away, and left the house.

I'd clutched her hand so hard, she'd complained about pins and needles as we strolled as casually as we could onto school property and told the receptionist we'd been invited to attend by the waitress at the diner.

Turned out, the waitress was also the deputy principal and came bouncing from the staff room, whisked Della from my hold, and promised to give her back at precisely three p.m.

And there I'd sat in my tree until three, glowering at every vehicle that entered and every person who exited, making sure no one ran away with my tiny responsibility.

When Della sprinted from the school as the bell rang, I was there to scoop her up and listen to her torrent of adventures from finger painting to a boy who said he had a dinosaur jumper like hers but it had mysteriously disappeared. He reckoned it was gremlins. Not that I had a clue what gremlins were.

I'd winced as she pitied him, all while hoping the kid wouldn't miss his jumper too much, and it was shop bought and common rather than grandma knitted and unique. What if I'd painted Della as a thief on her first day?

I made a mental note to destroy it and steal her something plain.

At home, she'd shown me everything she'd been given and true to her word, the waitress/deputy principal, had provided her with a red backpack full of crayons, exercise books, a drink bottle, lunch box, and a uniform that Della showcased for me with such joy, I'd struggled to remember why going to school was the most dangerous thing she could do.

Dangerous because as much as I lied to myself that we could run fast enough if we ever got caught, I knew the reality of that happening was slim.

When she was away from me, anything could happen, and I wouldn't be there to stop it.

I wanted to hate that cute red and white uniform with its dark grey pinafore, frilly socks, and black shiny buckle up shoes, but I couldn't.

I could only love it because it gave her access to a piece of life I'd been denied, and I wanted her to have it all.

From that day on, red was her favourite colour with only one exception.

Her ribbon.

Every morning, without fail, she'd have me plait or ponytail her hair and thread or bow her favourite blue ribbon. And every evening before bed, she'd have me free it and fall asleep with it wrapped around her fist.

I'd given her stolen teddy bears before. A stuffed unicorn. A talking hamster. But she wasn't interested in any of them—stuffed or plastic. Nothing, apart from that damn ribbon.

That first week, as we repeated the routine of the day before and I dropped her off to strangers while forcing myself not to threaten them not to touch her, was the hardest week of my life.

I lost weight because I stopped eating while wedged in my tree.

I grew cranky because I didn't sleep at night listening for noises of people sniffing around our house.

But as the days turned to weeks and Della returned time after time in her red and white uniform with pictures of smiling sunshines and squiggly writing as she learned more than I could teach her, I was forced to learn something, too.

I had to let go.

I had to allow life to take her the way she was meant to be taken and stop fighting the inevitable.

That was until everything changed.

Until the ninth week of school, when autumn arrived with bronze leaves and blustery chill and our time at Polcart Farm came to a sudden end.

Just like I knew it would.

Chapter Nineteen

DELLA

Present Day

THIS IS WHERE the assignment gets hard, Professor Baxter.

I can tell you right now that there are things in my life—sorry, my story—that won't be approved by some, won't be believed by others, and will be judged as downright idiotic by most.

You see, if you ask someone how many birthday parties they've had, they'd most likely list the number of years they've been alive. If you inquired how many pets they had, they could probably give you a definite answer.

I have definite answers, just not on those subjects.

My subjects are strange.

Such as I hear you asking…

Well, I can tell you that there were four times that Ren and I separated. Only four, but they were the worst times of my life.

The first was his fault.

The second was mine.

The third and fourth…well, I'll save those for another chapter.

Other topics that I have definite answers for are on trickier subjects than birthdays and pets. They are what you'd call confessions, I suppose.

Confessions of things I did because of hurt feelings and broken promises. Things he did because of loyalty and propriety and his unbreakable sense of honour. But again, I'm getting ahead of myself.

What I wanted to write today was the second time we separated, and how it was entirely my fault. He'd warned me what would happen if I went to school, but as a bold, invincible five-year-old, I didn't believe him.

I teased him for being such a worrier. I made jokes at his ever vigilante watching, and even went so far as to yell at him for never relaxing and trusting other people.

He was right.

I was wrong.

It all started on a Wednesday morning I believe.

Ren dropped me off and I went to class, I smiled at Jimmy who loved dinosaurs, I drank my carton of milk even though it tasted like paper and glue compared to the freshly milked stuff from Snowflake, and I enjoyed yet another day of education.

My teacher—I can't remember her name—made us copy a few math equations, and I think we did a science experiment…again, I can't remember, but what I do remember—and this isn't because Ren told me this story because he wasn't there—but after lunch we had Show and Tell.

I didn't know what that was to start with until other kids stood, talked about a toy or special possession, then sat down with praise from the teacher.

Sounds easy, right?

Yeah, I thought so too.

Seeing as I hadn't brought anything to school with me, I asked if I could borrow Frosty the rabbit, and beamed as the teacher carried the white rabbit's cage to the front of the class and smiled at me encouragingly.

I pulled Frosty from her hutch and held her tight just the way Ren taught me.

And then I told them what he'd told me.

I explained as detailed as I could how to kill a rabbit quickly and painlessly. How to nick its fur around its neck and then rip off its jacket in one move. How to gut it fast so bodily fluids didn't contaminate the meat, and how to cook it properly so we didn't die of rabbit fever.

I was so proud.

So self-satisfied as I stood before my class of students and nodded matter-of-factly; so happy that they could now fend for themselves—just like I could. I fully believed in my naïve little heart that I'd just delivered a perfect lesson on things everyone should know.

I didn't see the horrified glances until it was too late.

I didn't hear the sniffles and crying as children squirmed in their seats.

I didn't understand the jerky movements of the teacher as she snatched Frosty from my arms and stuffed her back into her cage.

And I didn't know why I was grabbed by the arm and escorted to a room with a stern-faced man and the nice lady from the diner who gave me cupcakes.

I didn't know any of that until Ren arrived.

And then…it was too late.

Chapter Twenty

REN

2005

SHE NEVER APPEARED at three p.m.

By 3:01, I was hammering on the receptionist's desk demanding to know where she was.

Instead of a worried woman bending over backward to produce my tardy Della, she gave me a grave look and quick shake of her head, ordering me to follow her. She said in an appalled, judgy tone that there'd been an incident. That the principal wanted to talk to Della's parents.

Alarm bells clanged in my head, drowning out the squeals and giggles of kids as they spilled from classrooms and into caregiver's arms. My legs were stiff wooden posts as I trailed after the woman, fighting every urge to kick her to the floor and run down the halls screaming Della's name.

She couldn't be here anymore.

I couldn't be here.

And there was no way to fix it because we had no parents to call.

My fists curled hard as rocks as the woman opened a door and said, "Go in. They're expecting you."

This was what I'd been afraid of.

This was why I hated walls and doors and locks.

Because once I stepped inside, there was nowhere to run. No way to get free. No gullies to disappear into or bushes to hide beneath. I would be *seen*.

I stepped back from the threshold as images of rain droplets on trees and sun dappling bracken filled my mind. If I left now, I could have those things. I'd never have to be trapped in a house with people again.

My heart galloped as I fought the overwhelming urge to flee, but then my gaze met Della's terrified one where she sat on a chair too big for her with her little legs dangling and hair tangled around her face where she'd yanked her ribbon from her plait.

She clutched it tight—tighter than I'd ever seen with a plea in her eyes to fix this.

Swallowing my matching terror, I squared my shoulders and strode into the room with every shred of rage and anger I could materialize. "What the hell is going on?" I went straight to Della and planted my hand on her small shoulder.

Her body quaked beneath my touch, and I squeezed her gently, wordlessly telling her to trust me. That we'd get out of here together.

A self-important man behind a self-important desk with degrees and accolades plastered to his walls ignored me, scowling at his laptop as he spoke into the phone held to his ear. "Yes, okay. Will do. We'll keep them here until you arrive. Thanks so much."

I pinned my glare on him as he hung up. "Who was that?"

The man smoothed his plaid suit with a quick glance at the waitress from the diner who looked distraught over whatever was happening. "That was Social Services. Our school has a policy to reach out if anything disturbing occurs." He cleared his throat. "Where are your parents? Before we release Miss Wild here, we really need to speak to an adult in charge."

I prayed my tongue wouldn't fail me as I prepared to tell convincing enough lies to get us free. "They're out of town."

"Oh?" The man raised his eyebrow. "How long have they been out of town?"

"Does it matter? I'm old enough to take care of her without their supervision."

"That's true." The man nodded. "But Miss Lawson here tells me that she's never met your parents. That Della's been coming to our school for over two months and no forms have been filled in or emergency contacts given." He gave the waitress/deputy principal a heavy scowl. "As she's new to the position and excited about educating young minds to the detriment of following protocol, I will overlook the lack of information we have on you and your sister and permit her to stay *if* we meet your parents, and *if* we have a strict conversation on subjects that are suitable in a classroom."

Della shrank into the wooden chair, her fingers twirling and twisting her ribbon.

I squeezed her again as I growled at the principal. "If you tell me what happened, I can give you the answers you need. Our parents are busy. They'd prefer not to be dealing with nonsense."

The principal shifted behind his desk, his greying hair slicked with oil. "This is not nonsense, boy."

"Don't call him boy," Della piped up, her girlish voice cutting through the tension. She cowered as all eyes landed on her, mumbling, "It's not Boy. It's Ren."

I smiled softly, letting her know how much I appreciated her having my back. "It's fine, Della."

She bit her lip, tears welling. "I'm sorry…"

"Don't apologise."

"But—"

I shook my head sharply. "You did nothing wrong."

"I beg to differ," the principal said. "She told her fellow students how to kill, skin, and cook a rabbit while holding the class pet. She's traumatized most of them, and I already have parents demanding to know how this could've happened." His brown, beady eyes narrowed at Della then slid to me. "Do you mind telling me why a girl of her age knows such things?"

I gave him the same condescending look. "She knows because I told her."

"Why tell her such terrible—"

"Because she needs to know the cost of life and death. She knows if she wants meat, she has to kill. She knows if she wants vegetables, she has to plant. She knows if she wants to survive, then things must die to achieve that." I crossed my arms. "Isn't that what education is about?"

"That may be the case, Mr. Wild, but we still need to talk to your parents." The waitress-deputy teacher smiled sadly. "I'm sorry, but we really must insist."

The atmosphere in the room changed from inquisition to punishment. My arms uncrossed, and I reached down for Della's hand.

She grabbed it instantly, wedging her ribbon between our palms.

"When our parents are back in town, I'll have them call you," I said smooth as ice. "But now, I'm taking my sister and going home."

Della leapt from the chair as I tugged her toward the door. The closed door.

"Let us out," I snarled at the principal.

"I'm afraid that's not possible. Not until Social Services have met Della, yourself, your parents, and investigated the type of home you are currently being raised in." He steepled his fingers importantly. "This is for your own protection, you understand. We're not here to be the bad guys; just making sure you and Della are in a healthy environment and are happy."

"We *are* happy," I snapped. "Now open the door."

The waitress stood from her chair beside the principal's desk. "You're free to leave, Ren. Go and call your parents and let them know how urgently we need to see them. But Della needs to stay here. I'll look after her. I promise."

Della blinked up at me, her eyes huge and hurting. "Ren...don't leave me."

My ribcage squeezed, making it hard to breathe. "Never."

A ghost of a smile twitched her lips, trusting me even though I had no idea how I'd keep such a promise.

My mind raced, charging ahead, doing its best with its limited knowledge and teenage capabilities to figure out a way to stop Della from being taken and to give us enough time to disappear.

A thought popped into my head.

A risky, terrible idea but literally the only one I had.

I wished I could tell Della.

I wished I could warn her.

But there were too many eyes and ears in the room. I just had to hope she forgave me once it was all over.

With gritted teeth and pounding heart, I pried her hand from mine and pushed her back toward the chair. "Sit down. Stay here. I have to go."

It took a moment for my voice to worm its way into her ears and drill a hole into her young understanding. "What?....*No*! No, you said you wouldn't leave me. No!" She launched herself at me, sobbing wet and loud. "Ren! I'm sorry. I didn't mean to. I'm sorry I told them about the rabbit. Please. I'm *sorry!* Ren, please!" She dissolved into tears, wrapping her shaking arms around the top of my thighs. "No. Please. *Please* don't go. Please, please, don't leave me." She looked up with blotchy cheeks and gut-wrenching sadness, and my heart literally cracked in two.

I bled a river inside, hot and red and painful.

I swallowed back the guilt and the all-powerful desire to stop her tears, and forced myself forward with the plan.

The *only* plan.

"Our parents arrive back today, remember?" I cupped her chin, willing her to understand. "The Social people will bring you to the farm, and they'll sit down with Mum and Dad, and this will all be fine, okay?"

Normally, Della would read between the lines—her whip fast intelligence picking up on my lie and realising, if not completely understanding, that this was a lie and lies were our weapons.

But today, her panic had overridden her ability to see, and she'd bear the brunt of believing I was about to abandon her for the second time.

Nothing could be further from the truth.

I just needed time.

Time to get things ready.

And even though it butchered me to press a sobbing Della into a cold wooden chair and leave her with people who didn't love her, I did.

I glowered at the principal, gave him the location of our farm, and promised that my parents would be there to meet him when he dropped off Della with the government officials.

He promised he'd be there at four p.m. sharp with my sister, and we'd get this nasty business sorted out.

I had forty-five minutes to pack up our life.

Forty-five minutes to figure out a way to steal Della, stop them, and vanish.

Chapter Twenty-One

REN

2005

IT TOOK ME twenty minutes to sprint home.

Ten minutes to zoom around the house, grabbing toothbrushes, clothes, towels, and food that would travel.

Five minutes to stuff the sleeping bag, tent, and every other belonging I could fit into my khaki and navy backpack, and another two to curse the zipper as it kept getting stuck on a sock shoved down the side.

My breathing was ragged and torn. My stomach knotted and coiled. My body covered in sweat from fear as well as exertion.

In the remaining eight minutes I had, I holstered every knife I owned down my boots, jeans, and back pockets, then jogged to the barn and opened the gate for Snowflake to leave her stall. She normally grazed in the field during the day, but now, I unlocked every fence and removed every obstacle, hoping she'd wander to a new home just like she'd done when she'd wandered into ours.

The chickens would survive without us. The house would still stand. The veggie patch would suffocate beneath weeds. And in a few short months, the farm would look just as abandoned as it had when we'd arrived.

I wished I'd had more time to steal thicker trousers and better jackets for us. I wished I'd thought up better travel arrangements and double checked the waterproofness of the tent.

I should've been more prepared for this.

I'd been stupid, and now, we were about to pay the price.

Gravel crunched as a car drove up the driveway for the first time in years. The house seemed to puff up in pride to accept visitors after so long of being cast out of society, hating me as I stood barring entry with my arms crossed on the front porch.

I forced my shallow breathing to become calm inhales. I clamped down on my jittery muscles and embraced ferocity instead of panic.

Panic that Della wouldn't be with them.

Panic that she'd been taken already, and I'd never see her again.

The headmaster climbed from the vehicle first, followed by the waitress who turned to open the back door and help Della out.

My heart kick-started again, revealing that it hadn't pumped properly since I'd left her forty-five minutes ago.

Such a short time but it had been a goddamn eternity.

Della wiped her running nose on the back of her hand, then spotted me and exploded into speed. She didn't get far. The waitress grabbed her gently, whispering something in her ear.

My fists curled.

I held my temper...barely.

Another car rolled up behind the minivan the teacher had driven. This one was black with an official looking logo and tinted windows.

The two front doors opened and out stepped a severe looking woman who resembled a stick insect in a burgundy suit and a man with a beard trimmed so perfectly it looked painted on.

I'd started shaving a year ago and barely managed not to gorge my face apart with cheap stolen razors let alone create facial perfection like he had.

"Mr. Wild?" The two Social Service agents prowled toward me like predators. "Ren Wild?"

I nodded, crossing my arms tighter to prevent throwing my knives at them or doing something equally as stupid. "I want my sister."

The man with his strange looking beard glanced at the waitress. "You can let her go. Thanks."

"Okay." She let Della go, and I held out my hand, begging her to come fast, come now, come quick.

Della saw my urgency, bolting up the steps and slamming against my leg. I wanted to bend down and tell her that she had to do everything exactly as I said, but we had an audience.

Instead, I smiled huge and fake. "Mum made you lemonade. It's on the counter. Take a glass and go out back to the pond, okay? I'll come play with you in a bit. The pond. Nowhere else, got it?"

Her face tilted to search mine, her eyes narrowed and uncertain.

Slowly, her confusion switched to enlightenment, and she nodded. "Okay, Ren. Pond. Got it." She took off, leaping into the house and vanishing into its darkness of living rooms and staircases.

The two agents climbed the steps, pausing in front of me. "Can we come in? Where are your parents?"

I cocked my head like I'd seen actors do on TV. The ones who pretended they were innocent but had just committed mass murder. "I can't let you in without their permission. Stranger danger and all. We're raised with strict rules, you see." I smirked as they looked at each other with annoyance. "But you can go and see them."

"We were told they were at home," the woman agent snipped. "Are you saying they're—"

"I'm saying they're behind you. In the barn." I pointed at the A-frame, paint-peeling structure where until a few minutes ago Snowflake had called it home. "They're milking our cow."

"A cow?" the Beard asked.

I nodded. "We're home grown here. Nothing but organic foods and good ole'-fashioned labour. That's why Della knows so much about the circle of life and the food chain. Not because we have a bad upbringing, but because we're not hidden from the truth."

"Right." The man nodded. "That makes sense, I suppose."

I smiled just as fake as before. "I'm glad. Okay then, go talk to my parents. I'm going to play with my sister and pull some carrots up for dinner."

The syrupy crap falling from my lips sickened me, but I'd dress up in smart clothes and quote the Bible if it meant they fell for my story and gave me time to keep Della safe.

The principal scowled but had nothing to say as the Social Service agents descended the stairs, crossed the driveway, and gave me one last look before disappearing into the barn.

The principal and his deputy followed.

I waved, animated and idiotic, cursing them under my breath as all four adults traded sunshine for shadows and vanished into the barn.

And that was when I made my move.

I flew down the porch steps, slammed the single wooden

door closed, wedged the piece of wood I'd made with the simple hinge to lock them inside, then sprinted as fast as I'd ever sprinted before.

To the pond.

To my backpack.

To Della.

* * * * *

"I'm sorry, Ren."

"How many times do I need to tell you? You don't need to apologise."

"But I ruined it."

"You ruined nothing."

"I did." She dragged the stick she'd been playing with through the dirt as I built a fire from gathered twigs and logs. Her red uniform, frilly socks, and shiny black shoes were now bedraggled and forest worn. "I shouldn't have said that about Frosty."

"I don't know who Frosty is, but you did nothing wrong."

"I told them how to eat a rabbit."

"And where is the harm in being honest?" I looked up, willing her guilt to stop beating her up. "Honesty is better than lying, Della. You know that."

"I know but...I don't think the kids liked being told how to gut a bunny."

"I'm sure they didn't. But that's the point." I broke more twigs into kindling. "It's because parents teach their kids that meat comes in packets and not alive like them that's the problem. Not you for pointing out the truth."

"Is it wrong to kill?" She looked up with nerves dancing in her eyes. "Are we bad because we eat meat?"

I stopped what I was doing, giving her my full attention. "People have forgotten so much, Della Ribbon. They've forgotten that behind their supermarkets and houses, beneath their fancy dresses and suits, they're still just animals. We're not bad for eating meat because we only eat what we need and don't waste. It's everyone else who doesn't appreciate the cost of things who are bad."

I dropped my gaze as I used one of my four lighters—ever the resourceful—to start the fire I'd built.

Della had been subdued all evening from the moment I'd skidded to a stop beside her by the pond, hauled on my backpack, then took her hand and jogged until she couldn't jog anymore, to now when all we could hear were crickets and insects, and our house had been replaced with a canopy of tree leaves.

I tried to hide my joy at being back where I belonged.

I tried not to smile or laugh in sheer pleasure at being away from cruel people and rotten societies.

I was happier than I'd been in a while, but Della was sad, and I didn't want to make her feel worse by treating this as a celebration rather than a serious escape from potential separation.

She poked a leaf with her stick. "I thought you left me."

"I promised I never would."

"But you *did* leave me."

"Only for forty-five minutes."

She stuck her bottom lip out, pouting dramatically. "You still left me."

I chuckled under my breath. "Okay, what can I do to make it up to you?"

She peered at me from beneath her brow. "I don't know yet."

"Well, while you're coming up with a suitable punishment, how about I put up the tent so we can go to bed?"

She nodded as if permitting me to do that one task but nothing else.

Despite our close call today, she was still the same opinionated five-year-old I cherished.

Traipsing through the soft undergrowth to where I'd propped my backpack against a huge tree, I unzipped it and began the process of yanking out almost every possession to get to the stuffed tent beneath. I also took out comfier clothes for Della. She'd no longer need her school uniform. Some animal could use it as a nest come winter.

As I shook out our shelter that hadn't been used since our last two-night camping trip a few months ago, I did my best to visualise where we were.

We'd cut over the farm, following well-known tracks and clusters of trees thanks to previous exploring during the summer heat.

Ideally, we should start to make our way south so we could avoid the cold for as long as possible. I had my compass. We could follow the autumn sun.

Wherever we ended up for winter would remain a mystery until we got there.

At least, we'd escaped this time. For hours, we hadn't stopped moving deeper and deeper into the treeline, and I'd pushed Della until she'd stumbled in exhaustion.

We weren't far enough away, but she was too heavy to carry for long distances, especially with an overstuffed backpack already killing my spine.

I gambled we'd be safe here for a night or two. No one had yelled or chased, and we'd successfully traded fields for forest.

We were just two unknown kids that adults would rather forget existed than file paperwork and begin a manhunt for.

We were alone.

And I wished I cared more about what we'd just left behind.

I wished I had some sort of homesickness for Della's sake, so I could understand how traumatic this sudden disappearance would be to her.

But I didn't.

I didn't dwell for a second on running from a house and saying goodbye to TVs and mattresses and couches.

All I felt was utmost relief and freedom to be back in a simple world where life grew all around me, creatures were safe to do their own thing, flowers and weeds grew side by side, and not one of them tried to trap or change us.

Once the tent was secured and our sleeping bag inside, I pulled out a few eggs that I'd wrapped carefully in our clothing and fried them on a rock warmed in the fire.

Della curled next to me as we ate, leaning against tree roots and watching grey smoke from our orange fire mingle with the black sky.

The taste was a thousand times better than anything cooked on a range. Smoky and earthy and seasoned by nature itself.

It wasn't just food that tasted different away from town.

The colours were brighter, bolder.

The night sounds deeper, wilder.

My heart beat softer, calmer.

Della nuzzled into my side as I leaned back and wrapped my arm around her. I couldn't give her language or history or math.

But I could give her perfect simplicity.

And a bedtime story or two.

Chapter Twenty-Two

REN

2005

FOR THREE MONTHS, we lived like feral royalty.

Washing in rivers, playing in forests, eating whatever we could hunt and gather.

It was just as perfect as the first few months I'd run from Mclary's—actually, it was better because Della had a personality now, voiced opinions regularly, and had an over inquisitive mind that learned fast and excelled at making fires, gutting game, and even cleaning a few rabbit skins to save for something useful later.

She said she remembered our life before Polcart Farm. She said she remembered the many nights we slept tentless and covered in stars and how much she'd hated roasted meat to begin with.

I didn't disillusion her and argue. I doubted she remembered any of it. Her daily awe and fascination of every little thing said this was her very first time.

But sometimes, she would surprise me and quip about hiding in that guy's shed with its piles of junk or hiding behind cardboard boxes in some family's basement.

I couldn't tell if she parroted the stories I'd told her or if she truly did remember. In which case, I made sure to teach her everything she wanted so if, heaven forbid, we were ever separated, she could fend for herself, light a fire, javelin a fish, and create a snare for smaller prey.

She even knew how to wield a knife without cutting off a finger and understood how to sharpen the point of a stick for cooking and other chores around the camp.

Overall, we excelled.

I'd always been strong thanks to the many hours of labour I'd been born into, but now, my muscles grew and height spurted and hair grew untamed or shorn.

Della often tugged on the slight patchy beard I couldn't trim without a mirror, calling me a hairy monkey. I'd try to bite her fingers until she'd squeal and run away, playing hide and seek in the trees.

The clothes I'd stolen before leaving grew tighter as yet another growth spurt found both of us and almost overnight Della lost the chubbiness of her baby cheeks, slimming, sharpening, showing glimpses of the young girl she'd become.

On those rare moments, when she sat like an adult or strung a complicated sentence together like any well-read philosopher, I'd freeze and stare.

I'd flash-forward to a future where she'd be a beautiful woman, strong and brave and based in reality, where hard work layered beneath her quaint fingernails and outdoor living whitened blonde hair and browned pink cheeks.

I was proud of her.

So damn proud.

And to be honest, proud of myself that I hadn't killed her yet through neglect or sheer incompetence.

Despite all odds, she'd flourished, and I only had myself to clap on the back and say good job.

Along with the many miles we travelled, we continued to supplement our rural lifestyle with quick forages where people massed and congregated.

Occasionally, we'd come across a small township where I'd leave Della on the outskirts while I slinked through oblivious city folk and help myself to toothpaste, packaged veggies, and canned fruit.

Della asked more than once if we could have lunch at a diner again.

It killed me to refuse, but I couldn't risk it.

We were still too close to our previous town, and I'd hate to put her at risk all over again.

I was older now.

Old enough to know I'd technically kidnapped her, and if Social Services ever found out her real name, my future would be worse than just living without her. I'd be living in *prison* without her.

At night, I battled with wondering if that was why I kept her hidden—for my own stupid sake. But when she bounced from the tent in the mornings, bright and happy and excelling at everything she did, I allowed myself to hope that my selfishness was really about her.

I loved that she loved the life I could give her.

I worried she'd hate the life someone else would force upon her.

So, even though I refused diner and city visits, I did my best to cave to her every other whim. I came up with crazy hair styles with her ribbon threaded as artfully as I could. I indulged her whenever she asked for stories, even if it was on a hike to our next camp and not just as a tool to make her drowsy. I let her wear my clothes and stuff one of my socks with soft moss to make an ugly toy snake.

Some days, when summer made a reappearance and chased off the autumn chill, we'd forget about travelling or hunting and spend the day sunbaking by the river and jumping into the cooling depths.

Those days were my favourite.

The ones when no responsibilities could find us and the world where men branded kids as property and women permitted their sons to be sold no longer existed.

At first, I'd worried about the new needs running in my blood and the pleasure my body insisted on finding sometimes in my sleep. I'd refused to skinny-dip and didn't let Della cuddle too close when we slept.

But gradually, the wariness I wore whenever we were around people fissured and shed, leaving me a boy once again.

A boy who might be turning into a man against his wishes, but out here…with nothing but trees for company and woodland creatures to judge, I could act stupid and make Della laugh. I could cannonball into the river butt naked and not feel as if I'd done something wrong.

I could be happy with my tiny stolen friend.

Nothing could make our life any better, or at least that was what I'd thought until Della rolled on her belly and poked my cheek as we lay side by side with our tent flap open and the sounds of night blanketing us.

"Hey, Ren?"

My eyes cracked open. "I thought you were asleep."

"I faked it."

"But I told you two stories, Della Ribbon. The deal is I talk, you sleep."

"I never sleep when you talk." She yawned. "I like your voice too much."

I narrowed my eyes. "You like my voice, huh?"

"Um-hum." She rubbed her chin where an indent of the sleeping bag zipper had pressed into her. "I like all of you."

The starburst of affection she caused made me choke. I cleared my throat, turning to stare at the tent ceiling and focus on the lining and seams. "I like all of you, too."

"No, you don't."

I scowled, risking another look at the blonde tussled kid who had every power to suffocate me beneath happiness and rip me to pieces in despair. "I don't?"

She giggled. "Nope. You love me." She blew kisses, then flopped onto her back and placed her forefingers and thumbs together to form a crude looking heart. "You heart me like this."

I chuckled at her impersonation of a cartoon skit she'd seen. I wasn't the best one to teach her what love meant. To be fair, I wasn't sure how to describe it apart from I felt for her the exact opposite of what I'd felt toward the Mclarys.

The cartoon explained love was when you wanted to do everything for the other person without needing anything in return. Love was simple with one rule: if you hurt the person you love, it would be as bad as hurting yourself.

I sighed heavily. "You're right. I do love you."

She wriggled under the unzipped sleeping bag, her little legs kicking mine. "Yay!"

A smile quirked my lips even while, for some inexplicable reason, I'd gone sad. Sad because I loved something? Sad that loving someone terrified me? Or sad because she was the first, and I'd missed out on loving the people who created me?

Either way, she didn't let me wallow, poking me in the cheek again. "I love you too, Ren Wild."

And that, right there, that made those few months back in the wilderness the best months of my life.

Nothing came close after that.

Nothing was ever that simple.

Nothing.

Chapter Twenty-Three

REN

2005

WINTER HELD OFF longer than I anticipated.

Some days, we didn't bathe as the thought of diving into icy water and walking back over frosty bracken wasn't exactly enticing. Some days, we went hungry due to animals snuggled up warm in burrows and towns too far away for a day's hike in the first snow fall.

Until the last week, it was liveable.

However, we'd stayed in the forest longer than we should. I knew that. I'd steadily grown more aware of how fragile we were as the weather became cooler.

If it was up to me, we would have found another abandoned building or some other alternative to survive the upcoming freeze.

But we were still here…alone.

No one knew we existed.

No one cared if we survived or died.

It was just me and Della, and Della had decided she didn't want to go back.

I'd rubbed off on her too much. I'd proven what a wondrous place simplicity could be, and she'd fallen in love with the life that had always lived and breathed in my heart.

But even I knew what we could overcome and what we couldn't. This was her fault we sat shivering in the tent, too lethargic and exhausted to do anything but try to stay warm.

Every time I mentioned we needed to find warmer, better shelter—that even though I agreed with her and didn't want to leave, we had to be smart and find a place to ride out the upcoming blizzards and heavy snow—Della would shake her head and pout.

She'd stomp her foot and snap her refusal, and that would be the end of it.

Until I brought it up again and again…and again.

For days, I tried to convince her. Until finally, I didn't pussy-foot around. I didn't tell her gently of my plan to head down the hill toward the small town we saw glittering through the trees at night. I didn't tell her to help me pack or to dress warmly for the journey.

What I did do was dismantle the tent with her still inside and wait until she crawled out in a huff before commanding her to move.

We were leaving.

This was stupid.

I wasn't about to let her freeze to death after keeping her alive this long.

Our dynamic was simple. I was older and in charge. Normally, she bowed to those points of authority, and our arguments were short and sharp, then gone.

But this time?

She threw a tantrum that gave wing to shocked crows, screams that ricocheted around the hillside and left her out of breath and hiccupping. She'd thrown a few tantrums as a two-year-old, but this was the first since then.

I'd done my best to refrain from yelling back, but after thirty minutes of her shout-sobbing that she never wanted to go back to a city, promising she'd hate me for eternity if I took her from this place, and vowing with snapping little teeth that she'd run far away and leave me, I lost my temper.

I shouted back louder. I stomped around harder. I cursed her with every swear word I deliberately refused to use. I dared her to run because if she ran in this, she would die without me to warm her at night and feed her by day.

She'd screeched that she hated me.

I'd roared that I hated her more.

She'd pummelled my belly with stinging little fists, and I'd held her hands until she'd torn away from me then threw her moss-stuffed sock snake in my face.

After that, I shut down.

I marched over to her, snatched her damn ribbon, and held it ransom until she calmed the hell down.

It took a while.

It took all day while I led the way from wilderness to civilization. Her disapproval stabbed me in the back as she followed, her newly returned ribbon clutched in frozen fingers and lips pressed tight together.

My anger faded with every mile we travelled, and by the time we reached the outskirts of town, my chest ached with regret.

I waited for her to catch up, her shoulders no longer stiff with temper but rolled with tiredness. She refused to make eye contact, and the ache in my chest wrapped tight around my heart and squeezed.

We'd never had a fight that lasted longer than a minute or two.

This grudge was new, and I *hated* it.

I didn't know how to make things right, and it hurt. It hurt so damn much to have the one person I loved withhold the love I'd become so accustomed to.

She was my one constant, and this was unknown, scary territory.

Turning to face her, I dropped to one knee and balanced with the weight of my backpack with my fingers jabbed into the dirt below.

She tucked her chin down, avoiding my eyes, twisting her ribbon with tight jerks.

Blowing out a breath, I wondered how to fix this. Her body language screamed not to touch her, but everything inside me needed to. I needed to bridge this terrible gap and I risked having my hand bitten off by cupping her chin and forcing it to rise.

Her beautiful blue eyes narrowed as she finally looked at me.

I stared into her for a long moment, trying to study her, to understand what I'd done wrong, and how the hell I could make her happy again. "I'm sorry, Della."

She flinched, ripping her face from my hold and backing away from me. "I want to go back."

"You know why we can't."

"I don't. We've lived through rain and wind. It's just snow."

"Snow can kill."

Her forehead furrowed. "We won't die."

"We would. Eventually." I smiled sadly. "We aren't equipped like the other creatures. We don't have furry jackets or warm nests."

Her bottom lip wobbled. "But I don't want to leave. I like it there. I like just being us."

"It will still just be us. It always has been, hasn't it?"

She paused, digging her dirty sneaker into the earth. "I guess."

Sensing a slight thaw in her, I rushed, "Nothing will change, Della. It will still just be us—as it's always been. When spring hits, we can go back. We can find another farm perhaps, or a tiny cabin somewhere. It will be fun, you'll see."

Her eyes skated to mine. "Fun?"

"A holiday." I grinned bright.

"Promise it will just be the two of us."

I drew a cross over my heart. "Promise."

"Good." She nodded sharply. "Because I don't want to share you."

I chuckled. "You'll never have to share me."

"Good," she said again. "Let's go then."

This time, she held out her hand and smiled without any remnants of our fight. My heart beat easier; I breathed deeper; my world was righted once again.

Only thing was, I should never have promised it would just be us.

Because I lied.

Without even knowing it.

Chapter Twenty-Four

REN

2005

IT TOOK THREE weeks of hiding in rickety sheds, occasional kid tree-houses, and a basement or two before life threw us another curve ball.

I'd searched for something permanent, but this town kept itself too well tended.

The streets were salted and swept of snow every day, the houses painted and cared for. Even on the perimeter of the town, no dilapidated buildings waited to house two homeless kids, and no farm promised space away from people but close enough to ride out the winter by stealing from their supermarkets and larders.

On the third week of searching, I came down with the flu. It was my turn to be shivery and achy, struggling through my daily chores of petty theft and cooking to ensure Della had a full belly to stay warm.

The first couple of days in town, I'd been able to steal her a couple of warmer outfits complete with ski jacket and trousers from a rich family who'd left their kids snowboarding gear on the front porch overnight.

I made do with jeans that got constantly wet and boots that pinched my toes from being too small. I forgot what it was like to be warm and did my best to hide my rapidly fading strength from Della.

She couldn't suspect I needed a rest. She didn't need to worry because I carried the worry for both of us. Only thing was, the stuffiness in my nose and cotton wool in my head made my reactions sluggish and instincts falter.

And that was how we got caught.

We'd steadily crept our way toward the boundary of the town and found a farm too far to see the twinkling city lights of its far away neighbours.

It wasn't abandoned.

Smoke curled from the chimney, recent footsteps melted the snow in the driveway, and the sounds of family laughter trickled through the starless night.

But it was late, and I was done—utterly unable to travel another step with the heavy backpack.

Keeping Della close, I guided her around the back of the cheery looking homestead toward the barn lurking in the darkness. Cracking open the double doors, I coughed heavily and stumbled toward one of the stalls.

Unlike our previous borrowed farm, this one was immaculate with polished brass fixtures, cobweb-free beams, swept cobblestone floor, and freshly-stuffed hay nets currently being munched on by two happy horses, warm and cosy in bright red rugs.

Della's eyes widened as the creatures snorted at us, ears pricked and swivelling in curiosity. "Can I go pet them?" She drifted toward their stables.

I pinched her shoulder, keeping her by my side. "Maybe later."

My eyes danced around the space. The tack room smelled of leather and oats, the racks of folded towels and bottles of vitamins and grooming gear sat dust-free and tidy. All this care and neatness meant whoever lived here took pride and time in their home. Our presence wouldn't go unnoticed, and usually, I'd run.

I wouldn't take the chance.

But right now, I would most likely tumble into a snowdrift and suffocate before we found anything else. It was this or nothing. And I desperately needed to sleep. I needed a new nose, new brain, new throat, new bones.

I needed to be taken care of, but there was no one to do that, so I sucked up my aches and fevers and smiled at Della who stood in rapture as the horses nickered then continued to devour their hay.

I daren't crash here where we would be found if the farmer came to check on his beasts. Instead, I looked up to where a loft held sweet-smelling hay and sacks of feed for livestock.

It was as good as it was going to get.

"Come on, climb up," I barked around a cough, desperate to shed my snow-wet jeans, peel off my icy-damp socks, and crawl beneath our sleeping bag. I was too tired to eat. Too tired to attempt to feed Della.

Guilt drowned my heart along with sickness, but I had nothing left.

I just needed to rest.

Della looked at me worriedly before scooting up the well-made ladder to the loft above. I started to climb after her, but the weight of the rucksack was too much.

I fell back down, tripping over a cobblestone and landing on my ass. I groaned in pain as my ankle rolled and my head snapped forward from the bulk behind me.

Della peered down from above, panic whitening her face. "Ren!"

"Quiet!" I whisper-hissed, very aware that this was a temporary situation with owners extremely close by. "I'm fine." I needed us to go unnoticed, so I had a few hours to catch up on some sleep before pushing on before dawn. "We have to be quiet, so we don't get caught."

She bit her lip, nodding once, even though the desire to climb back down and help shouted all over her tiny face.

With another wet cough and no strength, I shrugged out of the backpack and left it at the bottom of the ladder. Ripping open the zipper, I coughed again and again, cursing the rattle and noise as I yanked out the sleeping bag then hoisted my flu-riddled body up the vertical ladder.

A rush of light-headedness made me trip at the top, and Della squealed as I landed on all fours with the sleeping bag trailing in hay dust.

"Ren." Her little hands did their best to pull me upright, and I thanked her with a weak smile.

My body was shutting down, forsaking me, leaving me weak and wobbly and useless.

"I can manage, Della Ribbon." With the promise of sleep within reaching distance, with the knowledge of a roof above our heads, and shared body heat from animals below, my endurance reached its end and threw me head first into exhaustion.

I somehow crawled toward the stacked and inviting looking bales and barely managed to shed my jeans and boots before a deep, flu-congested sleep slammed into me.

* * * * *

"Ren, wake up." Something shook me. "Ren…please wake up."

I groaned and swatted at the annoyance.

My teeth rattled as I shivered with a bone-deep chill. I wanted to stay asleep, so I didn't ache so much, so I didn't struggle to breathe, so I didn't know what it was like to freeze to death slowly.

"Ren!" The shout was barely louder than a whisper, but it was delivered straight into my ear, along with the tone of terror and crippling urgency.

My eyes flew open even as my vision remained foggy and gritty. "Wha—" I coughed, loud and wet. Clamping a hand over my mouth, so Della wouldn't catch this awful bug, I waited for the tickle to pass, but it never did.

The ache in my lungs kept going and going, wrenching out air I needed, tightening around ribs I'd already bruised.

"Ren!" Della curled into me, diving her head over my shoulder in a terrified embrace.

I tried to shove her away. She shouldn't be close with me this sick, but she glued herself against me, trembling in fear.

I opened my mouth to assure her I was okay, to say the coughs sounded worse than they were, but then I heard what'd spooked her.

What I should've heard minutes ago.

What I should've never heard because I should've been smarter never to stay in a place so well loved by owners that only lived a few steps away.

Footsteps on the cobbles.

A voice murmuring to horses.

Daylight trickled weakly into the space from skylights above. *No!*

I shot upright, planting both hands tight over my mouth, willing the wheeze and urge to cough again to vanish.

Someone was below us.

Someone was about to find us.

Della shook harder as I froze in place. My jeans were across the loft where Della must've hung them over the ladder rail to dry. My boots were neatly placed out of reaching distance. My socks spread out and smelly on a sack of molasses-infused animal meal.

My bottom half was practically naked, and my top half could barely breathe.

A cough exploded through my fingers, uncaring that it had just condemned both of us to discovery.

"Who's there?" a female voice snapped.

A horse whinnied, followed by the sound of running footsteps then the creak of the ladder as weight shimmied up it.

"Ren." Della squirmed closer, seeking comfort and safety that in my stupidity and sickness I couldn't provide. *I'd* chosen this place. I'd been the one unable to wake at dawn. I'd been the one who didn't leave before we were noticed.

I was the one to blame for *all* of this.

Another cough spilled from my lips as my fever crested, and I blinked back teeth-aching chills.

All I could do was hold Della close and hope to hell I could talk my way out of whatever was about to happen.

A head appeared.

A head with long brown hair the colour of the bay horse below, green eyes, red lips—wariness and anger the perfect makeup on a very pretty face. About my age or slightly older, the girl's petite hands gripped the ladder as she locked eyes on me.

Three things happened.

One, my flu-riddled body threatened to pass out from added stress.

Two, my boxers tightened as my body reacted to stimuli it'd been denied for months.

And three, the strangest sensation of guilt and unease filled me, because even though she was my enemy, I wanted to *know* her.

The moment ended as suddenly as it'd begun.

She raised her chin, cocked her head, and snarled, "And just who the hell are you?"

Chapter Twenty-Five

DELLA

Present Day

SO...THIS IS where my story might turn a little odd, Professor.
I've told you pretty much everything you need to know up to this point.
I've introduced you to sweet little Della—the innocent child who looked up to her big brother, Ren. I've revealed the rapidly growing, ever inquisitive Della—the mischief maker and stubborn mule who idolized and sometimes despised her best friend, Ren. And now, I suppose the time has come to introduce you to complicated Della—the child who somehow became a girl with intricate complexities that even she didn't understand. The girl who suddenly knew Ren meant so much more but didn't know what.

And it all happened in a moment.

One second, I was secure in my world, protected and guarded by my love for Ren and his love for me. The next, I was full of things I didn't understand. Things that made sense for a woman to feel but not a child. Things I didn't fully accept or even have names for until many years later.

You see, that moment—that instant—when I heard the barn doors opening and Ren stayed catatonic beside me, I'd known our lives were about to change.

Horrors of being torn from his side like I'd been at school drowned me. Terrors at being clutched by teachers who spoke too close and asked prying questions about what Ren meant to me and if he ever touched me inappropriately made me want to leap from the hay loft and run.

I know our second separation wasn't a long time, but it affected me, it aged me, it changed me more, in a few short minutes, than a month living our normal happy life in the forest.

I'd already been kicked from childhood into the next part of growing up, so I suppose, it was only natural to be protective and guarded of Ren in return.

He was mine.

I didn't have much, but I had him, and I had no intention of ever losing him.

I know I'm rambling, but I'm trying to make you see that I felt different. Back then, I had no name or maturity to grasp how I felt differently. Now, of course I do, and as I sit typing this, I wonder if a child could feel those things or if I'm just placing such well-worn and long-lived emotions onto her.

That's possible.

Because what I'm about to tell you probably won't make sense.

It's time for my first confession. And I say confession because, well, there is no other name for it. It's twisted and wrong and one I've never told anyone…not even him.

Do you feel lucky that you're the first?

You shouldn't.

Because I've come to the conclusion that I can never show you this. The more I write about my past, the more I'm aware that I'll have to erase every word and burn every edit because realistically, Ren was right.

No one can know that my real name is Mclary or that he took me when he was ten or that we lived so unconventionally for so many years. Who knows the sort of trouble I'd cause him and the nightmare that might come after me.

And so, because I'm now entirely convinced I'm going to delete this, I can be more open. I don't know what I'm going to do when I have no assignment to turn into you, but now that I've started…I can't stop.

I want to keep going because it hurts.

Funny, right?

Every word I write about him hurts. The heartache I live with. The deep-seated longing that I've grown to accept has magnified tenfold since you gave me that piece of paper with this assignment.

You were the one who gave me permission to pull out dusty desires and polish them until they're so bright and blinding, I can't stop it anymore.

I can't pretend.

I can't ignore.

I can't lie to myself, and I don't know where that leaves me.

You see, there was never a day in my life when I haven't loved Ren Wild.

Every memory, he's there. Every experience, he's with me. And for that…I almost hate him.

There is no me without him, and perhaps this complicated mess is all his fault, but the sweet agony I'm putting myself through by writing this—the unrequited ache that I feel every time I recall how perfectly he raised me and how dotingly he adored me is nothing *compared to the agony of growing up loving him in a way I knew was wrong.*

Are you ready, Professor, to never read my darkest secrets? To never see the dirtiest of confessions?

No? Well, good because I don't know if I'm ready to write them, but here I go...

In my eighteen years, I've been guilty of all seven deadly sins: lust, gluttony, greed, sloth, wrath, envy, and pride. I was never innocent, and I'm not afraid to be honest and share them with you.

But how about I start with my first one?

Wrath.

My first true sin.

And it all happened the moment I met her.

Let's just say, I hated her.

From the second she popped up on that ladder to the many years and memories later, I hated her.

But...and this is the kicker, I also loved her.

Her name was Cassie Wilson, and she was the daughter of Patricia and John Wilson, sister to Liam Wilson, friend to my girlish adolescence, and biggest enemy to my fledgling womanhood.

When she found us, I clung to Ren—partly trying to protect him from her and partly wishing he'd protect me. Even so young, I knew our lives were about to change, and I knew it was all because of her.

She'd vanished as quickly as she'd appeared, slipping down the ladder with skills of doing it a hundred times before, and bolting across the farm to grab her father.

In the few minutes we had alone, Ren barked for me to grab his jeans and boots and used the last of his remaining energy to hoist on sodden, cold things and helped me safely down the ladder.

He'd tripped going down and tripped again as he struggled to haul the backpack onto his shoulders.

In his flu-fugue state, he'd left our sleeping bag upstairs—our one valuable piece of equipment second only to our tent, and he'd left it behind.

At the time, that terrified me.

To have someone so strong and invincible suddenly become so sick and lost rocked my small world.

Not that it mattered.

Because we didn't get far.

John Wilson arrived, flanked by his curious handsome wife, devious pretty daughter, and cute little son.

And that was when Ren pushed me behind him, stood to his full height, and spoke with the gruff and rasp of sickness to let us go. His hand flexed around the hunting knife in his jean's waistband, his knuckles turning white, then pink, white, then pink as he flexed in preparation.

He was my protector, and he'd promised I wouldn't have to share him with anyone, yet here I was...sharing him.

I wanted to run in front and scream for these strangers to let us go, but Ren kept a solid grasp on my bicep, keeping me wedged safely against him.

With my limited interaction with humans, I expected them to grab us and maybe murder us there and then.

I'm pleased to report, they didn't.

Instead, they changed our lives.

They welcomed us into their home, fed us a home-cooked breakfast of bacon and eggs, and called a doctor for my brother and best friend.

And through it all, Cassie Wilson never took her eyes off my Ren.

And my hate grew wings and flew.

You see, I loved her for being so kind to me, for everything she became to me.

But I hated her for taking something from me, for claiming the only thing I had, for stealing the boy I loved in all the perfectly right and terribly wrong ways that a sister ever could.

Chapter Twenty-Six

REN

2005

I DIDN'T WANT to be here.

I didn't want to be under the scrutiny or charity of John Wilson and his family.

But I had nothing left.

I could only accept their assurances that they meant us no harm, bow my head in gratitude as a warm-cooked meal filled the icy emptiness in my belly, and cough my thanks as Patricia Wilson led me into their guest room complete with donkey figurines and crocheted blankets thrown over yellow bedding and left me alone with a doctor they'd called on my behalf.

In my fuzzy state, I permitted them to close the door without Della by my side. In a flash of lucidity and rage, I remembered why Della had to be with me at all times, why I hated strangers, and how I could never trust anybody.

This might've been their plan all along—to lull us into a relaxed state, then steal her and kill me.

If my strength was at full capacity, I would've left right then.

Then again, if my strength was at full capacity, we would never have been in this situation in the first place. I wouldn't have slept too long, and under no circumstances would I have ever entered a house occupied by unknowns.

All I could do with my lacklustre brain power and my pathetic excuse for endurance was to immediately storm from the guest room and demand Della to stay with me at all times.

She was only too happy to wrap her arms around my thighs and take my command literally, even as Patricia Wilson tried to argue that I should be examined on my own and for Della to keep her distance so she didn't get sick.

Their logic tried to undermine my confidence.

A thread of fear filled me that she might come down with what I had, but it was a risk I had to take because I wasn't risking her in any other way.

I wouldn't leave her alone to be hurt by them, taken by them, or touched in any way, shape, or form.

Just because they hadn't punished us for sleeping on their property, shared their food, and called their doctor didn't mean I trusted them.

The only family I trusted was ours.

And Della would stay with me at all times.

Back in the guest suite with the doctor who'd patiently waited, Della wedged herself in the rocking chair and cuddled a pillow with an embroidered donkey on the front.

With one eye on her and one on the exit, I submitted to the doctor's many questions. I steeled myself against allowing him to use something that was cold and hard called a stethoscope and gritted my teeth with discomfort as he poked and prodded my chest and belly then felt under my throat.

I let him touch me more than any other human had before, and it drained me of my final reserves. I was a model patient, up until the end when his forehead furrowed and a strange new light filled his gaze—made worse when he found the brand on my hip and missing finger on my left hand.

He didn't ask questions but did ask to perform a full examination with worry in his voice. He looked at me as if I was worse off than just an annoying cough.

He already knew more about me from reading my body than I'd ever tell him verbally, and I had no intention of letting him guess more of our story than the lie I'd told the Wilsons.

The lie that Della was my baby sister and we'd been travelling on a bus to visit our cousins in some state far from here. The bus had broken down. And we'd hitch-hiked ever since.

I knew the tale had holes—my backpack was well-used and our gear adapted for life in the wilderness. I knew Della wore clothes meant for boys and her hair, even now, had leaves stuck between the strands.

She looked scruffy.

She looked wild.

Just like me.

But the doctor didn't give up, murmuring how he'd keep our confidence, that he knew there was more to us than we'd said, and his only interest was to help. He went on and on how he only wanted to ensure our full health and that Della needed examining just as much as I did.

He'd lost all my cooperability at that point.

I'd crossed my arms, did my best to stifle my ever-worsening cough, and told him to leave.

To my surprise, he did, with only a final word that he was around if I changed my mind.

The moment he was gone, I plotted a way to leave this farmhouse and the strangely nice family before they devised another way to delay us.

Only, Patricia Wilson knocked on the guest room door, interrupted my plans, and held out medicine while relaying the news from the doctor that the flu had turned to mild pneumonia, and I needed to start a course of antibiotics immediately so I didn't get worse.

I argued it was just a cold, but Della cried when Patricia shook her head and listed my symptoms. Each one she got right from the bruised ribs, continuous sensation of being out of breath, painful chest, and the incessant cough.

All of that didn't scare me—it only made me mad to be so weak—but what *did* scare me was the knowledge I was no use to Della in my current state. I couldn't protect her the way I wanted. I couldn't defend her if I needed.

Despite my desire to be far away from these people, I had to swallow those needs and accept help, for Della's sake.

I sat heavily on the mattress and grudgingly accepted the first tablet. With my spare arm, I held out my hand for Della to join me.

She threw away the donkey cushion and soared into my embrace.

Clutching her close, I eyed up the glass of water Patricia Wilson pushed toward me, then drank deep, washing the medicine deep into my belly so it might start working faster.

Patricia Wilson smiled kindly at us; her motherly instincts, already pronounced from raising her own kids, latched on to caring for us.

I didn't get the feeling she was cruel like Mrs Mclary or saw me as dollar signs like my own mother. With her red hair, freckles, and purple frilly apron, the only threat she delivered was her fascination with Della. She couldn't take her eyes off her, and my hackles rose.

Placing the glass on the nightstand, I stood and said around a cough, "Thank you for breakfast and the medicine, but we really need to go."

"Yes!" Della popped off the mattress faster than I'd ever seen, flying to the door where she wrenched it open, then promptly slammed it shut again as the girl with brown hair called Cassie peered in, catching my eye.

"Tell her to go away. I want to leave." Della stomped her foot. "I'll take care of you, Ren. You'll get better."

Patricia Wilson moved toward her and squatted down with a sad shake of her head. "Sweetheart, your brother is sick. He's lucky he found a doctor. Otherwise, he might've gotten a lot worse." Throwing me a look, she added, "You're both welcome to stay. In fact, I insist on it until everyone is healthy and no more coughing, okay?"

I didn't do well with instruction even when it came with a promise of being beaten and starved. And I definitely didn't do well with it after years of freedom and being solely responsible for myself and Della.

"But I don't want to stay." Della pouted, beating my refusal.

Patricia Wilson laughed kindly. "Are you sure? When the weather clears, you can go for a ride with Cassie if you want. Or maybe play snakes and ladders with Liam while having a treat of milk and cookies. He's about your age and loves new friends. Don't you want another friend, Della?"

My fingers clenched into a fist, regretting, in my weakened state, that I'd told these people our real names. At least, I'd said our surname was Wild—we had that element of protection—but if they happened to research any news or contact Social Services or decide to call the police…

We can't stay here.

I stepped forward, cursing under my breath as the room spun. A loud, painful cough shredded my lungs, sending me crashing back down on the mattress.

The bedroom door opened, and the entire Wilson family poured in. Liam, a lanky kid with short brown hair and green eyes like his father and sister, clutched a plastic lizard and ran to his mother who still squatted in front of Della. He looked Della up and down, then promptly shoved his lizard in her face.

Della stumbled back, indignation all over her.

I wanted to go and act as a barrier between her and all these people, but the girl with red lips stepped toward the bed, her arms crossed and one green eye covered by bay coloured hair. We stared at each other, her gaze flittering all over me while mine stayed transfixed to her face with the occasional stray to her full chest. Through her tight t-shirt, the indents of a lace bra showed.

I jumped as she said in her crisp, haughty voice, "Dad said you're not going anywhere."

My legs bunched to prove her wrong by walking out of there. I barely managed to stand again, let alone shove her out of the way to leave. "We aren't your prisoners."

"No, you're our guests," she snarled. "So how about you start acting like it instead of damn hostages?"

I blinked.

"Ignore my daughter, Ren Wild." Her father, John Wilson, stepped around Della, his son, and his wife to stand squarely in front of me. His height towered over me, his thick bushy beard putting my scraggly teenage one to shame. "I have something to say but before I do, I want your word that you'll hear me out and not use that knife in your waistband or try to push your way out of here, got it?" He narrowed his green eyes, waiting for me to speak.

Locking my knees as the room rolled and my legs threatened to buckle from lack of oxygen, I peered around him to Della who'd retreated to the rocking chair, glowering at everyone as if they were our mortal enemies.

And who knew, perhaps they were, but unfortunately, I wasn't at my usual strength, and I had to be smart about leaving that wouldn't end up with us split apart or me being shot by a farmer.

Because a bullet in my brain was a real possibility.

All farmers had guns.

Just because he didn't carry one right now didn't mean I was safe.

Sticking out his hand, John Wilson grumbled, "Do we have a deal?"

It took another few moments for my fuzzy head to clear, but I finally concluded I didn't have a choice. I had to continue playing nice and hopefully whatever drugs I just took would work fast and we could be out of here by this afternoon.

I nodded, keeping my hands by my sides. "You have a deal, but I won't shake your hand. According to your doctor, I'm sick, and I don't want you to catch it."

John Wilson cracked a smile. "Courteous fellow. I like that." Striding from the bedroom, he threw over his shoulder. "Come on then. Let's talk in the kitchen."

It took a few minutes for everyone to shuffle from the guest bedroom, down the wood-panelled corridor to the peach and cream kitchen.

Another minute later, Patricia Wilson had ensured each of her children, husband, me, and Della had a mug of something hot placed in front of us at the dining room table.

Once settled, John Wilson sipped his drink, looked me up and down, then glanced at my dirty, tired backpack wedged against his kitchen cabinets. "Okay…first, I'm going to start with the obvious."

My heart rate picked up. I wrapped my fingers around the hot cup to stop myself from grabbing Della and running.

"Obviously, you lied to us about a bus trip and visiting relatives. I understand why you did and appreciate your need to protect yourself and your sister, but that's the last lie you're ever allowed to tell me, understand?"

My teeth clacked together. I didn't reply other than narrowing my eyes in warning.

He continued, "Correct me if I'm wrong, but you two don't seem to have a home. If I was to put money on it, I'd say you've been living rough for a while. It's winter. You're going to freeze out there. To be honest, I don't know how you've survived with the cold snaps we've been having."

"Honey, don't go off on a tangent," Patricia Wilson piped up, smoothing her son's hair who sat next to her.

My eyes strayed to her daughter who sat directly in front of me, her gaze burning me with an intensity that prickled my skin and not from fever.

I sat back in the chair, resting my hands on my lap before Della's tiny one crept across and slipped into mine, squeezing me. Scooting my chair closer to hers, I did my best to resist the urge to cough and squeezed back.

John Wilson carried on, "I pride myself on being a good judge of character, and I like you, boy."

"Not Boy," Della immediately snapped. "Ren. He told you his name. It's Ren."

Cassie Wilson tossed her hair over her shoulder. "Ren Wild. Yes, we know." She rested her elbow on the table and rested her chin on her palm, studying me. "What I want to know is *who* is

Ren Wild? Why did I find you in our barn?"

Della squirmed, opening her mouth with some retort, but I squeezed her again and said, "I'm sorry we slept above your horses, but I wasn't feeling well."

Cassie cocked her head. "You weren't well, and you wanted to keep your sister from the cold. That's what you said before."

I nodded. "Yes."

"Where are your parents?" she asked, fast and sharp.

"Dead."

Her coldness suddenly thawed, her shoulders rounding and a sweetness she'd hidden filling her gaze when she looked at Della beside me. "I'm sorry."

"It's fine." I squeezed Della's fingers harder.

"Is my dad right? That you've been on the streets for a while?"

I shot her father a glance. He'd said I couldn't lie, but he didn't say I could omit the truth. "We've never slept on the streets."

Technically, it wasn't a lie. We slept in forests with tents and sleeping bags, never on empty concrete in heartless cities.

"I don't believe you." Cassie Wilson crossed her arms. "You look like you've just crawled from the jungle."

My lips twitched, not from her joke, but from pride. I liked that I looked more feral than civilized. I enjoyed being different to her even though the longer I stared, the more I found to notice about her.

Her hair caught the kitchen lights with golden strands as well as brown. Her eyes had specks of hazel and not just green. She licked her lips when she was angry or nervous. And she vibrated with energy I desperately needed so I could get better and leave this place.

She made me nervous, and I daren't analyse why.

"I don't care what you think of me," I muttered. "We made a mistake sleeping in your father's barn."

She waved her hand. "Meh, I don't care that you slept there. You didn't hurt my ponies, so you're already better than some of our old farmhands, and you care for your sister like I care for my brother, so that makes you kind. Dad says to give you a chance, so I will." Her eyes slipped back into suspicion. "But don't make me regret it."

"That's enough, Cas." John Wilson cleared his throat, then pinned his eyes on me. "Before Cassie steals this entire conversation, I better come out with it. My wife and I have discussed options. Our first instinct was to call the police and have them tell your parents where you are. You haven't told us your ages, but I doubt you're legally able to live on your own with a minor. I didn't invade your privacy and go through your bag, but if I'm right about you guys being homeless…that leads to the question of why."

"That's none of your business," I said coldly, calmly. "Our life is our own. It's not your place to call the police or—"

"Ah, see that's where you're wrong." John Wilson held up his hand. "It *is* my place if I believe you're at risk, parents are missing you, or if you're up to no good. We've dealt with a few runaways while operating this farm, and most of them we send directly home to parents who are sick with worry and only have love and honourable intentions for their children. Other times, we…" He looked at his wife, trailing off.

"Other times, you what?" Adrenaline filled my veins, already hearing horror stories of eating children for lunch or selling them like I'd been sold.

Such filth shouted loudly in my head, so I wasn't ready for him to say, "We give them a safe place to rest and figure out what they want to do. We don't pressure them to go home and we don't call the police with the understanding that there are no secrets between us."

He leaned forward, planting his large hands on the table. "I've been around a while, Ren, so I know a kid that's been abused versus one that has been loved. Winter is a slow time of year for a farm, but I'm willing to offer you employment, if you want it, and a place to stay with the only proviso that you tell me the truth."

I froze. "You're offering me a job?" A cough punctuated the end of my question, bending me over with wracking convulsions.

John Wilson waited until I'd stopped coughing before chuckling. "When you're better, yes, I'm offering you a job. For now, your only task is to get better."

I shook my head. "I-I don't understand. Why are you doing this?" I searched his face for an ulterior motive. I begged my instincts to strip back any falsehoods and help me see the fine print of such a deal.

No one could be that generous…surely?

"I'm doing this because a while ago, my eldest boy ran away thanks to a fight we had. He was missing for three years. We all believed he was dead and mourned every day from lack of news and guilt for failing him. I should never have lost my temper. He was just a kid—your age or thereabouts. It was my fault."

Patricia Wilson reached out and patted her husband's hairy hand. "It wasn't just your fault, John. Adam was as much to blame."

He smiled at his wife and shrugged at me. "Anyway, the good news is one day, a few years ago, we received a phone call from a family two counties over. They said they'd found our son sleeping behind their local supermarket. He was pretty beaten up, but when they'd tried to call the police, he'd hobbled away on a broken leg to avoid the mess between us. Instead of tying him down and calling the authorities, they took him in, cared for him, and believed him when he said he'd run from an abusive home and didn't want the police to send him back."

Pain shadowed the old farmer's eyes, a wince smarting even now. "Obviously, he lied to them, but they gave him shelter and offered him no judgment or expectation. They helped him find a job, earn some money, and mature enough to see that our fight was stupid and idiotic and not worth the estrangement anymore. Finally, my son told them the truth; that he wasn't from an abusive family, bore the brunt of their disappointment that he'd lied, let them call us with the news, and came back home."

Cassie picked up where her father left off. "What my dad is trying to say is now he has a debt to repay the kindness of the family who took Adam in. Without them, he would probably be dead. Instead, he's at university and about to graduate as a lawyer."

John Wilson nodded. "I've always felt humbled that complete strangers gave me back my son. If you need a place to stay, money to earn, and time to do whatever you need to do, then I want to give you that." He held up his finger. "Under one condition."

My thoughts raced, trying to unravel the story he'd just told and doing my best to sniff out the truth, but his gaze was clear and honest, earnest and fair unlike the evil that lived in others.

"What condition?" I asked around another cough, even though I knew what it was. Honesty. Truth I didn't know if I could share.

Della scooted closer, resting her head on my arm in sympathy.

John Wilson smiled at Della's move to touch me, understanding what anyone who wasn't blind could see—that our bond was tight and true. That we looked out for each other. That she cared for me as much as I cared for her.

He said, "That you tell me the truth about who you are and why you're running. Whatever your answer is, I swear to you my offer will not change. I won't judge. I won't call the police. I won't interfere in any way. If you've run away from a family who misses and loves you, then my one stipulation would be to call them and say you're safe and give them my number so they can contact you while you're away from home. Do that and the only reason my offer will expire is if you hurt my loved ones, steal from me, or I find out you were lying." The kind-hearted giant was replaced by a gun-slinging lawmaker with a single harsh look, hinting he was the reason his daughter had inherited a sharp tongue.

"So…" He crossed his arms, looking me up and down. "What's it going to be?"

I swallowed past the razor blades in my throat and looked at Della.

She shook her head, a whine falling from her lips. "Forest…please, Ren?"

It killed me that I couldn't give her what she'd fallen so in love with, but I also refused to kill her by *giving* her what she'd fallen in love with.

I didn't want to stay either.

But winter was our nemesis.

The moment the snow melted, we'd leave.

For now…this was our best option.

Sitting straighter, I locked eyes with John Wilson and gave him a blended version of truth and lie. I lied because I didn't separate Della from my own tale. We'd already said we were blooded brother and sister and not just two kids who'd found solace in each other. I intended to keep that secret for however long we stayed here.

And I told the truth because her tale was now my tale, and I wouldn't hide behind false veneers. I wasn't afraid of showing the ugly truth that went on behind closed doors.

I coughed, swallowed, and said, "We ran from a farm that buys children for cheap labour. I have a brand just like their cattle. I lost a finger due to their strictness. I ran before they could do such things to my sister, before they could sell us for cheap, or before they put us in the offal pit where other livestock go once they've died. There is nothing for us in our past, and I won't allow anyone, *anyone*, to jeopardize our future."

It was my turn to switch my tone from respectful to threatening, fighting off yet more coughs. "I know hard work, and

I'm not afraid of it. I'm strong. I'm skilled. I will obey and do what is required, but I won't do it for you. I'll do it for my sister, and as long as she is treated kindly, then I will be forever in your debt. But if there comes a moment when she's not, I won't hesitate to do what is necessary. Do *you* understand, Mr. Wilson? Don't see a kid who's sick. See a man who is prepared to do whatever it takes to protect what he loves."

John Wilson held my stare then slowly nodded. "I see a man who reminds me of myself. I understand."

Della pushed her forehead against my shoulder, knowing she'd lost the battle, and I'd condemned our next few months to be with strangers and not our chosen sanctuary of aloneness.

My gaze left John Wilson's and settled on his daughter, Cassie.

She gave me a look that wasn't full of suspicion or ridicule like usual. Instead, it was filled with fire that made my blood thicken and a feminine smile that made me feel strong for putting aside my mistrust and dislike of people and weak because despite myself...I liked one.

I liked her.

I liked her defending her family and home.

I liked her spirit and snap.

I liked her enough to know I should run far away from her, but I'd just promised to behave for the winter and work for her father.

It was a decision I would live to regret.

Chapter Twenty-Seven

REN

2005

WE STAYED AT Cherry River Farm all winter.

We made a temporary home in the single bedroom with its own bathroom off the barn. After that first afternoon when the Wilsons escorted us to the private quarters and showed us where we would stay, Della had shown a glimmer of acceptance at having our own place even though she still tugged on my hand to run.

I must admit, I'd sighed in heavy relief.

I hadn't considered where we would live, and if he'd given us rooms in the main house, we would've lasted a night before the loner inside me bundled Della into stolen jackets and vanished into the snowy night.

At least, even with our days filled with people, four evenings and nights were still ours...alone.

That first week took a lot of getting used to. I had no choice but to take it easy with my lungs sloshing with liquid, and Della paced like a caged tiger cub, desperate to run and leap while confined to a small cage.

I couldn't tell her stories to keep her mind off my commitment to be an employee because I coughed too much, and I couldn't ask for a TV to continue our unconventional education as I had no right to ask for more than what had already been given.

All I focused on was taking my medicine religiously until I no longer rattled with coughs, did my best to settle my jumpy nerves at being around people, and calm Della enough with promises and assurances that the moment we wouldn't freeze to death, we'd leave.

A few weeks passed where John Wilson gave me simple, easy jobs around the house, barn, and fields. He showed me his paddock boundaries, pointed out landmarks, and gave an overall rundown of what he expected.

His farm focused more on hay and produce rather than milk and meat and had more acreage but less livestock than Mclary.

This was a world I was familiar with, and my time in the forest had given me an even greater arsenal of skills so anything he tasked me with was easy.

I spoke politely, did what was asked quickly, and fought against the memories of doing similar chores for a much nastier boss.

It wasn't that I hated working—the exact opposite.

I adored working with my hands, twisting metal back into place on broken fences, chopping firewood, or hammering nails into posts. Despite the conditions back at Mclary's, I'd loved working the land, smelling the air full of animals and sweat, and waking up with the noisy cockerels every sunrise, knowing I was as connected to the land as I would ever be.

But there was something about working for someone else that itched and chewed, never allowing me to relax. I was still an asset to someone and not free. I didn't own anything. I didn't work my own stock or increase my own equity.

I was treading water, watching the frosts and judging when it would be time to run. I was fifteen, and although I had nothing and no way of knowing how, my dream was to have a place like the borrowed Polcart Farm with its boundaries in forest and bush.

I would have my own slice of wilderness one day where nothing and no one could touch me and Della without permission.

As the weeks went on, it wasn't just me who preferred evenings when the farmhouse turned quiet and I finished work for the day. Della found more and more excuses to hide in our one-bedroom home rather than accept the offer of hanging with the Wilsons around their warm fireplace.

She tolerated Liam, glowered at Cassie, and didn't let the adults get too close. She was a distrustful little thing, and I hated that I'd been the initial cause of such guardedness but also that her only experience with strangers had been good to begin with, then ended with teachers trying to rip us apart.

I didn't blame her for her wariness.

I shared it.

And despite Cassie's smiles as I worked around the farm and her offers of dinner with her family and the occasional gifted cookies as I repaired one of her horse jumps or helped stock hay nets, I never accepted an invitation.

Not because of the weird patter in my heart or tightening in my jeans whenever she was near, but because Della turned into a little monster whenever she saw us together.

I'd expected her to enjoy having another girl around. Instead, she took it as an offense whenever Cassie asked how she was or if she merely grinned her way.

I didn't say anything or ask why my sweet Della Ribbon turned into a nightmare whenever Cassie was around, but something niggled inside me to reassure her in some way. To prove she hadn't lost me. That we were still just me and her—an *us*.

On the third night at Cherry River, we'd pushed the two single beds together after being unable to sleep. We were too used to being within touching distance.

The bedroom was stark with its wooden walls and charcoal curtains but well insulated, protecting us much better than our tent.

We'd stayed sleeping with our beds together, hands occasionally touching, legs sometimes kicking, and I hadn't thought anything of it until Cassie poked her head in one morning at the end of the fourth week.

I looked up from tying a bow with Della's ribbon, securing a high ponytail she'd asked me to do. She might not like Cassie, but she copied her hairstyles often.

"Do you need something?" I turned from where Della sat on the bed to face the door, temper filling me that our sanctuary had been invaded. "I'm due to start work in ten minutes. I'm not late."

Cassie glanced around the room, her eyes narrowing on the rumbled sheets and pushed together beds. "You guys sleep together?"

Della jumped to the floor and grabbed my hand. "We do everything together."

"If I slept with my brother, I'd end up smothering him with a pillow." Cassie smirked, and I couldn't tell if she was being sweet or sarcastic when she rolled her eyes at Della. "Don't you find he snores?"

My shoulders stiffened as Della bared her teeth. "I like it."

"You like it even when he hogs the bed and kicks you?"

Cassie's eyes met mine, revealing her teasing. I didn't know how I felt about her teasing Della when she'd never been tormented by anyone other than me. But I let her continue, holding tight to the tiny hand in mine, willing the ice to melt and Della to calm.

I knew what she felt because I felt it, too.

Cassie fascinated me in all the wrong ways, from her curves and skin and smell. But she also terrified me because she had a habit of popping up from nowhere or hanging around longer than comfortable.

For two kids who'd adopted the forest purely because it was away from humans, it took a lot of adjusting and acceptance. I'd always thought Della would be the more adaptable one in that respect, but it turned out, she was a master at holding grudges and staying aloof.

"He doesn't hog the bed." Her pretty little chin came up, blue eyes almost as dark as her ribbon with challenge. "Go away."

Cassie giggled. "Feisty wee thing, isn't she?" She glanced at me. "Aren't you afraid you're going to wake up one morning with your fingers and toes nibbled on thanks to her tiny teeth?"

Della stepped forward, dragging me with her. "I'd never bite him. But I'd bite you."

"I'd bite you back." Cassie leaned on the doorframe, completely unfussed. Brown hair slung over one shoulder, thick boots and tight jeans barely visible under the long puffer jacket zipped tight against the cold. "I've heard little girls are tasty treats." Her eyes flashed to mine with a lick of her lips.

For some reason, my ears twitched at the way her voice lowered, and I swore an invitation echoed behind her joke.

Della looked as if she'd happily murder her. "You can't eat me. Ren won't let you. He loves me." She looked up, her eyes wide and wild, her cheeks pink with worry. "You do still love me…right?"

And once again, she successfully cracked open my ribs and ripped out my heart. Cassie was no longer relevant as I dropped to one knee and clutched Della close. With my face buried in her sweet-smelling neck, I murmured, "I will always love you, Della Ribbon. Until the day I die and even past that."

She threw her arms around me, trembling in a way that hinted she acted brave and brattish, but really, her fear was deep-seated and hurting her. I needed to spend more time with her. She should accompany me while I worked. We were so used to being in each other's pockets that this new dynamic wasn't acceptable.

"I'm sorry," she whispered into my ear. "Can we leave now? I'm ready to go."

I stroked her back. "We can't leave. It's still too cold, and I like you alive and not covered in snow."

"I could be an ice princess." She pulled away, rubbing at the quick glisten of tears on her cheek. "I'd keep you warm, you'd see."

I chuckled, climbing back to my feet and tugging her ponytail. "With your temper, you would keep me warm from fighting with you."

A smile appeared, barely there and still unsure thanks to Cassie invading our privacy, but at least whatever terror had clutched her was gone.

"Can I say something?" Cassie asked, pushing off from the doorframe and entering our bedroom uninvited.

I arched an eyebrow as she came closer, doing my best to assess her threat while very aware she was my boss's daughter. "What?"

"Not to you." She pointed at Della. "To her."

Della squared her shoulders, her blonde hair rippling with resentment. "I don't want to talk to you."

"You sure about that?" Cassie closed the distance then sat on her haunches in front of her. "Do you know what day it is today?"

"The day we can leave?"

"No, not yet, I'm afraid." Cassie shook her head. "That will be a sad day to say goodbye, not a happy day. For me, anyway." She flashed me a look, and once again, her tone thickened and eyes shot a message I didn't understand. The moment was gone as fast as it'd happened as she turned back to Della. "Today is much better than that. Want to know why?"

Despite herself, Della asked, "Why?"

"Because today isn't a normal work day. Ren doesn't have chores, and you don't have to stay in here all day."

"Why not?" Her eyebrows scrunched together. "It's not a Sunday. Ren works every day but Sunday."

"Not today, he doesn't."

I shuffled on the spot, fighting two polarizing emotions. One, I couldn't stop the warmth spreading through my chest at Cassie treating Della so kindly. I still hadn't made up my mind about her as a person, but the fact she spoke to Della as intelligent and not an idiot layered her with more than just physical appeal. And two, I struggled with the possession in my gut. The snaking, hissing knowledge that with every word she spoke, she cracked Della's coldness and made her interact.

She was making me share her, and I both loved and loathed it.

"Why not today?" Della wedged the toe of her sneaker into the threadbare carpet. "Tell me."

Cassie grinned. "Because today is Christmas!" Clapping her hands, she lost the sensual way she normally moved and acted like Della did when I agreed to tell her a new story. Excitement glowed on her face, making her so damn pretty that I had to move away to hide the evidence of my interest.

I had no idea what she was so upbeat about, but if it made her this attractive, I would have to avoid it at all costs. Strange heat bubbled in my belly. My lips tingled for something. Those frustrating, hated desires whenever I looked at dirty magazines returned in full force.

"What's Christmas?" Della cocked her head, her ponytail swaying.

"Oh, my God, did you just ask what Christmas is?" Cassie's mouth fell open. "How the hell do you not know what Christmas is?"

"Is that like when the TV families have a big meal, open gifts wrapped in bright paper, and then moan about eating too much?" Della nodded importantly. "I forgot. I do know Christmas."

Cassie rose to her feet, shrugging helplessly, and pinning me with a disbelieving stare. "Please tell me you know what Christmas is."

"Like Della said. We know the principal of it."

"But you've never celebrated it yourself?"

This was one of those questions that asked so much more than a simple query. Her tone said she didn't believe us. Her face said she pitied us if it was true. Her body language said she'd run to her father and tell him regardless of my answer.

I mulled replies in my head. I couldn't exactly say that our lifestyle meant we didn't follow dates, only seasons. I couldn't reveal the full truth that Della had been too young to remember, and I'd never had one since I was sold.

But then again, I *could* tell her because John Wilson had insisted on the truth, and I'd already told him we'd escaped from a farm that bought children for labour.

I was so used to lying that the truth felt bitter on my tongue. "You know where we came from. Do you honestly think people who buy kids for work would give them Christmas?"

I hadn't meant my answer to be a bucket of water on the cheery blaze of her excitement, but Cassie's face fell, her eyes darkened, and she looked at me deeper, harder, wiser than she had before. "You were telling the truth about that. I didn't think you were."

I shrugged.

"Can I see?"

"See what?"

"The brand you said is like a cattle mark."

Della shot toward me, clamping her hand over my hip. "No. He doesn't show anyone. Only me."

Cassie held up her hands. "Okay, fair enough. I get it." Struggling to find her previous light-hearted happiness, she said, "I came here this morning with two messages from my parents. One, today is a day off, and you're not to work. And two, if you'd like, we'd be honoured to have you join us for Christmas lunch."

It was my turn for my mouth to fall open. "You want us to join you?"

"That's what I just said, isn't it?" She smiled away the sharpness. "But, yes. Do whatever you need, then come to the house. I want to be the first to introduce you to Christmas."

She left with a smile at Della, lingering glance at me, and the sense that today would mark yet another change, a new adventure, a first experience…for both of us.

* * * * *

"Ren, can I talk to you for a moment?" John Wilson entered the cosy country lounge with large caramel couches and woven rugs where I sat beside Della on the floor beside a giant pine decorated in garish flickering lights and round coloured balls.

Somehow, Della and I had traded our aversion to company and accepted the invitation to Christmas. We'd eaten things we'd never eaten before like buttery brussel sprouts, juicy cranberry turkey, and pecan spun-sugar pie.

My stomach was no longer flat and hard but bloated with too much food.

It was a luxury I could get used to.

Without thinking, my hand found Della's head, and my fingers slipped through her long blonde hair. She'd undone her ponytail when the Wilsons had given her a small wicker basket full of ribbons in every colour of the rainbow. She'd compared her blue satin to the purples and pinks and yellows, her face brighter and happier than I'd ever seen.

The fact that the Wilsons had taken notice of her and seen her most prized possession was a tatty, dirty ribbon made my reserved nature falter a little. This family was the exact opposite of the Mclarys, proving good balanced out evil and kindness deleted cruelty.

Patricia Wilson doted on Della, giving her anything she wanted. More lemonade. Another cookie. Teaching her to plait the ribbons together to form one pretty braid. Setting up puzzles and games for Liam and Della to squabble over together.

She'd adopted her, and I'd been in a state of confusion all day thanks to the generosity of these people. I struggled to believe and not try to see past the truth, expecting the same rotting greed like the people I'd run from.

This was the family Della should've been born into.

This was the family that taught me not all humans were creatures to run away from.

"Ren?" John cocked his head toward the corridor, hurrying me along.

With a wince, I climbed to my feet, making sure to take the new knife Cassie Wilson had given me from under the tree. I hadn't expected presents. I didn't even know people gave gifts without requiring anything in return unless they loved them like I loved Della, but when I'd opened the blade and stroked the goat hide handle, I'd been speechless.

I still hadn't said thank you, and it ate at me every time Cassie smiled from across the room.

I had a feeling she knew the depth of my gratitude, though.

Her cheeks carried a pinkness that flushed whenever our gazes met. Her smile held a weight that sped up my heart and thickened my blood.

All day, I'd been aware of her and her of me, almost as if we were having a silent conversation while surrounded by our loud-spoken loved ones.

"I'll be right back." I looked down at Della.

She beamed. "Okie dokie."

Chuckling under my breath at the change in her, I followed John Wilson from the comfy lounge full of family laughter and scents of sugar to the spare bedroom where I'd been checked by the doctor.

Once inside, John turned to close the door.

My hackles instantly rose. My hands fisted. The knife in my

back pocket heavier and begging to be used. "What are you doing?"

Memories of Mclary taking girls into his house crashed over me. Fear that something similar would happen to me. Terror that all this time, he'd been the one lying, and I'd given him my truth to be used against me.

My breath came quick and fast; my heart exploding in my chest.

"Hey, son, calm down." John put up his hands, quickly opening the door again. "Easy, easy. Just wanted to have a quick chat in private."

I gulped back the sudden panic, rubbing my face with a shaking hand. "Sorry."

Where the hell had such things come from? I was a teenager now, not a boy. I'd lived on my own for years. Why the hell had a closed door made me react so stupidly?

My questions had no answers, and I shoved them to the side as John pulled out a crushed envelope from his back pocket and held it out to me.

I steadied myself before taking it, so he didn't see my weak tremble. "What's this?"

He nodded with his chin to open it. "Your first month's salary. I'll pay you fortnightly in the summer, but winter is always a little tight with more outgoing than incoming, I'm afraid."

"Salary?"

Would it reveal how much of an idiot I was if I admitted I didn't know that word?

Running my thumb under the glue of the envelope, my eyes shot to his when I saw what was inside. "This is money."

John scowled. "Eh, yes. I know it's not much, but I'll give you a few bonuses when we bale and sell the hay in summer."

I ignored that part and didn't bother reminding him I wouldn't be here in summer. All I could focus on was a wad of cash I didn't have to steal. A wad of cash that was given to me for services rendered.

Cash I'd *earned*.

My ability to count had drastically improved, but it still wasn't good enough to flick through the ten and twenty-dollar bills to find out what he'd valued my work at.

But it didn't matter.

Because I already had something in mind to spend it on.

Passing back the envelope, I said, "Thank you but keep it."

He refused to take it. "What? Why? You're my employee. You get how that works, right? You do what I ask, and I pay you for your time." He looked at me as if I was an imbecile. "I'm not taking it back, Ren."

"I want to spend it." I urged him to take it until he reluctantly held out his hand.

"On what?"

"On Della."

His face softened. "I see. What would you like me to buy her for you?"

I could've said trinkets and knickknacks, but we had no space for possessions. The only thing we had space for was education, and I knew how much it meant to her to learn. Every day she'd come home from school, she'd been a hive of energy and buzzing with new things.

I didn't want to keep that from her.

And the only way I could give it to her was while we had temporary permanency.

"It's complicated." I sighed, eyeing him, wondering if this man was as good as he seemed, or if I was about to get myself into a world of trouble.

"Give me complicated and I'll see if I can make it simple."

"Okay." I paced a little, needing to walk and think. "I want Della to go to school, but to do that, she needs people who will say they're her parents and an address for teachers to know she's taken care of. I-I can't give her that."

John crossed his arms, crinkling the envelope against his side. "So you want us to lie and say she's ours?"

"I want you to give her a chance, so she can become somebody better than me."

"Don't do that," he said sternly. "Don't put yourself down. She has a good role model in you, Ren, and if she turns out to be half as noble, then you've done well raising her."

I shrugged, uncomfortable with praise and ready to return to Della. "Will you do it?"

"School doesn't start back until next week. I can see if there's room to enrol her. I'll say we're her guardians, but her family is her brother, and all communication needs to go through you. Sound fair?"

"Yes."

"I'll do that for you, but you need to do something for me in return."

I froze. "What?"

"Take the damn money." He held it out. "School is expensive. Not to mention uniforms and books and excursions."

I backed away from the cash. "I know that. That's why I'm going to ask another favour."

"Go on."

"Keep everything I earn. Never give me a penny. But whatever you feel I'm worth, give it to her. Buy her new clothes. Give her books. Send her to the best school my skills can buy, and you have a deal."

John Wilson shook his head. "You're really something, you know that?"

"I know the responsibility I have to Della and mean to fulfil it."

"She's very lucky to have you."

I shrugged again. "And I'm lucky to have her."

"You know…" His eyes narrowed with thought. "Winter won't last forever. If she gets into school, she'll only be there a few weeks if you're intending to leave in spring."

My spine slouched.

I hadn't thought of that.

Here I was planning a future for Della that would end the moment the thaw came. She wanted to leave, but if we did…she'd never have what she deserved.

She'd never read and write properly. She'd never grow up with the skills to make her dreams come true.

I looked out the window at the silver moon on white snow and the silhouettes of trees beckoning me back into their depths.

The urge to run crippled me.

But my love for Della broke me.

She wouldn't like it.

I would hate it.

But this was about more than what we wanted. This was about what she needed, and any sacrifice was worth that.

Inhaling with steely resolve, I asked, "Do you need a farmhand for summer?"

A half-smile tilted his lips. "A kid with your skills and work ethic? I could use for multiple summers."

I looked once more out the window, toward the waving boughs of forests and promises of vacant untouched land, and then turned my back on it.

The rivers and forest would still be there.

For now, my role was to give Della everything I had to give.

Holding out my hand, I said, "You have a deal. Help me give Della things I can't on my own, and I'll stay for however long you need me."

Chapter Twenty-Eight

REN

2006

"YOU DIDN'T COME to the house last night."

My head shot up from where I was checking the blades on the hay cutter.

Cassie leaned over the tractor's front wheel, uncaring that dried mud and horse manure wedged in its big tread. "Where were you?"

I frowned. "Where was I?"

"Uh-huh." She nodded, licking her lower lip, dragging my attention to places it shouldn't go.

Clearing my throat, I grabbed the rag in my waistband and wiped away the grease on my hands. "In bed. Where I normally am once I've finished for the day."

"You do realise it was New Year's Eve, right? Dad said he invited you and Della to the house to watch the ball dropping in Times Square on TV."

"He did invite us."

"So why didn't you come?"

I glanced at the door leading toward the room I shared with Della. She'd been helping me all day—sweeping out the tack room, sorting out old bags of feed, and generally doing a tidy up. Poor thing was knackered. I'd found her having a nap face down on the bed when I went for a glass of water, and she hadn't emerged since.

Moving my attention back to Cassie, I brushed past her to grab another tube of piston grease resting on the tool chest. "Tired, I guess."

"You guess?" She followed me, crossing her arms and cocking her head in that annoying but somehow attractive way. "You don't talk much, do you?"

What did she want me to say? That I'd declined their invitation because, although Christmas had been amazing, it had drained me of all my reserves? That I'd reached my people quota and so had Della?

We'd spent the evening chatting about old campsites and wondering what the New Year would bring—both of us nostalgic for open air and cool streams.

When I didn't respond to her question, she tried another one. "Do you have any New Year resolutions?"

I shook my head, once again moving past her to return to the tractor and its hay cutter. "I didn't know I was supposed to."

"It's a thing."

"To make resolutions?"

"To have goals you want to do differently this year than last." She moved back to where she'd leaned against the huge wheel, watching my every move. "What did you guys do last year? Was my dad right when he said you'd been living rough for a while?"

I pursed my lips, pretending to be absorbed with using the squirting gun to apply grease.

"Silent treatment again, huh?" She rolled her eyes. "One of these days, I'll learn more about you, Ren Wild."

I flashed her half a smile. "Nothing to know."

"Oh, I don't believe that." Pushing off from the wheel, she pointed at the floor in front of her. "If you won't answer my questions, you better do something for me instead."

It was my turn to cock my eyebrow. "Do what exactly?"

"Come and stand here." She waggled her finger. "It will only take a second."

Doing my best to see a trap and unwilling to participate in whatever she wanted, I took my time to place the grease gun on the hood of the tractor and reluctantly moved to where she pointed. "What do you want?"

"I want what all girls want on New Year's Eve."

"And what's that?"

She waited until I stopped a few steps away from her. She licked her lips nervously, her cheeks pinking and feet fidgeting. "You honestly don't know?"

I jammed my hands into my jeans pockets, rocking backward on my heels. "Know what?"

"What happens at midnight on New Year's?"

"The clock switches to a new year. That's why it's called New Year." I frowned, wondering if I'd assessed her wrong, and her intelligence level was lacking instead of above par.

She sighed heavily as if I tried her patience. "No." She raked both hands through her hair, the brown strands cascading over her shoulders. "God, you're not making this easy." She laughed suddenly. "Normally, it's the boy making these moves."

My heart quickened. "What moves?"

A long pause, then an explosion of speed as she closed the distance between us, stood on her tiptoes, and breathed, "This."

Her lips landed on mine, freezing both of us to the spot.

I didn't know what the hell she was doing. All I knew was if her father caught us, I'd be fired and Della wouldn't be allowed to go to school anymore.

Tripping backward, I wiped my mouth from hers. "What the hell was that?"

"A kiss. But not a very good one." Her eyes locked on my lips. "Want to try again?"

I wanted to scold her like I'd scold Della for doing something I wasn't comfortable with. Instead, common-sense drowned beneath hot, hard need and my silence answered for me.

My brain emptied of reasons and rationality, and even the fear of ruining the bargain I'd made for Della's benefit didn't entice me to run.

Slowly, hesitantly, she stepped toward me again. Her hands fluttered by her sides, and my heart winged like a trapped bird. We didn't speak as she stopped with her shoes touching mine.

I wanted to stop her.

I wanted to grab her.

I stayed locked in stone as she once again balanced on her toes and pressed her lips to mine.

This time, I didn't stumble away, and she didn't disappear.

She smelled sweet and young and innocent. My eyes hooded, wanting to close, but I kept them open. I didn't know what I was supposed to do and didn't want to insult her by shutting her out.

With a soft breath, she moved closer, her chest brushing mine, twin roundness so different to my flat hardness. My arms twitched to encircle her, but I couldn't move.

My jeans hurt as my body swelled beyond normal. I wanted to readjust myself but daren't move in case she stopped whatever magic this was.

And then, the softest sweep of warm wetness and my eyes snapped shut on their own accord. Her tongue came again, and I gasped, opening my lips, letting her tentative quest go deeper.

My first kiss.

And hell, it was better than anything I'd experienced.

Cassie moaned as my tongue moved to meet hers—testing, learning, tasting. We stood there, hidden behind the tractor and kissed awkwardly, but somehow, that awkwardness only added to the blistering awareness and want.

My fingers curled to push her against the wall and kiss her harder.

My lungs gulped air to stop from going light-headed.

We slowly learned the other, and when it was over, Cassie smiled softer, happier than I'd seen. Her eyes were dewy. Her mouth wet from mine. Her steps floaty as she nodded once and whispered, "Thanks for my New Year's kiss, Ren."

With a lingering look, she left me to pick up my brain from the hay-dusted floor, wrangle the unbearable ache in my jeans, and somehow remember how to work.

* * * * *

That night, Della was subdued and not her usual self.

It took everything I had to lavish her with attention and be as supportive as I could when the only thing on my mind was a repeat of the kiss this afternoon.

When Della threw aside one of the few books we'd brought with us from Polcart Farm and curled into a tight ball, shutting me out and not responding to any of my suggestions to play, I lost my temper a little.

She wasn't sick. She didn't have a fever. She was just being a spoiled little brat, and I didn't have time to offer her stories or promises to do anything she wanted when all I earned was her skinny back and a savage little growl.

Leaving her to pout and deal with whatever mood she was in, I returned to the barn and found solace in Cassie's horses.

I didn't know their names, but they stuck their heads over the partition, nickering in the night for treats.

Stroking their velvet muzzles, I allowed the urge to spill my annoyance about Della's attitude to blend with the amazement of indulging in my first kiss.

The two extremes kept me standing there long into the night.

Confused.

Elated.

Frustrated.

And most of all, wary of what other surprises this New Year would bring.

Chapter Twenty-Nine

DELLA

Present Day

SO YEAH, I'VE been dreading writing this next part.

I've kind of been putting it off if I'm honest. Even knowing I'm never going to show you this assignment, it doesn't make typing it any easier.

I suppose there is no easy way to say this, so I'll ask a question instead.

How many times do you think a person can survive a broken heart?

Any ideas?

I would like to know because Ren has successfully broken mine, repaired it, shattered mine, fixed it, crushed mine, and somehow glued it back together again and again.

Then again, I don't need an answer to that question.

I'm living proof that a heart can be broken a thousand times and still function, still keep you alive—desperately hoping that it won't happen again, all the while knowing it will.

That cracking pain. That nicking, awful slicing has become horribly familiar to me now. I suppose my predicament could be seen as terribly romantic or horrendously stupid.

You'd think, after almost two decades of agony, I would've outgrown it by now...turns out, I'm stupid because I can't stop it.

Anyway, let's get on with the story...

The first time I caught him kissing her, I thought my chest would explode, and I'd plop dead right there where I hid in the barn shadows.

He didn't see me.

But, holy ouch, did I see him.

I saw his lips touch hers, his body tighten and breath catch, and I wanted to pelt toward them, scratch out her eyes, then kick him in the shins. I wanted them both to understand how much they'd wronged me.

But that was the thing…they didn't *do anything wrong.*

Ren was more man than boy, and I, as much as I despised it, was still a child.

I was trapped and hurting and ran back to our one bedroom with my heart gasping and insides smarting, curling around my agony with no clue how to stop it.

He got mad at me that night.

When he came to bed after kissing her, I couldn't bear to look at him. I couldn't let him see the depth of emptiness and loneliness he'd caused.

Instead, I ignored him.

He stormed off when I refused to uncurl and look at him. It took everything I had to hold in my aching tears, but once he'd vanished into the stables, I let loose the crushing agony and sobbed into my pillow.

I think back now and know my pain wasn't from seeing him kiss Cassie. It wasn't the fact I'd woken from my nap, bounced from our bedroom, and couldn't wait to help him with his chores again. It wasn't because, even though we lived across the driveway from the Wilsons, we were still separate, still us. And it wasn't because I knew that a kiss meant more was to come and as bodies grew closer so too do minds and hearts.

I was too young, you see.

I didn't know what kissing meant.

But the pain he injected into my heart? That was real and I felt betrayed, forgotten, and so terribly lost.

I was jealous that he was close to another when I was supposed to be the only one. I was angry that he turned to another for comfort and didn't come to me. But most of all, I was in shattered pieces because I wasn't enough anymore.

Crazy, right?

Such complex emotions for such a silly girl. I've read enough on the subject of unrequited love—especially when there are factors like age and experience separating two parties like they do with me and Ren—to understand my first broken heart wasn't about lust or sex or even understanding that a kiss like that eventually led to more.

All I knew was the one person who meant the world to me—the boy who kissed my cheeks and cuddled me close and kept all the monsters at bay—had betrayed me by liking another.

At least, I'm not unusual in my pain. Apparently, lots of children have issues with their parental figures when they start dating again after a failed marriage or other life situation. But that knowledge didn't help my fractured little heart, and it didn't help glue me back together again.

Funny enough…Cassie did that.

Remember how I said I both hated and loved her?

Well, I hated her for stealing Ren, but I loved her because she didn't just want his company.

She wanted mine, too.

I wish I could fill this assignment with slurs like she was a slut, a bitch, and a conniving little witch.

But...and this pains me to say...she wasn't.

She was reserved and protective of her family—just like Ren.

She was generous and attentive of her loved ones—just like Ren.

She was patient and kind, and little by little, she wore down my hate until I no longer hissed at her when she came into the barn to find Ren but ran out to meet her just as eager as him.

I can probably skip ahead a little because Cherry River Farm wasn't just a snippet of my life. It wasn't our home for just one winter like Ren had promised. It turned out to be my childhood playground until most of my earlier memories of tents and trees were overshadowed by barns, horses, and school.

Ah, school.

I almost forgot.

See, this is how Ren systematically broke and repaired my heart, time after time again. He broke it by kissing Cassie Wilson. He fixed it by sitting me down a few days later, while I still moped and sulked, and instead of scolding me for the fiftieth time about my unusual surly attitude, he held my hands, swept hair off my face, and told me I would be going to school.

Amazing how when you're a kid, you can switch from pain to elation so fast.

I didn't see it as bribery or search for an ulterior motive—not that there was one. I just threw my arms around his neck and squeezed as hard as I could. He still loved me. He still cared.

That first day of school, he helped me dress in a baby blue and navy striped uniform. John Wilson drove, and Ren sat in the back seat of the Land Rover with me as I bounced with barely contained energy. Instead of like the last school where my attendance was strictly temporary and based on people not asking questions, this time, it was legitimate.

Ren guided me down massive corridors and spoke proudly of me as we met the principal. And when it came time for Ren to leave me in my new classroom and return to work, I didn't mind in the slightest that he was going back to a girl called Cassie who I wouldn't be able to monitor or stalk whenever she spent time with Ren.

All I cared about was learning.

And I threw myself into it with a feverish addiction that comes from never knowing how long something good will last.

Every day, I woke up, tore around to get ready, and leapt on the school bus that stopped to pick me up. Every evening, I would do my homework and hang with Ren, and it was the happiest times of my life.

It wasn't until I finished an entire semester there and ice melted and snow turned to sun that the enjoyment faded a little thanks to the incessant urge to return to our camping way of life.

Ren had promised when the world thawed, we would be just us again.

But when the birds chirped at night and woodland creatures woke from hibernation and I asked when we would be leaving, Ren told me the second part of his bargain.

He'd agreed to stay working for John Wilson in return to sending me to school.

I'm embarrassed to say, I screamed at him for that. Here he was sacrificing everything for me, and all I could do was complain that the almost fairy-tale way of life before Cherry River was now forbidden to me for a regular one.

Even though I loved our regular one where he had a job and I had school and together we made friends with Cassie and Liam.

I'm making myself sound like an ungrateful cow, but I have to make you see the topsy-turvy world I lived in to understand how fragile my heart was.

How one moment I was queen of everything good and happy, and the next I was princess of everything bad and painful.

So much happened at that farm.

For me and for Ren.

And along the way, I lost count how many broken hearts I endured.

Chapter Thirty

REN

2006

SUMMER ALWAYS MADE everything better.

Longer days, warmer nights, happier animals, and a crap-load of work that needed doing.

When Della jumped on the school bus each morning, I'd throw on the cargo shorts and t-shirt that I'd stolen—that frankly needed to be replaced soon—and head to the back door of the main house.

There, John Wilson would meet me, try to convince me to share a cup of coffee with him and his wife—which I always refused—before listing what he'd like done for the day.

To start with, he came with me, not quite sure of my skills or abilities on using heavy machinery or trusting my methods on doing things.

Within a few days, I'd surprised him that I knew how to drive a tractor, how to attach different equipment like mowers and balers, and had the strength required to lift things even he couldn't lift.

Mclary had been good in that respect—he'd given me a crash course on how to build muscle that no ten-year-old kid should have, which only increased in strength now I was fifteen. He'd shoved me in his cantankerous tractor when my feet barely reached the pedals and expected me to figure out how to use it because if I didn't, I wouldn't be getting any scraps for dinner.

Thanks to that harsh education, I could make John's temperamental tractor purr like a sports car.

Occasionally, I'd catch him watching me with a mixture of

awe and sadness.

I didn't like that look.

I didn't like him pitying my past while being astounded at my present.

It made me feel like a freak.

However, slowly, as more time passed, and he trusted me with more and more responsibility, the more I grew into my belief that I was worth something, even if I only had nine fingers and a rusty knowledge of reading and arithmetic.

I liked being busy because it gave me something to occupy my time with until the school bus would trundle down the road, screech to a halt at the top of the Wilson's driveway, and Della would bound down its steps and charge to wherever I was on the property.

It didn't matter if I was in the furthest field or on the highest roof, she found me, demanded a hug no matter how sweaty and gross I was, then promptly sat down, pulled out two juice boxes from her rucksack, and gave me one.

The first time she produced a bag-warm blackcurrant juice, I'd raised an eyebrow and asked where she'd gotten it from. Thanks to John Wilson keeping my salary, he had the cash to buy food for Della as well as his own children, and when Cassie left for high school and Liam left for an all-boy's primary, Della was always third in line to receive a lunch bag full of fresh sandwiches, yoghurt, water, and a cookie or two.

I stood beside her every morning to make sure she said thank you and didn't miss the bus, so I knew what she had to eat and drink and what she didn't.

Turned out, she'd watched me closer than I thought whenever I'd steal something. She'd become a perfect little thief, and when the school provided extra juices to ward of dehydration during recess, she'd grab three. One for then, and two for later.

I warned her she'd get caught and wouldn't be allowed to go to school anymore.

But every day, she returned home and smugly gave me her pilfered juice box, proud and happy. She said she thought about me even when I wasn't there and wanted to make sure I had enough liquid while working out in the heat.

The fact that she cared and thought about me when I was so sure she'd be enthralled by new friends and teachers and forget all about me made my heart burst.

I couldn't believe I'd ever thought I didn't want her.

I couldn't stand remembering how I'd left her behind, if only for a few days.

My life wouldn't be nearly as rewarding if she'd never stowed away in my backpack and become my most favourite thing in the world.

And just like Della was my one and only, she was loved by each Wilson just as much. Liam would often search her out after he came home from school, and they'd play tag or swim in the river that cut through the Wilson's back paddock. Cassie took her under her wing and taught her how to be around horses safely, how to brush them, feed them, and even, on a muggy summer night, helped her climb aboard and led her around the paddock where Cassie jumped and schooled her horses.

Della had fallen asleep that night with the biggest grin on her face, legs and arms star-fished under the blankets in utter bliss. I'd watched her sleep for a while before sneaking from the bedroom and going to thank Cassie.

Her bedroom window was above a goldfish pond with pretty lily pads and noisy frogs. I often wondered if the position of the quaint pond directly beneath Cassie's window was to prevent her from easily scaling the flat roof and shimming down the ivy growing on the brick.

The more I got to know her, the more I learned who she was, and she had a rebellious streak. She might love her parents and brother, but she didn't necessarily like rules. She'd already tried dope, drank with her friends when she said she was staying the night to do homework, and generally acted like an adult when really, she was still a girl.

In many ways, Della seemed older than her with her serious attitude, utmost concentration on learning new things, and almost magical way she retained everything.

Where Cassie favoured sarcasm for laughter, Della preferred wit and a dry sense of humour. Where Cassie protected Liam and got angry with him over the slightest thing, Della cared for me as deeply as I cared for her, and we never had stupid arguments.

When we had arguments, they were never stupid, but hell, they were loud and long and drained me until all I wanted to do was kneel before my tiny ribbon and beg her to forgive me, even if it wasn't my fault.

That night, as I stood by the pond and threw a small pebble at Cassie's window, I knew I was crossing the friendship boundary that we'd danced around ever since that first kiss a few months ago.

She hadn't tried to kiss me again, and I was too much of a wimp to try myself.

Yet here I was about to do something that made my legs quake and belly knot, and in a way, it was thanks to Della.

It was her happiness that made me want to make Cassie just as happy because I was so damn grateful she'd befriended her. The fact that she let Della ride her prized pony was one of the most selfless things I'd seen her do.

Her window slid up on the third pebble, her brown hair mused from her pillow and one cheek red from lying on her side. "What gives? What's happened?"

"Meet me at the kitchen door," I whispered, keeping a close eye on her parents' blackened bedroom three windows away.

Not waiting to see if she'd obey, I jogged around the farmhouse, avoiding the perfect flower beds that Patricia Wilson spent hours tending, and waited nervously as soft footsteps sounded on the flagstone floor then the rattle of a lock and opening of the door.

"It's past midnight. Why am I out of bed?" Cassie blinked with blurry eyes. "You do realise Dad asked you to get up at dawn to do the first cut of the season, right?"

I nodded. "I know."

"That's in…I dunno, four hours or so."

"I know that, too."

"Well, how about you tell me what you're doing here, so I know if you've gone insane or not."

I smiled, climbing the small stoop so we were eye level. She was shorter than me but not by much. Her arms weren't as strong. Her legs not as fast. Her smile not as pure as Della's.

Funny how I compared the two.

Strange that I found both perfect in their own way.

"You're staring," she murmured, her voice dropping into the husky undertones that never failed to make me hard.

Clearing my throat, I said softly, "Thank you for letting Della ride your horse today."

She tilted her head so thick hair rivered over her shoulder. "That's what you woke me up to say?"

I shrugged. "I needed to say it."

"Well, I needed to sleep." She smirked, her cheeks pinking with pleasure instead of annoyance as she pretended.

"I also…" I coughed, doing my best to get up the courage. "I also wanted to do something."

"What something?"

Why was this so hard? How had she kissed me that night in the barn? It took a hell of a lot of guts, and it made me respect her that much more for being the first to do it.

"I—" Gripping the back of my neck, I squeezed hard. Doing my best to suck up my fear, I leaned toward her. "I wanted to kiss you again."

She gasped just as I closed the distance and pressed my lips to hers.

We stood frozen and awkward, her in the kitchen, me on the stoop, and my heart roared in my ears. I didn't know what to do next. I'd done this all wrong.

Cursing myself, I pulled back only for her arms to shoot around my neck and her mouth to seek mine. She yanked me to her, making me stumble against the doorframe and brace myself on the wood.

Her lips weren't innocent like last time. They'd had practice and now had a brave assurance that mine lacked.

Her tongue didn't flutter shyly, it didn't dance or ask. It pierced my lips and entered my mouth with a flavour of mint and teenage need.

Her arms tightened, deepening the kiss and wedging her body against mine.

And that was all I could take.

I'd come to give a heartfelt thank you and deliver a courteous kiss, yet Cassie turned it into a clawing, drawing need for more.

My hands left the doorframe and wrapped around her waist, jerking her against me, groaning at the delicious friction of her against every hard ridge of me.

She moaned as I spun her out of the house and crashed her against the porch wall. Our mouths never separated as our breathing turned quick, and our hands roamed with no direction.

Her tongue fought mine, adding another element to the kiss, turning it sloppy and violent. I didn't care about technique or learning how to do it better. I let her guide me, following her lead, kissing her as savagely as she kissed me.

And when her leg cocked over my hip—the very same one with a cattle brand and so many memories attached to it—I snapped out of the stupor she'd put me in and fell backward, breathing hard.

Stumbling down the steps, I stared at her, almost buckling

and returning for more.

She stood in cute cotton shorts and a nightshirt with bright pink flamingos, hair wild, lips red, chest panting, and eyes begging me to come back.

It was thanks to her blatant invitation and the fact I knew exactly what she was asking that gave me the power to walk away.

The night sky was my salvation from temptation as I put one foot in front of the other and dared let my hand wander and squeeze the excruciating ache between my legs.

Just before I reached the garden path, a sultry voice fell like starlight. "Della can ride my horses anytime she wants. I'll share everything with her…as long as you continue to kiss me like that, Ren Wild."

I didn't turn around as the kitchen door closed quietly.

* * * * *

The rest of summer was filled with late afternoon swims with Della, Liam, and Cassie; cold lemonade and barbecues thanks to Patricia and John, and a sensation of rightness as Della excelled at school and I indulged in my calling to work the land.

My hands were never fully clean from dirt. My skin was always browned from the sun. My body lean and strong, no matter how much Patricia tried to feed me.

I never saw a penny for the many hours I worked. It didn't matter if I started at dawn and finished long past dusk, John never gave me a dollar.

But it didn't mean he wasn't keeping tally.

During the busiest time of the year, when we had countless equestrians and fellow farmers coming to buy lucerne and meadow hay, and my life was a never-ending loop of cutting, fluffing, raking, baling, loading, and sowing, strange new possessions started appearing.

Patricia often stole Della to go with her and Cassie on shopping trips into town, and Della would return with sugar still rimming her pretty lips and her hands full of bags. She'd force me to sit on the bed as she tried on outfit after outfit, giving me a fashion show of colourful summer dresses, practical winter jackets, and frankly far too revealing swimsuits.

It was odd that the one-piece daffodil coloured swimsuit she wore whenever we'd swim in the river annoyed me more than skinny-dipping ever did.

There was something about the way it made Della switch from uncaring natural child to fledgling young woman who copied

Cassie's every move that made me look away as if I'd breached some sort of code by looking at her.

As Cassie prowled around in her black bikini with toned legs and perky breasts, Della would puff out her flat little chest and sunbake on flat rocks with her legs crossed in perfect imitation.

It made me uncomfortable but also indulgent.

I didn't like to think of her trading innocence for whatever Cassie dabbled in, but I also couldn't ignore that she was almost six years old—maybe already six years old, seeing as I didn't know her birthday—and time was speeding up.

Every morning, she seemed to look different with a wiser glint to her gaze and harsher pinch to her lips if I annoyed her. She kept me on my toes—almost as much as Cassie did.

I struggled most days around Cassie, and my body was in a total flux of pain whenever we'd swim together. She'd pin me with an inviting stare, her body lithe and tempting and I'd have to turn my back to avoid revealing just how much she affected me.

Little Liam was the easiest to hang out with because all he cared about was lizards and helping his mother in the garden. He wasn't growing up too fast or trying to lead me directly into sin.

Despite my growing awareness and steadily growing desire for what Cassie tempted, I loved working for the Wilsons. They were true to their word and among the many kindnesses they did for Della, they also ensured I had a treat now and again, too.

I did my best to ensure their farm ran as smoothly and productively as possible, and I guessed they appreciated it because one night, after a particularly gruelling day hauling hundreds of hay bales from the paddock and stacking them in the barn for winter feed, I lugged my tired, aching body to the one bedroom I shared with Della and heard music and voices coming from within.

A man's voice.

My heavy steps turned quick as I barrelled into the room only to find Della sprawled on her belly with her chin in her hands, watching a comedy on a brand new flat-screen TV.

"Where did that come from?" I plopped exhausted beside her on the end of the bed, laying my arm over her shoulders and playing, like I always did, with the blue ribbon trapped in her ponytail.

"Patty and John." She shuffled closer, uncaring that her clean skin pressed against my hay-covered sweat.

"Wow."

"I know." She nodded importantly. "I made sure to say thank

you."

"I think they deserve multiple thank yous."

"Cassie let me ride her horse today after school, too." Her face split into the biggest grin. "I got a gold star in class, got to ride a pony, and we have a TV again! Best day *ever*!"

I kissed her head, inhaling the sweet milk and honey shampoo she favoured and ignored my skipping heart. "I'm going to get clean."

"Okay." She flashed me a smile then turned back to the TV. As her attention fixed on the ridiculous show, I dragged myself to the shower and stripped.

I stood under cold water, trying to wash away heatstroke and prickly grass while doing my best to inject energy into tired muscles because I wouldn't be crawling into bed to fall asleep beside Della.

Not yet, anyway.

Della had ridden Cassie's horse.

And that meant I owed someone a kiss.

Chapter Thirty-One

REN

2006

I COULDN'T REMEMBER when I'd taken Della to the diner for our shared birthday lunch, but today was my only day off, and I wanted to spend time with her just the two of us.

The exact date didn't matter because it wasn't the right one anyway. All that mattered was marking the calendar of her turning six and me turning sixteen.

Instead of stealing a wallet to pay for a single lunch, I politely asked Patricia if I could pack a wicker basket of fresh ham sandwiches and some of her banana and raspberries muffins freshly baked and steaming on the windowsill, and head to one of the boundary paddocks where willow trees dragged long fronds on the ground.

Once there, I laid out a plaid blanket, served Della our birthday picnic, and when our fingers were sticky with muffin crumbs, I pulled out the only thing I could give her.

I had no cash as everything I made went to making her life easier. I had no income because I trusted the Wilsons to spend it better than I ever could.

All I had were my hands and snippets of time while Della slept softly beside me.

"That's for me?"

I nodded. Guilt that it wasn't something better and uncertainty that she might not like it rolled my shoulders. "It's not much but—"

"It's awesome."

"You haven't even opened it yet."

"Right." She smirked, stroking the orange striped dishtowel and baling twine I'd used to wrap it. "Can I open it?"

"It's yours. Of course, you can."

With her lip stuck between her teeth, she undid the bow and let the material fall away.

Inside, the carved horse gleamed from the hours I'd spent polishing it with saddle conditioner. The tiny girl atop the horse could've been anyone if it wasn't for the long ribbon trailing behind from her long hair.

It'd taken me hours and multiple attempts after snapping the delicate ribbon so many times while carving.

No one knew I'd done it even though I'd borrowed John's tools to make it happen. It wasn't perfect, and I hated a lot of it with my clumsy cuts and annoying mistakes, but it showed how much I cared. It revealed just how proud I was of her learning to ride and how terrified I was of her getting hurt. She'd taken a tumble a couple of times, and my heart literally quit beating until I knew she was okay.

My fear of her falling off a horse was nothing compared to the sudden terror drenching me as Della switched from chatty live wire to quiet, subdued seriousness beside me.

Silence fell, interrupted only by the breeze whispering through the willow leaves. I waited for as long as I could, my skin prickling with unease, my heart racing with dread.

Her fingers trailed over and over, stroking the carved mane, touching slightly too long legs, and studying not quite perfect nostrils.

I couldn't wait any longer.

Pinching it from her hands, I shoved it behind my back. "Forget it. I knew I should've asked John to buy you that laptop the school requests everyone to have. I'll-I'll tell him tonight. You might have to wait a few months while he saves up my salary to buy it, but I'll make sure you have something of use instead of—"

She sprang into me, bowling me over, slamming both of us to the blanket below. "Give it back."

My elbows bent awkwardly, my spine jabbed by the carved willow-wooden horse in my hands. "Wha—"

"My horse. Now. Give it back, Ren."

I wriggled beneath her as she sat on my chest, her shorts riding up suntanned thighs and lavender t-shirt right in my face. The sun silhouetted her, showing a faceless girl with curling white-blonde hair with her hand straight out and reckless determination bristling all around her.

"Now, Ren." Her voice turned sharp in the way she'd mastered from listening to Cassie telling me off.

Untangling my arms from behind my back, I lay flat and gave it up as a peace offering.

She continued to straddle my chest, snatching the horse and rider, the long ribbon sticking out between her fingers. "You can't give it to me then take it away. That's not how gift giving works."

Propping my head up with my hands, I tried to tame the clenching in my belly and did my best to accept that she liked it. Liked it enough to attack me to take it back, anyway. "It's not very good—"

"Zip it." She grabbed my lips between tight fingers, forcing my mouth closed. "I love it. It's better than all the shopping trips and all the ribbons." She squished my lips harder. "If you say one more bad thing about it, I'll...I'll—" She pouted, looking over my head toward the forests and fields. "I'll leave you here for something to eat."

I shook my head, dislodging her hold. "And here I thought you loved me."

"Not when you're being a moron."

"Hey, I just gave you a birthday present."

"And then took it away again." She scowled. "Not cool, dude. Not cool."

"Dude?" I chuckled. "Where the hell did that come from?"

Her personality had evolved leaps and bounds ever since she started hanging out with Liam and whatever kids she'd befriended at school. I'd even heard her curse the other day and told her off for such language.

I was fairly sure she hadn't picked that up from me seeing as I was super careful with how and what I said around her.

"Some girl in class."

"A girl you like?"

"I guess." She shrugged. "Stop changing the subject. Don't touch my gift."

"Okay, okay. I won't take it again."

"You better not."

I licked my lips from where her touch had been, tasting raspberries and sugar. "Now that we've got that sorted and you've attacked me on my birthday, what do you want to do for the rest of the day?"

She rolled off me, flopping onto her back and holding her

horse aloft with the sun sparkling on its glossy flanks. "Dunno. Something."

"Something isn't helpful."

"Something with you."

"Did you want Liam and Cassie to come?"

Her blue eyes locked on mine with fierce certainty. "No. Just us."

"In that case…" Climbing upright, I helped her stand. "Let's go home for the day."

Her face brightened as she spun to face the dense treeline on the edge of the Wilson's property. "Truly?"

"Truly."

Slipping her hand in mine, we stepped into tree-shadows just as she yelped, "Oh no! I forgot to get you a present. It's your birthday, too!"

I shook my head. "Just spending the day with you is enough."

"But Cassie said that sweet sixteen means you get lots of stuff."

I stilled. "What sort of stuff?"

"Dunno. Stuff."

"This 'dunno' business is getting old real fast, Della."

She clutched my hand harder as she rubbed the toe of her sandal into the grass. "She wanted me to tell you something, but I don't wanna."

I crouched down, pulling her closer. "Tell me what?"

Her face scrunched up as if she'd taken a bite of sour lime. "She asked where we were going on your day off."

"Okay…"

"I told her it's our birthday."

"And…"

"And she wished me happy birthday and promised she'd teach me how to jump on Domino tomorrow as my present."

"That's nice of her."

"No, it isn't. 'Cause I know what she gets each time she lets me—" She sighed as if she carried the weight of a thousand problems. "I mean…I guess so."

I stiffened. There was no way she could know the standing arrangement between Cassie and me, trading horse rides for kisses.

Pushing that stupid thought aside, I murmured, "Tell me what's eating you, Little Ribbon."

"Nothing." She sniffed, staring at the dirt.

"It's something."

I hated her being so glum but I also couldn't help if I didn't know what her problem was.

I reached out to touch her golden head but she jerked away at the last second, stabbing me as surely and as perfectly as only she could do. Della was the only one who could make sunshine live in my chest then suffocate it with perpetual night, depending on how she tolerated me.

I hated when she was mad because nothing felt right. My heart didn't beat right. My body didn't behave right. She made me sick and the only medicine was to earn her smiles and hugs again.

"What's wrong?" My patience thinned, batting away the ache at letting her down in some way. Even though I wanted to demand she spit it out, I forced myself not to push her. She had a habit of shutting down these days over things I didn't understand. She'd give me the cold shoulder if she caught me laughing with Cassie and hadn't been a part of the conversation. She'd glower if Cassie was there, handing me tools and giggling in her school uniform when Della leaped off the bus.

She'd always been an open book, so the silent treatment confused me.

It hurt too, but I didn't feel I had the right to be in pain when she was obviously hurting because of something she refused to discuss.

Dealing with a growing girl was exhausting.

"Della...it's okay. You don't have to tell me." I brought her tiny hand to my mouth and kissed her knuckles. "Let's just go for a walk—"

"She said she's going to give you a special birthday treat tonight because sixteen is a big deal and sixteen-year-old boys deserve special treats." Tears glassed her beautiful eyes as she yanked her hand from mine. "I don't want her to give you anything. You're mine. And I forgot to give you something, and now you're going to get all the things from her and forget all about me!" With an agonizing gasp, she tore off into the trees.

What the—

"Della!" I chased after her, following the crash and crunch of twigs, trying to catch up as she ducked under low branches and weaved around Della-sized bushes. "Come back here."

She didn't stop. She didn't slow.

"Della Ribbon, you get your butt back here this instant!" I leapt over bracken, grateful for years of hard labour and a body good at endurance. She was a speedy little thing, and I had no intention of letting her get away with shutting down this time. *"Della!"*

Goddammit.

Something crashed to a stop in front of me, sending me skidding on the brakes as I almost ran into her.

She looked up beneath a curtain of blonde curls, her eyes tight and lips thin but tears no longer glittered. I almost wished there were tears because the calm collectedness in her stare terrified me.

"I'm sorry that I didn't get you a gift." She let me grab her and wedge her into my stomach. Her thin arms wrapped loosely around my hips as she breathed hard into my lower belly. "I didn't mean to be a child."

"You weren't a child."

"I forgot. I'm not supposed to say anything about Cassie."

I peeled her away, staring into her face, but once again, that blank collectedness stared back. "What aren't you telling me, Della?"

"Nothing."

"There's something."

"Nuh-uh. I'm fine." She smiled bright and brittle. "See?"

I didn't buy it, but my brain didn't work fast enough to figure out what she was hiding.

I fumbled for something to say, some reassurance to utter, some way to bring back the happy kid I loved with all my heart, but I was too slow, and Della's truth slipped through my fingers.

"Wanna play tag?" she asked, already bouncing away as if the past few minutes never existed. "You won't catch me." The flavour of heartache vanished as she giggled and took off at a dead sprint, long hair trailing, ribbon twirling.

I stared after her, lost.

What had just happened?

Della laughed, already a fair distance away. "Ren! Come on, slow poke!"

Whatever it was wasn't over, but I didn't want to taint the rest of our day together.

For now, I let her fake normalcy and bought into her assurances that whatever worried her wasn't too overpowering that it stopped her from playing.

I'd protect her from everything, but until she told me what hurt her, I had to trust she was okay.

I took off, leaping forward into the trees I adored over any house or barn. "Oh, you're in so much trouble when I get you!"

Her happy squeal tried to delete the strange, painful moment from before.

But it never quite removed the shadow she'd painted on my heart.

No matter how long we ran like the wild creatures we were.

No matter how much time we spent in the forest that was our true home.

Something had happened between us.

And it would have to be dealt with...sooner or later.

Chapter Thirty-Two

REN

2006

THAT NIGHT, WHEN Della had fallen asleep and I lay staring at the ceiling beside her, a soft knock on our bedroom door told me Cassie had come to give me her present.

Glancing down at Della, part of me wanted to pretend I hadn't heard her while the other part desperately wanted to find out what she'd give me.

It took a minute of internal warfare before I slid out of bed in just my boxers and hauled on a pair of shorts that were my cleanest pair. I debated whether to stay shirtless.

Which would seem worse? Shirtless while hoping we were about to make out, or clothed while hoping we were about to make out?

I chose modesty and grabbed a black t-shirt from the floor.

Tiptoeing toward the door, I held my finger to my lips to keep Cassie quiet as I slipped through a crack, looking back once more at sleeping Della, her hair spread all over my pillow and tiny body tucked under cosy covers.

Cassie nodded, following me silently toward the stables until I stopped by the tack room.

I didn't know what to say because we both knew why she was here. I didn't want to be the idiot to ask what she wanted or pretend anything was wrong. Just staring at her told me everything I needed to know.

No words were uttered as she stepped into my personal space, stood on her toes, and kissed me softly. The familiarity of kissing her now didn't mean my heart stayed calm. Like always, it leaped and thudded as warm wetness and slippery intoxication turned my brain to mush and body to granite.

Wrapping my arms around her, I backed her into the tack room wall, pressing her tight and daring to wedge the length of my frame against hers.

She moaned into our kiss, her fingers slipping through my hair as she tugged me closer. Our heads tilted as we deepened the kiss, breathing hard, tasting, and licking—quickly losing propriety in favour of clutching hands and clawing need.

Her hands left my hair, slipping over my shoulders and running down my chest.

I gasped as her touch disappeared up the hem of my t-shirt and fingernails ran along my belly. She tugged the waistband of my shorts, murmuring, "Can I give you a birthday present?"

I could barely speak intelligently when I was of sound body and mind; asking me a question while blood pounded between my legs and my heart acted as if it was in a death metal band made me utterly unable to talk.

"I take your silence as a yes." Slowly, she dropped to her knees. Her eyes glistened, mouth gleamed, tongue flickered over her bottom lip.

The air prickled around us, full of forbidden danger and illicit taboo. I was playing with fire. I was touching the boss's daughter, yet really, she was the one touching me.

I trembled as she pulled my shorts and boxers down in one go, freeing me, sending a flush of embarrassment through my blood, and leaving the tight elastic of my underwear clinging to my upper thighs.

Her fingers traced the raised scar tissue from the Mclary brand that I'd never be able to remove. She looked up, eyes full of questions. Questions I would refuse to answer.

She bit her lip, deliberating.

I stopped breathing, waiting.

Then her touch moved away from the mark, slipping to cup around my length.

I jolted with mind-numbing awareness as her fingers pulsed, and her voice trickled into my ears, "Have you had a blowjob before, Ren?"

I gulped, shaking my head like an idiot. I'd always known Cassie was forward and far more worldlier than I was. I'd seen her kiss different boys if she got dropped off from school in muscle cars or dinged up 4WDs. I'd heard her father yell at her not to be so loose, and her mother to scold her on her friendship choices.

Although, nothing seemed to stop her from searching for something, trying new things, and sampling experiences she probably wasn't ready for.

She'd even told me that I kissed differently to an old boyfriend she'd dated for two weeks a year ago. She made me feel terribly young and stupidly inexperienced.

I didn't want to be taught these things. I wanted to be able to participate and blow her mind just like she blew mine. But despite her forwardness, she remained sweet and kind, making me worried that one day, she'd be taken advantage of.

She also worried me around Della.

Della was still too young to know what painful passion felt like, brewing constantly in your veins. She believed kisses on the mouth were for unconditional love between anyone—friend, parent, or anyone else who deserved it. She already had older views on body image thanks to Cassie in her bikinis, and I didn't want her growing up too fast that sleeping in the same bed suddenly went from comforting to downright unpermitted.

She was a kid.

My kid.

And I wanted to keep her that way for as long as possible.

Funny, when I pictured her kissing a boy like I was kissing Cassie, red anger hazed my vision. I'd kill any boy who touched her and didn't quite know how I'd deal with her when she entered her teenage years.

A flutter of hot breath on my upper thighs was the only warning I had.

My mind shot blank as a tongue met my hard flesh, and my knees threatened to buckle. I slammed one hand against the wall, my other landed in her hair. A grunt escaped me as her tongue came again. My head swam, and I felt nauseous and invincible and fragile and immortal all at the same time.

"I take it this is your first time?" she whispered around my length.

My fingernails dug into the wood and clenched around her hair, holding her tight, not knowing if I was allowed to pull her closer and stop her torture by making her do what she promised.

I managed some sort of non-cohesive reply before her head bent again and that intoxicating puff of air stroked my body.

"Happy Birthday, Ren Wild." Her voice licked around me just as her mouth sealed hot and tight *everywhere*.

My head flopped forward.

My oxygen rushed out.

And my body jerked in bliss.

I thought of nothing but the sensation of wet heat and the pulling deep in my belly.

I'd grown wiser than I'd been a few years ago when puberty first started making my life a living nightmare. I'd learned how to shave without bleeding and how to combat unwelcome erections—most of the time.

But I'd never been comfortable making myself orgasm.

Either I was working and didn't feel right while being paid, or I was in bed beside Della.

Animals didn't self-pleasure, even if those dirty magazines said men did. The thought of jerking off, touching myself, and searching for that ever-wanted release didn't seem ethical.

But right here, right now, with a girl sucking me and every single worry deleted, I didn't care.

I was entirely in her hands.

I was her student, and I would take whatever she taught me.

Her fingers wrapped tighter around me, squeezing as her mouth slid deeper.

The pulling in my belly evolved to an outright pain, travelling in quaking lightning bolts up my thighs into my spine and crackling between my legs.

I winced as her teeth caught the tip, adding a thread of agony to an otherwise mind-numbing experience, but instead of stopping the impending snarling release, it magnified it.

"Cas—" I groaned as she grasped me tighter with one hand and dug fingernails into my ass with the other. She yanked me into her mouth as she sucked with noisy pulls.

I honestly had no control.

I couldn't stop it even if I pulled away and ran as far from her as possible.

The release had already captured me, and as she sucked me hard, fast, and unrelenting, I came.

I jerked and bowed and blinked back stars as Cassie very generously gave me my sixteenth birthday present in the doorway of her tack room, in the very same barn where Della and I were found.

* * * * *

That first intimate moment set in motion regular meetings between Cassie and me.

Over the next year, she taught me that blowjobs could be used as a punishment as well as a reward, depending on if I'd pissed her off or pleased her.

Some weeks, we'd sneak to somewhere shadowy and private on a nightly basis. And some months, we'd return to just being friends as she entered a relationship with a new boy from school or some peacock masquerading as a cool almost-adult instead of a drop-out teenager working minimum wage at a local store.

We never went further than touching and kissing, and that was mainly because of me.

I supposed, with my unconventional childhood and learning everything by myself rather than having society or family teach what I should and shouldn't do, meant I had a wariness that took time to accept new things.

I was still a loner, and some weeks, I struggled with humans even as nice as the Wilsons. The only person I never grew sick of was Della, and that was probably because she felt the same way as me.

That kid adored school.

She came home with constant assignments and excelled in every exam. She put her hand up for extra activities and even joined a few sport-teams.

However, when school holidays rolled around, she'd spend the first few days in bed unable to stand being around people, claiming she was exhausted and needed space.

I understood her exactly.

And having a likeminded friend let me accept that part of myself and not change…for anyone.

My reserved nature drove Cassie crazy, but I didn't know how to stop it. Luckily, it didn't prevent her from teaching me how to touch her…all of her…and my first experience fingering a woman had almost made me come as fast as my first blowjob had.

It was unlike anything I'd ever touched, and I become an avid learner.

It hadn't taken long to switch Cassie's response from indulgent smile and soft instruction to heavy breathing and scratching nails as I made her come just like she made me.

The first time I'd successfully made her unravel, my wrist and forearm held lacerations from where she'd scratched me mid-orgasm.

The next day, Della had asked what happened.

I'd blushed and blamed the barn cat who fed on the mice

eating horse feed and burrowing into hay. She'd tutted and shook her head, telling me in her best parental voice to be more careful and to treat Blackie with more respect next time I tried to catch her.

Cassie had tried to laugh about it the next time we met, but that was one thing I never tolerated. She could laugh at Liam's escapades and discuss her family, friends, and boyfriend drama with me, and I would forever listen politely.

But try to pry into my background, try to make me laugh at Della's expense, or try to make fun of things I loved, and I shut down.

I didn't permit her to even mention Della unless it was to regale me with stories of her quickly improving equestrian skills or ask questions that would benefit their relationship.

I didn't know why, but I couldn't let my guard down about Della or relax enough to give Cassie answers to the questions she constantly asked.

Questions about the place where I'd been sold.

Questions about my mother.

Questions about how I ran away with Della.

I either turned mute or changed the subject—not because I didn't have answers but because something inside refused to give up that part of myself...to anyone.

A year after Della and I were caught sleeping in their barn, Cassie blew up at me for being quiet and elusive. I didn't know why she called me elusive when I made sure to be friendly and polite to every single one of the Wilsons.

She'd tried to enlighten me, saying she didn't know me at all even after a year of fooling around and seeing each other every day, that my refusal to talk about my past, that my preference to stay at home rather than head to the movies or gatherings, and the fact I didn't give anything of myself was a drain and a bore, and frankly, she wanted someone more outgoing.

After our fight, she'd announced that we could only be friends as she was with some new Nathan or Ryan or Paul.

I didn't mind either way.

I wasn't jealous of her with other boys.

I wasn't annoyed that I was passed over for what she called better alternatives. In fact, I rather liked being ignored because it meant I returned to a simpler lifestyle where my only desire was looking after Della and making sure she was as happy as I could make her.

Chapter Thirty-Three

REN

2007

ANOTHER WINTER CAME.

My work around the farm went from crazy to part-time, and with idle hands came the itch to leave. Every night that Della slept beside me, taller, prettier, more girl than child, I wondered where our future would take us.

There was no question that if I left she'd come too, but I was trapped by both returning cold weather and Della's love for going to school.

On the last week of her term, before winter closed classes down for a while, she seemed off when we ate together in our room. I'd taken to keeping produce that I'd helped plant and tend in a mini fridge that John Wilson had delivered to us a few months ago.

I had a camping stove and preferred to cook on my own rather than accept the nightly invitation to eat with the Wilsons in their snug home. Not because things between Cassie and I were strained right now, or even that, as I grew older, I became more wanderer by heart and outsider by nature, but because I enjoyed keeping my skills sharp.

One day, I would live off the land again, and when that day came, I couldn't be soft and useless when it came to skinning rabbits or preparing meals for two. I'd already let my talent at thievery turn rusty thanks to earning an honest wage, but it was never far from my mind.

I didn't think that mentality would ever fully leave me. Even at seventeen, I still studied unprotected spots in house defences, body language of easy prey, and weaknesses that I could exploit if I wanted to.

That night, instead of a normal Wednesday evening when Della and I curled up in front of the TV with a simple meal of simmered carrots and honey glazed chicken, my life took a swerve into terror territory.

She accepted her dinner with her usual politeness and even gave me a weak smile.

But something was off.

My heart, that usually calmed down and found happiness whenever I was around her, skyrocketed with anxious nerves. "You okay?" I asked softly, brushing aside hair that'd stuck to her cheek.

The instant my fingers connected with her skin, I yanked them back faster than a whip. Immediately, I took the plate she held listlessly, climbed off the bed, and scooped her from the end.

She didn't mutter one annoyance or frustration which layered my already anxious heart with more fear.

"Della..."

With as much tenderness as I could, I placed her on top of the bedspread and gathered her hair away from her back and neck so it draped over the pillow out of the way.

She groaned softly as if lying on a comfortable mattress hurt.

"Tell me what's wrong." I kneeled by the bed, hoping I looked in charge and strong when really, I was dying inside. "What is it? Something you ate? A cold? Tummy bug?"

We weren't immune to everyday illnesses, especially now that Della spent the majority of her time around grubby children and unhygienic school classrooms. We'd had enough colds to know the symptoms.

But this was different.

She'd been listless yesterday too but still chirpy when I pushed her. Then again, she'd only eaten half her dinner and none of her dessert, when normally, she wolfed whatever I put in front of her.

I'd stayed up late, watching her sleep, and she'd been deep under all night.

I should've been more diligent. I should've known she was worse than she let on.

She had a habit of hiding things—keeping secrets close to her chest. Most of the time, I could handle her need for privacy and lived in constant hope that one day, she would trust me enough to share her secrets.

But today wasn't that day, and I should've known better than to accept her lies.

She'd fibbed right to my face about her health and put herself in harm's way.

Didn't she know that was the worst kind of punishment? I loved her unconditionally, and she'd hurt herself yet again by keeping things from me.

My hands curled.

I wanted to tell her off, but instead, my mind raced with questions and theories of what could be wrong as my fingers rested on her forehead again, wincing at the heat radiating from her.

Goddammit, how had I not noticed?

Why did I let her go to school this morning?

"You lied to me. You said you were feeling better." I cupped her cheek, willing her to open her eyes. "Little Ribbon...what have you done?"

She moaned, her lips parting just enough for a flinched breath. "I'm sorry."

"Don't apologise. I just wish you'd said something."

"I had to hand in my science project that you helped me with."

I scoffed. "I think two caterpillars turning into chrysalis and butterflies in a jam jar could've waited if you weren't feeling okay."

A lonely tear leaked from her left eye. "I'm sorry."

I bent and pressed my forehead against her cheek, curling my arm around her head. "Don't. It's me who should apologise."

"But I made you mad."

My heart cracked. "You didn't make me mad. You made me worried. Big difference." I couldn't take my eyes off her as she winced and wriggled in discomfort. "You have me so damn worried, Little Ribbon, and here I am scolding you when I should be making you better."

"I'm sorry." She snuggled into my embrace even though her body was a mini furnace.

"Stop saying that." I held her tight, willing the chaos in my brain to settle enough to talk without bite and ask questions gently. "I'm the one who's sorry, and now I'm going to do everything I can to make you better."

Kissing her softly on her nose, I asked, "Tell me what's wrong. List how you feel." I'd watched Patricia Wilson deal with

Liam when he was regularly ill from kids at school. I'd lurked outside while Cassie recovered from a bad flu on the couch and she was doted on by concerned parents.

At the time, I thought them lucky to have such care—their only worry was to heal and be a demanding patient where all their wishes were met.

Now, I understood it from the panicked caregiver's point of view. The anxious hovering over their baby to ensure they were still breathing. The nervous voice when they asked how they were, dreading a reply of worse and begging for an answer of better.

Now, I was that parent, and I would do anything in the world to trade places with Della and suffer whatever she was going through.

She bit her bottom lip as she wriggled away from my embrace, sweat dotting her upper lip. "I'm hot."

"Tell me what else. Tell me how I can fix this." All I wanted to do was slaughter her pain and send it directly to hell.

"I'm thirsty." She blinked with wide eyes. "Um…I'm hot. My legs ache. I'm…tired." She yawned as if on cue, trying to roll onto her side.

I didn't permit it, holding her firm. "Anything else?"

Shaking her head, she moaned, "I dunno. Just…everything doesn't feel right, Ren." She tried to roll again, but I kept my hand clutched on her shoulder, dislodging her pink knitted jumper, revealing her back.

A red rash invaded the perfection of her porcelain skin.

Fuck.

Leaping clumsily onto the bed, I scooped her close and yanked off her jumper.

"No…" She protested weakly and not her usual spit fire attack. That alone made my belly knot and heart shut down.

All over her chest and back was a rash. An enemy infiltrating everything I loved in the world.

She batted me away with a feather-weak hand as I let her flop back down and undid the zipper on her jeans. Her head lolled on the pillow as I pulled them as gently as I could down her legs, my lips thinning and head pounding as I found yet more red rash.

Outside, snow had started to fall, and my mind regressed to when she was sick the first time, and we'd stumbled upon Polcart Farm. That place had saved her life. Perhaps Cherry River would save her this time.

Because as much as I would slay dragons for her, I was not a doctor.

I didn't have a clue what was wrong, and I couldn't stop my morbid thoughts from filling me with agony of her dying due to my incompetence.

Pulling her jeans back up, I hastily buttoned them, bundled her up in one of my jumpers, then clutched her tight.

Striding from the room, I carried her through swirling snowflakes and pounded on the Wilson's door.

* * * * *

Della was admitted to the hospital.

For three days, I paced those antiseptic corridors and slept curled up on a hard, cold couch at the foot of her single cot.

I hated that place.

I *despised* that place.

But I refused to leave even for a moment.

Della couldn't leave; therefore, I couldn't leave.

Turned out, thanks to scientific words I didn't understand and people I couldn't tolerate, Della had chicken pox. Normally, a kid contracted the virus and dealt with it no problem, but Della had a worse than normal reaction to Varicella, which according to some doctor I wanted to punch in the face, was the correct term for the red spots, obsessive itchiness, migraines, tiredness, and vomiting that Della endured.

She couldn't keep anything down, and her body looked more crimson than cream thanks to the invasion of spots and her tendency to scratch until she bled.

It ripped out my guts to see her in so much discomfort and not have any power to help.

This was the first time I'd been in a hospital since my finger had been cut off. Back then, I'd been given candy and a toy. Back then, I'd felt cared for and in good hands—until Mclary threw my gifts and their kindness out the window, of course.

But right now, I doubted everyone. No one had the power to stop Della's pain, and I hated them. I'd expected miracles, and Della had received subpar attention with lacklustre results.

Despite their un-miracle-working care, she slowly got better. I didn't give the tired looking doctors and harassed looking nurses any credit.

I gave it all to her.

Della was strong.

She fought hard.

And when she finally stopped vomiting and her symptoms

abated to an annoying scratch with no fever, she was released, and John Wilson drove us back to Cherry River.

Cassie, Liam, and Patricia all wanted to crowd and cuddle my patient upon her arrival, but I forbade them.

My possessiveness only grew worse now the doctors had relinquished her back into my care. Not that they had technically. They'd put her into the Wilson's care as I was still a minor.

Before, when I was young and terrified of having someone's whole existence hinge entirely on me, I would've been grateful to the Wilsons for loving Della as much as I did. If they had been the ones I left her with, I would've made the right choice.

But that was years ago, and things had changed. Della no longer needed me to survive, but I sure as hell needed her, and even with her sick, I needed her close.

At least the Wilsons knew she was mine and backed off after their initial welcome.

Della was my responsibility, and I ensured her every beck and call was met: applying lotion to her spots, duct taping her hands into my thick baling gloves to stop her from scratching, and feeding her whatever she wanted.

No matter that I was left alone to do whatever Della needed, I still couldn't get over the desire to growl at anyone who came close or snarl at those who offered help.

I acted like a controlling, dominating bastard but that was what Della's fragility made me become. I patrolled around her like a wolf would his cub, ready to bite anything that dared damage what was his.

I'd do anything to make her well again; including destroying anyone who got too close.

The Wilsons provided us with healthy soups and drinks—when they braved my temper—and when Della blinked awake one afternoon from yet another nap and her familiar strength started to glow beneath her illness, I found my selfishness at keeping her to myself fading.

I 'borrowed' John Wilson's Land Rover—which was so much easier to drive than a tractor—and headed into town where I used a handful of change found in the middle console to purchase Della's request for a Filet o' Fish happy meal.

For so long, we'd never had processed food, and I didn't particularly like that she'd grown to enjoy it. Ever since she started having lunches and weekend play dates with friends from school, her palate had adapted to not only enjoy fresh produce but also greasy takeaway.

I preferred to keep burgers and fries as birthday treats but Cassie called me old fashioned whenever I'd grumble about Della's new favourite foods.

John saw me arriving with the cab of his truck reeking of takeout but didn't say a word as I parked on his driveway and climbed out with the brown paper bag.

We stared at each other.

I tipped my head in gratitude along with the acknowledgment that I'd been a grumpy bastard and taken something I shouldn't. He nodded back, forgiving me and understanding.

Giving him another nod, I jogged back to Della to give her what she craved.

If junk food was the recipe to getting my favourite person back, then I'd do it.

I'd do anything for her.

Just like I'd stayed here past winter for her.

Just like I'd sacrifice anything of mine so she could have everything.

Chapter Thirty-Four

DELLA

Present Day

THERE ARE SO *many things I remember about Cherry River, but one of my sharpest memories isn't the itch and horribleness of chicken pox—to be honest, I don't really want to remember it so I probably shoved that part aside.*

What I do remember is what happened afterward.

What was that, you ask?

Well, the boy who nursed me back to health hadn't factored in his own invincibility against diseases we hadn't been around or vaccinated against.

Ren gave me everything he had those few weeks while I was ill.

He barely slept. He delivered my cravings. He gave me anything I asked for.

And what did he get in return?

Chicken pox.

I noticed it one night when his usual tossing and turning was eerily catatonic. Ren didn't sleep well. He never had. I'd been selfish and never minded because if he was awake, it meant I was safe sleeping beside him.

But this time...Ren didn't move when I whispered his name in the darkness. He didn't move just like when he'd had the flu-turned-pneumonia which led us to being befriended by the Wilsons in the first place.

That catastrophe had a happy ending.

I didn't want to tempt fate by seeing what would happen if he got terribly sick again. But those spots on the back of his neck and even one on his cheek above his five o'clock shadow hinted that he was about to endure what I'd gone through.

The next few days, he grew worse.

Somehow, as he grew sicker, I grew stronger, and our roles reversed. I was the one dabbing his flesh with lotion to stop the itch. I was the one dishing out painkillers for his fever, and I was the one carrying soup across the driveway courtesy of Patricia's awesome cooking skills.

Well, I was the one…until Cassie took over.

She infiltrated our bedroom and sat beside Ren on our bed. She touched his brow and whispered secrets, and all I could do was return to school, hiding the hissing jealousy in my heart and not able to focus at all on what the teacher said.

Cassie had school too, but she always seemed to be in my spot beside Ren when I got dropped off by the bus and there until late when it should just be the two of us.

My frustration steadily grew.

I'd sit in the corner chair with my legs bunched up and my arms wrapped tight around them, glowering at Cassie touching my Ren.

Every time she leaned in and touched his cheek. Every time she laughed at something he mumbled.

Ugh, it was times like that that I hated her all over again.

She'd been so kind and generous to me—letting me ride her favourite pony, teaching me how to canter and jump, and even letting me tag along to a local show when she competed.

I struggled because she was a genuine person and didn't hang out with me to get to Ren—I would've been able to tell; believe me, I was suspicious for a very long time—which made my despising her worse because I felt like a horrible, terrible child, and all I wanted to do was grow up faster so I wouldn't be so silly and petty.

Funny how I'm older now but whenever I think about Cherry River, I still have both love and hate inside me. I think, if I had to relive that time, I would be just as jealous as I'd been as a seven-year-old, only this time, I'd probably be arrested for murder.

Instead of just hero worship and parental adoration, I now have forbidden cravings and achings and all the things I know I shouldn't feel.

I know you're probably thinking…eww, how could you fall in love with your brother who is technically your father and definitely your uncle or some other untouchable life figure?

In my defence, I'll ask you a similar question.

How could you not fall in love with a boy like Ren Wild?

How could you not fall in love with a boy who puts you first in everything, protects you at all costs, worships the ground you walk on, gives you things you didn't know you wanted, who can hear your thoughts and see your fears? A boy who sacrificed so much without even telling you, leaving you heartbroken when you're old enough to figure it out for yourself?

If you'd been taken and raised and cherished by a boy who was closer to your age; therefore, he understood your childish tantrums better, could get in touch with his imagination easier, and have a better ability at discipline because he wasn't afraid to growl if you got out of line with no grudges or pause between instruction and praise, I think you'd fall in love, too.

Ren was simple.

Ren spoiled me.

Ren kept me in line.

No one else came close.

But it wasn't his skills at raising me that made me fall in love with him. Oh, no…

It was everything else that happened as I grew older, and he grew into a man.

I suppose you're wondering if I'm ever going to enlighten you on our third and fourth separation.

I haven't forgotten.

I'm just getting up the guts to tell you, because…the more you learn about me from here on out, the more you'll probably end up rolling your eyes, and thinking I didn't deserve all the sacrifices Ren made for me.

I had been his Ribbon—special, brave, and smart.

But then, through my own actions, I became argumentative, opinionated, and stupid.

I wish I could say I'd do things differently, but I honestly don't know if I would.

Crazy, right?

Crazy looking back at the heartache I caused both of us and still selfish enough not to change.

I was the reason we separated that third time.

I was the one who ruined everything.

For so long, I blamed Cassie.

I pinned all the guilt and regret onto her.

But it wasn't her fault.

As much as I wished I could type a lie and make you hate her just like I did.

I can't.

The fault was mine.

And I guess, eventually, I'm going to have to tell you.

But not right now.

Right now, I want you to continue liking me…for just a little longer.

Chapter Thirty-Five

DELLA

Present Day

ME AGAIN.

Strange, huh?

I closed my laptop a few hours ago, intending to put aside my past and the emotions that are tearing me up inside, but I can't sleep.

I can't stop thinking about Ren.

Always Ren.

I want to cry to relieve the aching pressure in my chest every time I think about him, but all I can do is laugh in the darkness and try to expand my ribs to contain the ever ballooning need that will never earn what it wants.

Melodramatic enough for you?

Too much for me, and I'm the one living this soap opera.

You know, until that last chapter, I've never actually said those words out loud...

Those terrible words that tear away the curtain and light up the truth in blinding stage lights with orchestras playing sad strings and empty amphitheatres pitying the poor wretched soul admitting such a tragedy.

Never really allowed myself to admit what I've known for so long.

I'm in love with Ren Wild.

It looks even worse in bold, doesn't it?

It looks like a life sentence I can never be free of...which, in a way, is exactly what it is.

I can't pinpoint the exact moment my childish affection turned to teenage crush turned to forever kind of addiction.

But what I do know is I will always love Ren.

I will always be in love with Ren.

And I also know I will never have him, and I'll end up marrying some other man who doesn't reach into my heart or has power over my every living breath like he does.

Anyway, enough of my present-day dramas.

You're not here to hear about that…not yet, anyway. There's still a fair piece of the story to go before I can share what I did yesterday or today or what I have planned for tomorrow.

Spoiler alert: I have no plans for tomorrow apart from ensuring my lies are hidden and my smiles are innocent, and my deep, dark desires are tucked far away.

Same as every day…nothing new, so I might as well give you something interesting.

Let's return to Cherry River.

I ended the previous chapter talking about Ren being ill with chicken pox and kind of went on another tangent about Cassie (grr) and my idiotic behaviour (ugh).

Cassie…

My favourite subject, and yes, I'm being sarcastic.

I know I keep flogging this subject, and this is the last time, I swear, but when it was just me and her…I loved her. I need you to see that.

I wholeheartedly adored that girl.

But when it was the three of us…well…what can I say that I haven't already?

Ren was mine.

Even as a kid, I'd known that. To a seven-year-old, my need for Ren stemmed from being the centre of his attention, the favourite in his heart, and confident in my place as first within his life.

Cassie threatened all of that.

And now, as an almost-adult, I can say she threatened my future too.

I didn't know it then, but over the years, she and Ren got close—even when they weren't sneaking behind barns or into stables to make out, they still had a fondness for each other.

Ren would often drop everything whenever she called on the emergency cell phone she'd make him have on the nights she'd sneak out with her troublemaker friends.

I'd tagged along with him for a few pickups.

Whenever that phone rang—way past midnight when John and Patricia believed their innocent daughter was safely tucked up in bed—Ren and I would 'borrow' the Land Rover and drive to wherever she was currently tipsy and partying.

She'd squeal my name, grab my hands as if I was her favourite person, then dash to the driver's side and plant a big, wet kiss on Ren's mouth.

I hated that, but I didn't mind her floppy and giggly in the back seat, regaling us with tales of bonfires and who hooked up with whom that night.

She was hard work, but she made it enjoyable by including us in her escapades.

Ren and I would share a look from where I sat up front with him. He'd roll his eyes and whisper things under his breath only I could hear—copying her or mocking her—our own little game.

In a way, Cassie made us become closer.

We had something in common, and we all shared a secret that the adults didn't know about. Even Liam didn't know what his sister got up to at night, and I enjoyed being in the big kids group even if I didn't understand what she meant when she used words like fucked and fingered.

During those conversations, Ren would turn on the radio and make me dance along with him. He'd drive one-handed while grabbing my arm with the other, distracting me with loud music from whatever naughty things Cassie was confessing.

Anywho, I did it again...I went on another Cassie tangent.

I'm not talking about her again for a while.

Ren.

I want to talk about Ren.

I better start by saying, he survived the chicken pox.

Obviously.

He healed faster than I did, bounced back to a boy full of health and was back on the tractor even before his skin was spot and scratch free.

Cassie returned to her popular world of friends and sometimes-boyfriends, and I was able to focus in school again, returning to the top of the class and hanging out with a girl called Celine who I swapped lunches with (she got chocolate while I got yoghurt...so naturally, I wanted what she had).

Life was good.

In fact, it was super good for the rest of the year.

During summer, I'd help Ren with his copious amount of chores around the farm, and in winter, we bunkered down just the two of us in our warm one bedroom.

I'm sure some days stood out where happiness was acute and misery was absent, but right now, I'm drawing a blank on anything super special to write about.

I don't mean to sound as if life wasn't amazing because it was.

Life on a farm was full of routine and new things every day.

Sunrise was our alarm clock, noon was our opportunity to stuff hungry bodies with delicious home-cooked meals, and evenings were spent with the Wilsons or ourselves.

The Wilsons gave me and Ren a safe place, and Ren gave his labour to ensure I lived a perfect childhood.

I couldn't have been luckier.

And that's why I'm going to start skipping forward to years I do remember clearly because, as much as this assignment is no longer for public reading, I don't want to bore myself. Especially, when I have some juicy memories just begging to be written.

Let's start with 2008.

The year started off awesome because it was just me and Ren camping in the hayloft in our old tent for New Years. It was smaller than I remembered and cramped, but we spent the evening eating candy, and Ren caved under pressure to tell me story after story.

He told me what he did during the days while I was at school. He painted pictures of himself saving a couple of sheep from a neighbour's farm who had tangled themselves in the boundary fence. He regaled secrets of getting too hot hauling hay on his own and jumping naked into the same river where we all swam.

He made me laugh.

He made me fall asleep knowing 2008 was going to be the best year ever.

And in many ways it was, but it was also full of embarrassing moments as I started to grow up faster than before.

For the past year or so, I'd been acutely aware that older kids and even adults kissed, touched, and did things that I was curious about.

I'd wanted to ask Ren why watching him kiss Cassie made my tummy go queasy, but a curiosity welled to know more, too.

But I never dared.

I never asked the questions burning inside me, swallowing things like: Why do you have different body parts than me? Why does Cassie rub against you like a moronic cat? Why does Liam have the same body as you but smaller? Do you rub against Cassie like a moronic cat, too?'

Silly things but things I desperately wanted to know.

Kids at school tried to educate each other thanks to overhearing parents talk, and so far, I'd gathered snippets about birds and bees and squirms infecting eggs and eggs being delivered by cranes which weren't really eggs like chickens laid but babies, and sometimes babies were caused by other magic when daddies touched mummies where pee comes out and then she got fat.

It made no sense to my unenlightened child brain, and I was too embarrassed to ask Ren.

I was even too embarrassed to ask Cassie.

So who did I ask?

Probably the one person I shouldn't as he was just as clueless as me.

I turned to Liam Wilson. Nine years old, boisterous but shy and still obsessed with lizards.

Including the lizard in his shorts.

And that was how Patricia Wilson found us one summer afternoon.

God, I'm blushing even now.

I can't believe I'm about to write this down, but here I go…

Liam and I hung out but not all that often.

I liked him, but I found him so young and silly compared to the calm, collected reservation of Ren. Liam squealed and charged. Ren spoke with rough serenity and moved with assurance.

Ren was mature with his rough-stubble cheeks and strong muscles. Liam was juvenile with his baby face and twig arms.

But Ren was too perfect to sully with gross things like what I wanted to know, so I figured Liam would be the perfect teacher.

Basically, I asked him to show me his if I showed him mine.

Obviously, I know now why he was only too happy to oblige. It seems all boys are happy to get naked for the right incentive.

We clutched hands, heat blooming on my face and scandalous danger welling in my chest as we left the house where Patricia was tending to her roses and walked quickly to the shaded grotto around the pond.

There, we stood awkwardly until Liam pointed at my summer dress with splashes of purple and pink and told me to pull it off.

I remember the rush of naughtiness even then, quickly swamped by shivers of fear.

Hiding my quaking hands, I grabbed the hem and jerked the dress over my head and stood bravely with just my white knickers on.

He nodded all business-like and the severest nine-year-old scowl I'd ever seen, then unbuckled his shorts, shoved them down his legs and ripped off his t-shirt.

I'd seen Ren naked many times—not so much recently, but I had memories of thick legs, hair-covered thighs, heavy flesh dangling between them, and a stomach and back rippling with light and shadow whenever he moved.

Liam was a sapling while Ren was the oak.

He shrugged in his white underpants, almost identical to mine. "Now what?"

"I dunno." I shrugged back. "Where are your squirms?"

His nose wrinkled. "Squirms?"

"You know, the things that make mummies fat, and then birds deliver babies."

"You're weird." Pointing at my knickers, he commanded, "Maybe you have squirms. Take them off and we'll see."

"You take yours off, too."

He nodded sharply, hooking his fingers into his underpants waistband. "Okay. One…two…three."

We both shoved down our underwear and kicked them away at the same time.

I stood barefoot.

He stood in his socks.

We stared at the differences in our bodies, moving closer in fascination.

"It's so small." I reached out to touch the worm-like thing between his legs. "Ren is bigger. Did yours shrink?"

He batted away my hand, poking his finger in my nipple. "You have no tits like Cassie. Did yours shrink, too?"

I looked down at my flat chest, so much like Liam's and not at all like Cassie's fullness. An awful pressure of inadequacy filled me, of fear that I was deformed, of terror that I needed what Cassie had to make boys like Ren notice me.

My shoulders slouched. "I don't know how to get tits."

Liam sighed. "I don't know how to get a bigger worm."

His melancholy matched mine, and I found a kindred soul. Wanting to cheer him up, I smiled. "It's a nice worm, though."

He returned my smile with a trace of self-consciousness. "Thanks."

We looked at the ground, exhausting our ability of conversation and not sure what to do next. Then I had an epiphany which well and truly got us into trouble.

"Liam?"

He looked up. "Yeah?"

"Do you know about kissing?"

His nose wrinkled again, but this time his whole face joined in, scrunching up like a prune. "Eww. Mummy and Daddy do it, but it's gross."

"Cassie and Ren do it," I confessed. "And I don't like it."

"I don't like it, either." He stuck out his tongue as if he'd tasted something nasty. "Yucky."

"Want to try?" I gulped, cursing the words but also eternally curious.

"What?" He backed up again, his worm bouncing. "Nuh-uh. No way."

"Just one. Don't you want to know?"

"I know already. It's gross."

"I know but how *gross?" I followed him as he stepped deeper into the grotto; his socks soaking up the damp ground and my bare feet skating over slippery leaves. "Don't you want to know why they keep kissing if it's so gross? Don't you want to know why they seem so happy afterward?"*

I rubbed at the fist wrapped around my heart.

Happiness was never something I'd begrudge Ren, but happiness from kissing Cassie drove me into a painful place that I couldn't untangle.

"I dunno." He finally stopped, not that he had anywhere else to go. His

back pressed up against the weeping willow, its fronds all around us like a magical fairyland. "Why do you want to know?"

"'Cause I'm sick of not knowing. I want to know everything." Brushing aside a frond, I stood directly in front of him.

He eyed me warily. "I want to go back."

"We'll go back after a kiss, okay?" I hated that I was the younger one, but I was the teacher in this. I didn't like it. Here, I was seeking answers, and instead, I was giving them to him instead of the other way around.

"One kiss?" He looked at me sceptical. "Then I can go?"

"Yup."

"And you won't tell anyone my worm is small? 'Cause if you do, I'll say you have no tits."

"Deal." I stuck out my hand, glad he made us promise because I didn't want that secret getting out. Tits were something older girls had, and I wanted so much to be an older girl.

I was sick of being in the dark and categorized as too young to know.

Liam placed his hand in mine, and we shook hard. Still touching, we brought our heads together while our naked bodies stayed put.

He puckered his lips.

I copied.

He sucked in a breath.

I copied.

Our lips met in a flurry of pressure.

It was over.

It'd been the same sort of kiss Ren had given me time and time again. There were no secrets, no answers, no wisdom to be found.

"Again?" I asked, tugging him forward, bitterly disappointed but determined not to stop until I understood why others seemed to enjoy it so much.

"Ugh, you said only one." Liam exhaled, yanking his hand back. "This sucks."

"One more and then you can go."

"Promise?"

"Cross my heart and hope to die." I drew an X on my flat chest.

"Fine." He leaned toward me, looking bored.

I leaned toward him, trembling eagerly.

And just as our mouths met a second time, our little experiment was shattered.

"Liam! Della! What on earth do you think you two are doing!?"

Liam squealed and took off.

And all I could do was turn around and stare at Patricia Wilson's sandal-covered feet, naked as the day I was born and still just as lost.

Chapter Thirty-Six

REN

2008

"DO YOU WANT me to talk to her?"

I hugged myself against what Patricia Wilson just told me. "No. I can deal with it."

How, I had no clue?

I had a mind to spank her. To pull her dress up like she'd done today and smack her bare backside until she understood that being naked around boys was never going to be an option for her.

I groaned under my breath, rubbing my face and trying to rid the images Patricia had put there.

Liam and Della.

Naked under the willow tree.

Kissing.

Goddammit, how the hell did I deal with this? She was eight, for God's sake, not eighteen. It had never crossed my mind that she would be like me and start seeking answers to her feelings inside. I'd been older than her when my first urges appeared, and I'd had the benefit of already knowing that two animals climbing on top of one another equalled a baby a few months later.

I knew that lesson so well, it was the main reason I hadn't let Cassie tempt me any further than fingers and tongues.

I did not want a baby.

I already had one.

And I'd ruined her by keeping information away from her.

Keeping my eyes downcast, I mumbled, "They didn't...have sex, did they?" I winced, already dreading her answer. The thought of someone touching Della, even if it was Liam, made things inside me hiss and howl.

Did that mean Della was pregnant just like the Mclary's ewes after one visit with his ram? And if she was, how the hell would we deal with this? How the hell would I get over the sick feeling inside?

"No, nothing like that. It was just kids being kids." Patricia shook her head, clutching a tea towel stained with berry juice from making jam. "They're curious, and it's my fault that I left the talk with Liam so long. I'll sit him down tonight and make sure he understands everything about sex and body parts and make sure it never happens again."

The minute I'd come in from the fields, Patricia had asked me to share a cup of coffee with urgent things to discuss.

I'd wanted to refuse.

It'd been a long day, and I suffered a little of heatstroke and wanted shade, cold water, and quiet in that order.

But now, Della had screwed up my plans by being as loose as Cassie was.

Perhaps, I better pack a bag right now and leave.

If Cassie's tendencies were rubbing off on Della, no way would we stay here. No way would I stand by and let her open her legs for the local boys and riff-raff in this town.

No *fucking* way.

My nostrils flared as my temper grew hotter.

The thought of it.

The images.

God—

Patricia noticed, standing up and moving into the sugary-smelling kitchen. "It's not the end of the world, Ren, and I'll gladly talk to Della as well as Liam. I've got a book with illustrations. I'm not embarrassed to answer any questions she might have."

My heart pounded.

A book?

I still couldn't read very well.

How the hell was I supposed to teach Della from a book?

As much as the thought of talking to her petrified me—worse than any farm incident or even a Social Services visit—I couldn't allow myself to pass the responsibility onto Patricia.

Della was my problem.

I'd deal with her.

"Like I said, I'll take care of it." Stalking toward the back door, my hand barely wrapped around the handle before Patricia said, "Be gentle on her, Ren. She's not being naughty. She's being a young girl transforming into a woman."

Great. All the things I'm not equipped to deal with.

Moving toward an overflowing bookcase by the fireplace, Patricia pulled a book free with a title in green and a man and woman smiling on the cover. "This is the book and has graphic pictures and explanations." She practically had to force it into my hand, patting my knuckles as she moved away. "She wants to know what her body is going through. She needs to be prepared for when her breasts start growing and pubic hair starts appearing and periods start hurting."

"Right." I wrenched open the door, desperate to get away from words like periods and pubic.

I'd only just recently found out about periods myself thanks to Cassie turning into a dragon at certain times of the month. At first, I had no clue why she was such a bitch, but she wasn't afraid to discuss what happened to her body or the by-product of not getting pregnant every month.

I knew animals came into season, but I'd never seen them bleed if they weren't mated.

Frankly, humans grossed me out, and I didn't want to know any more about it.

"Send her to me if it gets too much!" Patricia called after me as I jogged across the driveway to the barn and our one bedroom.

I waved once as I disappeared into the hay-scented building and prepared to do something I was woefully unprepared to do.

* * * * *

I found her curled up on the bed, her back against the headboard, her arms wrapped around her legs, her dress wrapped tight and tucked into her feet, and her face buried against her knees.

Her whole posture screamed 'leave me alone', and that was exactly what I wanted to do, but I had a job, and I couldn't rest until I'd done it.

She looked so young.

Far too young for what she'd done.

But she was the same age as the girls that Mclary would abuse.

The same age to know that her body was fragile when a man wanted it for his own pleasure.

The same age to be protected at all costs.

Images of her naked and kissing Liam exploded back into my head, and my temper that'd been steadily simmering overflowed.

Marching forward, I growled. "What the *hell* were you thinking, Della?"

She burrowed deeper into her dress-wrapped knees, not replying.

Tossing the book onto the covers beside her, I paced at the end of the bed. "Do you have *any* idea what you could've done? Do you know what happens when a man takes from a girl? Do you know how badly you could've been hurt? What are you trying to do? Give me a goddamn heart attack? You're a *kid*! You don't need to know about sex or babies or—"

Her head popped up, tears staining her face and matching anger red on her cheeks. "I'm *not* a kid. I'm eight years old. I *do* want to know about babies and kissing and—"

"You *know* what kissing is. We kiss all the time." I breathed hard, trying to get myself in check. "Kissing is a way to show love for each—"

"But you don't love Cassie, and you kiss her more than you kiss me. You kiss her with your tongue!"

My jaw dropped. "When have you seen me do that?"

I'd been so fucking careful.

I'd made sure Cassie never surprised me around Della. If Cassie kissed me in front of her, it was simple and innocent and exactly like what Della was used to from me and Patricia; hell, even Cassie kissed her.

"I'm not stupid. I know if I wake up sometimes and you're not here that you're off kissing her. I know where to find you. It's not hard. I've seen you touch her…" She gulped. "You know…down there. I've seen her kiss you…down there. I've seen so many things, and the kids at school tried to explain it to me but no one seems to know and it's making me so mad not to know and I'm sad that I'm stupid and I'm angry that you don't want to tell me and now I'm wondering if you actually love her more than you love me because you let her kiss you in more places and it hurts so much and I'm so confused—" Her rush with no punctuation or pauses ended as she burst into tears, wedging her face back into the wet patch already on her dress.

My temper switched from bubbling volcano to vast ocean full of condemnation and litres of painful guilt.

I exhaled slowly, letting the rage in the room seep through the door and cracks in the window until the only sounds were from my pounding heart and Della's soft crying.

Perching awkwardly on the edge of the bed, I picked up the book and stroked the smiling faces of the cover. "I'm sorry."

She hiccupped, her tears still loud.

I tried again. She deserved it.

Patricia was right.

I should've been gentler.

This wasn't her fault.

I'd done this by sneaking off whenever my libido got the best of me and not thinking she wouldn't notice.

"Little Ribbon..." I waited until she raised her head just enough for her red-rimmed eyes to meet mine. The moment she sniffed and stared at me, I let go of the aching fear I'd carried since hearing about her putting herself in harm's way. I let her see just how much I cared and just how angry I was that I wasn't prepared for her to grow up just yet.

I wanted to keep her for as long as I could, and now I'd been slapped in the face with the reality.

She wasn't a little girl anymore.

And I couldn't shelter her without serious consequences.

She had to know about sex, if only to protect her from men like her father.

"Can you forgive me?" I whispered. "And you're wrong about me loving Cassie more than I love you. No one will ever come close. You have my heart. You know that, and it kills me to hear you doubt it."

In a scramble of pink and purple splashes, she kicked away her dress and launched herself across the bed and into my arms.

Her weight was solid and warm and familiar, and it took everything inside not to give in to the wet ache to grieve over everything I was losing by saying goodbye to the kid I'd raised through impossibilities and miracles.

I kissed her hair, inhaling her scent; clutching her so tight, she squirmed for air but made no move to get away.

I wanted to smother her in hugs if it meant I could buy a few more innocent years, but when she finally sat up and her gaze fell on the book in my hands, I knew my time was up.

I felt the acres of distance that would slowly grow bigger and bigger between us as she read the title as easy as breathing and revealed that my sacrifices had been worth it.

"The Business of Babies and Everything in Between." Her voice cut me deep because I'd refused to hear it until now—underneath the

childish tone hinted a rich depth that would rival any woman's.

Husky and melodic with just enough sweet and sour to drive boys insane.

And she could read.

Better than I could at half my age.

She could understand.

Better than me at any age.

She wasn't just my equal anymore, she was my shooting star, sending her far out of my reach.

Keeping my arm around her tiny waist, I cleared away the heartache in my voice and smiled with all the light-hearted lies I could manage. "You want answers. Let's get answers."

She looked up. "Truly?"

"Truly." Opening the cover, I schooled myself not to flinch against the first graphic image. A penis with muscles and tubes and scientific sketches but still a penis and something far too crude for her eyes. Clearing my throat again, I said carefully, "Well, this…is a penis. And…um, you already know that, eh, I have one and…um, you don't."

My head ached with pressure and embarrassment. "You have a, eh…vagina. And it will get hair on it one day like…um…my penis did…remember? You asked why I had hair between my legs and on my face?"

She soaked it in, her cheeks pink, but her eyes alive and desperate for more. "Okay." She turned the page, reading aloud, "Males have penises that grow hard with blood in order to have int—inter—" She looked up, meeting my tortured gaze. "What's that word, Ren?"

My entire body flushed with humiliation.

I couldn't tell her that if she couldn't read it, there was no way in hell I could. The word was nothing but jumbled up letters.

Instead, I flicked to the next page where the sketches of a woman's vagina gave way to a detailed drawing of a penis inside it.

"I think they mean sex."

"Sex…" She rolled the word slowly on her tongue. "Ssseeeeeexxxxx." She insisted on making me suffer by asking, "What exactly *is* sex?"

I looked at the ceiling, wishing something up there would swap places with me, and this terrible evening could be over with.

I wanted to stutter. I wanted to stall. But I gulped deep and said quickly, "Sex is when a male animal puts his penis in a female animal. His hips thrust a little and then he comes and the stuff he releases makes a baby in the female, and she gives birth a few months later."

I dreaded how uninformative that was and how many questions I was about to receive.

"Is there squirms in the stuff?" she asked, deadly serious.

"Squirms?"

"At school, a boy said his mum told him that squirms make eggs turn into babies that are delivered by birds."

I groaned under my breath. "Sex has nothing to do with birds."

"Bees?" Her eyebrows rose.

"Bees, either."

"So all it is, is a man putting his worm into a woman's pee place?"

I hunched into myself. Hell, this was my worst moment so far. "Something like that."

She bit her lip, chewing over my terrible answers, obviously finding me lacking in the professor position. It wasn't like I had personal experience yet. This was all theory and barnyard knowledge, and I was failing...drastically.

A few minutes passed while she read the book, flicking a few pages to more graphic images of a man on top of a woman and her hands on his ass.

My own body reacted, and I unwrapped my arm from around Della, putting some distance between us.

She didn't notice, far too absorbed in her new friend.

"Ah! It's not squirms, it's sperms!" She tapped a line of text that looked like gibberish. "See, here? Men have sperms, and they swim like tadpoles up a woman's something after he's been on top of her."

"Awesome." I strangled, standing up and pacing again, anything to stop the sudden shyness about discussing this sort of stuff with her.

"Ren?"

I stopped, daring to look at her. "Yeah...?"

"What is so great about kissing Cassie?"

I swiped a hand over my face. "I'm sure the book will cover that."

"I want to know from you." She bit her lip again, worry and unease painting her pretty face. "Please?"

"Ugh, okay." I could never refuse her anything when she said that word. "Kissing is...nice." I did my best to conjure how I felt when Cassie had her tongue in my mouth. "It's different to normal kissing. It looks gross, but it feels warm and…comforting. And sometimes, my eh…"

God, I couldn't say that.

I couldn't admit that kissing made me hard and her wet and was the perfect prelude to sex. That would be too much, and I literally choked on the words. "Yeah, it's…nice. That's all you need to know."

"Would you show me?"

"No!" I stumbled backward. "That wouldn't be appropriate, Della Ribbon."

"Why not?"

"Because…kissing that way isn't done with family. It's done with a mate…a lover."

"Oh." Her spine rolled then straightened as she said, "Think Liam could show me?"

My temper fired back into full heat. "If you *ever* go near Liam naked again, I'll tie you to a tree and never let you come down."

She giggled. "I like trees."

"Believe me, you wouldn't like this one. I'd make sure to find a wasp's nest and put it up there with you. They'd sting you every time you thought about kissing someone."

"You wouldn't."

I narrowed my eyes. "Just try me and you'll see how deadly serious I am about you never being naked with another boy again."

She pouted. "You're mean. Why are you allowed to get naked with Cassie, and I'm not allowed with Liam."

"Because I'm older."

"So when I'm older, I can?"

"No."

"But you said—"

"Never mind what I said." Prowling toward her, I tapped the pornographic educational book. "Read this. It has all the answers."

She eyed me before finally nodding and turning her inquisitive gaze back to the pages.

For the next few hours, I sat in the chair in the corner, clutching the handles with white knuckles, and instead of telling Della about sex and kissing and everything in between, she told me.

She read the words she knew and stumbled over those she didn't.

She dashed across the driveway to see Patricia and came back armed with terms like Fallopian tubes and ovaries and clitoris.

And it was to my utmost mortification that she became the teacher on a subject she'd begged to be a student in.

A student who must never know she'd far exceeded the capacities of the boy who said he'd teach her everything.

The boy who now knew absolutely nothing.

Chapter Thirty-Seven

REN

2009

ANOTHER YEAR, another autumn, winter, spring, and summer.

Della and I celebrated our joint birthday where she turned nine and I turned nineteen. The day was simple and sweet, and we exchanged gifts that cost no more than ten dollars thanks to John giving me some cash from my salary instead of pre-empting what Della would need and spending on my behalf.

For the past year, Cassie had been dating a twenty-four-year-old mechanic who'd attended family dinners and been grudgingly approved of by her parents. She still hung out with Della, and they'd even gone to a local show jumping competition with Della riding Domino and Cassie riding HeatWave, earning a bunch of ribbons in the process.

Our lives had settled into the routine of living across the driveway from each other, and things couldn't be better.

The itch to leave still came with the warmer weather and shorter nights, but now, instead of leaving to search for better things, I had things I'd miss by going.

I'd miss Patricia Wilson's amazing lasagne and raspberry torte.

I'd miss John's steady guidance and unjudging leniency.

I'd miss Cassie's secret smiles and ability to make me mad and happy in the same sentence.

And I'd even miss Liam, even though I'd never truly forgiven him for what happened between him and Della.

Life marched onward.

One more year and I'd leave my teenage years behind.

And I was still a virgin.

These days, it wasn't because of my unreadiness or fear that Della would catch me or even the fact that Cassie was in a long-term relationship—I'd met some of her friends when they'd come round for dinners and two of them blatantly said the offer was always open for a booty call—whatever the hell that was.

I was ready.

If I was honest, I was dying with readiness, but I still couldn't take the plunge because I knew the consequences of sex, and as much as I loved Della and was grateful for her in my life and besotted with everything she did, I refused to raise another.

Sex talks and naked days and the terrible circumstances of watching her body turn from washboard to budding with breasts had drained me. Her body was no longer a kid's and had to be covered in public, making her self-aware, and stealing the remaining days of her childhood.

I was tired.

Frankly, I was exhausted, and I just wanted to give in to the thick desire in my blood whenever I looked at a pretty woman and forget about rights and wrongs and pregnancies.

But I couldn't.

Because I did *not* want to be a father.

And once I'd had sex once, I had no doubt I'd want it again and again and just like the stallion or bull who serviced an entire herd, delivering each mare and cow with a foal and calf, I did not want to have multiple Rens running around, killing me slowly.

That was my view on the world.

And because I never talked about my concerns, my beliefs became fact until one night when Cassie drove home with a squeal of tires in her second-hand red Corolla and bolted into the house.

Yells and sobs flowed from the farmhouse for hours, making me wonder what the hell happened.

Whatever it was made her angry and sad, and later that night, past midnight and almost at witching hour, a pebble dinged against the window above my head and I shot awake.

Della had always been a heavier sleeper than me, and just because she was flirting with puberty didn't change that fact.

Shrugging into a t-shirt and pulling on some shorts, I stumbled from our room to find Cassie pacing like a caged ferret with her hair wild, white nightgown flowing, and lips pinched with an aura of hurt female bristling amongst the hay and horses.

"You okay?" I asked, clearing the scratchy sleep from my

throat.

The moment she heard me, she barrelled toward me, snatched my hand and yanked me into a free stable. The moment the stall door closed, she shoved me against the wall, leapt into my arms, and planted her mouth on mine.

I stumbled beneath her weight, instinct causing my hands to cup her ass and my arms to bunch and hold her close.

Her legs wrapped around my waist as her tongue plunged deep, kissing me with a kind of passion I'd never tasted before.

It triggered something in me.

I went from courteous and willing to help to matching monster like she was.

Spinning around, I crushed her against the wall as hard as she'd slammed me.

Her moan only ignited me further, and our kiss turned savage.

We devoured each other with nips and thrusting tongues, struggling to breathe and spit slippery between us.

While our mouths attacked the other, our hands roamed.

Mine fisted her full breasts, kneading her with choking desire, being more aggressive than I'd ever been, unable to rein myself in.

I pinched her nipples, and she mewled.

I bit her neck, and she gasped.

I thrust the aching steel between my legs directly against her wetness, and she begged for more.

Her rapid fingers slipped down my front, cupping me, squeezing, fisting, jerking me off until I thought for sure I'd come.

As quickly as she'd grabbed me, her touch was gone, focusing on tugging down my shorts.

My brain was mush. My heart smoking. My blood black and thick with uncontrolled need.

I couldn't think or stop as she yanked out my pounding length and shoved aside the material of her nightgown.

The heat of her… *holy shit*.

The wet slick and tight promise pressed against my tip, and I groaned loud and long—a growl with every want I'd denied myself for so long.

I thrust upward, needing what she offered before my heart exploded and my life ended.

My aim wasn't right, and we slipped apart.

I stumbled to the side, crashing against a spade and sending it clattering to the cobblestone floor.

The noise reverberated around the stable, freezing us.

My heart kept thundering, obscuring my hearing as I did my best to look in the direction of my bedroom where Della hopefully continued to sleep none-the-wiser.

My chest squeezed as if I was doing something against her wishes. As if I was breaking her trust. Ever since our sex talk, we'd had an unspoken agreement that sex was an open topic. If she had something she wanted to ask, she asked it, and I swallowed down my chagrin to answer her.

She knew exactly what kissing meant, and what it led to, and what sex was between two parties.

She'd come with me to the neighbouring farm to watch ducks mate and pigs and dogs and even fish in the farmer's pond. She knew the mechanics now.

Therefore, she would understand what I was about to do with Cassie if she walked in.

Tripping backward, I unwrapped my arms from around Cassie's waist, dropping her to the floor.

My cock stuck out, glistening and angry beneath my t-shirt hem.

Cassie looked one last time toward the door leading to my room, then hissed with frustration. "She won't know."

"That's not the point."

She clamped her hands on her hips, looking girlish in her white nightgown with pink flowers and all woman with her puffy lips and tight nipples. "Then what *is* the point, Ren? Why do you keep stopping this?"

"Stopping what?"

She laughed with a trace of rage. "*This!* Every time we come close to fucking, you stop. You act all guilty and shy and shut down." She laughed again. "Do you know how many times I've returned to my bed, only to have to make myself come with wanting you? You're like the prized horse no one is allowed to ride." She smirked. "Get it? Not allowed to ride..." Her head lowered, brown hair cascading over one eye. "I want to ride you. I want to ride your dick so hard, Ren, and you shoot me down every time."

Her words and thick invitation sent more blood pumping to my cock.

Normally, I could ignore the punching, clawing desire, but this time, I almost buckled beneath it.

I struggled for a reason we couldn't do this. *Any* reason. I wouldn't tell her I'd jerked off to images of sex too, but she wasn't the one who starred in my daydreams. Some faceless female always did. Someone blonde and kind who didn't mind my inexperience.

And the fact that my ideal partner was blonde just ate more chunks away at my soul because how fucking disgusting was I to want an older version of Della.

Not that I wanted an older version of her.

But I liked blonde hair.

And I liked kindness.

And I wanted so fucking much to fuck something, but I didn't want to support more kids. I had no idea how Cassie had sex with so many men and never once got pregnant.

Maybe she was infertile.

And if she was, she was lucky she was human and not a sheep or cow; otherwise, her usefulness of reproducing would be replaced by the slaughterhouse and she'd end up on someone's plate.

"Are you going to say something?" She paced in front of me, her breasts high and tempting, her steps short and full of the same urgent wanting I suffered with.

I clenched my hands as the need to squeeze my tortured cock almost overrode my brain. "What about Kevin or Calvin or whatever his name was."

"Gavin and I broke up."

My eyebrows rose. "When?"

"Tonight. Bastard was cheating on me."

"I'm sorry."

"Yeah, well." She blew hair out of her eyes. "I wasn't interested in him anymore anyway."

"Oh."

Stagnant desire turned the stables full of festering appetite.

Knowing she was single again shouldn't add more fever to my already out of control yearning…but it did. I took a step toward her, only to take it back again as her eyes latched onto mine with a cat-like gleam and lick of her lips.

"There you go again," she moaned. "You want me. I know you do." Looking over her shoulder toward the door where Della slept, she did something she'd never done before.

I'd seen every part of her but only in glimpses and only with buttons undone or zippers half-mast. I'd never seen her fully naked.

But I saw her now as she tore off her nightgown and stood bare before me.

I swallowed hard, unsuccessfully silencing a desperate groan.

"See, you *do* want me." She walked toward me, her hips swaying, breasts bouncing, and wetness glinting on her inner thighs. "Help me forget him, Ren. Just for tonight. You never have to touch me again. Just...please...."

I scrambled backward as another flush of rebellious lust made me so damn hungry I almost forgot how to fight it. "Can't."

"Yes, you can."

I shook my head as fast as I could. "You'll get pregnant."

She froze. "Wait...what?"

Shit.

Her tone layered me with self-consciousness. I hadn't meant to say anything. I *shouldn't* have said anything.

But Cassie's face lit up and her edginess melted into the kindness I needed. "Is that why you've refused me all this time? Refused my friends? Never once tried to fuck me? Oh, wow, you think I'll get pregnant if we do?"

Her questions could've been condescending and cruel, but they weren't. Cassie was intricate and had two distinct sides. One side was all about her and she could be harsh without thought, yet the other was sweet and doting. And when it was activated, she could be an angel sent from above.

"Wait here." She scooped her nightgown off the floor, shook away the hay strands, and slipped it back over her head. "Don't go anywhere. I mean it." Slipping from the stable, she pointed a finger in my face. "I mean it, Ren. If you vanish, I'm going to tell everyone what a great lay you are and set up a revolving door of women. Won't that be torture for you?"

She vanished before I could admit that that would be my worst nightmare to have so many delectable beauties and not be allowed to touch a single one.

Not that she would do that...*would she?*

I had no idea why I stayed in that stable, standing deathly still in the dark and nursing an agonizing erection, but I did.

I didn't move to put my shorts on.

I didn't move to return to Della.

No way in hell could I climb into a bed beside her in this state anyway.

I either had to make myself come or think such gruesome thoughts that it went away.

Thanks to Mclary, I had more than enough gruesome thoughts to deflate myself—just a glance at my missing finger or many memories of our living conditions was enough, but before I'd been able to delete a tenth of my lust, soft footsteps sounded on cobbles and Cassie slipped back into the barn.

She didn't have anything.

She didn't look any different.

It didn't mean she was any less confident as she entered the stable with her chin high and nipples still pebbled.

"Come with me." Taking my hand, she gently led me toward a pile of horse blankets that had been dumped there last winter. Pushing me down, she held out her hand and revealed a tiny silver packet. "I can't believe you don't know about these things but...this is called a condom. It stops any sexually transmitted diseases and removes about ninety-five percent of risk of unwanted pregnancies."

She'd just talked witchcraft, but all I could focus on was the word disease. I didn't have a clue what sort of diseases you could catch through sex. Maybe it was another version of chicken pox, which I definitely didn't want.

I managed to keep my mouth shut about that, but I couldn't about the other fact. I stupidly asked, "Why only ninety-five percent?"

She sighed. "Not sure. I guess if you nick it with your teeth or fingernails or if it's not held down when you disengage. Who knows? My point is...you can fuck me. No more excuses. I'm actually on the pill, and you're clean, seeing as I'll be your first time, but you should learn how to use one of these for the future, and I want to teach you." She smiled softly. "I've enjoyed teaching you over the years."

I looked away, my mind racing.

Pill and clean and condoms...she spoke a different language. Pill for what? Clean from what? But my brain had relocated to my cock, and it'd just been given a free pass to proceed.

No more fear of pregnancy.

No Della spying in the shadows.

No reason to say no.

Grabbing the hem of her nightgown, Cassie once again switched clothing for nakedness, and I no longer had any arguments not to feast my eyes on her flesh or allow the quaking desire to gather between my legs.

"I want you, Ren," she murmured. "Do you want me?"

This time, there was no debate.

I nodded, licking my lips and reaching for her from where I

sat on the blankets.

"Oh, thank God." Kneeling before me, not caring about her knees on cold stones, she tore the tiny packet and pulled out something slimy and small. "This is going to feel a little strange, and you can't come while I put it on because I only brought one, got it?"

I bit my lip as she came closer, doing my best to control my trembling and the bobbing of my overeager cock.

Shifting the condom in her hands, she fisted me and pressed it on my tip.

She was right.

It did feel weird.

Weird good.

Weird strange.

Weird *'holy crap I don't know how I'm going to be able to control myself.'*

It took her an eternity to roll the slippery thing down my length, and when she'd finally finished, my vision was half-cross-eyed, and I panted as if I'd run to the paddocks and back.

I reached out to touch the casing around me, but she swatted away my hand and placed both of hers on my shoulders. Climbing up my body, she kneeled over me as I spread my legs out in front and ceased breathing as the scent of her arousal and the illicitness of what I was about to do almost sent me into cardiac arrest.

"Ready?" she breathed, leaning down to kiss me.

I'd passed the point of conversation and half-gasped, half-grunted as she slowly sat on me.

My mouth went slack beneath hers.

The sensation of her tight heat blew my mind.

The tremble of her thighs as she eased down and the small hitches in her breath as she threw her head back and let me fill her, activated the same trigger as before.

I was no longer Ren, the considerate teen thrust into fatherhood and homeless runaway. I was Ren the nineteen-year-old who'd been hungry for something for years and had finally found it.

She sank the final distance, her body clenching around mine, and I grabbed a fistful of her hair. Cradling her, I shot upright, spun her so she was on the blankets and slid her down until she was on her back.

And then I did what stallions and bulls and every male animal did when he was given access to a female.

I fucked her.

No other words.

I fucked her.

I thrust as fast and as hard as I could.

I turned animal as I bit her neck, raged upward, held her down, and punished her for making me unravel so completely.

And when that tickling, tingling warning came and my balls tightened and my cock swelled, I locked my mouth on hers and rode her harder.

And I came.

I officially entered adulthood.

I was a boy no longer.

Chapter Thirty-Eight

REN

2010

TWENTY and TEN.

This shared birthday was one of the more important ones because Della reached double figures, and I reached the milestone of any kid.

I was no longer a teenager.

I was a man.

A man who'd had sex—quite regularly, in fact—a man who still felt like a kid most of the time but was also no longer at the mercy of laws of minors or the judgment and pity of adults.

I was my own person, but it didn't mean our life changed.

It didn't matter the wanderlust in my veins switched from suggestion to downright obsession. It didn't matter, as I sat in an echo-plagued school hall and watched Della play the role of a Sandy in a younger, less suggestive version of *Grease Lightning,* that I suffered both pride and bittersweet sacrifice. And it didn't matter that as I grew older, the more I burned for something I hadn't found yet. Something I didn't know but wanted more than I could stand.

Even though my heart begged me on a daily basis to run into the forest and never look back, I knew I could never be that selfish.

The Wilsons had been nothing but good to us.

They'd given me the ability to grant Della the best foundation I could with her education and personal development. The fact that she had a surrogate brother and sister in Liam and Cassie meant the world because no way should she grow up with only me as her companion.

Not only had the Wilsons ensured that the hours I put into running their farm, increasing their bottom line, and turning a hobby crop where Patricia had to work part-time at a local accountancy firm and John picked up odd jobs here and there into a thriving income where they could retire, but they also taught me the basics in life.

Things like regular doctor and dentist visits.

The first time I'd taken Della and myself to the dentist, I didn't know who hated it more. Luckily, I'd ensured she kept up with regular brushing, and I was a bit obsessive when it came to cleanliness, even while living rough, so we didn't have too much wrong. A filling or two and we were done for another year.

Another year older.

Another year wiser.

And another year where I fought my lone-wolf tendencies and forced myself to stay for her.

For my Little Ribbon.

And it was the right decision because as the spotlight shone on her glossy blonde hair and her cherub cheeks glowed and her blue eyes twinkled like stars, she wasn't just Sandy from *Grease Lightning*, singing a song about a boy and summer.

She was Della Wild, and she was perfect.

* * * * *

Two things happened a month later that proved to me just how far apart our worlds had become.

The first, Patricia and John believed it was time that our two pushed together single beds should be split back apart, now that Della was getting older.

I'd swallowed back the denial that always followed when someone remarked how tall she'd become, how willowy and pretty and strong. I'd also gulped back the sudden terror that I'd never be able to sleep again unless I could reach out in the night and touch her—to appease my fear that she might be hurt in the darkness just like those kids at Mclary's barn.

The day when the bed we'd slept on for years was suddenly broken back into two singles and shoved to opposite sides of the room, the dynamic between Della and I switched again.

We'd been so used to our routine.

We didn't think anything of it or stopped to think that it might be strange for others to see a 'brother and sister' sleep side by side.

Even though I'd raised Della, I never truly thought of her as my sister. Somehow, even all this time later, when I looked at her, I saw her as a Mclary...not mine.

She looked nothing like her mother or father—which was a blessing—but she also looked nothing like me.

I was dark and angles and broody desire to be left alone.

She was light and curves and infectious kindness toward everyone.

Ten years separated me and my slavery at the Mclary's, yet it had carved something deep inside me, covering me with wariness, cloaking me with suspicion, and never letting me relax in company no matter how old I became.

I never stopped to think that sleeping next to her would be seen as inappropriate and never viewed our relationship from an outsider's point of view.

Della would kiss me often. Smacking my lips with a strawberry-lip-glossed mouth before running off to class or to play with Liam or help Patricia in her garden or ride with Cassie.

Her quick-fire affection always melted my gruff heart, and she was the only one who could touch something inside me—slipping past my walls, infiltrating my fortresses to remind me that I might not like many humans but I loved one more than I could stand.

Needless to say, both Della and I didn't sleep that night, or the next, or the next. Our hands somehow found their way from their covers to dangle over the edge and reach for each other, never quite touching no matter how much we wished.

Her ribbon would wrap and drip over her fingers, kissing the dusty floor and reminding me all over again that she wasn't a baby anymore, but she still had childhood ties.

Eventually, we got used to sleeping apart, and neither of us ever said how much we preferred sleeping in one large bed. I kept my mouth shut as I didn't want to overstep important boundaries, and I guessed she didn't feel the same way because after that first week, she went shopping with Cassie and purchased a bedspread covered with leaping horses frolicking in ocean spray, leaving my drab black sheets looking like a black hole in the corner.

The second thing to show the growing distance between us was a mid-summer evening where John opened his paddocks to the public to purchase hay bales directly off the meadow the moment we'd finished baling.

With over two thousand bales to sell and already a barn full of supplies for our own livestock in winter, John put me in charge of choreographing the countless arriving Utes, trucks, and trailer-pulling cars, directing them to appropriate fields and keeping tally of how many bales they took so I could grab the cash as they left.

I'd had a minor panic attack when he waltzed back to the house to do whatever he needed to do. That minor attack turned full blown when the first customer finished loading ten bales and drove toward me manning the exit gate.

The guy with his sunburned nose and stalks of hay on his t-shirt asked, "What do I owe you?" He cocked his head at the back with his loaded hay. "Ten bales at what price?"

I looked at the farmhouse, cursing John and wishing someone, *anyone,* would come out and help, but no one did. I sucked up my disgrace that all this time I'd never let John know the extent of my illiteracy. I'd never counted in front of him, never read anything. I'd always gotten around doing the books and tabulations because Patricia was an accountant by trade and enjoyed crunching numbers.

"Hey? You hear me? How much?" the guy pushed.

Rubbing the back of my neck, I muttered, "It's eight dollars a bale so…" I did my best to force a brain that had never been taught arithmetic to perform a miracle.

"Eighty bucks." The guy grabbed some cash from his pocket and peeled off four twenties. "Here you go."

Our hands met as he shoved the bills into my palm and gave me a quick nod. He drove away before I could hope to work out if I'd just been ripped off or if that was the correct amount.

A red car started in the distance with a trailer piled high with hay.

I gulped as it turned toward me and the gate.

Shit.

Wedging the cash into my back pocket, my eyes trailed back to the farmhouse, begging for rescue.

And that was when I saw her.

Della.

She leapt out of Cassie's Corolla, laughing at something Cassie said as they made their way toward the kitchen door. At the last second, Della looked up as if she sensed me staring at her.

Our eyes locked across meadows and driveways, and she waved once.

I waved back, adding a come here motion at the end.

I held my breath. She could go with Cassie. After all, it was school holidays, and she'd been spending a lot of time riding and going to the mall as well as playing with friends her own age.

I still didn't trust Cassie's loose morals wouldn't rub off on her, but I'd been fierce with her on our second or third time sleeping together. I'd flat out warned her if she ever let Della kiss, fondle, or fuck a boy while she was with her, I'd murder her with my bare hands.

She'd laughed.

I hadn't.

The subject hadn't been broached since.

Instead of continuing into the house like Liam would've done, Della said something quick to Cassie then tore toward me.

Her bony knees flashed beneath her yellow skirt, the matching yellow and white daisy top flopping on her shoulders while her hair gleamed as bright as the sun above.

Sweat glistened on her forehead as she finally careened to a stop beside me, squinting in the brightness. "Hey."

"Hey." I smiled as she threw herself into me, wrapping her arms around my waist. Sometimes, I was taken aback to find her head reached my ribcage when only yesterday her face was the very inconvenient height of my groin. "Have a good day in town?"

"Meh, it was okay. Just hung at the mall. I'm getting bored of doing that. Would much rather be here with you."

"I'd rather you be here, too." I kissed her hair as she pulled away, looking at the unusual traffic on the paddock.

Her nose wrinkled as two incompetent city folk struggled to lift a bale and place it into their shiny new Ute. "What's happening?"

"Free for all."

"Uncle John is giving his hay away for *free*?" Her mouth fell open. "Whoa."

"Not free, free." I moved position and rested my elbows on the moss-covered gate. "I have to charge them as they leave."

She eyed me carefully. "Having fun?"

I snorted. "Does it sound like something I'd do for fun?"

"Nope." Her giggle made me so grateful that I had at least one person I could be honest with. Who knew me. The *real* me. Not the Ren Cassie flirted with, or the Ren John and Patricia nurtured. Ren, the runaway who'd never learned how to read and write.

She climbed the gate, her white sneakers blinding compared to my dirt-covered steel caps. "I can help...if you want?"

I ordered myself not to nod like a demented dog. Instead, I cocked my head and looked at her critically. "Think you can handle adding up hay bales and then multiplying by eight dollars?"

She frowned. "I think so? I dunno…"

"Well, how about you try one?" I suggested. "If someone had ten bales, how much would they owe?" I had to look away, hating that I was using her to double check I hadn't been screwed over. A kid helping an adult do his job. What sort of asshole was I?

Della looked at the sky, her little lips moving before she announced with a flourish, "Eighty dollars."

Great, he didn't screw me.

I gave her a high five. "Awesome work. Your brain is a flawless machine."

She beamed. "So…can I help?"

"I'd love your help." The urbanites and their new Ute rolled toward us, their windows down and the wife fanning herself with her hat. "In fact, here's your first client."

Thank God, I had Della beside me because my heart itched with panic as my eyes flew over the stack of bales they'd chosen.

No way could I count and add that many.

The driver with his thin beard said, "We have twenty. What's the damage?"

I should be able to snap out a figure. I *wanted* to. But unlike when it came to building something or surviving in the elements or seed management and crop rotation, my mind shut down and went numb.

Della's soft, pretty voice piped up beside me, "That will be one hundred and sixty dollars, please." She flashed me a look as the guy fisted out the bills and passed them to me.

I grunted a thanks and shoved it into my pocket with the rest.

As the car accelerated, giving room for a new customer to trundle across the paddock, I inched closer to Della and squeezed her shoulder.

She gave me a sad pout. "I forgot. I'm so mean."

"Forgot what?" I whispered under my breath.

She kicked the gate, her spine rolling. "That you can't calculate."

I stiffened. "It's not something I need to know in order to live my life." Forcing a grin, I added, "That's why I have you."

She gave me a weak smile, moving away from my touch and toward the customers pulling to a stop in their black SUV.

The elderly man beamed at her. "We have three bales."

She looked at the sky, counted, then said, "That is twenty-four dollars, please."

The guy passed over three tens and Della turned to me. "Do you have change?"

Aside from yanking out all the bills in my pocket and checking what I'd stuffed in there, I didn't know. Instead of embarrassing myself, I shook my head. "Sorry. We did specify correct change only."

Della stood frozen. "What do I do?"

The driver assured her, "Keep the change, honey. Buy yourself something nice for the holidays."

He took off before I could punch him for calling her honey.

For the rest of the day, Della was my calculator, business manager, and boss.

And each time she gave a customer a figure, I battled with the knowledge that I would never be her equal again as she was utterly brilliant, and I would forever remain adequately passable.

* * * * *

That night, I lay staring at the ceiling, doing my best to figure out how people took one number and multiplied it by another to form a different one.

I did what the TV show had mentioned, but try as I might, steps were missing that I didn't have.

As much as I loved working with my hands and running the farm, I really should teach myself basic things like math and English.

Somehow.

Della's voice threaded through the darkness from her single bed across the room. "Ren...?"

My head turned on the pillow to face her. The slightly less dark of her bedspread and lightness of her hair were the only things I could make out. "Yeah?"

"These school holidays...can I? Um, do you want me to.... I can show you what I learned if you want?" Her voice dwindled before coming back sharp with determination. "What I learned at school. I'll show you. I mean, only if you want."

My heart fisted hard.

I didn't answer, not because she'd unmanned me or made me feel like an idiot, but because her offer was so perfectly her. So kind. So sweet.

When silence became oppressive, and I still hadn't said yes because I was so in awe of her generous offer, she murmured,

"Tomorrow, I'll show you a couple of things. You can decide after if you want to know more." She rolled over, giving me her back.

And I lay in the darkness, thanking her.

Chapter Thirty-Nine

DELLA

Present Day

A WHILE AGO, I mentioned I'd committed all seven deadly sins starting with wrath when I hated Cassie at first sight.

I was hoping I could skip over the others as I don't really want to reveal just how awful a person I became, but I don't think I have a choice. Not because I'm actually rather normal and felt nothing that someone else hasn't before me, but because I committed the rest of them all in a three-year period.

Clever, huh?

I went from innocent child to terrible human being all in the space of a few short years.

The first one I'll mention is pride.

And that one was Ren's fault.

I was taught at school that it was okay to be proud of achieving high marks if you'd studied hard and deserved it. It was okay to be proud of a drawing or accomplishment because that was the reward for striving to be better and succeeding. As long as you didn't brag or boast, a bit of self-praise was encouraged.

So, armed with that free pass, I already had a complex relationship with the meaning of pride seeing as I'd flirt with the feeling on a regular basis thanks to my love of learning and ability to recall most things that the teacher said.

I had a good circle of friends—only a few who I can remember names now—but I do remember a group bullying me and calling me a teacher's pet. Funny how I didn't mind. I was rather glad because if I was a teacher's pet that meant I was loved more because I did the right thing.

Or at least, that's what I figured it meant seeing as a pet was a family's pride and joy—not that Ren and I had one, and the barn cats that lived at the

Wilsons were there as hunters to keep the grain nibble-free rather than to be cuddled and pampered.

Anyway, I'm digressing…these tangents I keep chasing are becoming worse the longer I write. If I wasn't just going to delete this entire thing, I'd have some serious editing to do.

Anywho…

Pride.

Ren.

That's right…get back to the story, Della.

Where can I start?

Ren was my superstar. He was my hero in all things and never more so than the day when my eyes were no longer blinded by self-obsession. The day I helped him count hay bales and tally payment was the moment I grew up a little.

I didn't judge him or ridicule him for his lack of knowledge. I didn't laugh like the kids at school did when someone couldn't give an answer or screwed up a teacher's question. I didn't pity him or scoff that a boy so much older than me couldn't do simple math.

It made me sad.

It hurt my heart.

Because, all this time, I'd never stopped to think about what he'd given up to grant me my dreams. He'd stayed in a place so I could learn. He'd worked in a job so I could play.

He'd never had a childhood.

Never had a week off.

Never been given the gifts that he'd given me so often and so generously.

My offer to teach him what he'd made possible for me to learn wasn't something pure or offered out of the goodness of my heart.

No.

It was because of guilt. It was because of a child epiphany that I was literate and book smart all because of what Ren had sacrificed to make it happen.

And it hurt.

Because I'd been so selfish and only now seen the reality of what it had cost him.

I owed him. Big. Huge. Massive. So, for the next three years, I paid off that debt by teaching him everything I knew.

Every night during the school holidays, we headed to the hay loft where we'd first slept and sat on hay bales while I pulled out the box full of old work-books and texts that Ren insisted we keep.

I sharpened a pencil for him, gave him my brand-new eraser, and stumbled over how to teach a twenty-year-old boy primary grade English and math.

It took a few nights to find our groove.

I flew too fast through equations, and Ren grew frustrated.

I went too slow, and Ren felt like I babied him.

We bickered and squabbled about right terminology, and we ended for the night with clenched teeth and stiff posture from doing our best to work with each other while struggling with yet a new dynamic.

By the end of the second week, we had a system where Ren would read the text he could, point to the ones he couldn't, and wait patiently while I gave him what he needed.

I didn't try to interfere or pre-empt, and our scuffles gave way to happy cohabitation, hunched over workbooks, quietly studying side by side.

For most of my life, I'd believed I was special—mainly thanks to Ren's perfection at raising me, ensuring I was solid in the knowledge that I walked upon the stars in his eyes. My teachers had further cultivated that mind-set by encouraging me and being awed at my easy progress through the grades.

However, sitting beside Ren as he memorized and problem-solved, I felt the first kernel of lacking.

I'd always known he was unique.

I'd loved him far too deeply and for far too long not to believe he was magical and immortal and every prince, knight, and saviour I could ever need.

But I'd always envisioned him as a boy in dirty clothes, sun-browned and field-worn rather than a neat gentleman with glasses, all library-kissed and book-learned.

Ren Wild was all those things, but now he was something more to be looked up to.

He had a quick-fire intelligence that made me proud and envious—two sins in one.

He might not have had the chance to learn such things, but it wasn't from lack of cleverness. Even at his age and being fairly stuck in his ways, he soaked up numbers and letters as if he'd been thirsty his entire life for such knowledge.

And that was where my second deadly sin started to manifest.

Instead of going to bed frustrated at being teacher to a student far surpassing her, I fell asleep with pride tinting my smile that I was the reason Ren went from counting on his fingers to effortlessly reciting the times tables.

Without me, he still wouldn't be able to spell or read the words he used on a regular basis such as tractor, paddock, and twine.

Now he could spell all manner of things, and I beamed like a proud parent as we held spelling bee standoffs in the hay loft, testing each other, blowing raspberries when we got it wrong and giving high fives when we got it right.

Pride.

Pity it felt so good because every time Ren nudged me with his shoulder in gratitude or read aloud a text that would've caused his cheeks to pink and anger to rise with the unknown, I suffered more and more pride.

I glowed with it whenever he chuckled over a simple word with a strange spelling. I beamed with it whenever he surprised himself by adding up two large numbers and getting the total correct.

For three solid years, our routine never changed.

Some nights, especially in high-summer when Ren pulled fourteen and sometimes sixteen-hour days to get all his work done, we fell exhausted into bed without a lesson, but most of the time, we both looked forward to hiding away, just the two of us, and trading information.

Because what I taught him, he taught me in return.

He taught me how to drive a tractor on my eleventh birthday and sat me on his knee for the first time in a very long time as my legs were too short to reach the rusty pedals.

He taught me how to drive the Land Rover on my twelfth birthday, and even accompanied me to the movies with Cassie and some of my friends when I said I'd love to go see something with him because he'd never come into town with me before.

It was like asking a bear to leave his comfortable den and enter a world full of chaos and calamity.

His eyes never stopped darting. His ears never stopped twitching. His body always on high alert and ready to maul an enemy or protect a friend.

But he did it.

For me.

He happily drove me there, took me out for a burger and fries just like our first official birthday together, and sat beside me while we watched some animated cartoon that I caught him rolling his eyes at but gushed about afterward for my benefit.

He even refused to hang out with Cassie's entourage even though she practically begged him to go clubbing with them once I'd been deposited back home. She claimed he needed a birthday night too; her voice syrupy sweet with that hateful twinkle in her eye that reeked of sex.

She had no right to look at Ren that way, especially as she'd been dating some guy called Chip for six months, and Ren was far too good to be sloppy seconds.

The familiar wrath suffocated me, and it didn't fully go away even as Ren shook his head, escorted me back to the Land Rover, and drove home with me.

I didn't sleep that night, constantly checking his single bed was lumpy with him beneath the covers and not smooth with his absence.

During the midst of winter, we hired movies that we both enjoyed and held book discussions over reading material I brought home from the school library.

For three years, life didn't change too much.

We focused on learning, farming, and family.

And all the while, my girlhood slowly slipped away beneath teenage hormones. I forgot how to be innocent Della Ribbon. I forgot how to be anything, if I'm honest. I didn't know if I wanted to be sweet or sour or kind or cruel. I didn't know if I wanted my handwriting to be cursive or block. I didn't know if I wanted to be a rebel like Cassie or stay true to Ren and his many morals.

The constant war inside stripped me of my childhood values, and that was when the true sins began.

After pride came envy and my complex relationship with Cassie was no longer just black and white. I no longer just liked or hated her. I was twisted with awe and wanting to be her and dirtied with spite with wanting to be what Ren sought.

Over the years, Cassie finished high school and attended a local university. She was a middle-of-the-line student, but thanks to her background in horses and farming, she landed a full scholarship for Equine Science and Stable Management degree.

Her dream job was to event and scoop up the mega prize pools. In the meantime, she was wise enough to know she needed pieces of paper to her name to ensure a paid gig while she schooled herself and her horses to greatness.

Liam started high school in a county over being a year older than me, and I was left in the past, just waiting for my life to begin.

It also didn't help that my choices in TV shows and movies switched from feel good Disney to romantic comedies and everything in-between. Soap operas with brooding men and hurting socialites. Dirty kisses and naughty groping…anything to do with sex and connection was my kryptonite, and Ren often caught me starry-eyed and obsessed with a terrible show, crushing on the hero, my mouth tingling for kisses like they indulged in and wondering what it would feel like to have a boy touch me in places like the girls on the screen permitted.

The more I watched, the more envious I became and not just of Cassie.

I became envious of anyone with a boyfriend.

I tried to coax Liam into kissing me again, but he turned me down. I wasn't interested in him as anything more than a river-swimming, meadow-exploring friend, but it still hurt for him to wrinkle his nose and laugh about kissing me.

I wanted to shout that I was sure his worm hadn't grown any, but I was still nice enough to hold my tongue on hurtful things. Just because my tits hadn't grown past tiny bee stings didn't mean I should tear into his self-consciousness like mine chewed me every day.

My malice made me teeter on a knife-edge of tears whenever I caught Cassie flirting with Ren. Especially as he reshod her horse in the stable on a hot afternoon, bent over and shirtless, his torso glistening with sweat from hammering nails with harsh clangs into her latest warmblood cross.

He was so damn beautiful.

All muscle and masculinity, moving in that effortless way that used to make me feel safe but now just made me lick my lips and hide my gathering confusion.

Watching him was torture. Not because he made me feel things I'd only felt for movie heroes but because my mouth dried up, my heart pounded, and I hurt so much because I wanted something.

Something that made me itch and yearn. Something that made me snappy and hot-tempered whenever Ren gave me the smile reserved just for me and tried to gather me close to his sweaty bare chest in a joke.

Instead of slotting into his side where I belonged, I pushed him away because something inside no longer wanted innocent, carefree hugs.

It wanted what Cassie got.

It wanted more.

But how could I want it from Ren?

He was Ren!

Why suddenly did my eyes see him differently, my nose smell him differently, and my heart act like a cracked out raccoon whenever he came close?

I was thirteen and more confused than I'd ever been in my life.

The pain and hunger were excruciating when Cassie dragged a fingertip along Ren's back and rubbed her pads together, smearing his sweat and smiling that secret adult smile, making me want to tear her pretty brown hair out.

I hated this new vibrant painful world my emotions had thrust me into. I missed the simple days of girlhood where happiness came from riding Domino, doing well on a test, then hitching a ride with Ren on the tractor while he baled.

These days, I could do something I adored and still find ways to feel wrath and pride and envy.

And if it wasn't those three terrible sins, it was the other four.

Greed I often felt, especially around kids who had things I wanted.

Girls with boyfriends.

Girls with horses.

Girls with short hair or dyed hair or the freedom to paint their nails or dress with low-cut tops and high-waisted shorts.

Those girls attracted the boys.

The ones who were edgy and cool and smoked cigarettes stolen from their parents' private stash.

I was still the cute little good girl, and no one wanted her.

So yes, greed was a regular companion just like slothfulness. On hot summer days after a long day at school and a complicated day of soaring and plummeting emotions, I found myself hiding more and more from chores and farmyard duty.

Before, I'd bolt off the bus to wherever Ren was, desperate to help him, eager to be of service and earn his wonderful treasured smile. These days, I slinked off the bus and found a shady spot and curled up beneath stencil patterns of leaves. I'd stare at the sunny sky and lament about all the ways my life wasn't perfect.

In other words, I transformed into the brat who no one likes, and I look back now and wish I had the ability to reach through time and slap myself.

I want to shake my thirteen-year-old self and scream, 'Get over it! Your life was perfect. You were perfect. You had everything you were envious of and greedy for right beneath your stupid little nose, but you ruined it. You made it all disappear, and it was all because of the last deadly sin.'

Lust.

Chapter Forty

REN

2013

2013 STARTED LIKE all the rest.

Cassie tried to tempt me out to a local party where sex was guaranteed and liquor was compulsory. Even though I was twenty-three and of legal age to drink, fuck, and do all the stupid shit adults do, I still had responsibilities. I still had a girl dependent on me. I still had a life I valued and secrets I needed to keep secret.

So, just like all the other times, I declined.

And just like all the other times, Cassie promised she'd be back later and would give me my New Year's Eve kiss. It didn't matter she was getting serious with Chip. She believed that because I'd been in her life for so many years, I wasn't classified as cheating.

However, I was done being the other man.

I was done sleeping with her period.

Frankly, I'd grown tired of her games and immaturity a few years ago, but because I had no desire to find another girl to sleep with, I allowed my cock to keep me in an arrangement that offered no other satisfaction apart from a cheap release. But even that couldn't compensate for the shame I felt afterward, knowing some poor schmuck was in love with her and this was how she treated him.

Instead of doing the usual soul-crushing hook-up, I stayed in my room with Della and stayed up far too late laughing at some stupid TV show and falling asleep amongst chip packets and lolly wrappers.

We hunkered down through winter, believing nothing would

change and our content, happy lives had nothing to fear.

For months, we continued to study by night and go off to our separate lives by day, and Della continued to transform into a stunning young woman.

As much as I would like to, I couldn't call her a girl anymore. Sure, the softness in her eyes still said child rather than woman. Sure, the roundness of her cheeks when she smiled hadn't given way to the incredible sharpness of her cheekbones just waiting to sweep up and steal her forever from childhood.

Her body had hips with the fledgling hint of breasts. Her stare was full of both heartache and innocence, and sometimes, just sometimes, when she'd flick her hair and the rippling gold cascaded over her shoulders, I'd have to suck in a breath because I lost sight of the kid and only saw a beauty that I'd have to keep locked away so she wouldn't be devoured by hungry men.

She was far too beautiful, and it made me uncomfortable.

I cursed morning and night when she'd change in front of me.

Before, I didn't care if she'd strip off her top beside her single bed and slip into a nightgown. I didn't think anything of it when her jeans slid down her legs and she kicked them across the room with all the care of a teenager who didn't believe in housework.

For years, I'd refused to get undressed around her. I'd ensured I dressed in the bathroom after a shower and only swam in board shorts rather than skinny-dip.

She should follow those same rules.

But for some reason, I struggled to tell her to hide when it wasn't her with the problem but me.

Her innocence at strolling from the steaming bathroom with just a towel wrapped around her breakable, beautiful body made my eyes avert and heart stop because it wasn't right for me to look.

Not anymore.

Her growth from child to almost-woman should've been the first hint that things were about to change.

Drastic things.

Things we could never undo, and things that would ruin any future we might have had at Cherry River Farm.

Chapter Forty-One

DELLA

Present Day

OKAY, I'VE SLEPT on it, and I think I'm ready to tell you how I screwed up.

I'll tell you about our third separation.

My hands are shaking on my keyboard. My heart is rushing. My head's a mess with everything I did and everything I should've done differently.

Or better yet, never done at all.

I destroyed everything.

I was the idiot that took paradise and tore it to pieces.

How do I begin this?

I can't just jump in and say I ran away...because...well, you don't have context and will be wondering what the hell was there to run away from?

You'll shake your head and call me stupid, and I'd totally agree with you. Even knowing why I ran makes me shake my head and call myself stupid, so you're not alone.

If only I hadn't done what I did, I wouldn't have had to.

But I did, and I'll never forgive myself.

And he'll never forgive me, either.

Okay, assignment-that-will-never-be-turned-in-and-is-just-an-exercise-in-agony, let's do this.

Let's start two days before I ran away, shall we?

No wait, it was three days...no, you know what? I need to start at least four days before I ran.

Cassie.

Funny how it's always freaking Cassie.

I'm going to fast forward what happened until the important stuff.

I got up. I kissed Ren goodbye. I went to school. I learned stuff. I got *back on the bus. I came home. I hung with Patricia in her kitchen. I had dinner with Ren. We studied a little. We went to bed.*

A perfectly normal day. Innocent. Sweet. No incredibly idiotic screw-ups to deal with.

However, this perfectly normal day wasn't so normal. While I helped Patricia make rhubarb jam in her cosy kitchen, my lower belly started to ache. My head started to hurt, and by the time I'd finished my homework while Ren read my last terms textbooks, the ache had morphed into a terrible throb, radiating down my legs, my inner thighs, even up my back.

I did my best to sleep, but the discomfort never went away, and I woke up cranky and sore and with a zit the size of Antarctica on my forehead.

Ren kissed me goodbye as spring was a busy season with harrowing and replanting, and he started with the dawn.

I waved him away, doing my best to conceal the awful red spot destroying my confidence and was glad he disappeared because it meant I could curl up on my bed and nurse the terrible tummy ache I suffered.

Because I was normally a diligent student, no one suspected I didn't go to school that morning. No one came to check on me. And I spent the day alternating between great big wracking tears and hunching over in the bathroom as I endured a nightmare.

Blood.

Everywhere.

In my knickers, down my legs, on my sheets.

The pain intensified to the point where I grew light-headed with agony, moaning under my breath with every belly squeezing ache.

I knew what it was.

I'd read the books.

I'd devoured the articles online about what classified a girl from a woman and how they had to start menstruating to be called a proper adult.

My breasts ached and tingled.

My head crushed and pounded.

And my moods didn't know if they wanted to be angry with the mess, rage at the pain, or be grateful that I was no longer a kid.

It was one of the longest days of my life, and I didn't dare leave to get food because I couldn't risk running into Patricia or John.

I loved food, but the embarrassment at how disgusting my clothes and bedding had become meant I didn't move a muscle. I tortured myself with scenarios of Ren arriving home and seeing the bloodbath I lay in. Of him asking awful questions. Of him knowing that blood was coming out of me in places that I never wanted to discuss.

More tears came on the tailcoat of those thoughts, knowing I should get up, swallow some painkillers, and strip my bed and body of dirty things.

But the pain continued, and I just didn't have the energy.

I didn't know the time, but eventually the sound of Cassie's Corolla crunched on the driveway, and I hunched deeper into my pillow.

Normally, she came into the barn before going into the house, looking for Ren and sometimes me to say hi before the routine of dinner and homework.

Perhaps, she'd forgo her usual visit today, and my nightmare would go unseen.

I held my breath, hoping against hope that she'd stay away while also a huge part of me wanted to be cared for, for another girl to help me, and to be told I wasn't going to die with the amount of pain I was in.

Her footsteps sounded outside the bedroom door. Her gentle knock reverberating in my pounding my head. "Hello? Anyone home?"

I groaned under my breath, burrowing my head into my pillow, my face on fire and body in agony as she opened the door and found me.

"Oh, my God, Della." She dashed toward me, dropping her messenger bag and cupping my face with her cool hands. She'd grown from the rebellious teenager I looked up to, to a confident young woman who I envied, and here she was, being kind to me.

I burst into tears as she dragged me into her arms.

I could tell you in graphic detail how she helped wash me, dress me, strip and remake my bed, feed me comforting yummy food, and fill me with painkillers, but I won't bother. There's no point because you won't read this, and I don't feel like living that particular part of my life any more than necessary.

By the time she sat me on the couch in her room with music posters and trophies won at horse shows and dressage competitions, I felt somewhat normal and listened intently to the lesson she gave on pads versus tampons and what to expect during my new cycle.

A closeness blossomed between us, and I'd never felt so in-tune with her. She was my angel, and I'd never forget what she did for me.

By the time Ren returned, smelling of earth with dirt under his nails, my secret was hidden, my newfound womanhood none of his business, and now, for the first time, Cassie and I shared a smile that spoke of our own special secrets.

She didn't tell anyone I hadn't gone to school, and the next day, instead of heading to her uni classes, she took the day off and grabbed me as I forced myself out of bed.

I was still sore but nowhere near as bad.

"Is Ren gone?" she asked, looking around the messy one bedroom.

I nodded, struggling to get up the energy to haul on my school uniform. "Yep."

"Good. Get dressed in your joddies and boots. You're not going to school today."

"I'm not?"

"Nope." She grinned with her hair plaited with a ribbon similar to the one I wore every day. "My mum let me have three days off school when I had my first period. She bought me flowers and cakes and told me turning into a woman was something to be celebrated even though I wanted to yank out my womb and never have another one."

I giggled softly, standing in my pyjamas with one of the pads she'd given me between my achy legs. "Me, too."

Her eyes warmed. "You don't want me to tell anyone, so it's come down to me. I know you don't really like the mall, so we're gonna go for an all-day ride. I have a hot water bottle for your tummy in my saddlebag and lots of painkillers. I'm sure you probably don't feel like it, but the doctors always say exercise and endorphins help the pain."

She was so full of life and friendship that I couldn't say no.

I didn't want to say no.

This was Cassie accepting me as a friend not just as a younger nuisance, and she wanted to spend all day with me.

Needless to say, I loved her for that too. She let me ride my favourite of her horses—black and white Domino—and she rode her newest warmblood cross called Mighty Mo.

Armed with salad sandwiches and a slice of strawberry sponge cake, we headed off and spent the day riding, chatting, and being two simple girls sharing each other's company.

It was one of my favourite days, despite the lingering ache in my belly.

As we rode, propriety fell away, and we giggled at crude things, gossiped about people at her uni, and generally didn't care about right or wrong.

As our bond deviated from polite conversation to openness, more complicated topics filled my head. There were so many things I wanted to ask her, but embarrassment kept me silent.

That was, until she asked if I wanted to gallop over a rolling meadow after our lunch by the forest edge, and we'd ended up racing each other. Hair streaming beneath helmets, hands clutching reins, and legs tight against saddles.

The adrenaline hit me, making me giddy and chatty. Nothing was better than a gallop. I felt free. Not trapped by age or expectation. I was just Della, and she was just Cassie, and for once, we were equals.

She laughed as we slowed to a walk, rubbing her large breasts with a grimace. "These girls have been handy in the romance department, but holy shit, they hurt when riding."

I blushed a little, looking at my flat chest. "I don't have that problem."

She smirked, eyeing me. "Don't worry. Now that your periods have started, your breasts will grow almost overnight."

"Really?"

"Yup." She nodded wisely. "I went from surfboard to D's. My dad was horrified when Mum took me shopping, and I came back with bras bigger than hers."

I laughed under my breath, picturing all the upcoming trials of my life. Bras and tampons and girly stuff that I didn't want Ren knowing about.

We rode a bit more before I had the courage to ask. "Do the boys mind your...eh. When you're on your period, um..."

She raised her eyebrow. "Spit it out. I won't tell anyone, and you can't shock me. You should know that by now."

"Okay." I sat taller in my saddle. "Do boys care about periods? Like when you kiss them and stuff?"

"You mean can you have sex while on your period?"

My face flared.

I didn't know if that was what I meant, but I nodded so I didn't look stupid.

"I guess. I mean, some do. It's not exactly fun. But some boys aren't squeamish. It's natural, after all. Not our fault we bleed once a month."

I pouted. "Once a month is too often."

"I agree." Cassie sighed. "It does get in the way of some things, but tampons are great if you want to go swimming and stuff. And to be fair, a boy will normally stay clear 'cause of your mood swings, not just the blood."

"Does Ren stay clear of your mood swings?"

She laughed. "He seems to stay clear of me a lot these days." The sad wisp in her voice made me wince, partly because I was glad he avoided her and partly because I pitied her, because once you'd been graced by Ren's affection, it was hard to have it taken away.

"I do miss him, but I'm with Chip, and things are going well, so I guess I can't be greedy."

Greed.

That sneaky little sin again.

Questions exploded in my mind. Questions like 'Am I greedy wanting things like what you have? What is it like? Is Ren a good kisser? How often did you do it?'

But each one of those questions was guaranteed to rip out my heart and leave it in the hoof prints of my horse.

I swallowed them down, only for Cassie to somehow sense them and blurt, "I have no one else to talk to about him. I've never told my friends that I've been with Ren because I didn't want them thinking he was available, and I didn't want the news getting back to my parents. But..." She flashed me a pained look. "I really like him. Like...I think I might be in love with him.

Stupid, right?" She laughed and sighed at the same time. "When he's with me, he gives me his full attention, but getting him to that stage…it's hard work. It's like there's always something else on his mind, stealing his heart." She glowered at the reins in her hands. "Almost as if he's searching for something else, and I'm not it."

I sat deathly silent in my saddle.

Not even the sway of Domino's steady walk or the increasing ache between my legs now that the painkillers had worn off could distract me from the bitter sweetness of finally getting answers I'd begged for all while hoping I didn't get anymore.

"Have you kissed a boy, Della?"

I sucked in a gasp even as my head answered for me with a sharp shake, lying.

She smiled. "I envy you. That first kiss is the best."

"I…I kissed Liam once."

"Did you?! Oh, my God!" She burst out laughing. "Oh, wait. Is that when Mum got super mad and made Liam recite every body part so he knew what each did?" She laughed harder. "That's too funny."

I hunched. "I didn't find it funny. It wasn't good, and his worm…I mean…anyway." I shrugged. "I want to kiss someone soon. I'm a woman now. I should know what it feels like."

She flicked her plait over her shoulder, her ribbon fluttering like mine in the breeze. "Well, my suggestion is to kiss someone you love with all your heart. Don't settle for a cheap thrill. Save it for the person who means the world to you."

That advice, right there…did you see it?

Did you understand what my young foolish heart heard?

If you didn't…you soon will.

Cassie continued, "Sex isn't something to be done with just anyone, you know? You have to trust them impeccably. Love them. Want them. Believe in them. Know that they will never hurt you and always have your back. Okay?"

I nodded, still obsessing over her previous advice on who to kiss.

There was only one person I loved that much.

One boy who meant the absolute universe to me.

Doing my best to stop runaway thoughts, I asked the stupidest question I could've asked, "What was it like…sleeping with Ren?"

Her eyes narrowed, her breath inhaled, and she studied me for an eternity before admitting, "The best I've ever had."

I should've stopped there.

I should've known that something wasn't quite right with me that I wanted explicit details on the man who'd raised me.

I should've known nothing good could come from taboo conversation and dealing with amplified emotions while on my period.

So many reasons to stop.

I wanted *to stop.*

But this was adult territory, and I was an adult now.

I could handle it.

I could handle the filthy feeling inside at asking about Ren.

I could handle the strange greed, envy, and unfurling lust, even though all three emotions should've been massive alarm bells that I was broken in many ways. That I was on the precipice of doing something forbidden and disgusting and wrong.

But...I had no willpower.

And I'd been waiting for honesty like this all my life.

"How was it the best?" My voice was small, afraid, already hurting.

Cassie tore her eyes from mine as her hand found its way into her horse's mane and twirled the black strands. "How?"

"Uh-huh..."

Tell me.

Don't tell me.

Ruin me.

Don't ruin me.

"Because Ren has never been a boy. Even when he was younger, he was braver, stronger, more attractive than any of the boys who think they're men but are still just silly little children. He carries this melancholy melody inside him that just makes me want to protect him and have him protect me at the same time. When he touches me, it's like fire. When he kisses me, it's like drowning. When he pushes me down and thrusts inside me, it's like falling into space, trusting him to never let you go, all the while hoping he will let you fall and then fall right along with you."

Her voice dwindled away with longing. "He's aggressive in all the right ways. He's dominating and generous and ruthless and..." She shrugged helplessly. "Sleeping with Ren is the best thing I've ever done because he doesn't just live to deliver pleasure but because he gives so much of himself when he does. He has his secrets. He has his moods. But when he's in your arms...that's when he lets himself be seen. His kisses are full of tragedy. His touches are full of sorrow. And when he comes...wow..." She looked at the sky full of sunset-pink clouds. "He breaks your heart every damn time because he's everything you could ever want and everything you'll never have because Ren is wild. He's untouchable. And the knowledge that he'll always be that way tears off a piece of your soul, letting him steal it. He pockets it like his secrets, and he carves a hole inside you until you ache for one tiny piece of his in return."

She sighed with all the pain she felt and all the matching misery I was about to cause. "I'm in love with him, and he doesn't even notice. He doesn't care because whatever he cares about isn't me, and I'm done trying to be what he wants when I doubt even he knows. It's just...it's the perfect combination of grief and bliss, I guess. And I stupidly became addicted to it...just like I became addicted to him."

Now, I'm sure I've embellished what she said to me that day.

I've added flair that creative writing has taught me and put phrases into Cassie's mouth that an Equine Science student probably would never say.

I also, maybe, probably, put in my own bittersweet knowledge, because I understand her now. I might not have slept with Ren, but I know her pain. I recognise her craving because such catastrophe lives within me.

Of course, I didn't know that then. But...that's how I heard it.

I listened to a tortured tale of unrequited love and fell for it.

I'd never heard something so beautiful as being told Ren was unclaimable while in another woman's arms, and it sent my stupid adolescent heart wondering if I would be different.

If I was what he was searching for.

If he was what I was searching for.

If all of this was for a reason, a purpose, an ending that would complete whatever journey we were on.

It cracked open the blinders I'd had on all my life and gave me a glimpse at the man behind the boy.

The man I'd caught myself staring at.

The man I'd dreamt about.

The man who was my everything and would now become the reason for every tortured day thereafter.

I've loved Ren Wild all my life.

But it wasn't until Cassie Wilson ripped back the curtain that I fell in love with him.

I fell into the idea of him.

I fell into the idea of being his.

And unfortunately, once that idea was formed...there was no going back.

As we rode into the farm as dusk fell and Ren appeared from the stable with his reserved smile, tanned skin, and perfect love, I tore my gaze from his dark soulful eyes. As he asked about our ride and helped untack our horses, I kept my thoughts buried and my body averted from his hugs.

And when night-time descended, I lay in bed mulling over Cassie's words.

Over and over again.

Ruining myself, condemning myself until I had no other path to take.

"Well, my suggestion is to kiss someone you love with

all your heart. Don't settle for a cheap thrill. Save it for the person who means the world to you."

In bold, it looks just as bad as my last confession of being in love with Ren Wild.

Her advice wasn't meant to be taken the way I took it.

She didn't mean to kiss the only boy I'd ever known.

She didn't mean to set in action something that I'd regret for the rest of my life.

I knew that then, and I know that now.

But did it stop me?

Of course not.

Chapter Forty-Two

REN

2013

DELLA HAD BEEN out of sorts for the past few days.

I tried to ignore it and give her space. I trusted that if it was important, she'd tell me, and if it wasn't, then I didn't want to pry.

However, the day after she got back from her ride with Cassie, she was standoffish and strange. She refused to eat dinner with me. She gave me her back the moment she slipped into bed. She didn't want to watch TV or study or do anything that involved spending time with me.

I tried not to be hurt by her behaviour, but I lay awake most of the night missing my best friend and wondering how the hell I could fix what I'd most assuredly broken because her mood must be my fault.

Why else did she hate me?

By the time the next afternoon rolled around, I finished early, had a shower so I didn't smell of sweat and earth, and used the Wilson's barbecue to make Della's favourite: honey covered yams with brown sugar and soy sauce roasted chicken. I even threw on a few foil-wrapped bananas with maple syrup, indulging in her sweet tooth on all three elements of the meal.

When she returned from school, she gave me a weird smile, opened her mouth as if to say something, then darted into our bedroom.

She returned a little while later with blonde hair dark and damp down her back from a shower, and a turquoise summer dress with a heavy knit cream jumper to ward off the spring evening chill.

I cleared my throat. "I made us dinner."

The weirdness in her faded when she pulled up the barbecue lid and spied the deliciousness underneath. "Wow, everything I love." Her eyes gleamed with what suspiciously looked like tears before she blinked them away and beamed just like normal. "Thanks so much. You're the best."

The Della I knew and loved was still hiding, but for now, I'd settle for the reserved little woman smiling at me. I couldn't stop my arms from grabbing her in a bone-crushing hug.

I held her so damn hard, wanting to delete the strangeness between us, wishing I could ask what she hid from me.

There were too many unsaid things these days and it made me nervous, as if I'd already lost her when she was still in my arms.

She returned my embrace but not as fierce as she usually would, and when I let her go, she sprang away quickly, when normally, she'd linger. We always lingered around each other. We liked each other's company. I liked to know she was in reaching distance if she needed help. And she liked to snuggle up and make me laugh.

Where had that ease gone?

Why did her smiles make my heart thud in familiarity and foreignness at the same time?

It seemed she no longer needed that closeness, and I did my best to ignore the pain as we sat down on the outdoor picnic set at the bottom of the garden to enjoy our meal.

With birds roosting in trees, Della regaled me of tales about school and teachers and how she was excited to start high school because she wanted to learn the hard stuff and was done with primary.

I nodded and grinned and fixated on the shiny blue ribbon that she'd tied around her throat in a choker.

She'd often used the ribbon as a bracelet or even tied it around her ankle once, but this was the first time she'd used it as a necklace, and I couldn't take my eyes off the way it showed off her stark collarbones.

She looked like she'd lost weight.

She looked older, wiser, moodier.

If she was losing weight, why wasn't she eating? Was it school? Was she being bullied? I made a mental note to ask Cassie if she knew anything while I piled another piece of chicken onto her plate.

I merely shrugged when she raised an eyebrow in question.

Even though the atmosphere between us was a little strained, we smiled and laughed and pretended everything was normal.

So many things lately had been pushing us apart. The knowledge that something festered beneath the surface that neither of us was addressing itched at me just as much as returning to the forest did.

Strange to think I'd only been a boy when I'd found my calling of living in the trees, yet as a man, I'd never accept anything else for my home.

Regardless that circumstances like these made me hunger for space more often than when things were good between us, I forced away such thoughts and focused on Della.

I hated to think of her growing away from me, but at the same time, I welcomed it because it meant she was becoming her own person. I despised the thought of her one day not sharing everything with me and having her own secrets and shadows, but that was a guarantee and yet another piece of growing up that I had to accept.

I didn't know how John and Patricia did it—watching their kids grow from entirely dependent to utterly independent.

It was heart-soaring and soul-crushing all at the same time.

We finished our meal in silence, sipping on fresh glasses of milk and staring at wildflowers dancing in the evening breeze. The chill turned icy as I took her plate and told her to get warm in our bedroom.

She shook her head and followed me to the kitchen instead, standing beside me as I washed the dishes. She dried away the bubbles, and together, we walked from the Wilson's home to ours in the barn and closed the door on the world.

Normally, the sense of contentedness overflowed the moment we were back just the two of us.

Tonight though, nervousness flowed instead, and I didn't swap my jeans for pyjama bottoms like I usually did. For some reason, my instincts were on high alert, and the element of danger wasn't coming from outside the room but within it.

From her.

From my Little Ribbon who perched on the edge of her bed alive and brittle and not paying any attention to the movie we'd chosen.

To be fair, I didn't have a clue what we watched, and by the time she yawned and the clock said it was time to sleep, my heart whirred with smoke and anxious anticipation.

Of what, I didn't know, but as we said goodnight and climbed into bed, I lay in the dark waiting for an attack...just not knowing where it would come from.

* * * * *

I had a dream.

A nonsense kind of dream of darkness and trees and winter.

I'd lost something in the dark, and no matter how fast I ran, no matter how hard I searched, I couldn't find it.

It wasn't a simple trinket I'd lost but something fundamental. Something that would kill me if I didn't find it.

I kept searching, kept hoping, only to run through vast sections of emptiness, finding nothing.

I didn't know how long I ran for or where the trees disappeared to the longer I sprinted in nothingness, but eventually, sunlight beckoned, and I chased harder, faster. My legs burned. My lungs tore.

But I kept running, kept gasping until the one thing I wanted more than anything found me.

A figure appeared from the darkness.

A woman with flowing blonde hair and white angelic dress.

I slammed into her, halting my chase, welcoming me home.

I moaned at the feel of rightness. The sense of belonging. The knowledge of finding the one person I was meant to find after all this time.

Then I stopped breathing as perfect lips pressed against mine.

Soft and hesitant.

Innocent and testing.

I couldn't see the face of my dream-kisser, but I knew, without a shadow of a doubt, she was the one I'd been searching for. She was the one born for me. She was the one I needed to find before I lost everything.

I closed my eyes and gave into the dream.

I didn't try to see her face or know who she was.

All I wanted in that moment was to live beneath her touch, to taste what she gave me, to bow to whatever gift I was worth.

Lips pressed harder, hesitation mixing with determination.

It was as awkward as my first and just as intense.

My heart thundered all around me in the dark forest where I stood.

The innocence of mouths touching but no tongue or deeper invitation wrecked me until my knees buckled, and I collapsed before my dream-kisser.

Lips vanished. Breath caught.

And I groaned for more, to not be abandoned by those I loved, to not fear the future where I might be alone, to not have to clutch something so hard only to lose it anyway.

She heard me.

Lips returned, pressing sweetly, worshiping kindly, and I fell in ways I'd never been able to fall before.

No other kiss compared.

No other intimate moment existed.

This simple faultless, guiltless, sinless kiss was *everything*.

My hands came up, seeking to touch, to stroke, to claim.

My fingers met long, soft hair.

I opened my mouth to deepen the virginal affection.

But then a noise interrupted the purity.

A sound that wrenched me from the dream world, yanked me off my knees, and hurled me into an existence that was no longer fantasy but pure fucking hell.

Della bent over me in the gloom of our bedroom. Her hair was tangled in my fist, lips wet from mine, eyes as wide as blue moons, and her face as gorgeous as untouched snow.

No.

"Stop!" I shoved her away, my fingers burning as if I'd touched acid, my mouth twisting as if I'd ingested poison.

She stumbled backward, landing on her ass between our two single beds. Her nightgown rose up her legs, flashing me white underwear and cream-colored thighs.

I almost retched.

What the *hell* happened?

My body trembled so bad, I scrambled twice for my sheets before I was able to tear them away and leap out of bed. Standing over her, I gripped my hair with terrified hands, and barked with horrified rage, "What the *fuck* do you think you were doing?"

How could I do this?

How could I sleep through something so sick and twisted and wrong?

How could *she* do this?

What the *hell* happened?

"Della! Speak to me!"

I was a trapped animal wanting to slaughter something for having the one person I loved more than anything be the entire reason I'd just lost everything.

Pacing before her, I had to get out of there before I did

something I'd regret.

Wrenching open the door, I bolted into the stable and charged down the barn.

The scramble of feet and the flurry of mistake chased me. "Ren!"

I spun and swooped on her, grabbing her bicep, digging my fingernails in as hard as I could. She'd fucking *gutted* me. If I hurt her half as much, it still wouldn't be enough.

"Why?" I roared. "Why did you fucking have to do that?!"

Tears sprouted from her eyes. She tried to hold my gaze but couldn't match my fury. She stared at my bare chest as rivers spilled down her cheeks. "I'm sorry. I'm so sorry. I-I don't know what I was thinking."

I shook her. "You *weren't* thinking. That was the problem." I wanted an explanation. I needed it. Now. Before I went insane.

Was she sleep-walking? Was it involuntary? Perhaps a dare or something just as stupid but understandable thanks to teenage guts and idiotic attempts.

Shoving her away, I wiped my hands on my pants, desperate to get rid of the feel of her. The chilliness of her arms reminded me she'd stood over me, fucking *kissing* me, instead of snug and innocent in her bed. I rubbed my mouth, mad with the need to delete her golden taste.

I wanted to vomit.

I should stick my fingers down my throat and retch all over the cobblestones because that was the only way to get the devil out from inside me.

Della collapsed on the floor, her hands fisting her nightgown, her face bowed behind curtains of blonde.

She sobbed.

She begged.

And I couldn't do a damn thing.

I couldn't console her even though every tear cracked open my ribcage and took a pitchfork to my bleeding heart.

I couldn't hug her even though her quaking shoulders buckled my knees and ordered me to fall before her.

I couldn't do anything I would normally do because she'd just ruined everything normal.

Sudden tears filled my own eyes.

Shock and horror and the knowledge that we could never sleep in the same room.

That we could never return to age of innocence after this.

That it was over.

All of it.

"You ruined everything, Little Ribbon." My voice broke. *"Everything."*

She nodded furiously, gulping back tears, tripping over herself to explain. "I'm sorry. Cassie and I were talking about kissing, and I said I'd never been kissed, and I just thought about you and how much I love you and how nice it would be to share my first kiss with someone I love and how I know you'd never hurt me and I just wanted to *know.* I wanted to know, Ren. I'm *sorry!"* She crawled toward me, her white nightgown growing grey with dust and dirt. "I'm *so* sorry! It was wrong. I won't do it again. I promise. Please...please say you'll forgive me. *Please!"*

She reached for my ankles just as the barn door swung wide, and Cassie strode inside with her arms wrapped around her pink dressing gown and her hair mussed from sleep. "I heard noises. What happened?" Her gaze landed on Della collapsed before me, then to me with a rogue tear decorating my cheek and the aura of brokenness littered around us.

Della's sobs turned louder as she buried her face in her hands. "No! Go away! You ruined everything!"

Cassie's face, normally so trusting and up for anything, turned black with suspicion. "What did you do, Ren?"

"He didn't do anything. It was me!" Della yelled through clenched fingers. "Leave. Go away. You're only making it worse!"

Cassie ignored her wishes, running toward her and sliding to a stop beside her.

I backed away, unable to stop the sensation of waking up to kissing my little Della. Unable to stop the repeat of her taste and touch and the dream and the wondrous feeling of finding everything precious, only to lose it in a heartbeat.

The exquisite joy of my dream was now crushed beneath utter despair.

I couldn't breathe beneath the weight of it.

I couldn't exist beneath the horror of it.

How could she *do* this?

How could she break me so spectacularly after everything I'd sacrificed? After every year I'd given her. After every milestone and accomplishment I'd shared with her? I fucking loved her, and this was how she repaid me? By killing me with a simple kiss.

A kiss that could never be permitted.

A kiss that was as dirty and dangerous as everything

monstrous and evil.

Cassie locked her fingers around Della's wrists, forcing her to remove her hands and stare into her distraught, blotchy face. "Tell me what happened."

Della cried harder.

Cassie's gaze met mine. "Or you tell me. Someone better. Otherwise, I'm calling my father."

Della squirmed, trying to get out of her hold. "No, don't call him. Please!"

"You better tell me what happened then. Right now."

Her scolding worked, and Della's bottom lip wobbled with confession. "I kissed him. I-I did what you said and only kissed the boy I loved with all my heart."

Cassie fell back, ripping her hands from Della the same way I had. Her own heartbreak shattered all over her face as she looked back at me.

I couldn't do a thing but stand there with my head shaking and my hands opening and closing in helplessness.

"Is that true?" she breathed. "Did you *kiss* your baby sister?" Loathsome disgust painted her features. She switched from happy-go-lucky Cassie to judge and executioner. "What sort of fucking *pervert* are you? You let her *kiss* you? Are you insane? What the fuck else do you do in that one bedroom, huh?" She climbed to her feet, stalking me, backing me into a stable. "Have you fucked her, Ren? Is that why you won't like me? I'm too old for you? All this time, you've been sleeping with someone half your age. Someone who shares your blood?!" She dry heaved as she slammed the stable door with me inside and slammed the lock home. "Don't fucking move, you sick, twisted asshole. I'm getting my father."

The fact that I stood there, locked in place even as Cassie flew from the stable was a testament to how wonderfully Della had crushed me.

I had no energy to fight for my own freedom.

I had no ability to argue my defence so John Wilson wouldn't call the police for suspected incest and child abuse.

I just stood there, staring at Della on the floor.

Begging her silently to fix this.

To rewind time and never do what she did.

"Ren..." she murmured between thick tears. "I'm so, *so* sorry." She stood and wobbled toward me, grabbing the locked partition between us for support.

I backed away, deeper into the stable until the hay net stopped my retreat. "Don't come near me."

The desolate brokenness on her face matched the caving, crumbling destruction inside me, and we stood staring, silently cursing, painfully accepting that this was it.

There was no turning back from this.

"I love you," she whispered. "I didn't mean for this to happen."

Somehow, her wounded voice snapped me from my stupor, and I charged forward. Reaching over, I unbolted the lock and stepped as far away from her as possible.

I might not have anything to say in my defence, but I had plenty to say on behalf of Della's. I should never have returned that kiss. I should never have given in. Dream excuse or not, I should've known better. I should never have let her believe such boundaries could be crossed. I should never have encouraged hugs and kisses and affection.

This was my fault, not hers.

And if anyone was going to be punished, it was me.

John had to know the truth, and he had to know it now before the police came to take me away. Before they found out I was the runaway who stole a baby named Della Mclary. Before they found out I was a criminal who'd kissed that stolen child. Before they found out my past as a slave and knitted my sad sorry tale together and the newspapers wrote fiction, lamenting that anyone who'd been sold and forced into labour before he was ten years old was bound to have issues. That it was only natural for his story to end with him in jail for molesting the very same kid he stole.

I was *understandable*.

I was a statistic.

Della was not.

She was so many things.

So many wonderful things.

But she was no longer mine.

We were no longer Ren and Della.

No longer fake brother and sister.

No longer the Wilds.

Backing away from her, I grunted around my fury and grief, "Go back to bed, Della. I need to fix this."

I left her in the stables, crying and beautiful and perfectly screwed up from my lack of skills as a parent. *I'd* been the one to break her. I was the one to muddle her mind and make her think kissing me was appropriate.

And as I knocked on the Wilson's door and prepared to face the symphony that I'd conducted, I didn't think she'd ever disobey me.

I believed I would fight for her right to stay with the Wilsons.

I thought I would shoulder all the blame, be taken away in hand cuffs, and leave Della in the capable control of a family I'd grown to love as my own.

But just like I'd trusted Della never to overstep our friendship, I ought to have known what would happen.

I ought to have seen that as I entered the Wilson's house and prepared to do battle, Della Mclary would pack my old backpack, dress in warm clothes, and sneak unseen through the starlight, leaving me, leaving us, leaving everything behind until the only thing that was left was her twisted kiss on my lips.

By the time I realised what she'd do, it was too late.

She was gone.

Chapter Forty-Three

REN

2013

DELLA.

Every single part of my life, she was there.

Every single memory, she was in.

Every single achievement and ability, she was responsible for.

And now, she was the reason my heart was broken as I stood in an empty bedroom without her.

She'd gone.

She'd left.

Where, I didn't know.

For how long, I couldn't be sure.

Would she come back?

Should I stay or hunt for her?

What was the *right* thing to do?

My hands balled as a crippling wash of loneliness, despair, and confusion threatened to drown me.

How could she do this?

How could she rip apart our world and then run the moment I'd put it back together again?

How could she turn her back on me when I'd stood before the Wilsons and done my best to repair everything?

For the past few years, Della had spent her evenings teaching me spelling and multiplication and science. She'd traded the knowledge I'd bought her and gave me hours upon hours of her time.

She was selfless.

She didn't care about hanging out with girls her own age. She ignored the cell phone John and Patricia insisted she had and preferred to check my answers on tests she'd already aced, rather than respond to teenage texts.

Every night, I'd been gruff with her. I'd been impatient to learn faster. I'd been frustrated at her mercy and taken her tutorage, not with utmost gratefulness, but with tense irritation that my inadequacy stole more of her childhood.

Even though I sat stiff and surly through most of the lessons, it didn't stop my eyes from settling on her bent head or my fingers from itching to sweep away her hair so I could see her face.

I was in utter awe of her—in absolute wonder that my best friend was so smart, so capable, so perfect.

And that was the only reason I'd been able to hide most of my frustration and smile when she graded my division skills and laugh when she critiqued my sentence structures.

I'd never been more thankful for that gift as I'd stood before John, Patricia, and Cassie Wilson. I'd held my head high, able to use words I knew how to spell and give explanations I knew how to deliver, ripping apart their trust.

They'd welcomed us into their home under one condition. One measly condition, and I'd shattered it.

My lips still seared from hers. My dream still tainted my reality. Thanks to Della, I'd just had my world snatched away, all the while, she was the reason I was no longer an illiterate farmhand.

Pushing her out of my mind, I'd focused on ensuring this mess didn't ruin her future.

I'd make sure she had a *better* future.

One with firmer boundaries.

One that I didn't screw up.

John stood with his arms crossed, his maroon plaid pyjamas severe as a prison sentence. His wife stood with furious dots on her cheeks, and Cassie stared at me as if I was a stranger, hugging herself with white-knuckled fists.

No one spoke, but the air was heavy with condemnation. The phone rested in Patricia's hand either used to call the police or still waiting. Either way, I'd run out of time, so I said the only thing that mattered.

"She isn't my sister."

Cassie's mouth fell open, followed by her mother's.

John cleared his throat as if he hadn't been expecting such a confession. "Pardon me?"

I stood straighter, shoving aside the lies we'd told. "I did run away from a farm that bought children for labour. I did raise Della since she was a baby. Those weren't lies. And I do love her, with all my heart, but our last name isn't Wild and we're not related."

John scowled. "I…don't understand."

"She was the daughter of the people who bought me. Their name was Mclary. I don't know where their farm is. I don't know how much they paid for me or what my surname was before I was just Ren. Della was theirs. She was born the night after my finger was cut off for stealing food, and somehow, when I finally got the guts to run away, she was in the backpack I'd prepared with meagre supplies. I didn't mean to steal her. In fact, I tried to leave her with a family because I knew I would be no good as a parental figure. But…I went back for her. I took her with me, and I've kept it a secret ever since."

I stepped back, withdrawing myself from their world. "I know what you must think of me, but I never meant for this to happen. I don't know why she kissed me, and I definitely didn't condone it. She'll be disciplined, and I'll ensure she has better rules because I think it's time I left. She needs parents, like you, not a kid who doesn't know what he's doing. I'm not telling you this to excuse what happened. I'm as disgusted as you are. But I *am* telling you the truth, so you know how real I am when I say I'm sorry. You have enough information to ruin my life. I'm sure I'm wanted by the police. Della's been missing for twelve years…if her parents even care she's gone. Who knows? They might've been arrested for buying kids for all I know. But what I *do* know is, I love Della. I've loved her since I stole her. But that's all it is. I've never touched her. I've never kissed her inappropriately. I've never thought of her in any way apart from family. She might not be my sister, but I love her as one. And under no circumstances will I allow her to forget that, ever again."

Silence fell, heavier but friendlier than before.

Cassie was the first one to speak. "The brand on your hip. The one you said they put there. It has MC before the number…for Mclary, right?"

I gritted my teeth, cursing that permanent reminder. "Yes."

"And you swear on your life you've never done anything else? Never been tempted? Never gone too far in that one bedroom in the barn?" Her eyes blazed with distrust. "That kiss was the first and the last?"

I thudded a fist over my heart. "I promise on my life."

A thick pause settled around us, cushioning the night.

"I believe you," Patricia finally murmured. "I hear the honesty in what you're saying."

I nodded gratefully. "I'm sorry."

She shook her head kindly. "Nothing to be sorry for. She's young. Just like the day I caught her and Liam naked, she's merely exploring her sexuality and confused on where desire fit in."

I swallowed hard, refusing to let the word desire anywhere near the thought of Della.

John stepped forward, his face weary and wrinkled. "I think you better go. It's late. We'll all get some rest and deal with this in the morning."

"I can't sleep in that bedroom, sir." My voice thickened with urgency. "I...I can't stay here. I need to leave. That's why I'm here. I need you to take care of Della. I'll find another job. I'll pay for her upkeep. But—" I glanced at Cassie's whose eyes glassed with tears. "I don't think it's fair for me to continue trying to be her role model when I'm obviously failing."

"You can't go," Cassie whispered. "That's just stupid."

"I...I don't think I have a choice," I whispered back, wishing I could offer sympathy but sensing that to touch her now would be the worst mistake of my life. I'd always known something deeper lurked beneath Cassie's sweet affection and fierce tumbles in the hay. She pretended it was just casual sex between us, but occasionally, I'd catch that look in her eyes. The one she was giving me now. The look that petrified me because Della gave me the same look, only innocent.

It was love.

And love had hurt me enough.

"I'm sorry." I rolled my shoulders. "To all of you."

Patricia joined John, taking a few steps closer. "Don't be silly, Ren. We love you and Della. We want both of you to stay. Move your things into the hay loft if it will make it easier. We'll arrange for one of the stables to be converted into an extra bedroom. Now that Della knows kissing you is not permitted, things will go back to normal...you'll see. No one needs to leave." Her voice softened. "And besides, who will help John in the fields? You've been the best help we could have ever asked for. You're family, not just an employee, and we won't hear of this nonsense about you leaving."

I was trapped.

Trapped between trying to do the right thing and being given permission to do the wrong one.

I didn't *want* to leave.

The thought of walking away from Della ripped out my guts and left me dying, but how could I ever relax around her again? How could I speak to her without second-guessing if it was too affectionate? How could I ever touch her without fearing I was giving her mixed messages?

The carefree innocence we shared was forever lost.

John came closer and clasped my shoulder with his large, hairy hand. "I don't like that you lied to us, but I know you're a good man, Ren Wild. It's late. Go to bed. I'll come see you in the morning." His eyes flashed with more, but he held his tongue.

With nothing else to do, I murmured goodnight and returned to the barn where I'd assumed Della would be curled up tight in bed. I should've just headed to the hay loft to sleep amongst the grain and grass, but something made me check. Something clawed inside to see...to make sure she was okay.

She'd been just as distraught as I was and had no one to console her.

Part of me was glad she suffered—if it taught her the valuable lesson never to do it again, then so be it. But most of me twisted with agony, knowing she was sad and I hadn't been there to dry her tears and hug away her heartache.

My thoughts were tangled as I snuck into the bedroom, my eyes locking onto Della's bed.

Then nothing else mattered.

Not the kiss.

Not the mess.

Nothing.

Because she wasn't there.

Her bed was empty.

The barn, too.

It took me two minutes to learn that the emptiness inside the place we called home was just the beginning of the emptiness inside me.

I tore apart every hiding place she'd ever used. I galloped over the fields and screamed at the top of my lungs for a reply.

But she wasn't there to answer.

She wasn't there at all.

And now, after pointless wastage of time, trying to decide what I should do, I made the only decision I could.

I couldn't let her be out in the world on her own.

I couldn't forget her and turn my back.

I would *never* forgive myself, just like I would never forgive her for every disastrous consequence she'd caused by kissing me.

What was the *right* thing to do?

The right thing was to chase after her, keep her safe, and bring her back here...to where she belonged. I was the one who should leave.

My hands shook as I hurried to our one piece of furniture and pulled out one of the lined workbooks she'd given me to practice with. The shared dresser beneath our TV held a jumble of hers and my belongings—blending together, just like us.

Her socks on my socks.

Her dresses beneath my shorts.

Even our goddamn clothes liked to be close, and I slammed the drawer with a nauseous roil.

Perching on the edge of my bed, I quickly—or as fast as I could with my chicken scratch—wrote my third apology for the night.

Della had run, and I was about to vanish after her.

There were no times for goodbyes.

Dear John and Patricia,
What can I say?
I have to go after her. It's the only thing I—

"Ren."

My head shot up, my pen skidding across the page.

John stood on the threshold, his face tight and a black dressing gown thrown over his plaid pyjamas. "Can I speak to you?"

I stood, tossing the unneeded letter onto the mattress. "I need to talk to you, too. I'm leaving. She's run away."

"Oh, shit." His eyes turned forlorn as he nodded. "Of course. You must go after her."

I didn't know why he was here, but I was grateful he'd come, if only so he knew why I was about to walk out of his life with no guarantee of coming back.

John stood awkwardly while I yanked up my sheets and ducked to yank my old backpack out from beneath the bed.

Only, it wasn't there. Just a dust-free patch where it used to be, along with a skid mark from where Della had pulled it free.

"Shit," I breathed. *"Shit."*

Clambering upright, I glanced around the room. There was nothing else I could use to carry the supplies we might need.

"Eh, here…this is for you." John cleared his throat. "Take it."

An eerie sense of déjà-vu hit me. Years ago, I'd stood in their guest bedroom as he offered my first salary, and I'd traded it in for Della's well-being.

Now, he held out an even larger envelope.

"What are you doing?" I asked.

"It's the rest of your income and bonuses."

"But I thought you were spending it on Della's education and things?"

"She's in public school, and she costs very little to run with most of our produce coming straight from the garden. If Cassie cost half what she did, I'd be a rich man." He smirked half-heartedly. "Never a day went by that I didn't ensure I was paying you what you were worth. Patricia ran the books. With the bonuses and business increase you helped create, you have more than enough saved to put a deposit on your own place or do whatever you need to do."

My feet locked to the ground. I narrowed my eyes. "Why do I get the feeling this is charity?" Anger tinged my voice. "I'm not some homeless kid anymore. I'm twenty-three. I don't need your—"

"I know you don't, and it's not. This is rightfully yours, and I wouldn't feel right keeping it." The air thickened as he crossed the distance between us and forced it into my hand.

I swallowed as the weight of money settled into my grip.

And then I knew why he'd given it to me.

Tonight would never have had a different ending—regardless if Della had run away or not.

My fingers tightened around the cash. "You're saying goodbye."

John shoved his hands into his dressing gown pockets, looking at the floor. "Patricia is right. We love you like family. You're not just an employee, and I don't want to see you go. I love having you and Della here, and I'm eternally grateful for all your help. But…this is a small town, Ren. I know you said you and Della aren't blood relatives…but that doesn't change facts."

I sighed heavily, feeling disgusted all over again. "I know."

"If people find out. If Della tries it again—"

"She won't," I snapped. "Believe me. When I find her, she'll never wish to kiss another person again."

"That might be." He nodded. "But here, people believe you're brother and sister. If Cassie talks or even if Della talks, you stand a high chance of arrest just from local gossip. You've done well by that girl. No matter what you think, you are a good role model for her. But right now, this place would only hurt you if you stay."

Clutching the wad of money, goosebumps scattered over my arms. "You don't want us to come back."

He smiled sadly. "It's not that I don't want you. Hopefully, one day you'll visit, and things will be back to normal. But for now, you need to be somewhere that hasn't watched you two grow up and already have their perceived realities."

"There *are* no perceived realities." I growled. "There's nothing going on. We *are* brother and sister. No more. No less."

John backed toward the door with a wise smile that irritated and angered me. "Realities can change. I'm not blind. I've seen what's gone on over the years with you and Cassie. I never spoke up because out of all the boyfriends she's had, you were a good influence on her. But I also know it'll break her heart when she wakes up to find you gone tomorrow."

I glanced toward the farmhouse as if I could see through walls and witness Cassie asleep in her bed. "I didn't mean—"

"I know you didn't." He held up his hand. "But that's just who you are, Ren. You care about others so much they feel incredibly special. You give them the clothes off your back. You donate every penny for their benefit. You have no other purpose in life but to support those you care about, and that sort of dedication can be hard not to fall for."

"You're wrong." Guilt squeezed. "I was never that kind to Cassie. And I'm only generous to Della because it's my fault she has no parents—"

"I don't believe that. It sounds as though Della is lucky you took her that night. Her parents are monsters. And you treated Cassie better than most. Don't let that weigh you down. You're a good kid, Ren." He crossed the threshold, shuffling with reluctant steps. "But if I can give you any word of advice for the next few years of raising Della, I would say let her trip up occasionally. Pull back. Let her make mistakes. Let her know you're there for her but don't be her everything. Do that, and this passing phase will be just that—a phase. But if you don't...you'll have trouble."

I stepped toward him, desperate for guidance, while at the same time, wanting to run from any future problems. I just wanted her normal. I wanted things to be normal between *us*. There was no doubt in my mind that I would find her; even now, the urge to chase built every second until I struggled to stay in one spot.

But this was one of those moments that made the hair on the back of my neck stand up with importance. I hadn't been guided in my role as a guardian, and so far, I'd managed to keep her alive but not enforce the rules she badly needed.

I looked up to John, and if he wanted to share a piece of wisdom, then I wanted to listen. "What sort of trouble?" I asked softly. "What am I doing wrong?"

"You're not doing anything wrong. You're doing everything right. Too right. So right, in fact, you're giving her an unrealistic view of the male sex, and when she starts dating, the only person she'll have to compare them to is you, and she'll find them lacking every time." He smiled kindly. "Show her you're human, that you have flaws and a temper just like everyone else. Otherwise..."

"Otherwise what?"

"She won't just use you as an experiment next time. She'll fall in love with you and everything you've built together will vanish because you won't permit her to want you and she won't be able to keep living with something she can't have. You'll break apart, and the surname that links you together as surely as mine does to my wife and children will mean nothing."

He pulled the door to behind him, granting final words that stopped my heart. "Figure out a way to keep her as your sister, Ren. Otherwise, you won't have her at all."

* * * * *

I left Cherry River with far less than I arrived with.

I had no Della, no flu, no backpack, no tent.

All I had was an envelope of cash tucked safely in my waistband with two t-shirts on, a thick jumper, and my winter jacket. In my pockets, I had a spare set of underwear and socks, and on my head, a beanie with sunglasses perched for all types of seasons I might encounter.

John's words kept me company as I crunched down their gravel driveway one last time, turned in the direction my heart tugged me—all the while hoping it was the right choice to find Della—and never looked back.

I struck off into a jog.

My mind locked on finding my runaway Ribbon.

I didn't say goodbye.

Chapter Forty-Four

REN

2013

I LOST HER for two full days.

The first few hours, I wasn't worried.

I figured I knew her enough that she'd head to one of her friend's from school, follow the main road, get tired, and rest along the verge.

That theory was dashed by the time I arrived at the friend's house in question, and her mother informed me with sleepy frustration that there was no reason to get her out of bed at four in the morning because Della wasn't there.

I'd waited until dawn, sitting in their deck chairs on the lawn, waiting to see if Della would turn up, hoping she would, begging her to.

But by the time the sun warmed the world, I had to accept defeat.

She hadn't come this way.

By midmorning, fear crept over my anger, and I no longer thought about her with a thinning of my lips and discipline on my mind but with an ever-fledgling panic. She was no longer the bold girl who'd kissed me without permission. She was a child lost and alone and at the mercy of all manner of creatures.

Most of them men.

Heinous, horrible men who would gladly accept a kiss and so much else.

My heart never fell below a steady race as I jogged through downtown, visited her local familiar hang-outs, and racked my brain for her favourite places and people.

By the time another evening rolled around, I hadn't eaten or drank. I raged on terrified adrenaline. I didn't need fuel because the urgency to find her before another night fell kept me pumped and focused.

I'd exhausted all my options in town.

The next place I had to search was the first place I would've gone but not somewhere I'd expect her to find sanctuary in.

Especially on her own.

Doubling back toward the outskirts of town and keeping my eye on the horizon where Cherry River Farm had once been our home, I traded paved roads for bracken paths and shed off the city veneer I'd worn while living around people.

The forest.

My *real* home.

I relished in letting the wildness inside me take over and lengthened my stride until I covered miles upon miles, ducking around trees, listening for any animals complaining at having a human amongst their midst, doing my best to track her like any good predator would his prey.

But as another night fell, slicing me from Della for a full twenty-four hours, I had to rest.

I slowed to a walk, let my eyes adjust to the crescent moon glow, and padded as quietly as I could, hoping against hope to hear the girl I would die for.

* * * * *

Another morning.

No rest.

No luck.

No Della.

My stomach growled, and my thirst had gotten the better of me around two a.m., making me drink like a beast with hands cupped to my face from the river.

I'd followed the meandering water for a while, hoping Della would be smart and do what I'd taught her.

Anything was survivable as long as you had an abundant water source.

If she wasn't near the river, and she wasn't hiding with friends…where was she?

How would I find her?

How would I keep her safe?

My legs had turned to jelly hours ago, and I half-stumbled, half-jogged forward, always seeking, never finding.

I had no food.

I had no time to find food.

I had a waistband full of money, but it was utterly useless out here in a world of trees and woodland.

If I didn't find her soon, I'd have no choice but to return to civilization and gather supplies. I would turn the pointless dollar bills into practical belongings and never rest until we were back together again.

Another lunchtime and still no sign of her.

No noise.

No hint.

No clue.

I kept pushing forward, calling her name, peering into the hazy green foliage while stripping off overheating jackets and jumpers in the spring heat.

Another evening and still alone.

No progress.

No success.

No reunion.

And by midnight, when darkness thickened to its blackest and day-dwellers traded places with nocturnal, I had no choice but to put myself first, no matter how much it killed me.

My body needed help.

I had to be smart and feed the snarling emptiness in my belly, so I could find a way to repair the howling emptiness in my heart.

It took a few hours to switch direction and leave the river behind.

I cut through small tracks made by mammals and weaved around knobbly trees. I fell over at one point, almost too exhausted to stand, but I found my final reserves, hauling myself onward into an energy depleting march.

And lucky I did.

Because at the point when I was closest to giving up, that was the moment I found her.

Chapter Forty-Five

DELLA

Present Day

NOW...BEFORE YOU judge me...
Let's talk about that kiss for a second.
It was wrong; I know that.
It was morally gross; I know that, too.
It was all manners of bad, considering I took advantage of the boy who'd dedicated his entire life to making sure I was happy, cared for, and safe. I plotted silently in the dark; I willingly waited until his breathing changed and I knew he was asleep before I swallowed back the guilt, the nerves, and the shame to press my mouth to his.
I know everything I did was wrong, okay?
So you don't need to tell me how majorly I screwed up. The instant his lips softened beneath mine, and I felt something I'd never felt when kissing Liam, I'd known just how terribly I'd screwed up.
Hugely.
Monstrously.
Life-ruiningly.
When his mouth parted, and the sweetest, heaviest sigh escaped him, and his hand came up to twine possessively in my hair, I knew I would forever punish myself for doing something so far out of permission.
Not because Ren kissed me back.
Not because he tasted so perfect or the quick flick of his tongue made a fireball ignite in my lower belly, but because, in that fleeting moment when my eyes grew heavy and I closed them to concentrate on kissing someone I never should have kissed, I grew up in an instant.
I felt things no girl should feel.
I understood things no child would know.

And I condemned myself because, as fast and as innocent as the kiss had been, it had showed me that I would never be allowed the one thing I wanted with all my heart.

Again, this is where my past knits with my present, and I can't explain the true feelings I had then because they're so tangled with my current heartache that it's hard to distinguish the two.

What I can tell you is I didn't need to be punished because I'd punished myself. I didn't need to be told how wrong it was because I'd already whipped and cursed and shouted at myself. And I didn't need anyone to tell me that it could never happen again because the moment my lips touched his…I knew.

I knew he was off limits.

I knew he would never be mine.

And the pain…ouch, even as a thirteen-year-old, it was excruciating.

Now that I'm eighteen and I've lived with that pain daily, pretending that I only think of him as my friend, convincing him—and sometimes myself—that he is far too precious to me to ever risk another idiotic move like that—I know in my heart of hearts, I don't have much left.

God, it hurts so bad just saying that.

No amount of chest rubbing or false soothing can cut away the pain growing like a cancer inside me.

I'm an adult now.

And that means I no longer officially need him.

And because I no longer officially need him, I can move away.

I can cut ties.

I can put distance between us so our interactions will reduce to what normal families with children leaving the nest reduce to: the odd holiday gathering, the occasional phone call, a half-hearted text every other day.

I will be safe from ever being this wretched every time I look at him, smell him, laugh with him, adore him.

If I don't do something soon, then my entire life is going to be destroyed. I'll never find someone I can fall for. I'll never be able to love another the way they deserved to be loved.

Those two days when I ran—the days when Ren couldn't find me—were days I needed to glue shattered pieces back together in the best order I could. It was time I needed to talk to my younger self and tell her that she had her entire life in front of her and there would be plenty of other boys to kiss, to fall in love with, to want with such desire.

I wasn't ready.

Ren would never be ready.

Therefore, it could never happen.

I'd spent a night in a friend's house who I knew was overseas, and I happened to know where the spare key lived. I'd had the place to myself, but I hadn't slept or relaxed. I'd used the space and minutes wisely, doing my best to carve out the mess I'd made of my heart and return to the Della I'd been before I'd crept over to his bed in the dark.

I'd stared into mirror after mirror, desperate to reverse the time to when I didn't destroy myself or him.

I'd stared into my eyes.

I'd clutched the ribbon from my hair.

And I'd made a vow that Ren will never know.

I knew he would find me.

He would discipline me.

He would forgive me.

And I also knew, despite all of that, I would make him believe it was all a terrible mistake. I would sell my lies. I would believe my untruths. I would do everything required to make it all go away, because he must never know that kissing him might've been the worst thing I'd ever done, but it was also the best, the realest, the most truest thing I'd ever felt, and I would never apologise for that.

I would beg for his forgiveness purely to ensure our relationship was back where it belonged, and I would nurse my dirty secrets to protect him for a change.

I've failed at many things in my life, but I'm happy to tell you, I've never once broken my vow. I've been protecting him from that secret for years. I've been lying to him every minute of the day.

And now I'm exhausted, and writing this all down has shown the conclusion I didn't want to face: I'm not ready to say goodbye.

I'll never be ready but if I don't, how can I ever move on?

Chapter Forty-Six

REN

2013

"DELLA…"

Her head snapped up from where she'd been snoozing, sitting up against a tree stump. Her eyes blinked away drowsiness, slipping from joy at seeing me to guarded with trepidation.

She should be nervous.

Now that I knew she was in one piece and not molested or dead, my panic transformed into the hottest rage I'd ever felt. The catalyst of fury replaced my insides, making my nostrils flare with hot breath and temper fire with cruel words. *"Della."*

Before, her name had been a prayer of thanks. Now it was a curse of condemnation.

She scrambled to her feet, her head bowed, contrition all over her. "Before you say anything…I'm sorry." Glancing at me between strands of curling blonde, she breathed, "I'm sorry for doing something I shouldn't. I'm sorry for running away. I'm sorry I made you worry." She licked her lips, shrugging. "I'm…just very sorry, for everything."

Her apology tried to douse my anger, but I didn't let it.

Stalking the distance between us, I crunched over twigs and foliage, coming to a trembling stop in front of her. She was no longer as short as I remembered. No longer as young. She stood subservient and entirely ready to be scolded, but her eyes burned with the same sort of fire that hissed inside me.

A fire that did its best to confuse and convince me that she didn't deserve to be told off when it was the only thing she *did* deserve. She needed goddamn boundaries, and she seemed deaf to them unless I shouted.

My hands curled, doing my best to keep control. "Are you hurt?"

I'd wanted to yell, but somehow, my fear made me check she was capable of withstanding the violence I itched to give her first. My palms burned to strike. To imprint some sort of punishment for everything she'd done.

Hoisting the backpack—*my* backpack—up her shoulders, she shook her head. She'd dressed in jeans and a thick knitted jumper with her winter jacket tucked through the straps of the rucksack. "No."

Despite studying her appearance and finding no blood or broken bones to say she was lying, I took another step closer.

Her eyes flared then dropped to the ground again, giving me permission to nurse my terrible temper. "Where the hell were you?"

"At a friend's." Her voice was small. "I knew they weren't there, and I needed somewhere on my own...just for a little while."

"Didn't you think I needed somewhere, too? To figure out what the fuck you were playing at?"

She flinched.

I'd never used such foul language toward her until the moment she kissed me.

She fucking *kissed* me!

I couldn't control my rage's spit and snarl or the pain she'd caused. "You could've been hurt, Della. You could've been kidnapped or raped or killed. Did you stop to think about that, at least? Because I know you didn't stop to think before you fucking *kissed* me."

She bit her lip, shaking her head.

Weak from hunger and strung out from everything strange and wrong, I growled. "How could you, huh? What the *hell* possessed you to do something so sick?" Not waiting for answers, I paced away, snapping incoherent things. "You're so goddamn young. You're still a kid. And I'm...I'm ten years older. If that wasn't enough, we're *family*, Della. Do you know what that means? It means you love each other, but you don't fall *in* love with each other. You've taken everything that was so right between us and destroyed it because how can I trust you to understand the difference? How can I ever touch you again? How can I ever relax around you again?"

I slammed to a stop, breathing hard, facing her with spread helpless hands. "How can we ever go back to the way things were?" Pressure built behind my eyes as I stared at the girl I loved more than life itself. The girl who'd cracked my heart. The girl who would forever have the power to break me just like she'd broken me two nights ago and every hour in-between. "Do you even know the difference between platonic love and romantic? Is it my fault that I never explained the two? Have I failed you, Della?"

I was starving for food and affection.

I was thirsty for water and someone to assure me that it would all be okay. That I could have my Ribbon back. That I wouldn't have to worry if I touched her hand or brushed a kiss on her temple. That I wouldn't ruin her by making her believe that I wanted her the way a man wants a woman when I would *never* do that.

She was mine.

She was every hope and dream I'd ever had and the fabrication of every future I'd hoped for, and if I had to say goodbye to that...

Fuck.

I cleared the squeezing misery away and coughed into the night. "I...I miss you so fucking much, yet you're standing right there."

She sucked in a pained gasp, tears welling and overflowing in a second. Wriggling out of the backpack, she sprinted toward me before it even hit the ground.

With a rush of force, she ran into me, wrapping her arms around my waist, pressing her cheek against my chest. "Ren."

Two things happened.

One, no thought was required.

This was Della.

I'd hugged her a thousand—no, a million times before, and my body recognised hers as if it was a part of me—a part I'd lost but now had found, and it hurt almost as much welcoming it back as it was to lose it.

My body rejoiced at having her home in my embrace, and I clutched her so damn hard. I curled around her, inhaling her hair and smelling foreign shampoo. I pressed my lips to her head, but then the memories returned.

The dream figments.

The real yearnings.

The forbidden responses she'd drawn from me.

Shoving her back, I held up my hand, keeping distance between us. "You've even managed to ruin a hug."

She choked on a sob, hugging herself with fierce sadness. "I know."

You've made this impossible for me, Little Ribbon."

"I know that, too."

Silence slithered between us, letting her tears fall and regret ice over my temper, until we both stood drained and empty with no place else to go.

Finally, I sighed. "I knew keeping you would be full of complications. I lived an almost daily battle when you were young not to hurt you and an even bigger war as you grew older. I've leaned on you so much. I've taken all you've had to give. And I've given you the illusion that what we share is normal. That our closeness is what others have when it's not." I looked at her, wanting to burn her with the truth. "I've never had anyone. I had no love until you taught me what it was, and even as I slowly learned the opposite of hate, I've known all along that love would end up hurting me the most." I laughed sadly. "I was right."

Her spine rolled, letting my words whip her.

I breathed hard, completely drained and ready to leave this place, to leave behind these harsh truths and put everything back into the dark where it belonged. "Come on," I whispered, "I'll take you home."

Her eyes flicked to mine with blue surprise beneath black remorse. "How can we go back? I thought Cassie called the police."

I shoved my hands into my back pockets, adjusting the wad of cash stored in my waistband. "I spoke to them. They didn't call anyone. You'll stay with them."

"But...what about you?"

"I can't go back. Not anymore."

"No!" Her cheeks dotted with urgency. "I'm not going back without you."

"You have no choice."

"I do. I *do* have a choice!"

Her anger ignited mine all over again. "Like you had a choice when you kissed me?"

Her lips twisted, and her beautiful face warred with letting me remind her of her mistakes and fighting for forgiveness. "I said I was sorry."

"It's not fucking good enough. You should never have been so stupid!"

"I'll never do it again."

"Also not good enough. How can I ever trust you?"

"You can. You *can* trust me."

I shook my head sadly. "I thought I could. And I did. I trusted you with my life."

"And I trust you with mine." She wrung her fingers, twisting and tugging. Her blue eyes darkened as some sort of resolution shoved aside her despair. "I know things will be strained between us for a while. I get that. And I also get that I'm a danger to you—that I did something outside of your control. I also get how wrong it was, and that to outsiders, it will never be permitted."

"Not just to outsiders," I snapped. "*I* will never permit such things. *Ever.* Do you hear me?"

"Yes."

"Say you understand why it will never happen again."

"Because we're family."

My heart pounded at the word. For a second, I wished she *wasn't* family. I wished we'd never met, so this lacerating torture would never find me. But then, the thought of living in a world where I didn't have Della…

Fuck.

I'd rather be dead.

But that was my future now. I had to leave her behind. I had to walk away. She had somewhere to go home to, and I did not. Our lives were about to go in separate directions. I would miss her with every tormented heartbeat, but I would rather stay away if I was the reason for her confusion.

"Family don't hurt each other," I managed to say even though I almost choked on the lie. My own family had traded me for dollars. Perhaps that was why I'd failed Della? I had no decent role models of my own.

Della tucked unruly hair behind her ear as she stood straighter. "Can I say something?"

I narrowed my eyes warily.

When I didn't give permission, she ploughed on anyway, "I kissed you—"

"Stop." I cringed, falling back a step.

Before I could interrupt her with another scathing telling off, she added, "I shouldn't have done it, Ren. I *know* that. I've learned that lesson, and believe me, I know it will never happen again.

And, if I could do it all over again, obviously, I would never have done it…but I *did* do it. It happened. I can't undo it. I can't change it. And…well, I'm *glad* I did it."

My mouth hung open in disgusted shock. "*What* did you say?"

"I said I'm glad I kissed you." Her tears dried up, and every readable emotion on her face vanished beneath a cool veneer.

I fumbled with the change in her, hating the wall between us, cursing the sudden opaqueness I couldn't see behind. "What the hell has gotten into you? First, you do something you know is wrong and then you take back any apology—"

"I didn't say I'm not still sorry," she grumbled. "I said I'm glad it happened."

I spread my hands in surrender. "Please enlighten me because you've successfully confused the shit out of me."

Once again, she flinched at my cursing, but the blank shield on her face stopped me from reading anything else.

Standing tall and kissed by moonlight, she said, "I don't regret it because it gave me all the lessons you just mentioned."

"I-I still don't understand."

She sighed as if it cost her to explain. "You asked me if I knew the difference between platonic love and romantic. I thought I did. I've spoken to Cassie about her boyfriends. I know how sex works and what desire is. But learning theory is different to actual experiences."

She sucked in a breath, looking to the side as if to smooth out her tale with a script hidden from view. "In class, my teachers always encouraged us to learn with first-hand knowledge. They don't just let us read the textbook. They make us do stuff. Just like you do. You explained how to drive the tractor but until you let me change the gears and operate the thing, I didn't know what you meant."

Her argument was too well thought out. Too rehearsed. Too understandable. I hated that my hackles faded under a logical explanation.

"Love isn't the same as driving a tractor, Della."

"But don't you see?" She stepped closer. "It's exactly like that."

I schooled myself not to move, not to run as her body heat touched mine.

She looked up into my eyes. "I wanted to know the difference. And now, I do. I know you are my friend and my family. That kiss proved it. I felt nothing but warm love like I always do for you. There was nothing special from that kiss to any other we've shared over the years. I've kissed you on the lips before. Just like you've kissed me. Those weren't big deals, and this shouldn't be either."

Her voice sped up as if her carefully thought-out debate had reached the end, but she wasn't quite finished with convincing me. "I know the difference, Ren. And I know things are gonna be strange, but they'll go back to the way things were because nothing has changed. I promise. I'm still Della, and you're still Ren. I'm growing up now, and soon, you won't have to worry so much about me. I won't do anything bad, and I'll be on my best behaviour. You'll see. Just please…please…don't send me back to Cherry River if you're not coming. I know I made you mad, but I don't want to live with Cassie and Liam on my own. I want…I want to come with you. Please. Please say you'll forgive me, and we'll stay together."

Her chin tipped down as a glimpse of tangled things on her face hinted that her deliverance cost her. That there were other things. Deeper things. Scarier things inside her that she'd hidden.

The fact that she was old enough to be complex and have the ability to shield and reveal rather than blurt everything made wariness fill my blood.

What was she hiding?

What wasn't she saying?

I didn't trust her.

Not anymore.

Even if every part of me agreed with her that we'd been close in the past and affectionate in our actions, and those hadn't filled me with terror. Even if every inch howled at the thought of walking away when I truly didn't want that.

I wanted to stay with her.

I never wanted to say goodbye.

"This is too hard." I scrubbed my face with my hands. My stomach growled for the hundredth time, reminding me that making life-changing decisions with no food normally always led to bad ones.

Della stayed silent as if knowing I was in the middle of a seesaw. A lean in either direction, and the choice would crash to the ground.

The forest stayed silent and hushed. No creatures moved. No leaves rustled. We were utterly alone—away from judgment and history and the Wilsons who knew far too much about us.

This mistake was between Della and me, and, hopefully, with her promise never to do it again and my vow to make sure it never did, we could eventually find our way back to normal.

We could find another place to call home.

"What about school?" I asked quietly.

Just that one question showed her where my mind was. That I'd already come to terms with leaving. That I'd already agreed to take her with me.

She barrelled into me again, squeezing me tight. "Thank you, thank you, *thank you*." Her breath heated my t-shirt and chest.

I patted her shoulders awkwardly, prying her off me to look into her face.

The innocent girl was back.

The veiled mask was gone.

If she had any secrets, they'd sank far inside her, and I stood no chance at figuring them out now.

"Are you sure you want to leave behind your friends? Cassie? Liam?"

She nodded. "If you can't go back, then yes."

"And school? What about that?"

"I'll go to another one." She smiled. "I had to change anyway. I'm in high school now. This was my last term."

"Oh."

"But—I don't have to go back," she rushed. "I can get a job, too. I can pay my way—"

"Don't even think such things. You're finishing school, Della. University too if that's what you want."

She smiled with familiar love and devotion. "Okay."

"Okay." I smiled back, still not appeased and still tormented, but at least, for now, I didn't have to tear us apart.

That would come later.

"Come on." I strode toward the backpack forgotten on the ground. "I'm starving."

Chapter Forty-Seven

REN

2013

I'D LIKE TO say things went back to normal easily.

They didn't.

After that first night, where we headed to an all-night gas station and filled up with lukewarm Hot Pockets and processed snack foods, Della and I kept our distance.

We walked side by side but didn't touch.

We talked and laughed but didn't relax.

And when the sun rose on a new day and the decision to leave this place and the people who knew us as the Wilds cemented into reality, we headed to the local supermarket, filled the backpack full of provisions, checked over our old tent and sleeping bag, and traded some cash for another sleeping bag, rucksack, and a few other travel requirements for Della at the only camping store in town.

It felt strange not to steal the stuff we needed, even after years of earning an honest living. It felt even stranger breaking habits and saying goodbye to familiar landmarks that had been our constant for so long.

Not strange bad. Strange *good*.

I hated how easily I turned my back on everything. How I merely walked out of the Wilsons lives without a backward glance—focused only on finding Della. And now that I'd found her, I didn't care where we went.

I didn't think about Cassie.

I didn't worry about leaving John or Patricia without an employee.

Della was home to me, and there was something infinitely perfect just being the two of us again.

She might have upset me, messed up my mind, and ruined my trust, but nothing could change the fact that where she was, I was happiest, and she was all I needed.

I didn't know how to change that. And I didn't know how to make Della see that just because she was my everything, it didn't mean I wanted to be hers.

She needed to want others. That was part of life. John had advised me on such things.

His gruff voice echoed regularly in my ears: *"Show her you're human with flaws. Figure out a way to keep her as your sister, Ren. Otherwise, you won't have her at all."*

He was wrong when he said she'd ever feel more than a family bond for me. She'd told me herself, and despite my guardedness on her explanation, I tended to believe her.

She was ten years my junior, and I saw her as fresh-faced innocent and far too young to share the sort of relationship I wanted. But I'd forgotten something important. There were two sides to everything, and I'd failed to see how she must view me.

I'd been stuck-up to think she'd want me in any other way than as a guardian.

She had to be telling the truth because at ten years her elder, I was boring and surly and far too old to share the sort of fledgling romance she would eventually seek.

I didn't need to show her I was human.

She knew who and what I was.

She knew me better than anyone, and when the time came for her to meet another boy, then I'd show her exactly how flawed I was by interrogating the hell out of him before he could go near her.

John was incorrect.

Della loved me.

But it wasn't wrong or tainted. It was just as it had always been, and as the roles we'd played faded from view, and we turned toward the forest instead of the farm, I was grateful we were leaving.

Grateful to delete past expectations and remove outsider's opinions because no matter that they came from a good place, they didn't know us...not really.

No one truly knew the lives of another.

That was why I liked being alone, and by the time we reached the outskirts of the forest with our stuffed backpacks and wanderlust bubbling in our veins, I gave Della one last chance. One final choice—to admit this was truly what she wanted.

To run just like I'd done from the Mclary's.

To turn her back on everything and start new.

Unlike the last time we'd lived in the forest, Della had her own backpack with extra tools and equipment and would be expected to pull her weight. Our tiny tent would be a struggle, but at least we had separate sleeping bags. Washing in rivers would come with strict privacy, and dinners would be a chore shared by both of us.

This wasn't a vacation. This was real life. It would be hard. It would be constant. From here on out, we would be homeless until we found a new place to stay.

I needed her to understand that.

For her to accept the burden of running from people who cared because once we said goodbye, that was it.

"Are you sure?" I asked, glancing at the wind ruffling her butterscotch hair.

She didn't look at me, keeping her gaze on the beckoning trees. "I'm sure."

"Okay, then."

For better or for worse, we didn't look back as we vanished into the wilderness and said goodbye to civilization.

* * * * *

Unlike the other camping trips we'd taken over the many summers at Cherry River, this was different. What we carried was all we owned in the world. What we gathered as we wandered was all the food we'd have for that night or the next.

And slowly, gradually, the stress of living around people faded.

As a day turned into a week, and Della gave me no reason to worry, I smiled a little easier. I laughed a little louder. I didn't wince when she touched me in passing and didn't freeze when she pressed a kiss to my cheek.

The fear that she'd overstep grew less and less as our bond returned to what it had always been.

If anything, things grew better between us.

Different, yes.

Older and more grown-up, but still connected.

Before, when the stars woke and darkness descended, Della had been too young to talk before exhaustion put her to sleep.

Now, she stayed up late with me.

She was older, and I finally had no choice but to see the changes in her. To notice the roundness of hips and swell of breasts. She could've become a stranger as she lost her childish angles if it wasn't for the blue ribbon she still wore either in her hair, around her wrist, or in a bow around her neck.

I still recognised the girl I'd raised thanks to the untouched joy she showed when I agreed to tell her a story, and the unsullied sound of pure happiness when I made her laugh.

Della was still Della, despite my fears of losing her, and after we'd eaten and banked the fire for the night, we lay side by side squished in our tiny tent.

As our legs brushed and breaths found the same rhythm, our natural freedom and ease with each other erased the residual mess and balance returned.

Nothing felt forced.

Nothing felt hidden.

Our ages didn't matter as much out here, only our ability to survive.

By the end of the third week, I stopped bringing up the fact that we needed to find somewhere so she could return to school. I accepted, after multiple convincing from her, that the term was almost over, and she could slip into any educational system with her current grades with no problems.

I wanted to share her optimism, but we didn't have birth records or passports or even a place to stay to enrol her. Without John and Patricia's help, I didn't know how I'd get her into class without people asking too many questions. However, I couldn't shatter her dream and figured I'd solve that complication when we got to it.

For now, we agreed to spend the summer in the forest, remembering our old way of life.

Most days, we travelled a few miles before setting up another camp. Others, we stayed in a glen and swam and sun-baked.

Once a month, she'd turn extremely private, popping painkillers and staying subdued.

At first, I worried she was sick. But by the second time, I knew.

Della was no longer a child.

Her body was an adult, even if it hadn't fully grown into one.

I offered her sympathy and tried to help with her period pain, but unlike most times where she wanted my company, she wanted nothing to do with me.

When things passed, our bond would snap right back into place and life would be simple again. Hiking, exploring, swimming.

Della hadn't packed a swimsuit, but she didn't argue when I made her wear a t-shirt and underwear before getting wet. I made sure she was never around when I bathed, and I averted my eyes whenever she'd strip—sometimes catching me unaware with flashes of her perfect skin.

We shared tasks on building a fire or erecting the tent or preparing food, and overall, the lifestyle we shared was much easier now she was older and offered more help than hindrance.

For two glorious months, we travelled on back-roads and explored the stunning countryside. Occasionally, we'd stumble onto a campsite tucked high in the hills, or hear trampers in the distance, treading the trails we'd become so sure footed on.

The money stuffed safe in my backpack wasn't needed as I allowed every aspect of our lives before the Wilsons to return—including stealing.

I didn't take from those who had nothing and did my best to only pinch a few things. Items like toothpaste and deodorant, canned food and another lighter…things that didn't cost the large supermarkets much money but kept us healthy and fed.

Della asked me to teach her the art of thievery, but that was one thing I refused. I'd teach her anything she wanted—skinning rabbits, setting traps, sharpening knives, making fires—but never stealing.

There was too much risk.

And she was far too precious to get caught.

She might not need me as much as she once did, but I still had a role to play in her life.

A role I would gladly uphold until my dying breath.

To protect her.

At all costs.

Even if it meant protecting her from herself.

Chapter Forty-Eight

DELLA

Present Day

CRAZY HOW LIFE *can change so fast, right?*
How days can blend into months, and seasons can flow into years.
That was what happened with us.

Leaving behind Cherry River was sad. Some days, I missed Patricia, John, the horses, our one bedroom, Liam, and even Cassie so much, I almost asked Ren to turn around. To admit I'd made a mistake, and I wanted to go back.

I'd never stopped to notice just how privileged I'd been living there— learning to ride, running around in open fields, swimming in creeks, and attending a school that actually nurtured my dreams instead of ruined them.

I missed it.

But as much as I missed them, I would miss Ren more, and he was no longer welcome there.

Because of me.

I'd made it impossible to go back.

I'd taken away so much from both of us.

The guilt that caused was a daily passenger. Unfortunately, I had a steep learning curve to find there were many layers of guilt. Some days, I suffered shame. Some nights, I wallowed in disgrace. Others, I wanted to flog myself with blame and dishonour and somehow purge the skin-crawling chiding that I'd done something irrevocably wrong.

I'd been selfish, and stupid, and as much as I regretted everything we'd lost, I was just as guilty for being grateful for everything we'd gained as much as I was for losing it.

For the rest of summer and most of autumn, I had Ren all to myself.

He no longer left before I was awake to work on the farm. He no longer stayed out till dark doing chores and feeling responsible for the paddocks and meadows left in his care.

He lost the edgy hardness of being relied upon and returned to the serious, wild boy I remembered.

Every story he shared. Every laugh he indulged in. I remembered how to love him purely without any of the mess I'd caused. Some weeks, I honestly didn't remember why I'd risked everything by kissing him.

What was I thinking? I'd muse.

Eww, how gross. I'd conclude.

I merely saw him as Ren—the farmyard boy who I'd watched make out with Cassie, go through chicken pox, and get all stuffy with the flu.

But then...other days...a switch would flip inside me, and I'd struggle to see him as family and only saw things I shouldn't.

Forbidden things.

Things that had the potential not only to get me in trouble but to steal Ren from me forever.

I'd focused on the glisten of his sweat, and instead of thinking he needed a bath, I'd think how salty he would taste. I'd watched him break off dead tree limbs for our fire and instead of worrying he'd hurt himself, I only noticed how strong he was. How his arms bunched and his belly clenched and how everything about him was virile and perfect and just begging to be touched.

Things were alive inside me. Heat and hunger.

Sometimes, he'd look at me before I could bury my feelings and he'd freeze. His eyes would lock on mine, understanding the look of naked need even if he didn't want to.

I'd swallow it all down, let my hair curtain my eyes, and pretend all over again that things were normal and I wasn't drowning beneath right and wrong.

One dawn, when Ren slept beside me in our tiny tent, he rolled toward me as he sometimes did and gathered me close. I couldn't help myself. I let myself be gathered, melting into the way his front cradled my back.

He was asleep. I was awake. I knew who was innocent and who was not, but it didn't stop me from wriggling closer, my belly tightening as Ren's hips jutted forward with something hard and—

Yep, stopping right there.

I can't write the horror of what happened when I gasped and woke him up. How he'd ripped himself away from me. How he'd thrown himself out of the tent and refused to talk to me for the rest of the day.

It was yet another incident swept away, dirtying our relationship in ways I didn't know how to clean.

In fact, this whole chapter I should delete, but ugh, I don't like editing, and this is so close to being burned anyway.

I won't litter the rest of this assignment with teenage awareness of how his normally comforting face was suddenly a treasure trove of harsh jawlines, straight noses, and black eyelashes. I'm not gonna remember the beard he grew or the fact that it wasn't patchy like before but full and rugged and—

Why do I do this to myself?

Why do I insist on slicing through the sticky tape on my constantly breaking heart and stabbing it over and over again?

Can you answer me because I'm honestly at the end of my limit.

I know I can't have him.

I made him believe I don't want him.

Yet…I can't forget him.

I just want him to go back to being Ren.

So why won't that happen?!

God, you're no use.

This is a waste of time.

You know what? I'm done.

This is beyond stupid. It's become a mess of words and boring.

I'd get an F for this if I turned it in.

These secrets are just stupid really. I'm sure other people have the same issues. I'm not special. Just because I've been in love with someone I shouldn't be for almost a decade doesn't mean I can justify my heartache to you.

Ugh!

Okay, that's it.

No more.

Nice knowing you, assignment.

Deleting…

* * * * *

So…I'm back.

Yesterday was a bad day.

I always have bad days remembering the forest in-between the Wilsons and what happened next. Probably because it was the last time we laughed together. The last time we could sleep side by side—when Ren wasn't hunched against the tent to avoid me—and not have every other shit I caused become a third wheel between us.

God, I don't want to write this anymore.

Not because I'm afraid of bad grades because that no longer matters, but because the end is coming. The end of everything, and the end of what I can tell you.

But before I can write those two little words and be done with this horrible excuse of literature, I have to tell you what happened in the next five years of my life.

I have to tell you why our fourth separation has lasted the longest.

I have to tell you why it's my fault.

And I have to tell you why Ren will never forgive me even though he did in the forest.

I did something even worse than kissing him.

Wow, I didn't think words had the power to make me tear up and tremble, but they did. Clever, huh? I'm making myself insane. I'm dragging everything into the light that I've done my best to keep buried in the dark.

Let's see how my hands shake typing it again. Let's do it in bold, shall we? Just for even more dramatic effect…

I did something even worse than kissing him.

Yep, that got my heart galloping.

Bet you're wondering what the hell I could do, right?

What else could I possibly do to destroy everything I ever cared about? I'm sure you can probably imagine.

Maybe I should just let you imagine and not finish. My heart is done. I'm drained. I'm tired. I've been tired for far too long, and this is just ripping me into pieces.

All I know is, I can't write what happened in the forest.

All I can tell you is it was the best time of my life. It makes me miss him with a clawing, violent need that drives me mad. The freedom of living day to day. The joy at starlit nights full of talking and the lazy mornings with chirping birds.

It was total innocence.

Maybe one day, I'll be able to write a short story on the afternoons that stand out or try to describe the rose-coloured happiness and sun-warmed bliss we lived in. Maybe, I'll do a poem or haiku on how my love evolved all over again from crush to tenderness to fevered yearning.

Or maybe I won't.

Either way, it doesn't change how wonderful those few months were.

Ren and I found our way back to each other, and I wish, wish, wish we could've stayed in the trees and never come out. I've cried myself to sleep more times than I can count to stay in that joyful place and never slip into the Della I became.

But…it happened.

Winter found us, ice crept toward us, and snow drove us from our heaven back to hell.

And the stopwatch started ticking, inching me closer to the day when I would be alone.

The day when Ren would walk out of my life.

The day when everything would be broken.

Because I'm still here…alone…writing this sorry excuse of a story, pretending I can conjure him from nothing, desperately loving a memory, and killing myself with the knowledge that no matter how much I write about him. No matter what tales I tell you or secrets I spill, he's not going to be there to tell me off. He's not going to scold me for telling the truth. He's not going to notice or care.

I no longer need to pretend I don't love him.

I don't need to lie that I don't want him.

Can you guess why?

I've been lying to you, too, didn't you know?

I made you believe he stuck by me. That he would never abandon me no matter what disasters I caused.

But that is another lie.

Probably the biggest one.

Because Ren Wild…he's gone.

He left me.

And he's never coming back.

Chapter Forty-Nine

REN

2015

FOR TWO YEARS, things were back to normal.

It was just me and Della against the world, but I wouldn't lie and say I didn't think about what had happened between us.

Della had shown me two sides of herself in those few days that I hadn't seen before or since. Sure, there'd been a few incidents in the forest: a few heated looks, an early morning embrace that had been instinct and not thought, and even a couple of fierce arguments.

But we'd ironed out the kinks and found a new acceptable.

As time went on, problems were few and far between.

And that worried me.

Della had revealed she wasn't just the simple blonde angel I'd raised and adored, but a girl with evolving needs; a trickster who could hide behind a mask and successfully keep her secrets.

Lately, she'd been too amenable—none of her usual fire or willingness to get into trouble for speaking her mind. But no matter how many times I caught myself studying her and no matter how often I tensed in her embraces, there was never anything more to her affection. No tension or undercurrent.

Just natural, sinless love.

It was the same as it had always been: given freely, kindly, wholeheartedly, but most of all, purely with no underlying contraband.

Her smiles were innocently genuine.

Her touches appropriately platonic.

I did my best to relax, but no matter how normal things

became between us, I couldn't let it go. A niggle was always there, searching her actions and tones, knowingly putting a barrier between us that I didn't want.

She knew the wall was there, just like I did.

But we never addressed it, never tried to bulldoze it, and as time marched on, we learned to live with it. We accepted that the wariness would never fully dissolve and had become a fracture in our otherwise perfect relationship.

I hated it.

I hated that I'd lost the child I loved with all my heart and been traded a girl who had the terrifying capacity to destroy me.

Maybe it was all in my mind.

Perhaps the late-night dreams of phantom kisses with a woman I couldn't claim was turning me mad. Maybe I'd been ruined all along and that was why I could never give myself to Cassie.

Whatever caused my vigilance, I never found any reason to be suspicious.

Guilt drowned me because how could I pretend to trust Della, when night after night, I was waiting to catch her? And catch her in what, exactly? A confession that she actually loved me in a completely different way to what was allowed? A hint that she felt just as scrambled and confused as I did and couldn't find her way back to innocence?

At least, we still had each other.

That was all that mattered.

We fought against winter for as long as we could, but eventually, the icy winds and snowy chill drove us from our sanctuary and back into the cities we despised.

It took us a few weeks to adjust being around people again. And another few to figure out the rules as we navigated our way into well-oiled society where finding somewhere to stay meant paying rent and paying rent meant finding work and getting work meant providing references.

I had cash for a down payment on a rental, and I learned on the job how to walk into letting agencies, ask to view a place, and tolerate being chauffeured around, guided through the home in question, and sold on every benefit.

Even though Della and I had lived with the Wilsons, gone into town, and been around public before, this was on an entirely different level.

We couldn't hide behind the Wilsons anymore. We couldn't

rely on them to find us a place to stay or talk to the smarmy salespeople on our behalf. I couldn't work my ass off and ask someone I trusted to buy everything we'd need. I had to pre-empt Della's requirements with school uniforms and stationery. I had to plan groceries and living locations so she could get to school safely without a long commute.

There were no empty farmhouses for us to borrow. No perfect villages where we could happily live off the scraps unseen.

It suffocated me, seeking places to live where no trees grew or rivers ran. My brain battled daily with my heart, forcing me to give up house hunting and focusing on why we were there.

School.

Della had to go to the best school possible.

That was the reason.

And I clutched it hard even when finding a good school proved to be as much as a challenge as finding a home.

Della helped and researched online. She narrowed her results to two, and together, we walked from our hidden shack we'd commandeered as our winter abode on the edge of a campground, and did our best to hide the fact that we were still homeless.

The cracked weatherboards and grimy windows hadn't been maintained, but it had a small stove for the extra blizzard-filled nights and it kept us from freezing to death.

It didn't help with our bathing arrangements—having to melt snow and scrub down with the other person shivering outside to grant privacy, but at least the clothes I'd bought were fresh and new and Della's hair shone gold and her eyes glowed with intelligence.

Any school would be lucky to have her.

And thanks to her skills, she managed to enrol into an all girl's high school by acing the entrance exam and telling the headmaster to call her last school for her file.

I hadn't thought to do that and used the trick when we finally found a cheap one-bedroom place three blocks away, asking the listing agent to call Cherry River Farm and ask John Wilson for a reference.

They did.

And whatever he told them ensured within the week Della attended a new school and I'd moved our meagre backpacks into a bare essential, unfurnished apartment and chewed through a chunk of my savings paying bond, first month's rent, and Della's tuition fees.

Della and I transformed its empty spaces into a semi-liveable home, thanks to flea market bargains and the odd furniture found on street corners.

I'd achieved more than I had in my life.

I'd dealt with people and hadn't been recognised for being a runaway slave or for being the man who stole Della Mclary. My fears of being taken and sold were still strong, even though I was no longer a boy, and I preferred not to be too close or talk too long to anyone.

All winter, Della caught the local bus to school, bundled up in the thickest jacket, mittens, and hats I could afford, and returned straight after class ended.

I didn't mind she didn't make friends straight away. In fact, I was glad because it meant I had her company when I returned from work after toiling away at a local building site, and we spent the evenings together with our second-hand TV, street-salvaged couch, and snuggled under a shared blanket watching whatever was on.

The job I scored wasn't perfect and didn't pay well, but it meant I could keep a roof over our heads and dinner on our table without having to hunt and gut it first.

I never grumbled as I lugged timber and dug holes.

I was the bitch on the site, gathering tools and doing the chores no one else wanted to do. The foreman who gave me the cash job said I got the dregs because I wasn't a skilled builder, but I knew it was because I refused to drink with the guys or let them get to know me.

I didn't *want* people to know me.

That was where danger lay.

Every day, I hated trudging to work and enduring yet more snide comments and rolled eyes at my reserved silence.

I missed the fields.

I missed the smell of manure and sunshine and tractor diesel.

Now, the dirt on my hands was from concrete and lime, not earth and grass. The dust in my lungs was from cutting bricks and shovelling gravel, not from fluffing hay and hauling bales.

Sometimes, even though the guys hated me, they'd offer me the odd after-work gig. The rules were: always do it late at night and always be unseen by anyone.

I didn't understand the secrecy for tasks like removing old roof sheets or cracking apart ancient walls, but I followed their stupid rules and cleared away debris. No one else seemed to want to do it, and the money was double that of day labouring.

No matter that I was grateful I had a job, some mornings, when I left for work and Della left for school, I'd struggle to continue walking to the site. Ice would crack beneath my boots and breath would curl from my lips, and I'd physically stop, look at the snow-capped trees in the distance, and have to lock my knees to stop from bolting toward them.

Days were long and hard and taxed me of everything I had.

But the nights—when I wasn't working on secret demolition—made up for the struggle.

The emptiness inside from living in a concrete jungle amongst wretches and sinners faded whenever I was near her. Her comforting voice, familiar kindness, and almost intuitive knowing when I just needed to sit quiet and have her tell me stories for a change, repaired the tears inside me.

Watching her animate tales of school and teachers allowed me to forget about everything but her. It reminded me why I'd cursed her for overstepping a boundary. And why I could never lose her. No way could I ever survive without her, and that terrified me because with every day, the remainder of her childhood slipped off like a cocoon, leaving behind new wings dying to fly.

She was evolving, and I couldn't do a damn thing but watch her morph into something I could never keep.

For two years, I held that job and paid for Della's every need. For every whisper from the wind to leave, I was held in place by the knowledge I needed to stay for her. For every tug to run, I focused on the person Della was becoming, and it was completely worth it.

A month or so after we'd moved into our apartment and I'd decorated the bedroom with purple curtains and a foam mattress covered in lilac bedding for Della—while I slept on the pop-out couch in the living room—we received our first letter.

Because we'd used John Wilson as a landlord reference, he knew where we were and wrote to us.

The letter was short and to the point, making sure we were safe and doing well and that if we ever needed anything, their door was always open. I tucked his phone number and address safely in my memory just in case.

I missed them, but I didn't know how to say such things or to convey how grateful I was for their hand in our lives—I'd fail in person, and I'd definitely fail in writing.

So Della was the one who got in touch and thanked them.

She let them know I'd found her and apologised for any embarrassment she might've caused. I approved the letter she sent, making sure it held the correct tone and gave no room for imagination that we might be doing anything wrong.

But she didn't let me read the note she sent to Cassie.

She scribbled something, folded it tight, and placed it in the envelope, licking it before I had a chance to spy.

I wanted to know what she said, but at the same time, I respected their privacy and relationship. She had every reason to stay in touch while I had a lot to stay away.

I didn't send any letters. I didn't find her online. I didn't get in touch in anyway.

What was the point?

Cassie and I were friends out of convenience. She had used me just as much as I had used her, and she no longer needed me to cause any more stress than I already had.

But with one letter came more, and Della and Cassie stayed in touch with the occasional note from Liam. Eventually, their snail mail became emails and quickly evolved to Facebook messages.

Occasionally, once Della had dragged herself to sleep and left the cheap phone I'd bought her on the coffee table, I'd swipe on the screen and scroll through pictures of Cassie at horse shows or sunsets over the fields sent by Liam.

Those moments hurt my heart for the simplicity of the world we'd all shared.

The perfection of long summer evenings and cosy winter nights. The innocence of growing up without fences and traffic lights.

I missed sharing a bedroom with Della.

I missed birthday picnics and cherished handmade gifts.

I missed holding her close on a freshly harvested meadow and hearing the birds roost in the willows.

I would've given anything to be a farmhand again.

And I knew, over the course of the two years while we lived in a city I didn't care about, and life maintained a steady stream of work, school, and evenings together, that something had to give.

Something had to change.

Otherwise, I was going to go insane.

I wasn't cut out for a job where I hated the crew and the labour.

I wasn't cut out to live in a tiny claustrophobic basement apartment.

But each spring, when the ground thawed and Della murmured that we should go back to the forest, I forbid it. She had to finish school. That was my commitment to her to pay for her education and her commitment to me to learn it.

Despite our constant desire to leave, I was eternally grateful when a letter arrived for me this time, not for Della.

A letter from John Wilson.

There was no fluff or word wastage, just a short message letting me know a friend who owned a farm not far from where we lived had recently lost his head milking harvester. His dairy herd numbered in the hundreds, and he needed someone trustworthy to start immediately.

Della wasn't home from school yet, but I caught a bus as close to the city limit as I could and walked the rest of the way to his sprawling acreage.

The farmer, an elderly gentleman with yellowing teeth and balding head called Nick March, offered me a job on the spot if I could start at four a.m. every day.

The pay was double what I was earning, and I'd get to be around animals and open spaces again.

I didn't even think.

I shook his hand and celebrated with Della that night with an expensive tub of ice cream that I couldn't really afford.

And that was how two years bled into three, and slowly, our newfound routine faded in favour of upcoming complications.

And our lives got a lot more difficult.

Chapter Fifty

REN

2016

SWEET SIXTEEN.

I'd never wanted to deny Della a birthday before, but this one…I wished we could skip right over it.

Not because she'd transformed overnight from skinny to curvy. Not because she laughed with a depth and richness that made my heart skip a beat. And not because she'd taken to wearing clothes that revealed her perfect figure, announcing to horny teens and asshole males that she was no longer a kid.

Believe me, I knew she wasn't a kid anymore.

Living with a stunning teenager when I'd turned into a surly, angry twenty-six-year-old wasn't easy. She seemed to grant life whenever she walked into a room and steal it whenever she left.

If she got pissed at me, I felt as if my world would end.

If I got pissed at her, I wanted nothing more than to punish her so she never misbehaved again.

Our dynamic became more explosive as age both bridged us closer and cracked a wider ravine. Outside appearances might have ensured she matched me almost in adulthood, but our opinions and thoughts remained divided.

She had an uncanny way of wanting to touch and hug when I wanted nothing to do with softness and connection. I hadn't been with a woman since Cassie, and it had been a long few years sleeping in a house with a girl who'd managed to flip my world upside down with a simple kiss.

I hated the fact that I still guarded myself against her when all I wanted to do was relax.

I despised the fact I'd become afraid of dreaming because, without fail, whenever I started to trust Della's lovely smile or thaw from her innocent embrace, I'd dream that night of kissing a stranger.

Of chasing her.

Of catching her.

Of kissing her until my body ached and I woke with a desperate growl for more.

I didn't know who I dreamed of. I never saw her face. And I would never admit to myself that because of what Della had done that night, I'd forever stitched her to the sensation of feeling at home the moment I kissed my dream-stranger or the heart-shattering horror when I woke up feeling dirty and wrong and in serious need of punishment.

I was desperate to taste that sensation of wonder. I craved to relive the magic of falling so deeply and quickly, I'd belonged entirely to my dream figment in a single heartbeat.

But whatever my issues were, I never let Della see.

When we first slept in separate rooms, I'd been obsessed with checking on her—making sure she was safe and no monsters climbed through her bedroom window.

Now, I was glad we had walls between us because my body never obeyed me anymore.

I woke hard.

I struggled not to release the pent-up need in my blood.

And my mind turned to ways of releasing such painful pressure without getting involved with anyone.

Cassie had made me wary, and Della had made me nervous.

I didn't like getting close to anyone, which meant I buried my needs down deep and accepted I lived in a constant nightmare.

The one saving grace to my torture was no matter Della's beauty, most days, I only saw her as my Ribbon. I could allow the comforting swell of love when she smiled at me. I could permit the way my body warmed whenever she was close.

I might forever hate myself for kissing her back while asleep, but I was insanely grateful that while awake, I crossed no boundaries in my thoughts. I didn't covert that which I could not have. I didn't confuse my dream with reality.

She was my world and home and family.

It didn't matter her long legs meant when we hugged, her head met my chin. It didn't matter her strong arms could haul things I deemed too heavy or her quick brain surpassed me in everything.

She was still little Della who I obsessed over, and sometimes, I wondered if that pissed her off.

I'd catch her glaring at me if I indulged her rather than argued. I'd get the sensation she was hurt if I played along rather than acted serious.

But whenever those rare moments occurred, by the time I turned to look closer or cocked my head to hear clearer, the smoke in her gaze was gone, the tightness in her tone vanished.

I supposed we were both keeping secrets; both hiding certain things.

But that was life.

We had our own worlds we juggled during the day. She did things at school I would never know about, and I did things at work I never bothered to tell her.

As long as we returned to each other at night, then I was okay with that.

My family was a single girl who I would happily die for, and lately, that was exactly what she made me want to do.

She might be the sweetest person I knew, but she was also the meanest, and as much as she hated me to call her out on it, I knew why she'd started testing boundaries and pushing into territories I wasn't comfortable with.

Lust.

I did my best to remember the cocktail of confusing needs and rampant curiosities I'd felt at that age, but it didn't mean I wanted her to go through it.

I wanted her to stay the forest girl, not a boy-interested teen.

Not that it mattered what I wanted.

We were no longer in sync, and when I got home from work and took her out to a local diner for our birthday dinner, I learned just how much things had drifted.

The meal started nice and normal.

We chatted about generic things, asked questions, listened intently, enjoyed each other's company...that was until a group of people arrived.

A group she knew and a boy who waved in her direction and smiled.

My gut clenched, and my fist wrapped around my Coke glass.

The four teenagers came toward our table, and Della lit up in a way she hadn't in so long with me. Her eyes met the boy's, a familiar message shared between them, and I was no longer the most important person in her world.

Nothing, absolutely *nothing*, hurt me as much as Della laughing and joking with her friends while she was so careful with me. To see her liveliness return with these strangers ripped out my goddamn heart.

I tried to be happy that she had friends, even though she'd never mentioned them. I did my best not to clutch my bleeding chest when she turned to me with blushing cheeks and bright blue eyes and asked, "Do you mind if I finish my birthday with these guys? We...eh, we have an assignment to finish and probably should do some homework."

Her lie didn't hurt me.

It was the fact she couldn't wait to get away from me.

I glanced at her half-eaten burger and remembered a simpler time when she was five and made my world come alive. I recalled how she'd taken my loveless, painful existence and showed me that not all people wanted to buy and sell you.

She was the reason I wasn't more mentally damaged and physically scarred than I was.

And because she'd been the one to save me without even realising it, I found myself nodding with a fierceness that belied my agony.

This was life.

This was what had to happen.

"Of course." I cleared my throat, waving her away. "Go ahead. You should spend your birthday with whoever you want."

She bounced up, looked as if she'd come to my side of the booth and hug me goodbye, but at the last minute changed her mind, gave me a confusing-tormenting smile, then turned and walked away.

"Be home by ten, Della," I said softly.

She looked over her shoulder with blonde hair cascading with a single blue ribbon glittering amongst the gold. "I will." She blew me a kiss before giggling at something the boy said in her ear.

Sweet sixteen.

Just like my original discomfort and desire to skip over such a birthday, my resolution solidified with another memory of my own sweet sixteen.

Cassie had said I deserved something special.

I'd had my first blow job in the shadows of a stable.

Now, Della was sixteen and laughing with a boy I wanted to punch in the goddamn face.

I couldn't stop whatever she would or would not do.

All I *could* do was celebrate my twenty-six birthday on my own.

I paid for our uneatened burgers.

I returned home to an empty apartment.

And I sat and watched the clock strike nine then ten then eleven and still Della didn't come home.

Chapter Fifty-One

REN

2016

A FEW WEEKS later, Della asked me the dreaded question. The one I'd been expecting ever since I'd seen her happiness hanging with the group of kids from school on our birthday.

"Ren?"

I looked up from where I was trying to yank a splinter from my thumb. The bastard had gone in deep, and I'd left it for too long, ensuring a red infection and minor swelling. It was a fence's fault, catching me as I'd corralled the cows into the yard for milking. "Yeah?" I asked, distracted with a needle and tweezers.

Her bare feet appeared beneath my vision where I sat hunched at the dinged-up kitchen table. "It can wait. Do you need help?"

I smiled at her tangled hair from a long day and the pyjamas with a repeating decal of Cupid's arrows and hearts all over her arms and legs. Having her stand there ready for bed and eyes hooded with tiredness, I could almost forget she was slipping further from my reach.

Strange how you could miss someone when they were apart of everything you did.

Before I could reply, she stole the needle, pulled up the only other chair, and yanked my hand toward her.

"Careful," I warned as she prodded me with the sharp tip.

"I have to break a few layers of skin. You left it too long. It's grown over."

I groaned. "Great."

"Hold still." She bent over me, her hair obscuring her face

and tickling the tops of my jean-covered thighs. I hadn't had a shower from work, and the dust and filth from working cows all day dirtied her cleanliness.

Not that she cared as she bent closer and diligently dug into my thumb.

I flinched occasionally, but somehow, she managed not to hurt me even though a bead of blood kept welling, causing her to wipe it away with her own finger, continuing her splinter hunt.

She needed a napkin or something to prevent my blood from staining her fingers, but I daren't stop her. I might not let her resume stabbing me otherwise.

The scent of vanilla rose from her hair, hinting she'd bought a different shampoo than her usual. She still smelled of the girl I'd known for sixteen years, but there was a new smell, too.

Something that made my heart chug harder the longer she huddled close.

She was so real, so fragile, so beautiful.

My fingers begged to be allowed to run through her hair, to bring her close, to hold her because I missed her so goddamn much.

As she tended to my wound, a yearning gathered that had nothing to do with her and everything to do with me.

I missed being touched.

I missed being kissed.

I missed affection that didn't come with a price of losing my soul.

By the time she finally dislodged the splinter, I struggled to breathe, and my thoughts were full of killing rabbits and tractor mechanics—anything to keep my body in check and appropriate boundaries in place.

I told myself it was because I hadn't been close to anyone in so long, all the while truth danced behind my lies.

I was waking up; seeing things I didn't want to see. Feeling things I definitely didn't want to feel.

She blew curls from her eyes as she planted the tweezers on the table with an accomplished flourish. "There you are. It's out." Scooting up, she darted down the small corridor to the bathroom and came back with some antiseptic cream from the chipped-glass medicine cabinet.

She stole my hand again, and with soft, capable fingers, spread some of the cream over the puncture she'd caused, then wrapped my thumb in a Band Aid.

She patted my knuckles like a good nurse and smiled. "Well, you'll survive. That's the good news. The bad news is you might lose the thumb."

"Ha-ha." I chuckled. "Hope I don't. Can't afford to lose another finger."

Her gaze fell to my missing pinkie, and some of her playfulness faded.

Standing quickly, I did my best not to scatter pieces of silage and grain from feeding the cows onto the floor.

I'd only recently saved up enough to buy a cheap motorbike that ensured I got to work for four a.m. without having to rely on shitty public transport. I didn't have a license to ride it—seeing as I had no proof of who I was—and even having the convenience of wheels meant I still had to get up well before dawn. "It's late. You should go to bed, and I need a shower."

She looked away but not before her eyes skittered down my body, lingered on my crotch, then dropped to the floor. Inhaling quick, tension rippled over her then was gone. She nodded quickly. "Yes. Bed. Shower. Good plan."

Twisting on the spot, her hair spun out like a gold carousel as she headed toward her bedroom. A second later, she spun back, biting her bottom lip, her cheeks pinker than before. "Eh, Ren?"

Something in her tone froze me to the floor. "What?"

She studied me with painful blue eyes, her decision not entirely formed. "Umm…"

"Umm what?" I struggled to convert air into oxygen. The way she stared hinted she knew whatever she'd ask would wedge yet another problem between us. "Tell me."

"What I meant to ask you before…. Do you think…I…" She dragged a hand through her long hair, revealing her ribbon was tied around her wrist today. "Would you mind if I—"

"Spit it out, Della." My heart rushed to know, but at the same time, warned I wouldn't like what she was about to say.

She exhaled in a rush. "Can I go on a date with Tom?"

I stopped breathing. *"What?"*

"Tom…um, you met him? At the diner? The tall guy with brown hair like yours and um…" Her gaze landed on mine before bouncing away just as fast. Deep in their blue depths other things lurked. Things she didn't want me to see.

I stepped toward her, but she tripped backward. "So…eh, can I?"

Air was still hard to come by. Everything inside bellowed to deny her request. I wanted to lock her in the apartment and never let her out. She was still too young for this. Too delicate and special and perfect to let unworthy boys touch her.

I didn't want anyone touching her.

Period.

But it wasn't my place to prevent her from growing up.

I should say yes.

I *meant* to say yes even though it slayed me.

But somehow, what I meant to say transformed on my tongue into an unarguable, "No."

Her lips thinned, and the nervousness at asking me quickly switched to resentment. "Why not?"

Just because I had to dig the knife a little deeper into my heart, I repeated her question. "Why won't I let you go on a date with him?"

She nodded.

"Because."

"Because?" She planted hands on her hips. "That's not a reason."

"I don't like him." I'd backed myself into this corner and had no way out. Why the hell didn't I say yes? I'd meant to, for God's sake. Now we slipped into yet another fight, and I was *tired* of fighting. Tired of miscommunication and walking on eggshells.

I wanted her close and caring like she'd just done with my splinter. I wanted to know where she was at all times, so I knew she was safe.

"You don't even know him." She growled.

"I don't have to know him to know what he wants."

"Oh, really?" She flicked her head to the side, her nose wrinkled with familiar temper. "Just like I know what Cassie wanted with you all those long summer nights?"

I stabbed my finger in the air. "That's none of your goddamn business."

"Just like what Tom and I might do is none of yours."

"Oh, see that's where you're wrong, Della." I moved toward her until our chests almost touched. "Everything you do is my business. You're mine to keep safe, and I have no doubt he doesn't have any intention of doing that."

"He won't hurt me." She backed up. "He's nice."

"Nice doesn't exist when hormones are out of control."

"Hormones?" She laughed condescendingly. "What do you think I am, Ren, some animal who just wants to get laid?"

I flinched.

Words landed on my tongue, but I discarded them.

She wasn't an animal, but she was getting close to wanting sex. I could see it in her eyes, taste it in her voice. She wouldn't be content with just me much longer and that knowledge kept me up at night.

Before I could choose an appropriate response, she added, "Just because you were fucking at my age doesn't mean—"

"Language."

"Oh, please. You use worse all the time."

"Not intentionally, I don't."

"What's the difference?" She curled her lip. "You swear but don't let me swear. You slept with Cassie, yet you won't let me—"

My temper snapped. "You're not permitted to sleep with anyone. *Ever.* Do you hear me?"

"You can't stop me, Ren." She crossed her arms, trembling just as much as me.

We both trembled when fighting. I didn't know how it happened or how to stop it, but with every fight, my limbs turned shaky with frustration and helplessness because I knew I could never win.

She would do whatever she wanted.

I had no power, even if I liked to think I did.

The only way to stop her from doing things I didn't approve of was to cart her back into the forest and keep her tied to a tree. And as much as that idea appealed to me, she had school to finish, a life to grow into, and I had a duty to ensure I made that as easy as I could for her.

No matter how much it destroys me.

Lowering my voice but unable to lower my temper, I seethed, "I was nineteen when I lost my virginity. You have another three years to go."

She sucked in a breath as if shocked I'd shared something so personal.

Walking past her, I grunted, "You can go out with him in a group. You must be home when you say you will, and if you leave me hanging here like you did a few weeks ago, I'll spank you so hard you won't be able to sit down for a month and then I'll ground you for the rest of your life."

Her silence shot bullets into my back as I stepped into the bathroom and slammed the door.

As the stained, chipped mirror reflected my dirty face, I

whispered, "Give me a few more years, Della Ribbon. Just a few more before you leave me."

Chapter Fifty-Two

REN

2016

SCHOOL FINISHED FOR the holidays, and Della, ever the resourceful, refused to relax like she deserved after studying so hard. Instead, she wanted to contribute to our bills by getting a job.

I was too busy with the milking to argue.

After scoring the job with Nick March, I'd not only been made the head milk harvester but also the overseer for the rest of the staff on his dairy farm.

From figuring out how much protein and fibre to feed versus income per milk quart, to paddock rotation and herd streamlining, my time was booked from the moment I arrived to the second I left.

I loved being in charge and making a difference. I enjoyed working with the seven hundred head of cattle and ensuring happy stock, which in turn, made for ease of milking twice a day.

What I didn't enjoy were the long hours I had to put in and the time apart from Della.

I often fell asleep earlier due to the brutal wake-ups, and she'd stay up later texting who knew what and watching romantic programs that probably filled her head with ideas of sex and marriage and things I couldn't protect her from.

I'd wanted her to recharge during the school holidays, but in a way, I was glad she job hunted. It meant she had things to fill her days with, and no idle hands to date boys she shouldn't be dating.

And because she was intelligent and extremely capable, she landed a job within a few days, helping a local florist make bouquets and other gifts, spending her hours playing with flowers, plaiting ribbon, and turning nature into stunning works of art.

Whenever I'd come home, she'd have some sort of daisy, tulip, or rose waiting for me, tied with a snippet of ribbon on the kitchen table.

I never told her how much I adored the fact that she thought of me while at work. That she still cared enough that I was the one she kissed on the cheek and helped cook dinner with. That I still held enough importance in her life to spend time with, even if it was doing something boring like watching a movie with microwave popcorn and overly sweet cola.

Those nights were my favourite.

I could even pretend we were alone in our tent surrounded by trees instead of buildings if we pulled our curtains tight and huddled together on the couch.

Normally, I was so exhausted, I ended up dozing beside her watching some comedy or drama while she twirled and tangled ribbon, making rosettes and ribbon-flowers for basket decorations at the florist.

It reminded me of the Christmas present Patricia Wilson had given her that first year. Della had loved the colourful ribbon collection. She'd set it safely in our bedroom and never touched them because she didn't want the colours to get marked with grease and grime like her blue one had.

After a while, the ribbons were just there, seen but unseen in our bedroom until I carved her that wooden horse which then slept on the ribbons for the rest of its existence.

I supposed both gifts the Wilsons had either kept or thrown out when we left. Della hadn't taken them when she ran away, and I'd had nothing to pack them into.

It helped recalling memories when Della was still young and easily impressed. These days, she smirked rather than smiled, and sometimes I wished I could trade her with the cute little girl I'd raised instead of live another day with a beautiful brutal teen.

Some days, we were perfectly in tune—our communication effortless and easy. Others, we spoke the same language, but the message was all scrambled. I'd get on edge, and she'd get snappy, and neither of us could stop the secrets slowly driving us apart.

* * * * *

Halloween.

Just like we'd never celebrated Christmas until the Wilsons, we hadn't celebrated Halloween.

In the town where the Wilsons lived, it wasn't a huge thing, and Della wasn't interested in dressing up and door knocking on strangers. Mostly because I practically hyperventilated at the thought of her putting herself in such danger.

Humans were never to be trusted even on nights when it was acceptable to dress up like ghouls and witches and ask for candy.

This year, she wasn't a little kid with a plastic pumpkin bucket ready for sugar. This year, she was sixteen and had used her own income earned from the florist to hire a Victorian outfit with a dress that ballooned with skirts and lace, taking up the entire floor in our lounge.

The pearl-beaded corset was tight and pushed up her breasts, barely covering her nipples and revealing acres of white, perfect flesh. She'd coiled her blonde hair until the messy curls turned into corkscrews, piled on top of her head and tumbling down around her face.

Her navy satin gloves reflected the light from above as she waved an oriental-painted fan, and the baby blue material of her gown coupled with the cream bodice and Victorian lace made her eyes pop in a way that looked almost ethereal.

I might love Della unconditionally with no impropriety of lust or denial.

But that night, I struggled to see her as out of bounds. It didn't matter my body prickled or my heart pounded. I battled to remind myself that the stunning creature in finery wasn't some woman I desperately wanted to kiss, but a girl I would forever protect.

Even if it meant protecting her from myself.

"What do you think?" She spun in place, knocking over an empty water glass from the coffee table onto the threadbare carpet. It didn't break, but my stiff rules threatened to.

She was far too lovely, and everything inside begged to mess her up so other men didn't see how incredible she was.

I swallowed to lubricate my throat. "It's nice."

"Nice?" She blew away a curl that'd gotten caught on a fake eyelash—thick black frames around the most incredible eyes. "Just *nice?*" Her shoulders slouched a little. "I was hoping for more than nice. It was my entire week's salary. I should've rented a cheap stripper outfit for ten bucks."

My belly turned to a rock at the mention of a stripper.

No way in hell would that ever happen.

She looked at the ceiling with a huff. "Now I just feel like an idiot for spending so much when I should've given it to you to pay the elec—"

"Stop it." I stood from where I was sprawled on the couch. My hands tingled as I dared place them on her bare, glitter-dusted shoulders. "It's a hundred times better than nice." I squeezed her gently, ignoring the kick in my gut. "Believe me. You'll kill every boy there with a single stare."

Her charcoal-shadowed eyes studied mine, her lips parted as if searching to see if she'd killed me just like I'd promised.

And she had. She definitely had.

But I refused to let her see it.

It was better that way...for both of us.

Squeezing her again, I dropped my hands with a forced chuckle. "You're far too beautiful to go out."

She sighed as if aggravated at something I'd done but then covered it up with a giggle. "Well, I *am* going out. You can't ground me. Not tonight."

"In that case, I'm going to hog the couch and watch something gory. I'm looking forward to the peace and quiet." I stretched, reaching for the ceiling and working out the kinks in my spine. My grey t-shirt rode up my belly, drawing her gaze to my naked skin just above my belt.

She licked her lips, and my heart switched from nervous thrumming to out of control pounding.

The entire lounge filled with wildfire. The air crackled with lightning bolts just waiting to strike. My body hardened in ways it never should around Della. But I couldn't stop it. Every inch of me turned into a tuning fork, humming for something, begging for anything.

She sucked in a shallow breath as her eyes once again found mine. Only this time, they were hooded and darker, older and dangerous.

The invitation.

The *truth*.

Shit.

It was pure fucking hunger and it tore out my insides with how deeply she was starving.

For me? For sex? For anyone willing to offer pleasure?

I stepped back, combating the heavy pull to go to her, to touch her, to do things I never dared—

Knock, knock, knock.

The moment shattered as someone's fist announced guests waited outside our front door.

Della wobbled, blinking as if she'd transported far away and slammed back into reality.

I exhaled hard, dragging a hand over my face and turning my back on her.

What the fuck was that?

What had happened?

And whose fault was it? Mine or hers?

The swish of Della's skirts was the only noise as she bypassed the couch and headed to open the front door.

"Hi," she said, her voice breathy and papery, matching the shivery sensation left in my spine.

I needed to sit down. I needed to figure out what the hell happened and how to prevent it from happening again.

Turning around slowly, I ordered my body to behave as I glanced at the arrivals.

"Hi, yourself," a girl piped up dressed in another Victorian gown—hers in reds and blacks. Compared to Della, she was positively garish while Della was a powder blue angel tempting me straight to fucking hell.

The girl's gaze slipped from Della to me standing furious and dazed in the middle of the living room. She did a double take, her entire body slipping into sensual solicitation. "And hi to you too, handsome." She blew me a kiss, making Della freeze with a frosty glare. "Della didn't say how hot her older brother was."

I supposed I should be flattered, but all I felt was empty. She was so juvenile. So transparent and shallow and *young*.

Shit, she was Della's age, yet I'd never thought of Della sexually—

You did tonight.

You wondered...

My heart skipped a beat, remembering what happened between us before the knock. I was grateful for the interruption. Thankful that I'd been reminded of who Della belonged with and what my role in her life ought to be.

"Hello." I nodded politely, clearing my throat, eradicating any sin I might have committed.

Jamming both hands into my pockets, it was my turn to glower with hatred as another person entered my home.

Tom.

The boy from the diner.

Della instantly stiffened, flicking me a look before allowing herself to be gathered in a hug from the boy I struggled not to hate. She refused to meet my eyes as he kissed her cheek and wolf whistled under his breath. "Holy crap, you're gorgeous."

My hands turned into fists in my pockets.

She blushed. "Thanks."

"Are you ready?" Tom glanced at me.

My jaw clenched.

It never occurred to me that they might be an item.

That she might be dating already, right beneath my nose.

Della nodded. "Yep. Oh, almost forgot." Darting to the coffee table, she scooped up a little pearl bag and looped it over her wrist. Speaking to me, she said, "I have my phone and some cash. I can get an Uber or something home. You won't be able to pick me up on the motorbike in this dress."

I didn't trust myself to talk.

I wanted to ensure she knew the curfew and my many, many rules, but my voice refused to work. It was still a gravelly mess with things I never wanted Della to know. Things *I* didn't want to know.

"Ren?" she murmured, coming closer to me. "Everything okay?"

I nodded stiffly, stumbling back. I honestly didn't know what I'd do if she touched me. "Go. Have fun."

Even though I wanted to lock her in her room and ban Tom from ever seeing her again, I almost pushed her out the door so I could breathe again.

"Okay…" Her eyes danced over my face, a sliver of hurt hiding in them before she smiled, and it vanished. "My offer still stands. You were invited, you know. I don't know if you were listening a few nights ago when I told you about the party, but everyone is welcome."

Fuck, everyone?

"You mean…this isn't just school kids going?"

Tom grinned, self-important and making my life a lot more difficult by not punching him. "Nah, man. It's a frat party. Local uni is putting it on. There'll be booze and stuff, but I won't let Della have any. I promise."

My ears rang.

My temper slipped into an ice-cold single-mindedness.

"You're not going." I narrowed my eyes at Della. "No way."

I'd never been to a party as a guest, but I'd been to enough of the dregs when collecting Cassie on those nights she'd snuck out and called me for a ride home. Della had accompanied me enough to understand why this was non-negotiable.

The amount of used condoms and spewing kids. The reek of sex and trouble.

No. Fucking. Way.

I crossed my arms as Della looked back once at her friends then swooped toward me. Her perfume of something light and floral invaded my nose, her body heat made me sick with want, and her breath against my neck as she hissed into my ear made my knees almost buckle.

I hadn't expected her closeness or her fight, and my silence gave her the perfect battlefield to destroy me.

"Don't mess this up for me, Ren. I'm not asking this time. I'm going to this party, and you have my word I will behave. I won't drink, and I won't fool around, but this is my life. These are my friends, and I want to hang out with them."

Everything she said was for my ears only.

The two strangers lingered by the door, giving us a confused glance.

Della pulled away but not before I lashed out and grabbed her wrist.

She gasped, her eyes dropping to where I held her, her soft inhale ripping through my defences and making my fingers squeeze against my command.

I clutched her hard, unable to let go even though everything inside screamed to back the hell off. "Don't threaten me, Della."

Her eyes widened then hooded to that sultry stare I had no power against. "I'm not threatening you. I'm telling you what's going to happen. Come if you want. I *want* you to. If only to get out of the apartment and live a little."

"You know I don't like crowds."

"Well, stay then."

"You know I can't. Not now."

"Because you don't trust me." Her tongue licked her bottom lip as once again my fingers squeezed her wrist in reprimand. The feel of her tiny bones. The rush of blood in her veins. The electricity infecting both of us that wasn't there before.

Fierce.

Forbidden.

Off-limits.

She shivered, leaning closer.

It took everything I had, but I released her and stepped back, rubbing my fingertips from the residual burn from touching her.

"Because I don't trust *them*."

Or myself.

"Fine." She stood tall and any hint of being affected by our whispered conversation disappeared. "Come then. I'll see you there. It's the house four blocks away toward the campus. Follow the music and pumpkins."

Without another word, she grabbed Tom's hand, smiled at the girl, then dragged them out the door, closing it with a slam.

Chapter Fifty-Three

DELLA

Present Day

AH, DATING.
So much fun, right?
Wrong.
The minute I met Tom in line at a local McDonald's of all places while I did English homework with Tina, I'd been rather smitten.

He went to a school not far from ours and regularly used our school's facilities like the basketball court and track as part of the physical education offered.

To be honest, the first thing that attracted me to Tom was his sable hair—almost the exact same colour as Ren's in autumn just before winter made it dark and summer made it bronze.

Instead of Ren's dark soul-deep eyes, Tom's were a startling green. Instead of Ren's well-honed and work-hard muscles, Tom's was gym perfected on a body still growing into manhood.

But despite his youth, Tom was cute. And compared to Ren's fine lines around his eyes and the aura of impatience and intolerance that came from hating people and growing up with the loner deep inside him, Tom was different enough to remind me I wasn't dating him to replicate my fantasies of being with Ren, but he was similar enough to ease that ache in my heart.

Sick, I know.
Twisted, I agree.

But...I always warned you I wasn't a nice person. That the more I followed this road, the worse I became.

I mean, most of the fights between Ren and me were my fault.
Shocker, right?
I know, I know, not a shock at all.
Most of the days that were full of tension and miscommunication were

because those days...I couldn't hide how I felt about him, and instead of blurting out that I was madly in love with him, I made him think I couldn't stand him.

And those were the nights I fell asleep torturing myself with imaginings of what it would be like to share my first real kiss with him and be touched in places no one had touched and have him climb on top and—

Anyway, back to Tom...

He was sweet. There isn't much more to say.

I suppose, while I'm at it, I'll confess everything else I did wrong while Tom was in my life. I was cruel to him because I knew he liked me more than I could ever like him. Not that I could ever tell him why. When he texted me pages of ardent affection and how much he missed me when we weren't together, I focused on giving him something I could all while hiding the bits that I couldn't.

I couldn't give him my heart.

But I could give him my body.

But even in that way, I used him again because my physical desires...well, Ren had nailed it when he accused me of being an animal wanting to get laid.

I wasn't quite ready for sex, but holy cow, I was ready for something. Just a kiss, a touch, a fumble in the dark.

I'd been ready for months, but something had held me back.

Ren.

Of course, it was Ren, but not in the way you'd expect.

His blurted, extremely surprising honesty that he hadn't slept with Cassie until he was nineteen had effectively dampened my libido.

I honestly thought he'd been screwing her for years as I slept stupidly in the room next to the barn. The looks they'd shared. The kisses they'd stolen—it all hinted at full blown sex.

So how had he waited so long?

Why had he waited so long?

And just how the hell was I supposed to do the same?

Look, I'm getting ahead of myself again, and there's a reason I'm going to reveal exactly what happened that first Halloween.

It was the first stepping stone to Ren walking out, and I think I'd always known it. I'd known it, and even though it lurked like a shadow between us from that moment on, I couldn't seem to stop myself.

You see...I used Tom to hurt Ren.

Another terrible confession.

What seven deadly sins does that fit into?

I'm too brain-dead and emotionally exhausted to figure it out.

Adultery perhaps? Even though Ren and I had nothing to cheat on.

I was single. He was single. And I was ready to live a little, even if living meant existing in constant pain. Even if it meant seething in jealousy when Tina hit on him. Even if it meant, eventually, I'd have to smile away my heartache when Ren found someone else.

God, I never thought I'd be so tired writing this. I didn't think memories had such a power to strangle and soothe at the same time. All I want to do is delete this and go to bed. To forget I ever started this tale and spend the last few days before my assignment is due writing something I can actually hand in.

But I also can't end here.

I'm so close.

Just a few more chapters…and then, well, then I can rest, and perhaps the past won't haunt me so much.

Are you ready?

Ready for more terrible Della?

I'm not, but let's see if I can remember exactly what happened that night. Some of it is a blur, and it's not like you need to know it anyway.

The typical party stuff.

I arrived with Tina and Tom, dressed to my eyeballs in glitter and powder and two-hundred dollar Victorian gowns, wanting desperately to feel older and wiser and irresistible to someone, and realising that no matter how much cleavage I might have or how fluttery my eyelashes were or how I stared and licked my lips, Ren was immune to me.

If anything, he just got mad and made me feel even more of a fraud than I already was.

At least, Tom seemed to love my effort, and his hands never strayed from touching me, appeasing my jealousy over Tina's constant whispering about how gorgeous Ren was and if he was available.

I tried to ignore her. I wanted to tell her he was a monk or someone who despised being touched. I threw myself into Tom's attention and encouraged his hands to rest in the small of my back and linger on my waist.

I should've shivered at having him touch me in places that sent goosebumps leaping over my skin, but all I could think about was how Ren had snatched my wrist and held it so tight and unforgiving, leaving a circlet of his fingers for minutes after he'd let me go.

Tom was so tame compared to Ren, and that taboo, forbidden factor just wasn't there, either.

Perhaps I'd become addicted to the fact that I couldn't have Ren more than the actual reality that we weren't actually compatible.

Ha!

Even now, that lie doesn't work. I tried to convince myself that if Ren was my age and available, I wouldn't truly want him. That I'd find him boorish with his rules and stuffy with his diligence.

But yep… it doesn't work.

I didn't want Ren because I couldn't have him.

I wanted Ren because he was everything that made me appreciate, adore, and burn for. He was utterly perfect from his snappish temper to his doting devotion, and yep…I'm back on the crazy torment-myself-with-falling-all-over-again-for-the-boy-who-left-me train.

God, I'm crying.

Why am I crying?

This…ugh!

No!

I haven't cried since the day he left. I didn't let myself and now…now I can't stop.

I…I can't do this.

I need a break—

* * * * *

Sorry.

Jeez, I seem to be apologising to an assignment a lot.

I couldn't finish yesterday. Not unless I wanted to drown my laptop in tears and have to buy another one. It seemed I had a weak day, made worse by a brain that refused to stop thinking about Ren, Ren, Ren.

You know? Some days, I literally do hate him. I hate his damn guts. Those days, I feel somewhat normal and can honestly say I don't want him to come back. Leaving was probably the best thing he could've done for me.

Because I now have no choice but to get over this stupid infatuation and move on.

But other days that hate transforms back into love and, holy ouch, it fills up my heart until it bursts with need, infecting my entire body until I feel as if I have the flu.

Funny, huh?

The love flu.

Stupid man has made me eternally sick, and there is nothing I can do.

Right, enough feeling sorry for myself.

Today, I'm determined to tell you about Halloween.

Where was I? Let me just skim over what I wrote yesterday and try not to roll my eyes at the patheticness of unrequited love.

…

Ah yes, okay, the party.

We arrived.

Tom got me some punch that unfortunately was alcohol free, and Tina and I bounced around in our skirts and fanned our pretty fans, enjoying the stares of young students and wiser university goers, steadily growing more and more silly as the night went on.

For an hour, I refused to let myself think about Ren.

I pretended I didn't care if he didn't come. I spun and laughed and flirted all for me, not to get back at him. So it killed me to realise how fake I turned out to be because I knew the moment he arrived.

My skin prickled. My heartbeat quickened. And everything inside me slipped from chaos to calm.

In the middle of a manic Halloween party filled with Frankensteins and vampires and zombies, I knew the second the matching piece of my heart arrived.

Sad right?

Poetic?

Star-crossed?

Screwed up?

Probably all the above.

But probably not as screwed up as the next part.

You see, I knew the second Ren arrived, and instead of going to him, being a good hostess, and smoothing over the troubled waters between us, I grabbed Tom and clutched him close.

We slow danced with werewolves and fairies, and when he gathered me closer, I mewled in invitation, and when he grinded his hips against me, I gasped in appreciation, and when his head lowered, and his eyes sought mine, and his lips crashed down, I dove my fingers into his messy sable hair and threw away all the decency and morality left inside me.

I became a husk. A chewed-up disgusting person who willingly kissed a boy all the while pretending it was someone else.

And by pretending it was someone else, I kissed harder, deeper, sexier than I ever had before. My first real kiss, and it was with a ghost of the boy I truly wanted.

I let go. I lived my fantasy.

I clawed at his hair, I tangled my tongue with his, and I fell so deeply in love with my illusion that when I opened my eyes and snuggled into his chest, I breathed the wrong name.

"Ren," I moaned with my body aching and breasts swelling and wetness gathering.

And Tom had pulled me away with a terrified look in his green gaze. We'd stood motionless on the dance floor while others swirled around us as he stared into my ripped apart secret and knew.

He knew.

And there was no going back.

* * * * *

I wish there was more to the tale.

But I've sat here for a while thinking what to write, and honestly, there isn't anything else.

I wished I could say that Ren came stalking from the mismatch dressed up crowds, yanked me out of Tom's arms, and planted his mouth on mine in punishment for ever kissing another boy when I'd always been his.

But it didn't happen.

Tom went to get us more drinks, this time with alcohol laced in its sugary depths, and Tina and I continued to dance, but my smiles were brittle and my laugh hollow.

Tom stayed close, but things had changed—awareness had been shown, harboured secrets blown wide apart. His touches were just habit, and that night, we agreed that it was fun and all, but it was better if we went our separate ways.

I wasn't sad. I was relieved. And that was yet another nail in my otherwise rotten coffin.

Meanwhile, as I was getting dumped for hurting two people in one, my heart constantly zeroed in on where Ren was.

Occasionally, he'd appear in the crowd, arms crossed and leg cocked over the other as he leaned against the perimeter, an outsider to the party, a watcher on the wall, close enough to protect me from harm but willing to let me make my own stupid mistakes.

I didn't know if he'd seen me kiss Tom.

I didn't know if he'd been hurt or didn't care—perhaps he was relieved that I was manhandling someone else for a change.

I didn't know.

But when it was time to go home, he walked with me.

He carried my high heels and gave me a pair of flip-flops he'd thoughtfully stashed in his back pocket, and guided me through streets filled with ghosts and demons back to an apartment where he went to his bed and I went to mine, and through the thin walls, I heard him tear apart the meagre furniture we had, howling at the moon.

All the while, I cried into my pillow.

Chapter Fifty-Four

REN

2016

WE DIDN'T EVEN make it to Christmas before another catastrophe found us.

For weeks, I kept the fact that I'd seen Della kissing Tom hidden. When she looked at me over breakfast of toast and cereal on the weekends, I tasted the question she wanted to ask. When I arrived home from a long day at the milking yards and she had a home-cooked meal for two, I heard the query she wanted to know.

And I ignored each look and stare.

Not because I still didn't know how it made me feel—sick to my stomach mainly—but because I worried about her. I worried what sort of person kissed another with that much heat and desire—practically making love on the damn dance floor—and then broke up with them that same evening.

I knew the feeling of not wanting to get close to someone, but she'd taken it to a whole new level. She'd used him, and as much as I loved the fact that she'd broken up with him, I couldn't get over the way she'd kissed him.

Over and over, I replayed it, ripping my heart out little by little until I was more lost and more afraid than I'd ever been.

I hadn't hugged her in weeks.

I hadn't snuggled with her on the couch.

I barely touched her.

And she didn't call me out on it or demand to know what was wrong.

We both knew what was wrong.

Lines had been crossed again, and I desperately wanted to

draw more in the sand and ensure they stayed steadfast and true.

Regardless of how I felt about watching her stick her tongue down another boy's throat, she seemed to shut everything down and act normal—if we even had a normal anymore.

She never once mentioned Tom again, and I couldn't think about the kiss she'd given him without getting hot and angry and hard, and not necessarily in that order.

I hated that she'd kissed someone, but that was my own selfish reasons wanting to keep her protected. I was hot because all the men in that place watching that kiss had felt the passion dripping off Della. And I was hard because, goddammit, it reminded me how long it'd been since I'd felt the delicious friction of kissing and I was obscenely jealous.

Jealous of Della's freedom.

Jealous of Della's courage.

Jealous of Della being with anyone when all I wanted to do was lock her in a tower.

It made me sick that I couldn't entangle proper and improper thoughts anymore. I *hated* that I couldn't trust myself around her, when before, she was everything I ever needed.

I didn't know if that was her first proper kiss, or if she'd been practicing a while, but holy fuck me, she knew how to do it.

The way her leg came up to hook over his hip. The angle her head tilted to give unfettered access to her mouth, and the way her hands roamed and nails dug as if she'd drown if she didn't get more.

I could understand the awe on student faces who'd watched such a thing. Even the girls had parted their lips and wanted what Della was having, but for some reason, I didn't think it was Tom who was the excellent kisser.

It was all her, and that was what screwed me up even more.

Why was she so talented at something I wanted to shield her from for years?

And why had I only just noticed what a sexual creature she'd turned out to be?

It made my own needs spring loud and cruel to the surface, and I often thought about my experiences with Cassie. Of our kisses and thrusts; of hands in dark places and tongues wet and dancing.

I'd enjoyed sleeping with Cassie, but I hadn't felt a tenth of violent hunger as Della had shown on the dance floor that night. Perhaps, she was right and I was wrong. Some people were just more sexual than others, and I was hurting her by not letting her be free with whatever she needed to find.

Maybe she'd outgrown me in more ways than I'd ever imagined.

It fucking gutted me, but the very next day, I headed to the pharmacy while she was still in bed and bought a packet of condoms. Afterward, I booked in a doctor's appointment for her to arrange a better in-depth sex talk than I was capable of and to discuss birth control arrangements.

Thanks to Cassie, I knew about the pill and STIs and the minefield of what sex entailed. It was time Della did too, so at least I didn't have to worry about her getting pregnant or sick.

I assumed Della found the condoms with the note I'd left on her bedside table.

Simple and to the point: *If you're going to do things outside my control, please be safe. Use these. At all times.* With a big black arrow pointing at the twelve pack of condoms.

My heart hadn't stopped pounding in agony every time I thought about her using them. But my job wasn't to prevent her from living. My job was to keep her safe while she did.

It didn't matter how I felt.

It was all about her.

And that was what I tried to remind myself when the phone call came.

* * * * *

Normally, I was the one who screwed things up. I took the blame. I shouldered the consequences. But more and more, Della was the reason things turned ugly.

Two unconnected events made one very nasty conclusion.

I came home a few nights after I'd given her the condoms to find the bathroom door wide open and steam curling down the corridor.

The scents of liquorice body wash and melon shampoo—her current favourite scents—gave me a clear path to her bedroom where she sat in the middle of her bed, dressed in innocent pink pyjamas, reading a textbook and doing science homework.

Everything was right with that picture apart from her hair.

Her gorgeous, golden hair was now a rich blue to match her ribbon.

The same ribbon tied at the end of her plait, draped over her shoulder in a vicious shade of cobalt.

"What the *hell* did you do?" I stormed into her room, barging past the door, and not caring that it slammed against the wall. She'd transformed from angel to nothing but trouble.

Trouble that I no longer knew how to handle...in so many complicated ways.

She looked up, blue eyes even brighter thanks to her new hair.

She winced at my temper. "I knew you'd be mad—"

"Of *course,* I'd be mad. Your hair is goddamn blue! What were you thinking?"

"It's not permanent."

"I don't care. Wash it out. Right now."

She shrugged, her pen in one hand and the end of her plait in the other. "It...um, it'll wash out in twenty-four showers or so."

"Twenty-four! You have school tomorrow."

"They won't mind."

I laughed, full of exasperation and annoyance at how stupid she could be. "Oh, they'll mind. There's nothing natural about that, Della. The dress code states no makeup, offensive jewellery, or embellishments of any kind."

"Why the hell do you remember the dress code?" She pouted. "Can't I have a little expression?"

"I remember because I remember *everything.*" My eyes burned, sending their own message that I'd seen her kiss, and I remembered every mortal detail about it. Before she could read that stupidly sent information, I growled. "And no, expression is for after school. School is about learning to follow rules and—"

"It's stifling me, Ren! I can't be who I want to be there anymore. I can't talk to anyone about...things. I'm sick of telling lies about who we are and where we come from. They don't understand. No one understands—"

I shook my head. "I never thought you'd become one of those self-obsessed whiners like those stupid TV shows. This is *life,* Della. You need an education. You're not there to find out who you are. You're there to learn skills you'll need for when you do."

Her shoulders slouched. She had no rebuttal, and my temper stalled.

We waited in a room heavy with argument, slowly fading the more we breathed.

Finally, she murmured, "I'm sorry, okay? I just...I needed to do something. It's been a tough couple of weeks."

I did my best to relax, backing up and leaning against the doorframe with my arms crossed. "Why? What's going on?" There was no surer way to make my anger dissipate than thinking she was hurt or sad. "Tell me, Little Ribbon."

She glanced up with an unhappy smile. "Do you know you hardly ever call me that anymore?"

I opened my mouth to argue, racking my brains for a time when I last used it. Sadness filled my heart when I found none recently. "You're right. I haven't."

"Why?" Her question ached with so much more than just that one request. My bones physically throbbed to cut across the distance and sit beside her on the bed. I wanted nothing more than to gather her in my arms and crush her close. To hug like we used to. To kiss like we used to. To promise her that this might be hard for both of us, but we would never drift apart the way we seemed to be drifting right now.

The silence stretched, this time scratching my skin and drawing blood.

I forced myself to stay in the doorway, no longer comfortable to enter her bedroom with all the strangeness flowing between us. "You know why," I murmured.

I hadn't meant to say that.

I hadn't meant to say anything.

She stiffened, her lips smashed together as her eyes glowed with something that took an axe to my chest, cleaving me in two.

We stared.

And stared.

And when my body prickled and blood boiled, and I was so close to doing something I really shouldn't do, I cleared my throat and the moment was gone.

I smirked, going for light-hearted, when really, I ought to scold her for such a reckless colour. "I should probably march you to a hairdresser and get that colour stripped out, but…it suits you."

And it did. It suited her too much. It made her skin pop white and lips burn red. It made her look older, which was not a good thing.

Her shoulders fell, her tension rippling away to settle on the bedding beneath her lotus-crossed legs. "Thanks." She tugged on the end of her cobalt plait. "I know you don't understand, but sometimes…well, sometimes it feels like we're still alone in the forest, you know? Surrounded but with no one to talk to. At least, in the forest, the trees can't repeat your secrets."

"I miss it, too. But you know why we can't go back…not yet, at least."

"I know." She sighed. "But it's hard when I feel so…" She shrugged. "Look, I know I can't tell people the truth about where we came from or mention my real last name or tell people that we aren't truly related, but sometimes, I just wish I could blurt out everything." Liquid glossed her eyes for a second before she swallowed and smiled bright. "Sorry, like I said. One of those weeks."

My hands clenched into fists, holding myself in place not to go to her. "What do you want to talk about that you can't discuss with me?"

She barked a laugh as if I'd said something hilarious. Rolling her eyes at the ceiling, she chuckled in a tortured-exasperated way. "Gosh, *everything.*"

The hair on the back of my neck stood up, hating that she felt trapped and alone. "I'm always here, Della. If it's girl stuff or periods or whatever. I can handle it."

Her nose wrinkled. "I'm good. Thanks."

"If it's not that, then tell me what's bugging you."

She dropped her gaze to her bedspread, her fingers plucking the pages of her text book. "I can't."

"Why?" Despite myself, my feet stepped into her bedroom, needing to go to her when she seemed so forlorn. "What's wrong?"

Her blue hair shivered as she shook her head. "Nothing's wrong."

"Something's wrong."

Her eyes flashed with warning not to push her. "Like I said, I'm good. Don't worry about it."

My legs locked in the centre of her carpet. "Don't get mad at me. I'm only trying to help."

"Yes, and look at the great job you're doing!" She launched upright, kneeling on her bed. "Just…I can't do this right now. I need to study and you—you just—"

"I just what?"

"You make it worse, okay?"

I froze. I had no reply. Only the pain she'd caused and the knowledge that I'd somehow failed her. Nodding curtly, I backed toward the door. "Fine. Study. You know where I am if you need me."

I turned around and left before the argument could fall into trickier territory.

* * * * *

The very next day, our lives changed once again. The catastrophe hit with lashing accusations and howling consequences.

I was commanded to visit the high school where Della attended. When the phone call came, I was herding seven hundred plus cattle into the milking shed and could barely hear the snippy tone of the principal's assistant ordering me to pop in for a 'chat.'

I'd barked back, asking if Della was hurt or lost or missing. Did I need to save her from yet more Social Service agents or was it not as dire as that? The urge to run and vanish into the protection of the forest sprang into an undeniable urge.

All the woman would give me was Della had been served detention for her blue hair, and they wanted to discuss the matter.

My need to grab Della and disappear faded a little. I'd told her she'd get in trouble for such a ridiculous colour, and it turned out, I was right. Frankly, she deserved a bit of punishment, and if being detained after class and earning a stern talking-to by the principal was the price, then hopefully she'd learn her lesson.

For the rest of the day, I lived with a recipe of uncertainty and curiosity, and by the time I sped my way on a beaten-up motorbike that needed new parts and some serious care, I was wired and ready to kill someone.

I didn't care I had grass stains on my work jeans or my plaid shirt was covered in dirt. I made an honest living, and the scents of earth and cow were more acceptable to me than asphalt and metal.

Striding through the school corridors, I peeked into classrooms full of posters with correct etiquette and current assignments. A science lab smelled of sulphur. A lecture room still hummed with a projector someone had left on even though no students were there to learn.

The place was foreign, but I wondered what it would be like to attend. What did Della think when she arrived early in the morning and soaked up knowledge in different environments?

I got lost in the labyrinth of corridors and cut across the wrong campus forecourt until I found the admin building where the principal's office was housed.

The moment I stepped into the stuffy, low-ceiling building, a woman with spectacles and greying hair looked up from typing something on a computer. "Ah, you must be Mr. Wild?" She said it as a question, but with a knowing gaze that unsettled me.

"I am." My eyes drifted over the space, instinctually seeking exits and keeping a safe distance from myself and this new stranger.

"Great. Della's detention is almost over. She'll head here accordingly. Please." She nodded at a closed pine door where a bronze plaque announced a Marnie Sapture was in command of this establishment. "Ms. Sapture is expecting you."

Gritting my teeth, I strode to the door and opened it without knocking. The principal would've been pretty once upon a time, before she let stress pile on the pounds and too much makeup try to hide the heavy lines on her forehead. "Mr. Wild?"

I nodded.

"Good. We need to talk."

"As I've been told."

"Please, sit." She waved at the chair in front of her. A moment of déjà vu hit me of entering another principal's office and hearing a tale of how Della informed a bunch of five-year-olds how to skin and gut a rabbit.

The memory gave me mixed feelings of amusement and terror. She was so different to everyone else, but her differences meant we never seemed to stay in one place for too long.

Sitting down but with all my weight in my feet ready to leap up and run, I waited for Marnie Sapture to tell me why exactly I'd been summoned. The familiar weight of my goat hide knife that Cassie gave me whispered to be used.

To unholster the blade and threaten this woman the same way she was threatening me.

She ran her hand through her black short hair, shuffling paperwork with the other. Finally, she cleared her throat importantly. "I'm sure you're aware, Della came to school today with blue hair." She looked up, narrowing her eyes. "And I'm sure you're aware that our policy on uniform and conformity don't permit such unnatural colours."

It didn't matter that I'd said the exact same thing last night.

Telling Della off on my own was one thing; having a stranger do it made my need to protect her at all costs surface. "Blue isn't unnatural." I shrugged. "Blue is the colour of the sky. It's one of the most common colours around."

She pursed her lips, causing more lines to appear. "That may be the case, Mr. Wild, but blue in the clouds and blue on one's head are two completely different things."

I held my tongue, waiting for any other reason I was here. Della's detention was hardly breaking news to call in a caregiver. The hair on the back of my neck stood up as Ms. Sapture's cheeks reddened, and her righteous voice slipped into disgusted. "I'm sure you're also aware that in this state, there are rules about unnatural relationships between family."

This time, she didn't look up as if she found making eye contact with me repulsive.

"Excuse me?" I hissed.

"I said unnatural relationships between fam—"

"I heard you." I shot to my feet, hands balled. "And just what the hell are you implying?"

She stiffened but dared look up. "I'm implying that some information has come to light that you and Ms. Della's bond is more than brother and sister." She tapped some papers with a pink-painted fingernail. "This is Della's enrolment application. You signed as her brother, yet a student here informed us that a more worrying connection might be at play."

I couldn't breathe.

I couldn't see past the red haze in my vision.

All I wanted to do was grab Della and run. What had she done? Who had she spoken to? What the fuck did she say?

"Whoever said such things is lying," I bit every word as if killing them with my teeth.

"That might be, but whenever accusations like this arise, it is protocol to call Child Protective Services."

I backed toward the door. "You have no right."

She stood behind her desk, eyes gleaming. "I do have a right, Mr. Wild. In fact, I have an obligation. I invited you here today to state your side of the argument, but if you have nothing to say on the matter then—" She picked up the phone on her desk. "I suppose I might as well make that phone call now and get this over with."

Fuck.

What did I do? Waste the precious time I had trying to make her see reason or bolt now and pack up as much as I could? Where the hell was Della? I couldn't move until I knew she was safe and—

Commotion sounded outside, the receptionist's high-pitched voice arguing against one I knew better than my own.

Della.

Before I could spin and open the door, she shoved it open and stumbled over the threshold. Every nerve demanded I grab her, but I had to bury those urges because she wasn't alone.

"What the—?" I said under my breath as she dragged Tom,

her ex-boyfriend, into the small office and slammed the door. She held his hand with a death grip, her fingernails making white indentations in his flesh.

"What is the meaning of this, Ms. Wild? Why is another student from a different school in my office?" the principal snipped. The phone dangled in her hand, unconnected and silent on its horrible message that Della and I did something immoral.

"I know who started the rumour, Ms. Sapture," Della said, yanking Tom closer. "And it's just that. A stupid, silly little rumour that's gotten out of hand."

I didn't understand what the hell was going on, and Della refused to make eye contact with me.

I'd been forgotten about as Tom gulped and hung his head. "It was me, Ms. Sapture. I started it. I wanted to make life difficult for Della."

The principal gave him a harsh stare. "What do you mean?"

"I mean…" He flinched as Della dug her nails harder into him. "Della and I were going out, but then she dumped me, and I got jealous and made up the lie that she broke up with me because she was in love with her brother."

Holy shit.

I stumbled backward, dragging a hand over my mouth.

Della flicked me a glance, then fixed her stare back on the principal. "As you can see, Ms. Sapture, my brother is as horrified by this as I was. I couldn't think of a more terrible thing to say." She glowered at Tom beside her. "Jealousy makes us do strange things."

Ms. Sapture slowly sat down in her chair, her witch-hunt game-face fading in favour of the truth. The *only* truth. That Della and I weren't blood, but we were family through and through.

Aren't we?

Della let Tom go but not without a heated, warning look. "So you admit it? You and Tina have been spreading lies about me?"

Tom gritted his teeth as if he wanted to argue but nodded stiffly. "Yes."

"And you have no evidence to back up this lie? No photo or video revealing the vile things you said?" Della's eyes glittered a ruthless blue. Her blue hair matched, contrasting with the auburn and browns of her school uniform.

"None." He blew out, his tall frame sinking. "I made it all up."

Della crossed her arms, nodding once at Ms. Sapture. "You

see? Stupid student gossip. I don't know why it started, but it's over now. Not a word of it was true and I'm sorry to waste your time."

Ms. Sapture looked put out, struggling to get control of the situation that Della had so successfully commandeered. Finally, she waved at the door with bored impatience. "I'll accept your explanation for now, Ms. Wild. However, I wasn't born yesterday, and I've been around enough students to understand rumours usually start from some kernel of truth." Her gaze found mine as she leaned forward almost in a threat. "One more sniff of such a thing and I'm calling CPS, regardless of your dramatics."

I glowered back, refusing to let her intimidate me.

Della brushed past me, opening the door and letting Tom step out before her.

"Oh, and one more thing, Ms. Wild," Ms Sapture clipped. "I want that colour gone by tomorrow, do you hear me?"

Della didn't answer, and with a flick of blue motioned for me to follow her.

Chapter Fifty-Five

DELLA

Present Day

I KNOW, I know.

I was stupid. Incredibly stupid. So stupid it almost meant we were separated again, but if it hadn't have been for detention with my blue hair, I would never have heard the rumour until it was too late.

I'd been under the illusion that Tom was trustworthy, and my minor slip after our kiss didn't bother him too much—not enough to tell people about. Yes, were dating, but he was wanted by a lot of girls, and I was nothing special.

Saying the wrong name after kissing him had been my error, but I'd apologised and believed him when he said it didn't matter. I stupidly accepted his assurances and didn't think anything more on it.

Turns out, he started making out with Tina, my so-called best friend, and she decided to rat on me. We'd gotten close over the few years, Tina and I, close enough for me to slip occasionally and reveal things I shouldn't about me and Ren.

I never came out and said I wanted him or that I was in love with him, but I supposed she read between the lines.

And yes, I know you're calling me names, and I totally accept them because it was idiotic to confide in someone, but…I had no one to talk to. No one to help settle my nerves every time the overwhelming desire to kiss Ren pounced on me. No one to be a shoulder to cry on when the wanting became too painful. And no one to offer advice on how to move past such a horrible situation and just accept that things would never change between us.

All I told Tina was there was a boy I liked.

A boy who liked me but not in the same way.

When she asked if it was one of Ren's friends, I hesitated. Tying Ren's name into any of this was dangerous but making it be an older guy who was no longer at school and who couldn't be researched made sense.

So I gave in.

I found myself spinning a tale of unrequited love with one of Ren's friends—not that he had any—and how I'd kissed him once but that was it.

Tina was sympathetic and sweet and acted as if I had a terminal case of the flu and needed constant mothering. At first, I loved it. I loved having someone nurse my achy breaky heart and be there whenever I needed to vent. But then, her questions became more prying, her eyes more suspicious, and I stopped telling her things.

I stopped muttering secrets like: when he's near me, it's all I can do not to reach out and grab him. When he's cooking beside me, my mouth waters and not for the food. When he's asleep, I wage a battle to stay in my bed and not go to his and repeat the mistake I made last time.

By the time I met Tom, Tina was sick of my wishing over a boy I could never have and encouraged my crush on Tom. He could be talked about freely, and I shared intimate details with Tina because she shared them with me. I knew she wasn't a virgin anymore and I knew she'd bled when a guy called Scooter took her to the movies and ended up banging her in the back seat of his car.

She was worldly to me, and she gave good advice on how to seduce Tom and what to expect when I first jumped into bed with him.

Unfortunately, armed with her prior knowledge of me pining for a boy who I wouldn't name, when she found out Tom had broken up with me after kissing at the Halloween party, she couldn't understand why.

She'd badgered and badgered for answers, until finally, in a moment of utter moronic weakness, I told her that I'd said the wrong name afterward kissing him. I'd said the name of the boy I was in love with. Ren's friend.

I thought I'd covered my tracks pretty good.

I patted myself on the back for keeping her away from the truth.

Funny, how it was the exact opposite.

Tina messaged Tom, telling him off for breaking up with me. They'd had some hate-lust-text-war for a few weeks before hooking up behind my back. Then, of course, it was just a matter of time before Tina mentioned my sad, hopeless situation of being in love with someone who wouldn't even notice me, and Tom told her the name I'd breathed after our kiss.

Perfect explosion.

But you know what I'm most mad about?

I'm mad that neither of them came to face me. That they didn't ask for my side of the story before they jumped to conclusions, figured I was boning my brother, and spread gossip loudly enough to get the principal involved.

So yeah, dying my hair blue was stupid. But at least it landed me in detention right next to Tina, who smirked and asked if I'd been summoned to the principal's office lately. I waved the slip in her face and she giggled. She told me to expect a certain brother waiting for me, along with a few other people who wanted to discuss our 'family dynamics.'

I'd bolted from detention without gathering up a stitch of my belongings. My backpack left opened on the floor; my pencil case on the desk, and my notebook on the page of my current homework assignment.

I left it all behind as survival instincts overrode everything and I hopped onto the nearest unlocked bike in the bike shed and hoofed it over to Tom's neighbouring school.

There, I'd yelled his name until someone pointed me in the right direction. The moment I found him in after-school woodworking, I grabbed his wrist and dragged him to my campus, all the while telling him the truth.

The only person I ever told the entire truth to.

I held nothing back. I told him my last name was Mclary, and I'd been rescued from monsters. That Ren wasn't my brother. That he was the reason I wasn't dead in a ditch somewhere. And that yes, I was in love with him, but it was fine because he wasn't in love with me and nothing inappropriate was going on. Not that it was any of his business because Ren and I weren't related, so even if we did get together, the only law being broken was the fact I was a minor and he was not.

And once I'd spilled everything, dragging my ex-boyfriend to fix what I'd broken, I made him swear to secrecy. And because I didn't trust his vow never to breathe a word, I added a threat. One that would surely put me in hell because it was yet another of the seven deadly sins. Lying. Or, at least, I think it's a deadly sin. If it isn't, it probably should be.

Doesn't matter.

The point is, I told him I'd spread a rumour how he'd fucked me against my control. How he'd gotten me drunk at that party, had his wicked way with me, then spread a different kind of rumour about me to take the heat off him.

His eyes filled with hatred, but I didn't care. All I cared about was ending this nightmare before it ruined everything.

You see, I only had one year left of high school.

The next time Ren and I ran, I wanted it to be for good. I never wanted to have to tie Ren to a new place so I could go to school. I never wanted him to feel as trapped as I did. I wanted to be free because maybe, just maybe, away from people and rules and constant reminders, Ren might slip enough to realise he loved me, too.

Chapter Fifty-Six

REN

2016-2017

FOR TWO MONTHS, our packed backpacks rested by the door ready to grab at a moment's notice. I'd never opened a bank account as I had no identification to appease the paper pushers, and the cash I'd diligently saved was hidden in a small box under the rickety floorboard beneath the couch—ready to be snatched and taken.

I'd wanted to run the day we got home from the principal, but Della had picked a fight and we'd argued well into the night. Her reasons for staying were she didn't want to move schools when she was so close to finishing, that she'd fixed it so the rumour would fade and the teachers would chalk it up to stupid teenage drama, and that I was too flighty.

I'd roared at that one.

Flighty?

How about fucking wary that even though Della was more adult than kid these days, she could still be taken away from me. Excuse me for not caring about anything other than her. Running meant abandoning my work and our apartment, but I would gladly give up everything over and over again if it meant she stayed safely by my side.

But even in the wake of my temper, she'd won in the end— just like she always did.

I bowed to her pleas to stay, just for a little while, and gamble with time to see who was right. If Tom kept his mouth shut, we would be free to stay. But if he didn't, it might be too late to run next time.

I hated it.

I hated that I didn't just grab her and leave rather than listen to her debate and bow to her conclusions. But something else made me agree and not just her excellent arguing skills.

I agreed because of the rumour that'd called me in to the principal in the first place. The rumour that Della was in love with me.

My heart had stopped and hadn't beaten correctly since. It was just a silly rumour, but I agreed with Ms. Sapture: truth lived in rumour, and if such a thing was said...

Could it be true?

Who had started it?

And how could they screw up my mind by making me fear that my love for Della wasn't pure, after all. That it was tainted and no longer black and white.

I withdrew even more from her.

I stopped using her nickname.

Whatever physical contact still existed between us, ceased all together.

She obeyed me and stripped the blue from her hair but that was about all she obeyed me in.

We became strangers living in the same apartment, and I couldn't stop it because every time I looked at her...I wondered.

I wondered what she felt for me.

I wondered what she kept hidden.

I wondered about so many things I shouldn't wonder about.

For eight long weeks, I ignored her when she was home, yet made her text me after each class. Just a quick *I'm fine* to let me know she hadn't been taken by CPS. It was the only way I could focus on my work and not get trampled by the cows. And ignoring her at home was the only way I could be civil and not tear into her, demanding answers to the sick questions inside my head.

Was she in love with me?

And if she was...where the fuck did that leave us?

The incident should've ended up with us homeless and running again, but somehow, it was swept under the rug and life continued as normal.

All of it, from the threat of Social Services to the rumour of Della's affection for me, was never mentioned again.

It made me nervous.

It made a ticking clock hover over my head, speeding up time and somehow slowing it down.

Christmas and New Year's came and went.

We didn't celebrate it.

Spring arrived, and as snow left the world a more habitable place, Della withdrew from me as I'd withdrawn from her, causing an even worse strain between us.

God, I missed her, but I had no idea how to fix something I didn't understand.

Then, two weeks before our joint birthday, I broke my wrist.

The pain of being kicked by a cow while trying to hook it up the milking machine was a price I'd happily pay all over again because it gave Della back to me. If only for a little while.

She swooped toward me after I'd driven home one-handed, turned off my bike, then stomped down the stairs and into our tiny apartment.

Her eyes widened with worry, taking in my swollen ugly wrist, instantly losing her wariness around me and fussing as kindly and as sweetly as she had with the splinter.

She bustled around, fear and affection thick in her voice as she charged to the mostly-empty freezer to find something cold for the swelling.

With jerky speed, she flew back to me, skidding to a stop and falling to her knees before me. Her focus entirely on making me better and no other mess from before.

Having her close.

Having her care.

Fuck.

I couldn't help myself.

I reached out to cup her cheek as she rested a bag of frozen peas on my skin, so grateful to have my Della back.

The moment I touched her, she flinched and melted at the same time.

The nastiness of pushing each other away vanished, and with a bone-deep sigh, she rested her cheek in my palm.

It was all I could do to stay touching her innocently. My body bellowed to clutch her tight, to stop thinking about everything, to just give in to whatever pulled us together.

The sensation of holding her was one of coming home after being lost for so long, and I *ached*.

I ached with a need so hungry, so raw, I couldn't think.

All I wanted to do was slip off the dining chair and pull her against me. Words and apologies filled my mouth with bitter regret. Why had I been so cruel to her? How had I forgotten how much I cared for this girl?

We stayed like that for far too long, me bent over her with my hand on her cheek and her curled on the floor with a heart-stealing wish in her eyes.

My lips tingled. My fingers fluttered. And Della arched up on her knees.

My attention fell to her mouth.

Her blonde hair—no longer blue or fantastical—hung over her shoulder, tickling my knuckles, and I wanted something I'd never wanted before.

I wanted things to be different. I wanted things to be innocent between us again but finally ready to accept that that would never happen.

She licked her lips, breaking the spell, inviting me to do something I desperately wanted. I needed to kiss her. But I needed it to be right. I'd had enough wrongness between us to risk losing her again.

I sat taller in my chair to kiss her forehead. To kiss her like I was allowed.

The moment my mouth touched her skin, she inhaled sharply, swallowing a quick moan. She bowed into me, pressing herself against my legs.

My thighs bunched as my body hardened against my will, and lust that I had no right to feel became excruciating.

With clenched teeth, I dropped my touch, removed my kiss, and tore my gaze away.

Standing with a wobble born from everything she made me feel, I stepped around her still hunched on the kitchen floor. Breathing for the first time since I'd kissed her, I headed to the dresser where my clothes waited, grabbed a cleaner pair of jeans and t-shirt, then walked down the corridor to change in the bathroom away from her heated eyes.

It took me twice as long, awkward and painful with only one working hand.

If things were simple between us, I would've asked for Della's help. I would've chuckled as she wrangled me from my t-shirt and teased her as she unzipped my jeans.

But things weren't simple. And that would be a complication I couldn't afford.

By the time we made it to the emergency room, taking the bus to the downtown hospital, my wrist was three times the size and an angry blue to match Della's ribbon.

The nurse checked us in, asked for a deposit up front as we didn't have documents or identification for insurance, advised I'd need X-rays and most likely a cast, and finally that the wait was long.

I told Della to go home. She had school in the morning, and who knew how much time we'd waste in this place.

She nodded to appease me but never left.

She sat beside me, reading trashy magazines, getting me coffee and water, never leaving my side for longer than a few minutes. Every so often, I felt her watching me through a curtain of blonde, her fingers tracing her lips. She'd avert her gaze the second I noticed, leaving me confused and achy and in more pain than before.

It was the longest evening of my life sitting in that room. Not because of my wrist but because of her.

It was a constant fight not to hug her close and kiss her softly. All I wanted to do was be free with my actions and affections. I just wanted to touch her to reassure myself that she was still here, despite the stress of the past few months.

But I couldn't.

I was no longer allowed to hug and touch because my thoughts were no longer clear.

When I finally saw a doctor, underwent X-rays and learned the news that a couple of fingers as well as my wrist had been broken, I wouldn't wish it away for anything.

The cow that kicked me gave me a night I'd never forget. It deleted the stilted strangeness that festered between me and Della, and I had my best friend back.

We went home together that night, me in a cast and Della with her arm looped through mine. We sat in comfortable silence on the bus home, had a midnight snack of cereal and milk, then she took my hand and instead of saying goodnight and going to our separate rooms, she led me into hers.

I baulked at the doorway, staring at her double bed, seeing it not as a place to rest but a battlefield in which I'd never stop fighting.

But I couldn't stop her when she tugged me forward, whispering, "I miss you, Ren. Please…just for one night."

I'd never been able to deny her anything.

And so, despite my better judgment, I stayed.

Together, we stripped to underwear and slipped beneath the covers.

We didn't touch, lying stiffly in the dark, but having her so close I could hear her breathing and feel her heat and smell her lovely scent...I was happier than I'd been in a very long time.

* * * * *

"Happy Birthday, Ren." Della gave me a card with one of those tinsel rosettes stuck to the envelope.

We sat in a burger joint with red vinyl and grease-stained music posters. Tradition demanded our birthday meal took place in a diner, but I ensured it was different to the last one where she left me to eat with Tom.

"I thought we agreed we weren't buying each other presents." I put down my fry and wiped salt-dusted fingers on a serviette. "Now I just feel like crap because I didn't get you anything."

"Ah, well." She shrugged. "I saw it the other day, and I had no choice. It had your name all over it."

I frowned as I tore at the glue holding the envelope shut. Sliding my finger under the seam, I ripped the paper and pulled out a card with a picture of a forest wreathed in fog.

My heart thudded harder, knowing it belonged there over anywhere; my legs tensed to run to wherever this photo had been taken. "It's beautiful." I looked up, smiling. "Thank you."

Della rolled her eyes. "Open it, you moron." Wearing a black dress with her hair slicked in a high silky ponytail, she was pure elegance. She'd grown up, and the change in her from sixteen to seventeen hurt my chest whenever I stared too much.

I'd loathed her wardrobe choices lately; mainly because they were far more revealing than before. She was beautiful in whatever she wore, but the tight shorts and skirts, the tops that clung to her...it all drove me mad trying to stop myself from hunting down the men who stared at her in appreciation.

She deserved to be appreciated—just not by them.

Not by *any* man.

Including me.

Cracking open the card, another picture fell out, this one torn from a hunting and fishing catalogue. Picking it off the table, I flipped it over until I looked at a four-person tent with a small alcove for gear and two sleeping pods off the main living. The price had been blacked out with a picture of a scribbled balloon.

"What..." I looked up. "You bought me a tent?"

She scooted her chair closer. "Uh-huh. It's the perfect size for when I finish school and we leave again. You won't have to feel awkward sleeping with me squished so close, see?" She tapped the picture in my grip. "We would each have our own wing and our stuff would be safe in the middle. It's brown like your hair, so it will disappear in the forest, and the fly screens are green. It's perfect, don't you think?" Her blue eyes danced with futures I hadn't dared think about.

My life until now had been a monotony of riding to work, cows, riding home, and staying close but not too close with Della. I hadn't dared think about what would happen when she'd finished school.

About what I wanted.

About what I needed.

The past few years had been a different chapter to our normal world—totally unrelated to who we truly were. An episode of treading water until we could go home, be happy, and figure out how we fit into each other's lives after so much.

The concept that we could leave this place...*run*.

Just us.

Fuck, I wanted it more than I could stand.

Her voice dropped when I said nothing. "You weren't planning on staying here...were you, Ren?"

I blinked, dragged into the conversation against my will. Unprepared to show her how desperate I was for something different...something better and bearable between us. "Well, no. I mean, I hadn't thought—"

She dragged a fry through her tomato sauce. "We need to start thinking about it. This is my last year of high school. We can leave soon."

Leave...

I cleared my throat as that promise did its best to wrap around my heart and free me from every restriction I'd put in place. "But what about *your* future? What do *you* want to do?"

"I want to go back to the forest. I've told you that."

"There are no jobs out there, Della. No boys to make a family with. No future apart from—"

"Apart from with you," she whispered.

I froze, studying her face and the naked desire there.

The restaurant disappeared. Silence descended, turning the world mute.

I stopped breathing.

She stopped breathing.

The only thing we survived on was the vicious, violent bond that we'd always shared but had somehow magnified from virtuous to blistering.

Her eyes filled with promises, pleas—things that filled the chambers of my heart with crucifying futures I could never have.

We stared for an eternity, drowning in each other, before I closed the card with a snap and shoved it back toward her. "I can't accept this."

She flinched. "Too late, it's in our apartment. I didn't bother bringing it with us as it's bulky, but it's already yours."

"How did you buy—"

"With my salary from the florist. I still do the odd weekend. Enough to save up some spending money."

I nodded.

I'd known that. Every time she came back from that place, she smelled utterly devine. Honeysuckle and rose petals drove me insane sitting beside her on the couch, pretending to watch TV when really I counted down the seconds for her to go to bed so I could be alone with my traitorous body.

This was too much.

My cast clunked on the table as I shifted uncomfortably, seeking something normal to say. "If you could have anything you wanted for your birthday, what would it be?"

Her eyes burned like blue coal. *"Anything?"*

I swallowed, cursing her. "Within reason." Terror at what she'd ask for locked me to the spot. This was a stupid idea.

Her forehead frowned as if thinking of every gift she'd love but knew better than to ask for. Eventually, she murmured, "A tattoo."

I coughed on a mouthful of Coke. "Excuse me?"

"I've wanted one for ages, but I knew you wouldn't approve."

Normally, I would agree with her. I'd had a panic attack when she'd come home one afternoon with her ears pierced, let alone her skin inked, but that was then and this was now. Della had once again unsettled me with talks of futures and forest freedoms. I needed to change the subject with something—anything to stop the electricity humming unpermitted between us.

"Okay," I whispered.

Her eyes widened. "What did you say?"

"I said okay. Let's go get a tattoo."

"You're—you're serious?" Her head tilted to the side, her hair swishing down her back in one long rope.

"Deadly. If you want to permanently mark your skin and regret it later, who am I to stop you?"

"I'll need a guardian who is over eighteen to sign the paperwork." She stood, inching her way around the table to stand in front of me, her tight black dress showing off every sinful curve. "Is that going to be a problem?"

I shook my head. "No problem. You want a tattoo. You can have one." Keeping my attention on her face, I stood. "Your decision."

"Yes!" She threw her arms around me, wedging her breasts against my chest, deleting space I dreadfully needed to keep between us.

I swallowed my groan as I nuzzled her against my will, hugging her fierce, missing her hard.

She trembled in my arms, her breathing quick and shallow. Her leg slipped between mine, inappropriate and far too close. "I've missed hugging you, Ren. So much." Her lips pressed against my t-shirt.

My body reacted, my heart smoked, and even though I had to fight every muscle, I pushed her away with a careless shrug as if she hadn't just crippled me all over again. "A birthday hug before your birthday tattoo."

She nodded sharply, liquid suspiciously bright in her gaze. "Right."

It physically stung not to gather her close again, but I held out my arm, the only form of contact I could handle. "Come on. Let's go get your seventeenth birthday present."

She looped her arm through mine.

And we pretended things were perfectly normal.

Chapter Fifty-Seven

REN

2017

SHE GOT A ribbon.

Of course, she did.

A long blue ribbon that wrapped twice around her ankle with one end flared on her calf while the other trailed down the bones of her foot, twisting into a shape that looked suspiciously like an R.

When she showed me after two hours in the tattooist chair, I'd almost beaten up the artist. They'd shown me the original sketch that was drawn and printed on her skin prior to inking and that ribbon had ended with a kick in its tail.

Normal.

This one, the *permanent* one, looped over itself and back across in a letter not a shape. A letter that happened to be the first of my name.

Della hadn't even tried to act ashamed, high on marking her skin with an unforgettable, unforgivable symbol.

With shaking hands, I paid the artist and was grateful when he wrapped Della's leg and foot in cellophane, blurring the design enough so I could pretend I'd seen something that wasn't there.

By the time we'd returned home, my temper was short, my mind a mess, and the tent resting in its untouched box on the coffee table just made me tip into places I could no longer run from.

Grabbing Della, I marched her to the couch, shoved her down, and kneeled before her.

"What are you—"

"Shut up," I hissed, hell bent on finding answers I was afraid of.

She gasped as I tore at the cellophane, unwrapping the plastic, revealing the slimy aftercare cream and the vibrant blue ribbon forever inked into her skin.

Two hundred dollars and she'd fucking ruined me.

My teeth hurt I clenched so hard as what I'd feared stared back at me.

Not an ordinary ribbon but one with a goddamn message. "What the hell is this?" I looked up, seething and ruthless. My fingernails dug into her foot as I held it on my thigh.

She tried to yank it away, her black dress riding up her legs, the flash of red underwear sending yet more rage into my already out of control temper.

"Nothing."

"It's not *nothing*, Della."

"It's nothing, okay?" She shrugged with a worried look in her gaze. "It's a ribbon. That's all."

My hands, despite themselves, feathered up her calf to her knee. I couldn't stop them, and I couldn't stop her reaction as her legs parted and her lips sucked in desperate air.

She should hate me for touching her.

She should leap away and smite me for even *thinking* of touching her.

But she did the opposite.

Her entire body beckoned, clouding my head, making me sick with—

"What the hell are you doing?" I groaned as I shoved her aside and stood on trembling legs.

I needed to get laid.

I shouldn't have blocked myself from other people's affection just because I preferred Della's company over everybody else's.

I wasn't naïve.

I knew Della was experimenting and testing, and this was just another push to see what I would do. Only problem was, I didn't know what I'd do if she pushed me any further.

Raking my hands through my hair, I paced the lounge as Della shuffled higher on the couch, her eyes dropping to her newly inked ankle and foot.

I couldn't look at her. Couldn't stand to see what she'd done to herself.

It hurt.

It hurt so damn much to love her so fucking dearly but be so confused. I loved her in so many ways, but here she was, trying to get me to love her in an entirely different one, and I honestly didn't know if I could.

How was I supposed to see past the little girl I'd raised?

How was I supposed to be a man with her when I would forever be her boy?

How was I supposed to be okay with the changes in my need for her?

The answer?

I couldn't.

I was projecting my desires onto her, making myself believe she sent me messages when really, they were entirely innocent.

She wasn't inviting me.

She wasn't messing me up.

This was *my* fault.

I was reading into things that weren't there.

There was no message. No ulterior cry for more.

I was the one turning innocent into dirty, and it had to stop. *Right now.*

She confirmed I was the one making a mess of everything by murmuring, "Ren, I'm sorry. You're right. I did ask him to make it wrap like an R. I didn't think you'd be so mad. I thought you'd appreciate it."

I spun to face her, willing to hear the truth after my stupid mind muddied everything. "Go on."

She spread her hands helplessly. "I love you. I'll *always* love you. You're my family. Is it so wrong that I wanted a reminder of you on me at all times?" She blinked back tears, urging me to believe. "I'm sorry. It doesn't mean anything, okay? I know we never talk about it, but that kiss at Cherry River has been infecting everything between us for years. It's a toxin that I don't know how to get rid of, and it's changed how you see me and I *miss* you, Ren. I miss you so much. I miss that I can't hug you and say silly things without you tensing and thinking I'm trying to get you into bed. I miss that I can't get a tattoo that represents both me and you and explain that it's a symbol of togetherness and nothing more. That's all. That's it. If you were a girl who'd run away with me and been there every day of my life, I would feel the exact same way. I would want something permanent to remind me of all the amazing times we've shared and all the sacrifices you gave me." A single tear rolled down her cheek. "Please, it's nothing more than that.

You have to believe me."

I backed up, hearing the truth beneath her shaky promises.
This was all my fault.

"I'm sorry, Della." I wanted to use her nickname, to prove to her that things hadn't changed so much that I could no longer say it. But my skin felt foreign, my heart a stranger, and I needed to fix myself before it was too late.

Stalking to the front door, I grabbed my keys and my phone.

Tonight, I'd reached my limit.

I needed companionship that would hopefully clear my head. I needed to be away from Della in order to do that.

Not looking back, I said, "Don't...don't wait up for me."

I slammed the door before I could fall before her and beg her to forgive me.

Chapter Fifty-Eight

DELLA

Present Day

THAT WAS THE *beginning of the end.*

If I could, I'd rewind time and never get that ridiculous tattoo. I couldn't explain what came over me as the artist bent over my foot and dug his needles into my virgin skin. Ren had paced the front of the shop, studying blown-up pieces on the wall, flicking through books with tattoo designs.

I'd thought I would be happy with the simple design, but the longer the tattooist dragged his needles, the more it felt like only half of the puzzle. The ribbon had been a part of my life since the day I could remember...just like Ren.

It wouldn't be right to draw myself without him there to weave into the tale, too.

With Ren's back to us, I'd whispered to the tattooist to flow the ribbon into a capital R. He'd given me a strange look, glanced at Ren who'd signed the paperwork with his matching last name to mine, and shrugged as if it wasn't his business.

He'd finished the piece quickly, and my heart swelled as the formation of the first letter of the word I loved most in the world came into being on my foot.

Only, I hadn't thought ahead.

I didn't guess how rattled Ren would be or understand how much he was cracking beneath the constant mixed messages I sent him.

He was right to doubt me.

I promised myself I kept my secrets about loving him hidden. I lay in bed congratulating myself on being able to lie to his face and laugh about something silly when all I wanted to do was climb into his lap and pull his lips to mine.

But...I wasn't as good an actress as I believed.

I couldn't have been because if I had, Ren would never have suspected any other meaning than sweet connection thanks to the freshly finished tattoo.

It was my fault he demanded to know what I meant.

It was my fault I couldn't answer him truthfully.

It was my fault he went out that night.

And it was my fault he stayed out until dawn and when he came back, lipstick stained his t-shirt and his hair was mused from another's fingers.

I didn't know if he'd slept with someone, but he'd definitely made out, and it ripped me apart.

I'd been hiding for years and I'd finally reached my limit.

I stayed away from him the next day and the day after that.

I made sure to wear socks long enough to cover my new artwork and even wondered if there would be a way to laser it off so I could pretend I'd never been so stupid.

For a week, our conversations consisted of stiff hellos, goodbyes, and how were your days, but it all came to a head on a Friday evening when his phone chirped on the coffee table.

He was in the shower after a long shift at the milk farm.

Normally, a Friday meant pizza or takeaway and a chilled evening in front of the TV, recharging after a long week.

Not this Friday.

This Friday, I picked up his phone and brought up the notification.

Ren Wild, the boy from the forest and avoider of company, had joined a hook-up site.

He'd been matched with three women in the area and had obviously messaged one because her reply was a simple: I'm interested for no strings. I don't want commitment, either. I'll meet you at Paddington's at ten p.m. Bring a condom.

* * * * *

Can you understand why I did what I did next?

Can you put aside your judgment just for a little while and give me some slack for being a bratty, stupid teenager who didn't grow up fast enough? Who chased away the one person she'd ever loved? Who ruined everything when it had all been so good?

If you can't, then I don't want you reading anymore—not that you will as I'm burning this in a few short days, anyway.

But if you can, then keep torturing yourself because it only gets messy from here.

Super messy.

End of the world, Ren leaving me, kind of messy.

Let's see…first there was Tom.

Then there was Larry.

After that…some boy I didn't get his name but tasted like blueberries from the lollipop he'd been sucking on.

The nights that Ren left and didn't come back till late, hopping in the shower almost the second he walked in the door, and unable to meet my eyes the next morning, were the nights I stopped wishing.

I stopped hoping that one day...Ren and me...well, I stopped being so young.

I finally accepted what he was telling me. There would never *be a Ren and me, and it was time I stopped killing myself over it.*

The best way to do that was to find a replacement.

I only kissed the boys.

Or at least, I did at the start. By the time Blueberry came around, I was itching for more, if only to erase the blistering emptiness inside me.

I let him touch me.

I let him kiss my breasts and press his fingers inside me.

And I felt nothing.

I think that destroyed me the most.

Here I was doing my best to move on, but my body was just as broken as my mind. The things Tina told me should happen like the tensing and the quickening and the sparkling orgasms never happened.

All I felt was the probing of unskilled fingers and the swirl of tentative tongue.

Some nights, when Ren stayed out super late, I'd feel so rotten, so sick, so twisted, that the next evening—regardless if it was a school night or not—I'd find a party somewhere and crash. I'd dance like a slut and encourage like a whore, and when a boy finally kissed me, I'd want to vomit with tearful disgust.

For almost a year, we co-existed in shame.

Him doing whatever it was he was doing, and me doing my best to move on.

I didn't want to be this doormat. I didn't want to be this weak. When I hooked up with a guy, I pinned all my hopes and dreams on him and truly listened to what he had to say. I laughed at his jokes, even if they weren't funny. I answered his questions, even if they were hard, and I truly did my best to make a connection so I could find some self-worth after so many years of self-hate.

But it never worked.

No matter how much I tried to release myself from Ren, returning to him every night, living with him, loving him...it tied me up into knots I could never be free from.

I often thought about leaving.

Of running away so I could stop being so weak.

But every time I thought about waking up without him, of living in a world without him, I couldn't do it. I'd unpack the bag I'd hastily stuffed in the darkness and accept that this was my punishment for every sin I'd committed.

The one saving grace was Ren never saw a woman twice.

Believe me, I knew.

I became a master of reading his phone when he was in the shower, skimming over past messages and investigating new ones.

For some reason, even knowing he was running to these women to fuck, I still felt better than them because he returned to me afterward. They might borrow his body, but I ruled his heart, and he was still mine.

Until…one day, that assurance and kingdom that I'd always treasured was threatened to be invaded by infidels.

A second date.

A woman who went by the name Rachel989.

Her message carved out my heart with an ice-cream scooper: I had fun last night. I know we agreed it was a one-time thing, but there's something about you. I'd love to see you again.

I would've deleted it and hoped Ren never saw it.

If it wasn't for his reply: Okay. Tonight. Same place.

I'd rushed to the sink and thrown up.

Dramatic right?

Yep, I said so to my body. I schooled it for the long minutes that Ren was in the bathroom, and I plastered on a fake smile when he came out dressed in a black button-down and faded jeans that hugged him like a second skin. His sable hair was tussled from rough towel-drying. His lips pouty and almost sad. His eyes dark with unshared things.

He was drop-dead gorgeous, and he didn't even know it.

Of course, this Rachel989 would want a second date. She would want him for a third and a fourth and marriage, too. And I'd finally been slapped in the face with my reality.

Ren was twenty-seven, almost twenty-eight. He was at the age when people settled down and started families of their own. He would eventually replace me with his own sons and daughters…and wife.

And as he kissed my cheek and asked what I had planned for the evening, I marvelled at how steady my voice was. How I could fib so effortlessly when every piece of me was breaking. How I could stand there with my bones shattered and organs splattered on the kitchen floor.

That was my true performance because he never knew how much I sobbed the moment he closed the door, promising to be home soon.

I sobbed so much I couldn't breathe, and my tears were no longer tears, but great heaving, ugly convulsions where hugging myself didn't work, where lying to myself didn't work, where promises that it would get better definitely didn't work.

I'm sure you can probably guess what I did next?

If you can't, then you've never been in love with someone who was off making a future with someone else.

Wiping away my grief, I crawled to my phone and went on the Facebook group listing campus parties in my area. There was one that a student at the local university that I'd considered applying at for their creative writing course was hosting.

It was late.

The party was probably winding down by now, but I stripped and climbed into the shower. I shaved every part of me. I styled and painted and slipped into the little black dress I'd worn on the night of my seventeenth birthday.

Unlike that night, when I wore new red lingerie that I hoped peeked out beneath the black straps, tormenting Ren at dinner, this time, I wore nothing.

I wasn't playing games anymore.

I was done, and this was war.

I caught an Uber to the party as my killer heels would break my ribbon embroidered foot before I could arrive, and I sashayed my way into the tipsy crowd, looking for a particular kind of prey.

A boy of pretty origins, slightly drunk, single, and up for fun.

And when I found him, I pulled him to the side and told him the truth. I hid my cracked voice behind a sultry beg and said, "I'm in love with someone else who doesn't want me. I'm a virgin who doesn't want to be innocent anymore. I want to forget…about all of it."

I'd pulled away, expecting him to run but needing him to understand that I wasn't going to be an easy lay. I would be skittish and jumpy and most likely cry at some point, but I'd chosen him and all I expected him to do was relieve me of the one thing that I'd started to hate.

I didn't want to be a virgin anymore because Ren most definitely wasn't.

He'd waited until he was nineteen but on the cusp of my eighteenth, he'd well and truly ensured I had a fair number to sleep with before I caught up to him.

Any idiotic concepts I'd had of saving myself for him—of him waking up one day and climbing into my bed with words like how stupid he'd been and how much he loved me and wanted me and needed me and then he'd kiss me and touch me and fill me and…

I sighed, blinking with my freshly painted eyelashes and waited for this pretty stranger to save me.

To make his life easier, I opened my beaded bag and pulled out a condom.

The first condom from the box of twelve that Ren had bought for me.

Inside my bag, all I had was some cash, my phone, and two more condoms. Because who knew if once would be enough to ease the agony in my soul?

"What's your name?" the pretty stranger asked.

I paused, wanting to use a fake one to protect me from any future pain but determined to ruin myself as much as I could, to prove I was brave enough to survive anything. "Ribbon. Della Ribbon."

He rubbed the back of his neck, disrupting his dark blonde hair, blinking with baby blue eyes, looking the exact opposite of Ren.

I was glad.

I wanted to look into this stranger's face when he was inside me and have no doubt that he wasn't Ren.

"And his name?" he murmured as he stepped closer, cupping my chin and studying me. "The guy who's just thrown you away?"

My eyes burned, but I kept the sobs away. "Wild. Ren Wild."

It was the first time no one believed we were related. Two different last names. Two different futures.

"Well, Della Ribbon," the stranger said. "He just made the biggest mistake of his life." Drawing me close with his fingers on my chin, he kissed me sweetly.

I suppose I should stop there.

I should fade to black and let your imagination fill in the blanks, but I'm feeling extra martyr-ish today, so I'm going to tell you what happened.

It was nice, really. Exactly what I'd asked for.

First, I kissed him back.

I willed my mind to blank and gave everything had into his control. The kiss was innocent to start with, warm lips and soft touches, but then he took my hand and guided me through the stragglers still lolling on couches and drinking against walls and led me upstairs.

My legs shook and the draft from not wearing underwear reminded me exactly what I was about to do.

Part of me screamed not to do this, that I wasn't ready, while the other stabbed her pitchfork into the dirt of my soul and screeched that it was.

I was ready to be an adult.

I'd been ready for so, so long.

"Don't you want to know my name?" the pretty stranger asked as he guided me into a room with a queen bed, white bedding, and a mountain of pillows.

It was a girl's bedroom.

I didn't know whose house this was or where this room's owner was, but I didn't care as the stranger spun me around and pressed me against the wall.

"Do you?" he asked again, his eyes blazing blue, his lips wet and waiting.

"Is it wrong if I say no?" I dropped my gaze, expecting him to leave. I didn't know why I didn't want to know his name. After all, I needed something to remember him by. He would forever be part of my life—taking my virginity would tie him to me regardless if I wanted it to or not.

But he smiled softly, nodding as if he understood. "Are you going to pretend I'm him?" He kissed me gently, waiting for me to reply.

Against his lips, I murmured, "I don't want to, but I can't promise anything."

How lucky was I? How incredibly lucky to be honest and not have to pretend to be brave and sexy. I didn't have to hide my shakes. I didn't have to fake my fear.

He kissed me again, and I opened my mouth, licking him. When he pulled away for a breath, I moaned, "I don't want to think about him. That's the point."

"Well, think about me then. Think about where I touch you..." His fingers trailed down my face to my breast, cupping me with a pressure that wasn't enough. "Think about where I kiss you..." He pressed his mouth to my neck, sending coils of desire through my belly. "Think about where I'm going to fill you..." His fingers drifted down my thigh and hooked under the hem of my dress. With locked eyes, he shoved aside the material and skated his touch, up and up.

I bit my lip, breathing fast as he touched me between the legs and found I wore no underwear.

A firework of surprise showed in his blue gaze as his fingers feathered over my newly shaved mound. "You truly came here to do this...didn't you?"

I nodded as he pressed a finger inside me.

The condom in my hand fluttered to the floor as his mouth found mine again and kissed me deep.

I sighed, clutching at his shoulders and letting my bag drop to where the condom landed.

The stranger could kiss.

His fingers felt better than other boys who'd touched me.

And it didn't take long for my body to shed its sadness and welcome any other feeling but heartache.

I spread my legs, pressing my spine against the wall and hooking my fingers into his belt.

He groaned as I cupped his erection, tracing the hardness, learning that his length and girth were impressive and would most likely hurt me.

I shivered harder, a mix of terror and lust making me jumpy. My mind was nothing but fog—a mist where no thought could find me apart from touch.

Kiss.

Finger.

Sex.

No Ren.

No breaking hearts.

No Rachel989s.

My hand worked harder on his belt as he made me wet. His one finger morphed to two, stretching me in all the right ways. My head turned heavy, my eyes hazy as I struggled to free him.

Ducking to his knees, the stranger hooked my leg over his shoulder and kissed me in a place no one else had before.

His tongue ran over my smooth seam, flicking on the clit I'd been told did wonderful things but still had yet to learn them.

My knees almost buckled as lightning bolts appeared from nowhere. I latched my fingers into his hair, a flash of Ren filling my head with his sable copper locks.

I bashed my head into the wall behind me, wanting him out, needing him gone so I could enjoy this.

This wasn't because of him.

This was because of me.

And he was once again ruining it.

"Della Ribbon..." the stranger moaned as his tongue entered me, and I collapsed into his arms. Pressing me against the carpet, he climbed on top of me, his hips thrusting between mine, his metal zipper cold against my heated wetness.

I squirmed beneath him, needing more, instinct making me reach for him and unbuckle his belt.

His hands fumbled for the condom on the floor as I successfully unbuckled his belt then unzipped his jeans. The minute I shoved them down his legs, followed quickly by his boxers, I gasped at the size.

I didn't want to get hurt, but ouch, I couldn't imagine how he'd fit inside me.

"It's okay," the stranger murmured as he arched his hips and rolled the condom on. Once sheathed, he cupped my cheek again. "I'll do my best not to hurt you."

I nodded. I didn't know what for, but I was grateful. Out of all the horny teenagers I could've chosen, this boy wasn't like them. He took his time. He kissed me sweet. He smoothed my trembles and wiped a rogue tear away as his kisses swept me away from Ren and delivered me to Ren at the same time.

"Do you want me to stop?" he whispered as my legs tried to clamp around his hips, feeling the strangeness of hard man against the soft yielding of me.

I paused, biting my lip, staring at the ceiling with a chest full of icicles and dread.

Did I want him to stop?

Not really.

Did I want him to hurry?

Yes.

Pulling his head back down to mine, I kissed him with heat and demand. "I want you to finish this."

His eyebrows knitted together as if I'd hurt him, but his lips sought mine again as his hand wrapped around my hipbone. "I should do this in a bed for your first time." His other hand disappeared between us, guiding the tip of him to my entrance.

I stiffened as the first press of him warned that this wasn't a joke.

This was happening.

"I don't care."

I was about to lose every shred of innocence I had left to a boy I didn't know his name.

"Wait." I pushed at his shoulders.

He gritted his teeth but didn't try to enter me. "You changed your mind?"

Resting my hands on his ass, I pulled him into me, making his eyes widen and mouth pop wide. As he sank into me, I shook my head. "No. But I want to know your name."

He groaned as his length slid inside me, then hit an obstruction that pinched and burned.

He looked at me, looked through me, looked right into the person I was and said, "My name is David."

David.

Della and David.

It had a nice ring to it.

We poised on the point of no return, his elbows jamming into the floor beside my ears, holding himself above me. "Do you want me to finish, Della Ribbon?"

My heart gave one massive kick of denial before I nodded. "Yes..."

And the rest is history.

He thrust inside, tore apart my virginity, and tried to be as gentle as he could. All the while, tears leaked from my eyes, and I kissed him with a ferocity that ended up with us rolling around on the floor as I fought him for power.

I wanted him to pin me down and take everything I had to give. Instead, he let me manipulate him. He allowed me to roll him onto his back and ride him on top, not caring that my insides hurt or the pleasure in my blood was mixed up, screwed up, and so far away from heaven that it sent me plummeting to hell where I surely deserved to live.

It lasted longer than I thought it would.

His thrusting sent ripples through me, his harsh breathing and tattered groans made me feel powerful and wanted, but when his pace increased and his fingers tightened and his kisses deepened, I didn't leap into the void with him.

He came.

I didn't.

He kissed me.

I kissed him back.

And then my cell phone rang, putting a full stop on one of the strangest paragraphs of my life.

Funny how Ren knew the exact moment to call. Almost as if he had some sixth sense telling him what I'd just done.

I ignored it.

Most of the time, I got home before Ren even noticed I was missing.

But not that night.

Unfortunately, or fortunately—depending on how you look at it—he caught me on the worst one, ringing me again, just as I was wiping a Kleenex between my legs and marvelling at the smear of blood.

Once again, I let it ring as I exited the bathroom attached to the bedroom where I'd lost my virginity and padded barefoot to David.

He pulled me into his arms, kissing my temple and hugging me close. "I'm sorry I wasn't who you wanted."

I kissed his chest before letting him go to put his t-shirt on. "You were the best person for me to lose it with. I'm glad it was you."

He smiled. "Well, I'm honoured." Buckling his jeans, he stood awkwardly by the door as I rearranged my dress. "Do you want to…eh, stay in touch?"

My heart fluttered at the way he looked at me. At the fascinated puppy dog crush that no doubt made him feel all protective and smitten with a girl who begged for sex in such a sad, pathetic way.

I smiled, picking my beaded bag off the floor and stuffing the two unused condoms inside. "It's fine. I knew what I was doing. You don't have to worry about me."

My phone danced around again, chirping its annoying little chirp.

"Are you going to get that?" he asked.

"Why? It only hurts."

He held open the door for me to exit the room. "Want me to talk to him?"

I laughed. "That would be interesting."

The chirping grew louder, and I sighed. "He'll be concerned about me."

"In that case, you better answer it." Tucking a curl behind my ear, he murmured, "Come find me after. We'll have a drink. Get to know each other

a little."

The fact that he liked me enough to want to hang out even though he'd already gotten me into bed made me warmer than I'd been in a while. "Sure."

With a handsome smile, David left me alone as I sucked in a steadying breath and smoothed down my dress one last time.

I pressed accept on the call. "Hello?"

My voice was empty and flat like it was most of the time these days, and I didn't have time to fix on the Della false brightness and strength that Ren was used to hearing from me.

"Della?" His tormented tone slipped into my ear making tears stab my eyes. "Where are you?"

"I'm safe, don't worry."

"That's not what I asked."

I let silence gather between us as I stared at floral wallpaper in some stranger's house.

"Della?" His voice dropped to a whisper. "Tell me where you are. What happened?"

Now, there were two scenarios I could've done and knowing the outcome of the one I chose, I should've gone for the other one.

I should've told him I was fine, and that I'd be home soon. I should've kept my secrets just a little longer, hidden my heartbreak for just a little more, but with my insides bruised from another man and that same man actually wanting to spend time with me, I was done playing this part.

I was through pretending and wanted to ensure the canyon that'd formed between us could never be repaired.

And I had the perfect way to do it.

"Della, answer me," Ren commanded.

So I answered him.

I told him things I should've taken to my grave because who wants to hear about another being so vindictive and lost they'd practically do anything for a sliver of happiness.

"I'm at a house party a few blocks from home. I Ubered here in my little black dress with no underwear, and I selected a boy from the dwindling crowd."

His harsh inhale sounded like thunder in my ear.

"Do you want me to continue?" I breathed, rubbing at the fiery ruin of my heart.

"Yes," he strangled. "Finish. Tell me."

"This boy kissed me and took me upstairs, and I told him I was a virgin who was tired of being a child. I asked him to relieve me of it." Tears cascaded down my cheeks as I confessed, knowing full well I broke his heart as well as mine. "And...he did."

Ren hung up.

Chapter Fifty-Nine

REN

2018

IT WASN'T HARD to find her.

Whatever Facebook group she joined, I joined too.

Whatever event she tagged as interested in attending, I clicked the button too.

Thanks to social media, I knew more about Della's schedule than she thought, and tonight was no different.

I killed my bike outside the house.

Music still filtered from cracked windows with a few shadows of people dancing in the living room. I wanted to stab out my heart that this was the place where Della had come for comfort instead of confiding in me.

I'd failed her so fucking much.

When she'd answered on the third call, I'd been relieved but furious. I'd wanted to tear into her to delete some of the panic in my blood, but that was before I heard her voice. Before the hollow defeat replaced her normally beautiful tone, hinting that tonight...something had happened.

I'd wanted to yell at her for leaving me. I'd wanted to demand her excuses why I'd come home to an empty apartment after meeting a girl I'd met online for the second time.

I'd come home early.

I should never have gone.

It was a mistake.

Every meeting was a mistake.

I'd had a drink with her and let her down gently, my only thought of returning to Della and laughing with her at something stupid on TV or debating the pros and cons about a new camping device.

Each woman I hooked up with was just buying me time, even though I felt it running out. I told myself things between me and Della would go back to the way things were if I got my rampant desire under control. That it wasn't her I dreamed about but some nasty side effect of not having sex for so long.

I'd done my best to believe my lies. I'd honestly wished they were true as I smiled at faceless women and touched unwanted places.

It didn't matter that my lust was being controlled, it didn't stop my dreams becoming more graphic or my days become more difficult the deeper I fell into Della.

I could fuck every female I could find but in the end...no one could cure me but her.

And now, I'd hurt her so much she'd snapped just like I had.

She'd willingly chosen self-harm because it was the only way to leach out some of the pain.

So yes, I wanted to be livid with her. I wanted to strike her, grab her, kiss her with every red-tinted rage, but hearing such desolation from the girl I loved, I couldn't do it.

All I cared about was her safety, her happiness.

All I needed was to get her home.

I clutched at my hair, digging fingernails into my scalp, doing my best to get myself under control. I didn't want to think about what she'd told me. I didn't want to visualise what she'd done. And I daren't focus on how crippled I was knowing she was no longer a virgin.

"Yo, man, party's over." A tipsy boy waved my way, his arm slung over some brunette as they made their way down the garden path. For a house party, the place was well tended with manicured bushes and lush grass.

I didn't know why that bothered me. Why this place was ten times nicer than the apartment Della and I shared or that whoever had accepted her invitation to sleep with her might come from much better stock than me.

He might have money, manners, and mansions.

And what did I have?

Fucking nothing because Della had deliberately torn out my heart and ensured nothing would ever be right again.

Swinging my leg over the bike, I ignored the leaving couple and marched up to the front door. Pushing it open, I entered the cream foyer and narrowed my eyes at the reek of booze and weed.

Only a few lights were on, scattered like islands in the darkness as I made my way through the living room to the kitchen to the den.

No signs of a blonde girl in a black dress.

With sick despair, I followed more rooms, past making out students and giggling girls until I stumbled upon the one thing I couldn't live without.

Curled up in another man's arms, her cheeks pink as he murmured something in her ear.

His hand on her thigh. His lips on her throat.

It was more than I could fucking bear.

Della ran a fingertip along the rim of a champagne glass looking every inch an adult. There was nothing girlish about her with her sex-tussled hair, tight dress, and jaded look in her stunning blue eyes.

I stumbled at the sight as the man grabbed a blanket from the back of the couch and draped it over her lap, stroking her softly. She smiled in thanks, tucking it behind her, hiding the long expanse of beautiful legs, sneaking away the ribbon tattoo complete with its R.

I thought I couldn't stand seeing him touch her before. But it was nothing compared to the shredding, slashing sorrow now.

"Della," I breathed, marching as steadily as I could toward them.

She froze. Her eyes round and shooting to mine. "Ren...what—what are you doing here?"

My hands curled as the man looked me up and down, studying me, judging me, waging war with just one glance.

Tearing my eyes from my enemy, I said, "I came to take you home."

She sipped her half-full champagne. "I'm not ready to go home yet."

Anger sneaked over my pain, granting me safe haven from my misery. I latched onto it, desperate to feel anything but the grief I had no right to feel. "Don't argue with me."

"Don't command me then."

"I'm not commanding you."

"Yes, you are." Her eyes narrowed. "I'm a big girl, Ren. Run along back to Rachel989."

I stiffened. "What?"

"You heard me." She slugged back the rest of the drink in

one mouthful.

"I can take her home. Don't worry about her," the man dared to say.

I didn't look at him, keeping my eyes fixed on Della as I tried and failed not to see the change in her. The new knowledge in her gaze. I'd hoped...

Fuck, I'd hoped it was a lie.

That she'd said something so hurtful on the phone just to punish me, but now, I knew.

She was telling the truth, and she'd fucked the guy currently holding her close like I wanted to do.

And *shit*...that fucking hurt.

"Della. Now." I growled, quickly losing my temper. I'd never beaten someone up before, but if I didn't get her out of his grip soon, I would.

Shoving off the blanket, Della swooped upright. Fire blazed in her eyes as she stalked in bare feet and stabbed me hard in the chest with her finger. "You don't get to boss me around any longer. I'm almost eighteen, Ren. You don't get to baby me anymore."

Grabbing her wrist, I jerked her through the space and toward the front door. "You and I need to talk."

"Hey!" She struggled. "Let me go." Her fingernails scratched my skin, but I didn't release her.

The front door beckoned, night sky and streets to get lost in before we had a conversation that would probably end us forever.

"Oi!" A hand landed squarely between my shoulder blades, shoving me forward.

Stumbling, I instinctually let go of Della so I didn't make her trip with me then spun to face who'd dared touch me.

The man.

"David, don't!" Della called, tripping to get between us.

But it was too late.

All the pain and regret manifested in my fists, and I swung without thinking.

David ducked, his blond head narrowly missing being hit.

He rammed his shoulder into my chest, sending us both slamming to the ground.

"Stop! Both of you!" Della screamed.

We didn't listen.

I kneed him in the ribs, sending him rolling to the side. He shot to his feet, trying to punch me again.

I punched him first.

I wanted to *kill* him.

My broken wrist, long healed from being cow-kicked, twinged as I swung hard and true and connected with his jaw.

He reeled backward, right into Della.

Oh, fuck no.

I charged forward, intending to throw him off her, but she pushed David to the side and leaped in front of me.

Slamming on the brakes, I managed to avoid bowling her over. "*Move*, Della."

She crossed her arms. "No."

David stood behind her, his eyes glittering with malice and triumph. He knew he'd won because he'd had what I couldn't. He'd taken the most precious thing in the world to me, and fucking gloated about it.

I couldn't help it.

I couldn't walk away from this without making him bleed. He'd fucking destroyed me; it was the least I could do.

I swung again, aiming over Della's shoulder at the bastard's face. Only, she shied the wrong way. David bumped her, sending my fist half into his jaw and half into Della's temple.

"Fuck!" Catching her as she fell, I choked on worse pain I could've imagined. I'd come here wanting to hurt someone, and I'd ended up hurting her.

She moaned, cupping her head with a wince.

David tried to grab her, but I snarled in his face. "Touch her and I'll kill you." I wasn't joking. I didn't need any other reason to murder him. I *wanted* to kill him. Needed to.

He heard the raw truth in my tone.

He froze, allowing me to hoist her into my arms like a groom would carry a bride and stumble through the house to the front door.

Della mumbled something under her breath, her fingers tangled in blonde curls as she rubbed where I'd hit her.

"I'll make it better. I promise," I groaned as I carried her down the steps and across the garden to my bike.

Standing on the threshold, David didn't follow us as I gently placed her on the back of the bike, mounted, revved, and sought her arm to latch it tight around my waist.

She still had strength even if I'd dazed her, and the feeling of her hugging me even if she didn't want to sent my heart smoking with sadness.

"This is my place, Della Ribbon," David called over the rumble of the engine. "Come by anytime."

I fed gasoline to the rumble, turning it into a snarl, ripping from the curb and away from all manner of agonies.

The entire time I drove, all I could focus on was David calling Della by *my* nickname.

She'd allowed a stranger to share something so intimate.

She'd allowed a stranger to take her innocence, and all that was left between us were past mistakes and future heartbreaks.

* * * * *

Home.

A word that was supposed to mean contentment, safety, and love.

Now, it meant nothing as Della leapt off the back of my bike the moment we arrived and cleared the stairs to our apartment before I'd even turned off the engine.

I sighed heavily, killing the rumble and locking up.

Coming home to an empty place before had been a nightmare, but heading inside with a pissed off female who had every right to be angry was even worse.

My boots thumped on the steps as I went to her, stalking over the threshold before closing and bolting the door.

I found her sitting on the couch with a bag of frozen peas held against her temple.

Shit.

Raking hands through my hair, I lingered by the coffee table, not knowing how to fix this. "Della, I'm…I'm sorry."

"You're sorry?" Her eyes flashed as her head snapped up. "Sorry for ruining my night, sorry for punching my date, or sorry for hitting me?" She threw the peas at my face. "What *exactly* are you apologising for, Ren?" She laughed coldly. "Maybe you're apologising for sleeping with half of the female population over the past year? Maybe you're apologising for walking out night after night and leaving me here alone, wondering where the hell you are and who the hell you're doing." She crossed her arms tightly as if warding herself against me. "What do you want to apologise for because I'm confused."

"I didn't sleep with them. Well…" I rubbed the back of my neck. "Not all of them."

"Oh, excuse me for thinking you'd turned into a man whore." She flung up her hands. "Really, you're just a regular male, aren't you? Sleeping around, looking for someone to make you happy."

"You. *You* make me happy."

"Ha! Yet you've never tried to sleep with me."

"*What?!* No, of course not. You're Della! You're—you're—"

"I'm what? Too innocent for you, Ren? Too young? Do you look at me and still see a child because you better open your damn eyes. I haven't been one in a long time." She smiled thinly. "And now I've joined the ranks of adulthood. I'm not a virgin—"

"I don't want to hear it." I held up my hand. "Stop."

"Oh, you don't want to listen? You don't want to know how he took me or what it felt like? Then again, I'm sure you don't need to know. I almost forgot. You have enough experience of your own to fill in the blanks."

"Della, just stop."

"No, how about *you* stop, Ren. You know what I realised tonight?" Her cheeks flamed red as her eyes welled with furious tears. "I realised I hate myself. I hate what I've become. I hate everything I stand for, and I'm done. You hear me? I'm *done*. School is almost finished and instead of moping about wishing for things I can't have, I'm focusing on my future. Did you know David goes to the college who hosted the party tonight? I told him I'm interested in creative writing…that I might want to be a storyteller like you used to be or maybe a journalist or writer or I dunno…. All I know is, I'm moving on. No more thoughts of running back to the forest with you. No more make believe. This is real life, and I'm letting it pass me by. I'm going to enrol next week, so I know where I belong."

Her shoulders slouched with weariness I hadn't seen until now. "I'm weak for giving up, but I tried. I really did."

I stepped toward her, hesitant, wary. "Tried what? What aren't you telling me?"

Her fatigue faded with yet more crackling rage. "Are you really that blind? Do you honestly not know? Or maybe it's because of me. Maybe because you raised me, you can't see past the mess of being sole guardian to an entirely reliant child. And maybe that's my fault for not realising that sooner; for believing that the love we share wasn't just one-dimensional but could grow into something different."

She glowered at the ceiling, tears trailing paths down her cheeks. "God, I've been so *stupid*."

Every inch of me begged to go to her, to hug her close and do my best to shield her from her unhappiness, but I couldn't move. I daren't do anything because right here, right now, the end gaped wide between us, and I didn't want to fall into the abyss.

I didn't want to be faced with the reality that had been slowly gathering ever since Cherry River.

"Della...don't," I begged. "Don't do this."

I didn't understand what I pleaded for, only that I wasn't ready. I'd *never* be ready.

She cocked her chin, shaking with blonde hair wild and a red mark I'd graced her with on her temple. Her ribbon tattoo flashed on her naked foot, snaking up her ankle.

She was gorgeous, and she was wrong that I'd been blind.

I'd seen her changing. I'd watched her transform from sweet girl to stunning woman, but I was responsible for her well-being. I was the one who had all the power whether she acknowledged it or not. And having that sort of power was a terrible burden to bear.

I would always be hers, but I couldn't be what she was looking for. I couldn't block her from growing into who she needed to become. I couldn't put my own hopes and dreams onto her and read between lines that weren't really there, hoping that there might be some way, some chance, that our friendship could be something more.

Something that wasn't sick and twisted.

Something that wasn't morally wrong.

"Let's go to bed. It's been a long night. We can finish this in the morning." I wanted a truce, a peace treaty until daylight chased away this corruption.

But Della pinned me to the floor with an angry sniff and a flash in her blue eyes. "No. I'm done waiting." Grabbing the hem of her dress, she yanked it over her head.

I stumbled back as she tossed the scrap of material to the floor and stood naked before me.

My heart hissed with possession. My body hardened with need. And my eyes feasted on curves and shadows of the most beautiful woman I'd ever seen.

I was utterly spellbound and trapped. If she moved toward me, I wouldn't have been able to run. If she kissed me, I would've have been able to stop what I desperately wanted to do.

The end would've come in a totally different form.

And who knows where that path would've led us.

But she didn't chase.

She didn't try.

Instead, she held her head high as if proving to herself that standing naked before me wasn't as poignant as she'd believed. That it wasn't anything special when it was the most special thing in the world.

My heart cramped with so many things as she planted her hands on her hips, pinned me to the floor with a merciless glare, and said coldly, "Take a good look, Ren Wild. See for yourself what you've been trying to deny. I'm not a girl anymore. I haven't been for a long time, and now…it's too late."

I couldn't breathe as she added, "You know…for so long I was terrified that I'd strip in front of you and you'd scold me like a little girl. That I'd bare everything I've become and you wouldn't see. But the way you're looking at me…you *do* see. You see but it's not enough. It will *never* be enough."

Stepping with willow legs and fairy grace, she closed the distance between us and whispered, "I lied to you, Ren. I've been lying for years, but this time, this time I'm speaking the truth when I say, I don't need you anymore. I don't want you. I can survive without you no matter what life throws my way. Isn't that what you wanted to hear? To know I'm self-sufficient? That I won't make your existence any harder than I already have?" Cupping my cheeks, she breathed, "Cherry River was a mistake but not in the way I led you to believe."

I trembled beneath her hold.

I was so fucking close to snapping.

Her fingers so soft and sinning on my face.

"I made you believe that I kissed you as an experiment and maybe I did, but that wasn't the real reason." Her tormented gaze drifted to my mouth. "I kissed you because I wanted to. I deliberately waited until you were asleep to have *you*—the boy I loved above everyone—give me my first kiss." She laughed under her breath, tortured and hollow. "Up until tonight, I'd stupidly hoped you'd be the first of so many things. That can never happen now."

I swallowed back a wash of grief, once again slammed with the knowledge she'd slept with someone else. Someone had been inside her. Someone had loved her who wasn't me.

I wanted to punish her for that.

I wanted to touch her, kiss her, press her against the fucking wall and screw the consequences, but then I was crushed beneath mental pictures of her naked, back arched, and lips kissed as that bastard traitor from the party thrust inside her.

I stumbled backward, burning beneath hot jealousy. I gulped

back every need and looked at her sternly. "Go to bed, Della."

"Oh, don't worry, Ren. I'm going. But not before I prove to myself I'm stronger than I thought." Her touch reached for me again, softening to a caress as her thumb traced my bottom lip and she stood on her tiptoes, bringing her mouth to mine.

I froze as she kissed me.

Innocent.

Sweet.

It was the hardest thing I've ever done not to kiss her back.

Not to ruin that innocence.

Every muscle turned rigid at the invasion, the seduction. My eyes begged to close. My lips pleaded to part and give in.

I was seconds away from throwing it all away and taking what I wanted, but then she was gone, dropping her touch and smiling with every nightmare in the world. "Goodbye, Ren Wild. Goodbye to fallen dreams and impossible fantasies."

When she turned her back on me, I couldn't tear my eyes off her perfect ass as she walked bravely across the lounge to the corridor.

Every part of me wanted to follow, still spellbound and broken.

Just before she disappeared into the darkness, she looked back.

Her eyes locked on mine.

Her lips parted.

Her breath caught.

And we stood trapped in a physical embrace even while apart.

My willpower cracked enough to put one foot in front of the other as I *begged* to have her.

Then she shattered it by smiling soft and sweet like she'd done since she was a girl and dropped her eyes. "I'm sorry, Ren…for everything. But things will be better now. I promise. I'm done making life difficult…for both of us."

She left without a backward glance, leaving me in the rubble of our lives, stupidly believing anything could be better now everything had been destroyed.

She didn't come back even though I stood there, silently screaming her name over and over for her to find me.

This couldn't be it.

This couldn't end.

We couldn't end.

But…we had.

We'd been honest for the first time in years and it had successfully proven what a dangerous game we'd been playing. We'd been willingly hurting each other. Twisting all that was good between us until there was nothing left.

My chest ached. My body throbbed.

I stood there for far longer than I should have.

Long after she'd headed to her bedroom.

Long after I heard the springs of her bed bounce and the click of her light signal she'd cocooned herself in the dark.

Only when my legs threatened to collapse did I trip across the lounge and grab her dress discarded on the floor.

I hugged it as I fell heavily on the couch.

I rocked with it as my mind flickered with images of her fucking another while flashes of her as a child made me sick.

I couldn't untangle the two. I couldn't accept the Della I loved with all my soul was now an adult. And not just any adult, but a woman who'd torn out my heart.

I switched from filthy obsessions to a racing track of warning.

Dawn wasn't far away.

A new day where even sunshine couldn't fix what was broken.

Della didn't need me anymore, but somehow, I needed her more than ever. I needed her more than I could stand. More than I could ever let her know.

She'd been honest with me tonight, and it was time I was honest in return.

We were both miserable. Both searching for answers when we only gave each other questions. Both looking for permission to circumstances no one could understand.

I had no excuse for my behaviour. I was haunted by a dream-kisser. In love with a figment of my imagination that disgustingly believed Della was my fantasy.

When really…she could never be.

Della was mine, and I was hers.

I was her protector. She was my best friend.

I'd seen her grow from baby to child to woman, and no matter how I felt about her, I would never be allowed to have her in any other way but family.

I would burn in hell before I did.

I should be able to happily stand by as she found a lover, a husband, and be proud that I gave her such a life.

So why did the thought of her finding such gifts make me

want to tear out the remainder of my heart and deny her everything? Why did I want to trap her in this one-bedroom apartment for the rest of our lives, never letting her see others, never letting her be happy unless she was happy with me?

That wasn't right.

That wasn't healthy.

I would end up smothering her, and I loved her far too much to destroy her.

I couldn't have her, and I couldn't watch her walk away.

So there was only one thing I could do.

She was right.

She didn't need me anymore.

I'd done my part; I'd given her everything I had to give and now, I had to give her her freedom.

Once the idea manifested, I was grateful for the guidance. I didn't second-guess as I pushed aside the couch and pulled out the cash I'd saved under the floorboards. I moved quietly as I checked the contents of the forever-packed backpack and lashed the new tent Della had bought me to its bulk.

I wanted my removal from her life to take years. For something to say we were so entwined, so tied together that there was no possible way for me to walk away. But I didn't come across any knot or rope that couldn't be undone with the simple choice to leave.

Within thirty horrible minutes, I had everything I needed.

I stared at the corridor where she rested and took two steps toward her before I grabbed control again and nodded with determination.

This was what had to happen.

I'd hurt her.

I continued to hurt her just like she continued to hurt me, and we both shouldn't have to live in agony any longer.

Placing the cash on the coffee table, I looked around the apartment one last time. Grabbing a spare pen and a Post-it always housed next to the TV remote, I wrote the hardest letter of my life.

Della Ribbon,

I love you so much it hurts—

My hand paused.

My brain full of everything I wished I could tell her.

There was so much to say. So many confessions to share.

But in the end, I couldn't write any of them.

Goodbye, Della.

I put the pen down next to a years' worth of rent, picked up my backpack, and walked out the door.

UPCOMING BOOKS 2018

The Girl & Her Ren
The Body Painter
The Argument

For more up to date announcements and releases please visit:

www.pepperwinters.com

PLAYLIST

Details by Sarah Reeves
Wolves by Selena Gomez and Marshmello
Who we are by Imagine Dragons
Hurts like hell by Fleurie
Broken by Lund
I want something like this by The Chainsmokers and Coldplay
Heartbreaker by Pat Benatar
Human by Rag N Bone Man
Madness by Muse
Somebody I used to know by Kimbra and Gotye
Someday by Milo Manheim and Meg Donnelly
Nothing left to say now by Imagine Dragons
What you want by One Republic
Demons by Imagine Dragons

ACKNOWLEDGMENTS

This will be short and sweet.

The Boy & His Ribbon exploded from nowhere and I'm still entirely wrapped in their tale while I write The Girl & Her Ren. I've never had a book flow so easily before, nor written one so fast—that in itself is something I'm hugely grateful for because writing went from fun to almost magical.

Thank you for giving this book a chance and reading something different from me.

Thank you to my beta readers, I couldn't have done this without your encouragement and equal excitement every time I sent a chapter via messenger.

Thank you to Ari, the covers were so hard to design but I think you nailed them.

Thank you to Nina, for loving this book as much as I do and thinking outside the box with getting it into as many reader's hands as possible.

Thank you to my readers, for letting me tease you with snippets of The Body Painter only to release The Boy & His Ribbon instead. Thanks for understanding that when a muse like Ren pops into your head, you have no choice but to write what he tells you.

Thank you to my hubby, for putting up with me and for letting me write even when I got sick with pneumonia (nothing could keep me away from writing this book).

And finally, thank you to Ren and Della, for popping into my head when I had a case of writer's block and pouring your tale through my fingers in just one month.

I'm so incredibly lucky to have the chance to write a story like this and it will forever be a favourite of mine.

I hope it will be one of yours, too.

DISCARD

28399941R00236

Made in the USA
Lexington, KY
15 January 2019